THE LEGACY OF
GRAZIA DEI ROSSI

Also by Jacqueline Park

The Secret Book of Grazia dei Rossi: Book One

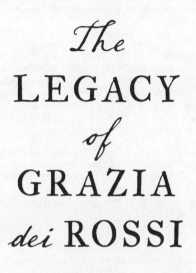

The LEGACY *of* GRAZIA *dei* ROSSI

BOOK TWO

JACQUELINE PARK

ANANSI

This edition published in 2014 by
House of Anansi Press Inc.
110 Spadina Avenue, Suite 801
Toronto, ON, M5V 2K4
Tel. 416-363-4343
Fax 416-363-1017
www.houseofanansi.com

Distributed in Canada by
HarperCollins Canada Ltd.
1995 Markham Road
Scarborough, ON, M1B 5M8
Toll free tel. 1-800-387-0117

House of Anansi Press is committed to protecting our natural environment. As part of our efforts, the interior of this book is printed on paper that contains 100% post-consumer recycled fibres, is acid-free, and is processed chlorine-free.

18 17 16 15 14   1 2 3 4 5

Library and Archives Canada Cataloguing in Publication

Park, Jacqueline, author
The legacy of Grazia dei Rossi. Book 2 / by Jacqueline Park.

Issued in print and electronic formats.
ISBN 978-1-77089-892-9 (pbk.). — ISBN 978-1-77089-893-6 (html)

I. Title.

PS8581.A7557L43 2014   C813'.54   C2014-902726-5
C2014-902727-3

Library of Congress Control Number: 2014938783

Book design: Alysia Shewchuk

The inscription on page 259 is from "I am the Sultan of Love" by Suleiman the Magnificent, translated by Talât Sait Halman, http://raindropturkevi.org/jackson/50-literature-sman-the-magnificent

The inscription on Rumi's Tomb on page 268, "Come, come, whoever you are," was translated for the author at the site when she visited the tomb.

The poetry excerpt on page 271 is from "My worst habit" by Rumi, translated by Coleman Banks with John Moyne, The Essential Rumi, New York: HarperCollins, 1996: 52.

The excerpts on pages 350 and 351 are from The Odyssey by Homer, translated by Robert Fitzgerald, New York: Farrar, Straus and Giroux, 1998: 367, 368.

Canada Council   Conseil des Arts   ONTARIO ARTS COUNCIL
for the Arts   du Canada   CONSEIL DES ARTS DE L'ONTARIO

We acknowledge for their financial support of our publishing program the Canada Council for the Arts, the Ontario Arts Council, and the Government of Canada through the Canada Book Fund.

Printed and bound in Canada

RECYCLED
Paper made from
recycled material
FSC® C103567

For Heather Reisman

CONTENTS

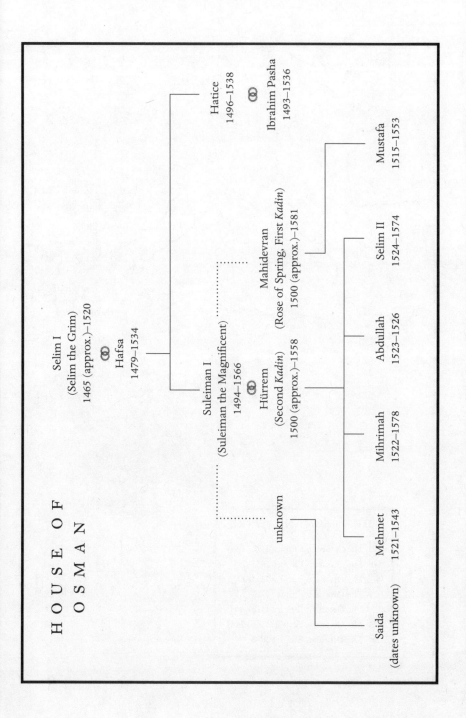

HOUSE OF OSMAN

Selim I
(Selim the Grim)
1465 (approx.)–1520

Hafsa
1479–1534

Hatice
1496–1538

Ibrahim Pasha
1493–1536

Suleiman I
(Suleiman the Magnificent)
1494–1566

Hürrem
(Second Kadin)
1500 (approx.)–1558

Mahidevran
(Rose of Spring, First Kadin)
1500 (approx.)–1581

unknown

Saida
(dates unknown)

Mehmet
1521–1543

Mihrimah
1522–1578

Abdullah
1523–1526

Selim II
1524–1574

Mustafa
1515–1553

THE OTTOMAN EMPIRE

▨ The Ottoman Empire 1359
⬚ The Ottoman Empire 1451
▦ The Ottoman Empire 1451–81
▨ The Ottoman Empire 1512–20
⬚ The Ottoman Empire 1520–66
▨ The Ottoman Empire 1566–1683
▨ The Ottoman Empire 1856

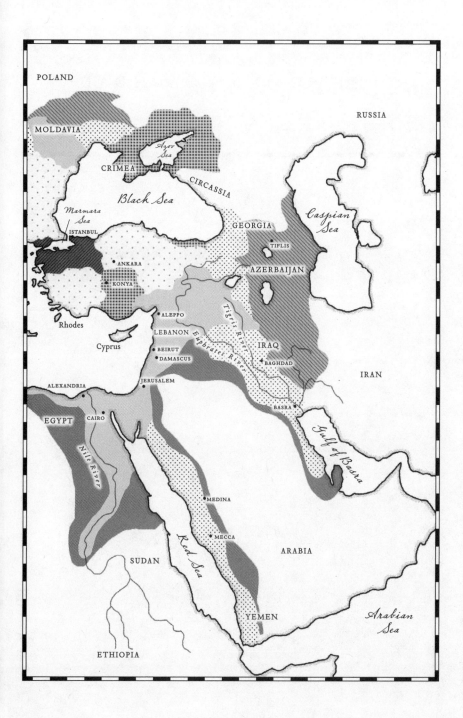

THE ROAD TO BAGHDAD

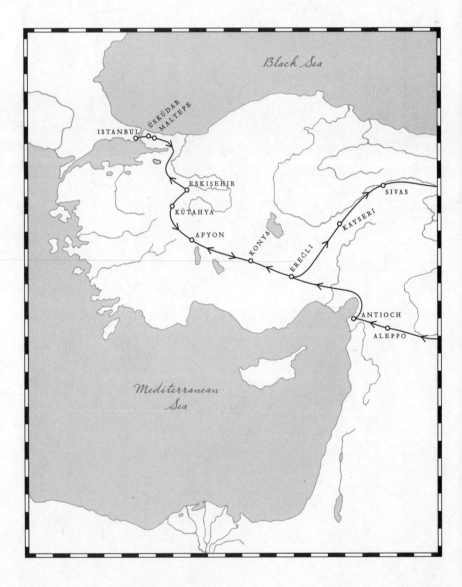

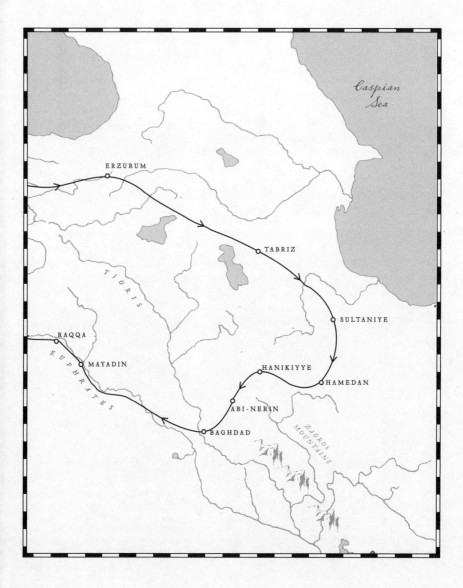

ISTANBUL

I

RANSOM

AFTER A LONG AND SUCCESSFUL CAREER IN THE SERVICE of the great and powerful, Judah del Medigo was not surprised when out of the blue a courier arrived in Rome ordering him to report immediately to his new master, Suleiman the Magnificent, at Topkapi Palace in Istanbul.

Sudden arbitrary orders were the price the doctor knew he would have to pay when he signed on as the Sultan's new Chief Body Physician. Just as he knew that doctors do not say no to sultans. So the doctor reluctantly kissed his wife and son goodbye and boarded the first ship bound for the eastern Mediterranean, leaving his family behind in Rome to pack up and follow him.

When news reached him at the Ottoman court that the city of Rome had been sacked and burned soon after he left, del Medigo was not unduly alarmed. He felt sure — with good cause — that his wife and son would escape the sack unscathed. He had left them in the fortified Colonna Palace in Rome under the protection of his wife's patroness, Isabella D'Este, the Marchesana of Mantova, and he knew Isabella to be a woman of infinite resources and a practiced survivor.

Not until the doctor had heard nothing of his family for some weeks did he begin to worry. Even then, he mentioned his concern only casually to the Venetian *bailo* when they met at the Ottoman court. He knew that the Venetians made it their business to pick up odds and ends of information, and sure enough, that very evening the *bailo* presented himself at the Doctor's House with a rolled-up dispatch from one of his informants.

Wordless, the Venetian pressed his spy's report into the doctor's hands, gently patted him on the shoulder, turned on his heel, and left without a word. When the doctor unrolled the document and read it, he understood why.

Madonna Isabella D'Este reached home safely, he read. *Sadly, members of her household were captured by Mediterranean pirates off the Isola D'Elba. Their ship, the* Hesperion, *put up a brave defense, but its crew and passengers were lost at sea.* Then, being Venetians, they added, *Most of the lady Isabella's valuable treasures were also lost.*

The blow hit the doctor with the force of a pole axe. He had never doubted that the indomitable Marchesana Isabella would protect his dear ones. Isabella was an Este by birth and, say what you will about the Estes, they take care of their own. Now suddenly the Marchesana was apparently safe in her palace in Mantova, but her confidential secretary, the doctor's wife, Grazia dei Rossi, and their son, Danilo, had been lost at sea.

Judah del Medigo was an observant though not a believing Jew. The day he received the news, he locked his doors, covered his mirrors, and settled down on a low stool in the basement of the Doctor's House in the Third Court of Topkapi Palace to weep and grieve. Being a realist, he did not pray to have his loved ones brought back to him. There was no reason to hope they might still be alive. The Venetian report had left no doubt as to their fate. Yet before dawn on his sixth day of mourning, the Sultan's Chief Body Physician found himself scrambling across the dark silent streets of Istanbul in response to a ransom note that had been slipped under his door on the previous night.

The woman is dead, the note read. *The boy is safe. You have until dawn to appear at Pirates Cove with 2,000 gold ducats. If the ransom is not paid at sun-up the boy will be delivered to the Istanbul slave market and sold to the highest bidder.*

The ransom note read like a fraudulent ruse to extract money from a grieving parent. And the doctor knew better than to trust any bargain made with the Corsican pirates who prowl the waters of the Mediterranean. But what if just this once, the Corsicans proved to be as good as their word? What if his son was still alive? He could not afford to risk that chance.

So the next morning, well before sun-up, the Sultan's Chief Body Physician was found plodding through the sleeping city of Istanbul clutching a pouch full of gold coins. When the doctor clambered down the bank of Pirates Cove he saw no sign of life in the woods that ringed the shore or on the beach. Only one small portion of the landscape moved in the stillness: a deserted fishing boat bobbed up and down against the small dock anchored in the curve of the cove. If anything, the tattered sail that fluttered from the flagpole of the abandoned skiff underscored the flat emptiness of the scene.

By now a rim of sunlight had appeared on the horizon. The witching hour had come and gone, but there was no one there to collect the ransom.

As the doctor stood gazing into the void, reluctant to give up his last remaining glimmer of hope, he heard what seemed to be the sound of a twig breaking behind him in the silent woods.

When he turned his head toward the sound, he was taken from behind by a pair of unseen arms and felt hot breath on the back of his neck.

"Did you bring the gold?" The question was voiced in a growling, deeply accented Corsican dialect.

The doctor nodded his assent.

"Hand it over."

He reached into his pocket for the pouch, only to find it yanked from his fingers by a hairy hand that made immediate use of it to rap him smartly on the back of his head. A sharp pain flashed through his body. Then blackness.

When he opened his eyes his attacker had made off with the gold, and the woods behind him were as unruffled as they had been when he first arrived at the rendezvous. He had been duped. How could he have been such a fool as to put his faith in a passel of Corsican pirates?

But wait. Out of the corner of his eye he became aware of something moving on the deck of the abandoned skiff. Transfixed, he watched as a trap door was slowly thrust into view from below the deck of the craft and two pairs of bronzed, muscled arms emerged bearing what seemed to be a black-hooded body wrapped in a tarpaulin.

Mesmerized by what he took to be a mirage brought on by the blow to his head, the doctor stumbled to his feet expecting that at any moment the illusion he was seeing would disappear into the wind. Instead, the sailors carrying the wrapped figure moved forward to the prow of the ship where they propped it up against the mast and began to unwind the straps that enclosed it.

They did say he was alive, the doctor reminded himself. But could he take them at their word?

One of the sailors pulled out a knife. *Oh my God, they are going to kill him in front of me.*

But no. The sailor used his knife to slit the black hood at the neck, releasing a single golden curl onto the forehead. Then a nose. Now a chin appeared. Above it, a mouth. Then a pair of clear blue eyes. At last a whole living boy was revealed, arms stretching out toward the shore.

The sailors led their captive down a small gangway from the deck of the skiff to the pier. And, with a gentle push, Danilo del Medigo was released into his father's waiting arms.

It was at that moment that Judah del Medigo became a believer in miracles. And if a battle-scarred, somewhat arthritic old campaigner can be said to have floated through the streets, the Sultan's Chief Body Physician floated home from Pirates Cove that day to the Doctor's House in Topkapi Palace, cradling his son in his arms.

There he settled his son on a pallet beside his own bed and wrapped him in a lavender-scented quilt. But not before he had washed and barbered and massaged the boy into a state of cleanliness and ease.

At the same time, the physician in him managed to conduct what he hoped was an unobtrusive examination of his son's physical condition. And Judah del Medigo fell asleep that night with the miracle boy nestled beside him, confident that, considering the shocks he had suffered, the boy was amazingly fit. No broken bones or bruises, no signs of being starved or beaten.

Not until the next day did Judah become aware that, although his son was healthy enough, he seemed to exist in a state of passivity, hardly moving, not speaking unless spoken to. Perfectly obedient and accommodating, never rebellious or defiant, this pale wraith bore little resemblance to the vigorous, lively boy his father had left in Rome just a few months before. When the doctor tried to distract him with tempting morsels of food or chat, the boy accepted the offerings with a nod but showed no sign that he enjoyed his father's pleasantries any more than the eggs and meat and pilaf that Judah poured into him, hoping to renew the energy that had always been so much a part of his nature.

Certainly the doctor was beyond joy to be reunited with his lost son. He thanked God every morning in his prayers for the boy's miraculous delivery. Yet he couldn't shake off his awareness that come spring, he was bound to the Sultan on campaign and would have to either leave the boy behind or take him along. Could he in good conscience leave his troubled son behind in the care of strangers? Or expose him to the hardships of campaigning? Or must he now resign his position in order to devote himself to the boy's rehabilitation?

While he was struggling to come to a decision, a note from the Sultan arrived. Suleiman was proposing that during the upcoming campaign, the doctor's son join the royal children in the so-called Princes School attached to the Sultan's harem, where he would be as well taken care of as a prince. The offer was tempting. But after two sleepless nights and many prayers, Judah regretfully tendered his resignation as Chief Body Physician, pleading pressing family obligations.

In the interim he would bend his efforts to find a replacement body physician to serve Suleiman on the battlefield. Knowing that his decision was the right one put his mind at ease.

But Suleiman the Magnificent was not a man to be denied his will by a mere doctor. Like the popes at Rome and certain Christian princes whose instinct for self-preservation exceeded their religious scruples, the Ottoman sultans favored Jewish doctors. Unhampered by medieval Christian screeds against "pagan science," Jewish physicians had continued to practice the teachings of Asclepius and Hippocrates. Armed with this knowledge, they had emerged from the Middle Ages as an elite cadre of medical practitioners, Judah del Medigo foremost among them.

The Sultan had pursued the renowned Jewish physician through the courts of Europe for several years before finally bagging him. And he was not about to allow the unexpected appearance of a motherless boy to rob him of his campaign physician. Certainly not at this moment when the gout that it was said only Jewish doctors had a cure for was beginning to make it uncomfortable for him to mount a horse.

To initiate what he confidently expected to become a fruitful dialogue, Suleiman called in his physician for a friendly chat, reminding him that the campaign season would not commence for many months, that there was no urgency to make such an important decision, and urging the doctor to take some time to reconsider resigning.

"You have my assurance that in the Harem School your son will do his learning as a part of my own family under the watchful eye of my own mother, the Valide Sultan," he coaxed. "Surely," he went on, "that would be a much safer arrangement than dragging the boy off to the battlefield or leaving him behind with strangers." Then, to add a little sweetener to the sherbet, he offered to assign the boy an armed guard to escort him from the Doctor's House in Topkapi to the Princes School in the harem each day that Judah was absent on campaign.

The prospect was tempting. Judah wavered. His head told him that the Sultan's offer was a solution to his problems. But his fatherly heart told him that the boy was not yet ready to deal with yet another abandonment by the only parent now left to guide him through the labyrinth of dark memories that haunted him.

What the Sultan was offering the doctor was time to ferret out what had happened during the boy's captivity on the pirate ship, and to find the key to his son's despair. A boy's natural grief for the loss of a much loved mother could account for weeping, fainting, even vertigo—but not for virtual paralysis. What cruelty had the damned Corsicans inflicted on Danilo to cause such damage?

That question might never have found an answer had not some lost soul stumbled in the dark into the Sultan's personal domain, a swampy moraine outside the wall of the Third Court. If an interloper ever managed to get anywhere near the Sultan's *selamlik*, a warning fired from a Janissary's musket would have scared him off, pronto. Which is what happened that night. But as the shot reverberated across the palace wall into the Third Court, it also shattered the silence in the Doctor's House, where Judah del Medigo and his son lay sleeping.

At the sound of the shot, the boy sprang up from his pallet as if he had been hit, clutching his heart in terror. "Stop, don't shoot!" he pleaded. "Noooooooo..."

Then came a blood-curdling shriek of anguish. "Not Mama. Not her, I beg you. Take me...take me."

The musket-shot had released a flood of dammed-up memories. And finally, between the sobs, came a confession.

"It was all my fault. The pirate ordered me to abandon my perch guarding Isabella's baggages. Mama begged me to climb down. I wouldn't listen to her. If I had come down the pirate wouldn't have aimed the gun at me and she wouldn't have thrown herself in front of me to take the bullet. She would be here now. Alive." A long pause. "I killed her."

A glance at his son's face told Judah he could not allow this madness to go on. Gently but with great firmness he took the boy's pale face between his hands and addressed him sternly. "Did you have a gun?" he asked.

When no response came, he demanded with fatherly authority, "Answer me."

"No." The answer was barely audible.

"So who did have a gun?"

"The pirate they called Rufino."

"Then it was the pirate Rufino who killed your mother with his gun. Not you."

"No. No." The boy wrenched himself from his father's grasp. "You weren't there. You don't know what happened."

"Tell me," the doctor urged him softly.

Somehow Judah had struck the right note. His son took a deep breath, straightened his shoulders, and began to relive his memory.

"Madonna Isabella left the *Hesperion* to finish the trip to Mantova by land because she was seasick," he began, hesitantly at first but with increasing assurance as he went on. "Before she quit our ship she asked me to guard her baggage with my life and bring her things home safely to Mantova. There were treasures packed in those cases—a tapestry by Raphaello that she said meant more to her than her own life. When the pirates attacked the *Hesperion*, the crew put up a brave fight, but the ship sprang a leak in the hold and started to take on water. That was when Rufino and his crew began to remove Madonna Isabella's valuables from our ship to theirs. All I could think of was my promise to watch over her goods. I climbed up on top of her cases to guard them. Rufino ordered me out of the way. I didn't move. He said he would count to three.

"'One.' The pirate raised the musket to his shoulder. I saw Mama moving toward us.

"'Two.' He placed his thumb on the trigger.

"'Three.' He squeezed. The shot rang out just as Mama threw herself into the line of fire. Nothing seemed to happen...then she fell at my feet."

There were no tears in the boy's eyes when he spoke. Simply a blank emptiness. "That bullet was meant for me. I killed her."

"That bullet was shot by the pirate, not by you," Judah insisted.

"But if I had stepped down..."

"It would still be the pirate that killed your mother. There is no pity in these men. Murder is their business. When I first saw you at Pirates Cove you were tied up in a tarpaulin. They had bound your ankles, taped your wrists, and covered your head in a hood. You were their prisoner. They would have killed you."

"You don't understand, Papa. They never would have killed me. They tied me up to save me from drowning. They saved my life."

"Are you telling me that these bandits rescued you out of pity?"

"Of course not. I may be confused, Papa, but I am no fool. I know they saved me to sell in the slave market in Istanbul. But they did fish me out of the sea and save me."

"After they threw you in?"

"No, after I jumped in. They put Mama's body in a wooden box and shoved it off the side of the ship. When I saw her body sinking under the waves I wanted to follow her, to be dead like her. So I jumped in. That's when they tied me up, so I wouldn't try to do it again."

Judah had convinced himself that if he learned the secret of his son's suffering at the hands of the Corsicans, that knowledge would guide him to a cure for the boy's malady. But having relived his ordeal, the boy remained pale, silent, and still. Clearly reliving his nightmare had done nothing to alleviate Danilo's guilt and pain. It would take months, even years, to rescue his son, Judah thought, from the pit of despair into which he had fallen. If there had been any doubt in Judah's mind, there no longer was. There would be no campaigning this year for the Sultan's Chief Body Physician. Danilo's needs were far greater than the Sultan's, and Judah's first duty was to his son.

2

THE SULTAN'S GIFT

T O THE MEMBERS OF THE SULTAN'S INTIMATE CIRCLE
his manner of dealing with the Chief Body Physician's
defection was mystifying. In the strict code of Ottoman
service, failure to answer a call to the battlefield promptly, and
with enthusiasm, was tantamount to treason. Yet this Jewish
doctor who, it was said, had refused the Sultan's order to serve
in the spring campaign, was still occupying the Doctor's House
and walking about the palace grounds unpunished. There was
only one possible explanation for such a violation of protocol.
The doctor had cast a spell on the Sultan. He was a sorcerer.

Then again, if Judah del Medigo did possess magic powers,
how was it that he could not bring his own son back to good
health? The boy continued to wander the grounds pale, listless, and silent, never seen to express the trace of a smile much
less to laugh aloud or to show signs of behaving like a normal
eleven-year-old. For his part the doctor's disappointment in his
son's recovery gave him little hope of remaining at his post as
the Sultan's Chief Body Physician. Still, the Sultan was making
no effort to find a replacement for his body physician. Or so it
seemed.

Then one morning, a cart pulled up in front of the Doctor's House unannounced, hauling a horse van driven by a groom with the Sultan's *tugra* embroidered on his cap. When the doctor's servant answered the bell, the groom announced he had come bearing a gift for the doctor's son, Danilo del Medigo.

Hurriedly, the boy was washed and dressed and led out sleepily to receive his caller. Whereupon the Sultan's groom opened the rear door of the horse trailer and led out a brindle pony — clearly a thoroughbred — caparisoned with a gilt-edged saddle and a bridle etched in gold.

Standing at his door with a protective arm around his son's shoulders, the doctor was perfectly positioned to witness a vision he had all but given up hope of ever seeing. The moment the boy caught sight of the pony, his eyes widened. And when the groom offered him the animal's lead, he sprang forward to take the rein in hand as would any eleven-year-old boy who had been offered a thoroughbred pony.

"Is it for me? Can I keep it?" he asked his father with an eagerness he had not shown for any one of the many distractions the doctor had tried to tempt him with.

Giving the doctor no chance to reply, the groom answered for him. "In the Ottoman Empire it is an insult to refuse the Sultan's gift," he announced. "The pony is the Sultan's gift."

The matter was settled. And, with Judah's lukewarm acquiescence, the groom led the boy and the pony out through the Gate of Welcome to the Sultan's stable in the Second Court, where a stall was set aside to house the animal.

What occupied Danilo for the remainder of that day, his father could only guess. Although he did take note that the boy, who had walked the animal away to the Sultan's stables on a lead that morning, had returned in the afternoon mounted on the animal's back. But not until Judah witnessed with his own eyes his son's evident pleasure as he rode his brindle into the courtyard did it occur to him to wonder why he had never thought to tempt the boy with a pony. Yet the answer was obvious. Judah del Medigo took no pleasure in a horseback ride.

Given his choice, he always picked a coach or a litter. And if a mounted steed was the only available mode of transport, the doctor far preferred a docile mule to a frisky thoroughbred. With such a limited feel for horseflesh, he could only acknowledge that a daily gallop offered his son a distraction so demanding as to overcome the boy's searing memory of his mother's death. What the doctor did not understand was that, far from helping Danilo to forget his mother, galloping over the fields on his pony brought back to him many happy years of his daily rides at her side; that in the saddle, he was in her presence.

Nor was Judah witness to the scene at the end of each day in the horse barn, where the princes of the Harem School stabled their ponies and gathered to groom them at the end of their afternoon ride. All young, all competitive, it was inevitable that an occasional pony race should break out among the riders when they met up on the bridle paths, and that they would quickly move on to compete with each other on the jumps behind the Harem School.

When Danilo cleared the highest hurdle with room to spare on his first try, he instantly earned himself a place in the fraternity of princely athletes. True, the new boy was unable to converse in any of the civilized tongues (these being Turkish, Arabic, and Persian), but among the princely athletes, the fastest pace and the highest jump easily trumped a lack of language skills. The Ottomans were still, in their hearts, people of the horse. They were also famously devoted to the principle that merit is rewarded over birth, race, and personal eccentricities like yellow hair. And when his new companions challenged the foreign boy to a jousting contest with the *gerit*, and he proved to have a flair for that popular Turkish lance, his place among them was firmly secured.

With so much to occupy him away from home, Danilo began to spend less and less time at the doctor's side and more and more time at the Harem School with his new comrades. As the weeks went by, the doctor found that the only times his son was with him were the evening and day of the Jewish

Sabbath, when they attended services together. The Sultan's plan was unfolding. Without anyone noticing, the doctor's son became an unofficial student at the Harem School. And Judah's reasons for refusing to leave the son whom he hardly ever saw evaporated.

Quite informally, a pattern for the boy's life was established. Weekdays and Sundays he would ride back and forth from home to school and school to home, accompanied by a groom. Saturdays, he pursued his Jewish studies at the Ahrida Synagogue, the oldest synagogue in Istanbul, founded in the previous century by Jewish traders from Salonika. Ever since their expulsion from Spain in 1492, Jewish refugees had been welcomed by the Ottoman sultans. So by the 1520s, when Judah del Medigo arrived to serve the Sultan, the Jewish population of the capital supported close to a dozen synagogues, and a canny liturgical shopper could take his pick among Sephardic, Roman, and Ashkenazi rites.

Of them all, the little Ahrida Sephardic congregation appealed to Judah as a house of worship because the Sultan's Jewish physicians had always worshiped there. And that congregation became the center of his son's Jewish life when the doctor went off to campaign. Thus, with his father's half-hearted acquiescence, the boy began his life in Istanbul dodging nimbly between Muslim weekdays in the Princes School and Jewish weekends in Balat, soon becoming adroit at straddling the gap between the two worlds, overseen in his father's absence by the first lady of the land, the Valide Sultan.

The Jewish part was easy. The members of the little Ahrida Synagogue were quick to offer warmth and welcome. But in the Princes School the language barrier proved far more impenetrable than did the high hurdles.

The Sultan had given his word that the doctor's son would be as well educated as a prince. But the boy's lack of fluency in the common tongue stood in his way from the beginning. And, as the weeks went by, Danilo felt himself falling farther and farther behind his classmates in his studies.

What was to be done? In desperation, his teacher turned to the Valide Sultan, a woman who had spent her life finding remedies for problems her son didn't even know he had.

Like herself, the Valide's solution was elegant and practical. Clearly young del Medigo needed a tutor, someone to read with him every day to accustom his mouth to the Turkish tongue. Any one of the older princes would have done. But best of all, thought the Valide, would be her ward, the Sultan's motherless daughter Saida. Just short of eleven years old, the princess was far and away the best student in her cohort; Saida would be the ideal mentor to keep the foreign boy occupied with his lessons, while his father was absent on the Sultan's service. In making this arrangement neither the tutor nor the student was consulted.

Given a choice, Danilo would never have picked a girl as a tutor. But he understood he had no say in the matter and decided simply to learn quickly and rid himself as soon as possible of the encumbrance of the girl.

Had Saida been asked, she also would have refused the favor. This Danilo looked oddly pale to her, with straw for hair and eyes of a bright blue more suited to floor tiles than human eyes. But she was too well brought up to express herself outright. However, she did make her displeasure evident with a small pout.

"What is the difficulty, Princess?" asked the teacher. "The stranger is clever and will learn easily."

Her mouth set in a tight little knot, the girl muttered, "He slouches."

"He what?"

"He slouches," Saida repeated. "He is not well mannered." In her grandmother's book of etiquette, a straight back was the key to a place in paradise.

"But he does not slouch when he's in the saddle," the teacher pointed out tactfully. "Tomorrow, watch him in the riding ring. Watch how he sits his mount."

The next afternoon, as she cantered around the ring, Saida

took careful note of Danilo del Medigo and, to be sure, she had to admit that the very moment he put his foot into the stirrup his spine straightened and that, once in the saddle, he sat his mount as tall as any of her brothers. Reluctantly, she agreed to take him on.

Having been given her choice of a text for them to study, the princess picked a Turkish translation of *The Thousand and One Nights*. It was a volume that had been given to her by her father, the Sultan. From the first page, the tale of Scheherazade, a young girl forced to spin out stories night after night to save herself from being beheaded, became her favorite.

Had Danilo been asked, he would have preferred to be reading one of the old Turkish epics of *ghazi* warriors. But these the princess disdained as suitable only for soldiers and peasants.

"We will study *The Thousand and One Nights*," she explained as if to a backward child, "because the great difference between those of us who are educated in this *saray* and those educated outside the palace derives from our familiarity with a fine style. Besides, this old story contains many words in Persian and Arabic for you to learn."

No boy likes to be ordered about by a girl, especially by a girl younger than him. It was humiliating. "She's more bossy than an old *lala*," Danilo complained to his father.

But he had played enough games to know when he was outclassed. So he agreed to his tutor's choice with good grace, and in the space of a few months, the princess managed to lead him through the adventures of "Aladdin and His Magic Lamp," "Ali Baba and the Forty Thieves," and "Sinbad the Seaman." As Danilo read each tale aloud, the princess corrected his pronunciation. By the time they were ready to take on the less popular, longer tales, Danilo had become as much the captive of Scheherazade as the husband who had a habit of marrying virgins and murdering them the morning after the wedding. In the end, like thousands of readers before him, the boy was unable to resist the magic, the adventures, the disasters, and the jokes that had kept Scheherazade alive over centuries.

It was a few days after they began to read "The Tale of the Porter and the Three Ladies of Baghdad" that their tutorial took a sudden turn. In this story, the porter is picked up in the marketplace by an honorable woman who wears shoes bordered with gold and spends money like water. When the porter is invited to accompany her home, he doesn't hesitate to accept, not for a moment.

The lady leads him through a gate made of two leaves of ebony inlaid with plates of red gold and into an elegant salon. There he is introduced to a second lady—a model of beauty, loveliness, brilliance, symmetry, and perfect grace. In Saida's text, the woman's forehead is flower white, her cheeks ruddy-bright like the anemone, and her eyebrows shaped as is the crescent moon which begins Ramadan. These details, which the princess relished, left Danilo cold. *Who cares?* he thought to himself.

But the porter in the story is dazzled. After some wining and dining and dancing and laughing, the porter, now drunk, begins to carry on with both women: kissing, toying, biting, handling, groping, fingering.

As Danilo read he became intrigued in spite of himself. And he was more than a little put out when Saida announced in her pedantic little way that it was time to stop for the day. He found himself pleading to read just one more page. She acceded. He read on.

Now one of the ladies is stuffing a dainty morsel into the porter's mouth, and the other slaps him and cuffs his cheeks. This porter is in paradise. It is as if he is sitting in the seventh sphere among the houris of heaven.

Just then, as tended to happen in Scheherazade's stories, a visitor knocked at the gate. It was the Caliph of Baghdad, Harun al-Rashid, gone forth into the night from his palace to see and hear what new things are stirring in his kingdom.

Harun al-Rashid. The name echoed in Danilo's memory. In his head he heard it spoken in the soft musical timbre of his mother's voice. He had heard his mother, Grazia the Scribe, speak the name Harun.

"Why do you stop reading?" the princess asked.

"Because I have heard of Harun al-Rashid. More than once."

"You have read the story of my ancestor before?"

"No. But the name Harun al-Rashid comes from a poem my mother used to read aloud to Madonna Isabella D'Este and her ladies in Rome. The story is all about the Emperor Charlemagne and his paladins. It is called *Orlando Furioso*."

She was noticeably unimpressed. "And what has this French emperor to do with my ancestor Harun al-Rashid?" she inquired.

"Harun was a Saracen," Danilo explained politely. "He was an enemy of the Christian emperor."

"Harun was a great caliph." She drew herself up proudly. "He was the fifth son of Abbas, brother of Caliph Musa al-Hadji, son of al-Mansur, and Commander of the Faithful. He is a great hero in my family."

"He was the enemy of my forebears," the boy informed her. They were both on their feet now, glaring at one another.

"Then I, too, am your enemy," she declared.

"And I am your enemy," he retorted.

When she heard this, she wheeled around and stormed out of the room, leaving Danilo not entirely certain of what had happened but feeling somehow at fault.

"Princess!" he shouted after her.

He caught her before she reached the main classroom. "Please forgive me for raising my voice to you. I must apologize."

She did not lift her eyes to meet his.

"You have been very kind to give me so much of your time and knowledge," he went on. "I have repaid you with rudeness. Perhaps, if you will allow me to explain myself..."

She raised her eyes.

"You see, I have a personal interest in the Emperor Charlemagne," he explained. "His paladins were the first knights of chivalry. And my father was—is—a knight."

"Your father, the doctor, is a knight?"

"My legal father, the doctor, was wounded in battle at Pavia while serving King Francis the First of France. The King sent him home to Venice in care of a member of his court, Lord Pirro Gonzaga. My mother was overwhelmed with gratitude to this knight. Nine months later I was born. I am the first child to be born in the Venetian ghetto."

This was the kind of story the princess had been educated to appreciate. "Are you saying," she asked, "that your blood father is not the doctor but a Christian knight?"

There was still time to deny the truth that he had inadvertently revealed. But Danilo was urged on by his deep pride in his blood heritage.

"I am the son of a brave Christian knight and I am what is called a 'love child,'" he told her.

Not surprisingly, the revelation of his bastardy hardly caused a ripple in the mind of the princess. She clapped her hands delightedly. To her, reared in the harem, irregularities regarding parentage were the stuff of everyday life. She took his soulful confession as just another of the countless tales of illicit love told in *The Thousand and One Nights*.

"Your apology is accepted." She held out her hand in a gesture of forgiveness. "I also raised my voice to you. But, like you, I have a personal interest in Harun al-Rashid. As Commander in Chief of the Faithful, he was ancestor and hero to my father, who himself is now Commander in Chief of the Faithful. We do not like to hear Harun referred to as a Saracen. The last foreigner who spoke that word in my father's presence lost his head for it. If you take my advice, you will not use the word Saracen in this court unless you fancy seeing your head mounted on a pike outside of the Gate of Felicity."

She hesitated, as if troubled by what she had just said, then smiled cheerily and added, "I misspoke. You could hardly see your own head if it was on a pike, could you?" And, with a toss of her curls, she flounced off, giggling.

Strange girl. Mind you, she did not seem to think any less of him for his bastardy. Of course, to a girl who cut her baby teeth on *The Thousand and One Nights*, secret paternity could hardly be a novelty. Come to think of it, if Danilo had to make a reckless disclosure to anyone, he couldn't have chosen a better recipient. Still, he had revealed a fact that Judah del Medigo had not seen fit to share with his patron, the Sultan — the fact that his recently arrived son had been fathered by another man. And princes do not like to be lied to. Not that the doctor had actually lied, but the Sultan might not see it that way. And it was not his son's place to reveal his father's secret.

The echo of his mother's voice had undone Danilo. Hearing it in his head saying the name Harun al-Rashid had brought on a rush of longing so fierce that he had to bite his lip — hard — to hold back his tears. Then, as quickly as it had descended, his grief was overcome by fear. What if Princess Saida should happen to mention the identity of his true father to her grandmother, the Valide Sultan? And what if the Valide should mention it to her son, the Sultan? It would be a neat bit of gossip to pass on to him. And, in a world rife with plots and betrayals and deceit, the Sultan could easily get the wrong impression.

First thing the next morning Danilo pulled the princess aside. "I shouldn't have told you about my blood father, but I did," he confessed. "Now I must ask you to keep the confidence."

To his surprise, she agreed without hesitation. That ought to have been the end of it. But that night he dreamed he was a boy again in Marchesana Isabella's Roman salon, pressed into service as a page during his mother's reading of the French romances that her patroness doted on. Even in the dream, he could feel the scratchy surface of the starched white *camicia* he wore on those occasions, and the weight of the heavy silver salver that it took all his boyish strength to hold steadily aloft as he offered glasses of spiced wine to the Marchesana's *demoiselles*, to his mother (who liked to sip as she read), and to the great lady herself, fat and puffy but imposing nonetheless with her twisted strands of pearls and her bejeweled fingers.

From the square below could be heard the muffled sounds of the sack of a great city. Screams, curses, and blasts of powder seeped into his dream. And through it all, his mother continued to read from Ariosto's poem, *Orlando Furioso*. Poetry was read aloud daily in Madonna Isabella's court in Mantova, and—sack or no sack—she insisted on maintaining the ritual in Rome.

But suddenly, as happens in dreams, the drawing room was overrun with wild, black-haired Saracens who seemed to have climbed up the palace walls from the square below. They were led by the blackest and wildest of all: their leader, Harun al-Rashid. His mother had stopped reading. The *demoiselles* were screaming. Madonna Isabella swooned. Danilo woke up in a sweat.

The next day, when he came again to the name of Harun al-Rashid while reading, Danilo broke off and found himself once more confiding in the princess.

"It is the name that takes me back," he explained. "When I read the name of Harun al-Rashid, I could hear it coming from my mother's mouth. The Este family was very fond of French romances. They had a library full of them."

She seemed puzzled, and indeed he was hard put to find a Turkish equivalent for the term *roman*. But now that the flood-gates of memory were open, he had no will to stop the flow.

"You see," he found himself telling her, "my mother was the private secretary to the Marchesana Isabella D'Este, wife of Marchese Francesco Gonzaga of Mantova."

"Marchesana?" Her query was more of a conversational courtesy than an expression of interest.

"Marchesana is what you call the wife of a marchese." Seeing no sign of comprehension, he decided that a degree or two of rank inflation was in order. "A sort of Italian princess," he explained.

Now he had her attention. Princesses were something she understood.

"I was not aware that your mother was secretary to a princess." She spoke with a new respect in her tone. "I thought she was just one of those clever Jewesses who go shopping for the ladies of the harem."

"My mother was no bundle-woman," he hastened to assure her. "Her name was Grazia dei Rossi. She translated many books into Italian from Latin and French and was renowned as a scholar."

"And this princess she served?"

"Isabella D'Este is daughter to the Duke of Ferrara. In Europe they call her La Prima Donna del Mondo, the First Lady of the World."

Saida nodded approvingly. Titles were something she also understood.

"The Lady Isabella and her family used to commission works of poetry." He paused, then added, "As your father does." Again he was greeted by a nod and a smile of approval.

"And my mother was in this lady's service," he went on, "when Ariosto dedicated his poem, *Orlando Furioso*, to Lady Isabella D'Este in honor of the birth of her first son. He even gave her name, Isabella, to one of his heroines."

Better and better. The Ottomans were even more enthusiastic dynasts than the Estes, if that were possible.

In all the months since he had arrived at Topkapi Palace, Danilo had spoken to no one about his life in Italy, about his escape from Rome, or about his mother's death. Now, having begun, he could not stop himself.

"I had a dream last night," he found himself confiding— confiding!—in this girl. "I saw Harun al-Rashid breaking into Madonna Isabella's salon during the sack of Rome."

"I have heard of that unfortunate event," she chimed in. "My father told me of it. But you are mistaken. Harun al-Rashid is not the villain of the piece. The attacker was King Charles of Spain, who calls himself the Holy Emperor even as he attacks his own Pontiff, Pope Sir Clement the Seven."

She spoke this garbled version of these European titles with such assurance that it took all his patience to refrain from setting her straight.

But, this time, he took the high road. "Quite so, Princess," he agreed. "Quite so."

To which she responded, "Please tell me more about your dream."

At this point, he might have excused himself from further confidences. But instead he went on.

"In my dream, I confused Harun al-Rashid with the true

villains of the sack of Rome, the Emperor's German soldiers, his *landsknechts*."

"The so-called emperor," she corrected him sweetly.

"I was brought up to think of Charles the Fifth as the Holy Roman emperor," he advised her.

"The Venetian *bailo* told my father that people in Venice say that this Charles is neither holy, nor Roman, nor an emperor," she said.

"They also say that in Rome," he admitted, "but they still bow down to him. It all depends on how you look at him, doesn't it?"

She sniffed.

Not about to be intimidated, he went on. "What my dream taught me is that you and I live in the same world, Princess. Although we speak different languages, our stories are inhabited by the same heroes and villains. We may see them differently, but we share them in our dreams."

This was clearly a new thought to her, and she took several moments to consider it before she spoke. When she did, her voice was quiet and modest. "I would like to know some of these romances that you speak of. Especially the favorite story of your mother's patroness—the Princess Isabella D'Este."

"I could read that story to you," he ventured. "My father, the doctor, keeps my mother's manuscript of *Orlando Furioso* on his shelf."

Again, she took a moment to consider, and during the silence a plan formed in his mind.

"What if I translate the story of Isabella from Italian into Turkish and read it to you?" he asked. "Then you can correct me as you do when I read stories aloud from *The Thousand and One Nights*. That way"—he was finding himself increasingly at home with the idea—"I will still be doing my Turkish lessons and you will be hearing one of my stories."

By now, his hours spent with Princess Saida had given him a fair notion of what would suit her: the simple account of an event studded by incident, few digressions, and jeopardy lurking at every turn. And he seemed to have found these requirements in Ariosto's tale of Princess Isabella—a story that had been Madonna Isabella D'Este's favorite, a story with a heroine that the poet had named after the great lady herself. He set to work that very evening, full of zeal for the project and blissfully unaware of the pitfalls that lay in wait for him buried among Ariosto's doubled quatrains.

What Danilo had not realized was that although Ariosto's epic was a collection of many separate stories, the Italian poet had chosen to tell his stories not sequentially as in *The Thousand and One Nights*, but by picking them up and putting them down throughout the text the way a knitter saves out bundles of stitches for occasional use throughout a pattern. The task of sorting out a single story demanded patience and scholarship. And, in spite of his mother's efforts to train him, Danilo del Medigo was neither patient nor scholarly.

Damn Harun al-Rashid! Damn Isabella! Damn the poet! Why had he made such a rash offer? He had been better off with Scheherazade, who turned out to be not nearly as boring as he had expected. Still, he could not bring himself to give up and admit failure, certainly not to a girl. Besides, something else held him to the task. He might be a bastard, but his mother was no *puttana*. Grazia dei Rossi had been a respected scribe and a true scholar, and in some way he had taken on this impossible task to honor Grazia the Scribe. Why?

Maybe because this was the kind of task his mother would have tackled readily and accomplished brilliantly. So he kept at it.

Meanwhile, Princess Saida was getting impatient. He began to work at his translation secretly, under a quilt, while his father was asleep. One night his candle set fire to his quilt. One day he fell asleep on the back of his horse. But when he finally reached the tragic end of the romance of the doomed Isabella and her lover, Zerbino, he was as certain as one who is in thrall to royal whims that this tale was just the bait to entice Saida into his world.

3

THE PRINCESS
AND THE PALADIN

THE PRINCESS HAD MADE IT ABUNDANTLY CLEAR THAT what appealed to her about Ariosto's epic was purely and simply the love story of Isabella and Zerbino. Any reference to the larger tale of which it was a part, or to its origins in the world of French chivalry, she met with a barely disguised yawn. He knew that if he was to capture her attention and hold it, he must jettison Ariosto's opening cantos and leap into the middle of Canto 13, where the knight-errant, Orlando, out for a gallop in the French countryside, discovers a maiden being held prisoner in a cave. She is not much older than fifteen, and even though her eyes are tear-swollen, such is her beauty that she makes her filthy prison look like a paradise.

"Full well do I know that I may suffer for having spoken to you," she tells her rescuer, "but I will tell you my story even if I pay for it with my life."

Danilo could not resist sneaking a peek at his princess to see if she had taken the bait and was rewarded with an expression of rapt attention. So far, so good.

"I am Isabella, daughter of the King of Galicia," the captive maiden goes on. "Once I had a happy life. I was young, beautiful, rich, and esteemed. Now I am poor, wretched, and debased."

"Young, beautiful, rich, and esteemed," Saida repeated. "How does that sound in your language?"

He checked his text. "*Felice, gentile, giovane, ricca, onesta e bella,*" he read.

She repeated the strange words slowly, turning them over in her mouth as if to taste them. "And now she is?"

"*Povere, infelice e vile,*" he read. "Poor, wretched, and debased . . ."

"Poor princess . . ." She dabbed at her eyes.

This was going even better than he expected. "She tells Orlando that although she used to be the daughter of a king, she no longer is," he continued.

"How can that be?" Saida loved a puzzle.

"Because she is now the daughter of grief, misery, and sadness. And it is all the fault of love." He hesitated before continuing. "That is not quite right. The Italian words are *colpa d'amore.* There is a suggestion of her being heart struck."

Saida clutched her breast.

"Shall I go on?" he inquired. Need he have asked?

He continued: "The damsel sets off to seek refuge in a convent to dedicate the rest of her life to the service of God. Not that she will ever forego either her love for Zerbino or the possession of his mortal remains. Wherever she is, wherever she tarries, his corpse accompanies her and is with her night and day."

The delicacy of this final detail brought new tears of admiration to Saida's eyes.

It had been months since the tutor and the pupil returned to *The Thousand and One Nights.* And now Saida was the one begging for more, and Danilo was the one parceling out his daily readings in miserly increments.

"Of course, Princess Isabella is destined never to reach her refuge. Not far from the convent she encounters a savage Saracen, an African king named Rodomonte, who does not immediately kill or dishonor her. But Isabella knows that every hour she spends with this man increases the peril she is in. She conceives a plan ..." Danilo stopped his tale, unable to voice the words he was about to read. "I cannot go further. The end of Isabella is too cruel for your young ears. Even Madonna Isabella D'Este could not bear to have it read to her. And she is a grown woman."

Saida said nothing. She simply pursed her lips in that stubborn way she did when her mind was made up.

Reluctantly, he began to trace Isabella's downward spiral into the arms of death.

"In the brightness of the early morning, before Rodomonte's head is clouded by wine (a habit against his religion that the villain has picked up in France), Isabella makes him a provocative proposal," he said. "'If you leave my honor safe,' she says, 'I will give you something of far greater value. Search and you can find a thousand comely women to possess, but no one in the world can give you what I have to offer.' Artfully, she leaves the precise nature of this priceless gift shrouded in mystery.

"Intrigued, Rodomonte accepts her offer, knowing that once he has the gift, he can easily break his word and take the woman along with it. Isabella takes Rodomonte out into the woods to search for a certain herb that when boiled with ivy and roasted over a fire of Cyprus wood, and then pressed between innocent hands, produces a magic juice. 'Whoever bathes himself with this juice three times,' she tells him, 'so hardens his body that he will become proof against fire and steel.'

"'I shall bathe myself with it from the crown of my head down to my breast,' she tells him. 'Then you must turn your sword upon me as if you intend to cut off my head, and you will see the wonderful result.'

"Whereupon she bathes herself in the juice three times, then steps forth to offer her bare neck to be severed. Completely convinced by her charade, Rodomonte unsheathes his sword and in one slice lops her fair head clean from her shoulders."

"No!" The cry escaped Princess Saida's lips like a moan.

"Yes, three times. The poet is specific," Danilo insisted. "And from that head a voice can clearly be heard calling the name Zerbino." He paused. "Shall I read what the poet has to say about this?"

She nodded, dumb with grief.

"Here is Ariosto's benediction: 'Depart in peace, beautiful spirit, and take thy seat in the skies,'" Danilo intoned in a sepulchral voice. "'If my verses had the power, I would work to the limit of my poet's skill to give them such endurance that, for a thousand years, the world would have knowledge of the illustrious name Isabella.'"

"I will pray for her." Saida folded her hands under her chin and lowered her head. Then, after a suitably solemn pause, she raised her head and announced briskly, "Now we must begin again."

"Again?"

"Yes. We go back to the beginning of Isabella's story. Let us begin this very day, leaving out no detail. But this time" — he noted that her mouth was set in the now familiar, determined pout — "this time, I will speak for Isabella. You may read all the rest. But I will be Isabella. And you must teach me her words."

So they began again to recite Ariosto's poem, the two of them now. Then one day Saida, quite overcome by the perils of Isabella, tossed away her notes and began to act out her part, embellishing it as her fancy dictated.

From then on, the Princess and the Paladin became a kind of mode that they slipped in and out of whenever the inclination and the opportunity permitted. Gradually, the game insinuated itself into the riding ring, the archery court, and the ball field in the form of brief intervals of wordplay, teasing, and tag. They acted out Isabella's rescue by Orlando, Zerbino's death, Isabella's sacrifice, sometimes complete, sometimes in part, depending on the time available.

Although secrecy was never mentioned, none of their fellow students was ever included in this play. And when the fine weather came and the class was rewarded with weekly picnics on the little island of Kinali, the Princess and the Paladin found their perfect setting surrounded by a dense forest that eerily resembled those so prominently featured in *Orlando Furioso*. Saida was very good at melting away from the others undetected, and Danilo became an expert at picking up her signals and following her surreptitiously.

Alone in the woods they found glades that might have been cleared explicitly for the purpose of jousting and caves ideal for the imprisonment of princesses. They even uncovered a fountain, dried up and battered but a fountain nevertheless, of the sort likely to be encountered by any paladin galloping over the countryside or any princess escaping the clutches of a villainous Saracen. It was as if nature herself had created the ideal setting for Isabella's tragedy.

How could such things have happened under the watchful eyes of the nurses and teachers and *lalas* of the Harem School? Perhaps because it came about innocently. Princess Saida and the foreign boy were so young. Both were thought to be children, much too young to present any threat to each other. And the boy was mastering the Turkish language at a formidable rate. Soon he would move on to a European school of his father's choosing. And the princess would, of course, marry.

Was it the certainty that, in the very near future, these children would be leaving their childhood behind them that blinded the adults to what was happening between them in the here and now? Whatever the case, their ferocious chases on horseback, their muttered little exchanges as they shot off their arrows during archery practice, and their occasional absences from their fellow students went unremarked, and they remained free to play the game they had invented.

Then, as unexpectedly as it had begun, the little idyll came to an end. With the threat of puberty looming, the time arrived for the children of the Harem School to put away childish things and move into adulthood: the boys to enter one of the all-male pages' schools, the girls to be immersed deep in the harem to prepare for marriage.

Oddly enough, the event that ushered in this sudden change

was marked by a seemingly unrelated ceremonial occasion: the circumcision of three of Suleiman's sons. And Danilo's first intimation of what lay ahead arrived in the unlikely form of an invitation from Prince Mehmet, the Sultan's first son by his Second *Kadin,* to take a walk in his mother's garden.

Since the prince was younger—just the age at which Danilo himself had come into the Princes School—contact between the two boys had been limited to nods and smiles. So Danilo was puzzled by the sudden offer of a princely arm. What could this boy want of him? He quickly found out. As soon as they were out of earshot of the other students, Mehmet dropped his formal manner and got straight to the point.

"I know that you were circumcised because all Jews are cut," he began. "Tell me, please, did it hurt?"

What was Prince Mehmet after? Whatever it was, Danilo had nothing to lose by telling the truth. "I can't remember," he replied with perfect candor. Then, his curiosity piqued, he asked, "Why do you want to know?"

"Because we've been told that two of my brothers and I are going to be circumcised on the twenty-third day of June, and I have to know how much it hurts in order to prepare myself. They say it hurts like burning hell. Does it?" And, when Danilo did not immediately answer, the young prince added, "They say you never forget the pain."

"I can't remember." Danilo was beginning to feel himself inadequate to conduct this bizarre conversation. "You see, I was only seven days old when I was circumcised. That's when we Jews do it."

"Damn!" The boy slapped his hand against his thigh. "No one told me that. And now you think me a fool."

"Of course I don't, Mehmet. You can't be expected to know everybody else's customs."

"I'll bet you do," the boy answered. "Everyone knows how clever the Jews are. I learned that from my great-grandfather, Bayezid. Do you know what he said when he heard that the Catholic king of Spain had expelled the Jews from his country?"

Danilo shook his head.

"My great-grandfather said, 'People tell me that Ferdinand of Spain is a wise king. I ask, how wise can he be? A king who impoverishes his country by expelling the Jews and enriches the Ottoman Empire by sending them to us must be stupid.'"

"Your great-grandfather said that?"

"In 1492," the boy assured him confidently. "Even then, we Ottomans knew that the Jews are the most clever of all races. My father told me that story. He also told me that the Jews are skilled craftsmen, astute merchants, and brilliant doctors. That is why we have always welcomed them into the Ottoman Empire. Did not your father, the physician, cure my father of his gout when all the Arab doctors failed?" Then, without waiting for a confirmation, he added, "And now I see for myself an example. How clever of you to do it to babies."

"Clever? Babies?" Danilo was having difficulty making the leap.

"Because babies don't feel anything. We Muslims leave it until so late that we always remember the pain. But that is not why I am afraid." He stopped abruptly.

"Why then?"

The boy looked down at his boots, silent, then peered up through the fringe of shiny black hair on his forehead, bit his lip, and looked Danilo straight in the eye, having decided, it seemed, to give up a secret.

"I am afraid that I will disgrace myself by crying out," he whispered. "The pain will pass, but the shame will never go away. People always remember that you cried out at your circumcision." He paused, then almost as if speaking to himself, asked, "But what if you can't stop yourself?"

The question was accompanied by a look so woebegone that Danilo found himself wrapping his arm affectionately around the younger boy's shoulder. "You have nothing to worry about, Mehmet. You are a brave boy just like your namesake, Mehmet the Conqueror. Everybody says you resemble him."

"They do?" The boy remained solemn but looked slightly less woeful. "We must learn to be brave, my brothers and I, because there is nothing ahead for us but certain death."

Danilo was well aware of the Ottoman practice of eliminating all fraternal rivals to the throne each time a new sultan was crowned. But he had stored it in his memory as an ancient custom, not something that really happened to the real princes he knew. Now, suddenly, he found himself looking into its human face.

"But there were no executions when your father, Suleiman, came to the throne," he temporized.

"Only because he had no living brothers. But my mother tells us that, on the day that my half-brother, Mustafa, comes to the throne, he will exile her and have us all killed."

"Oh, surely Mustafa wouldn't do a thing like that," said Danilo, knowing as he spoke how foolish he sounded.

"It was my ancestor, Bayezid, who authored this law," the boy explained. "He did it to preserve the succession. Do you wish to hear his exact words?"

At Danilo's nod of assent the boy began to recite his forefather's dictum. *"It is proper for whichever of my sons is favored by God with the sultanate to move immediately to execute his brothers in order to prevent the outbreak of a civil war."* Then, striking a pose, the little prince continued, *"What is the death of a prince compared to the loss of a province?"*

After delivering the rhetorical flourish, the prince went on in the same composed tone he had adopted at the beginning of the conversation. "That is why my brothers and I must die. But since it is against the law to shed the blood of princes, we will not be beheaded. Each one of us will be strangled with a silken bow string."

The bizarre logic behind this final bit of protocol only exacerbated Danilo's dismay. He tightened his hold on the boy's shoulder as if to shield him from his fate. Then, realizing he must offer some kind of verbal consolation, he said, "I don't think the pain of the circumcision is as bad as they say and I know you will not cry out, Mehmet. I am certain of it."

The reassurance sounded hollow in his ears. But, sure

enough, on the day of the circumcision ceremony, everyone commented favorably on the extraordinary forbearance of Prince Mehmet, who did not make a single sound when the knife cut his foreskin.

4

HALCYON DAYS

THE FESTIVAL OF THE ROYAL CIRCUMCISIONS SO
dreaded by young Mehmet turned out to be a fateful
occasion for Danilo as well. In the week after the
circumcisions, the *Kapi Agasi* made one of his rare appearances
in the little school on the edge of the harem garden to
announce the news. Now that the present cohort of boys had
passed the bar of circumcision, it was time to make way for the
next class in the Princes School. The crown prince, Mustafa,
would be sent directly to an outlying province as an apprentice
governor, accompanied by his mother and a covey of *lalas*. The
lesser princes, raised from infancy by their mothers in the
harem, would now be assigned places in one of the Sultan's
elite schools for pages, there to be groomed for leadership in
an all-male society by eunuchs.

For the boys' sisters and female cousins, little would change.
The girls would continue to be educated in the harem, never
again to be seen unveiled even by their male cousins. No more
calcio, no more racing on horseback. Once a young girl entered
the state of womanhood, she was immured behind the walls of
her father's harem until she married into her mother-in-law's

harem. From the day Saida's fellow students entered the class, the Valide Sultan, ever watchful for her granddaughter's well-being, began to notice subtle changes in the girl. It seemed that day by day, the fire that put the sparkle in Saida's flashing eyes and the color in her cheeks was being slowly doused by her new routine.

The princess was of course still permitted her daily ride, but now she rode alone accompanied at a respectful distance by a groom—no brothers or cousins to challenge her at the jumps or chase her around the race course. Yet she was still far too young, in the Valide's judgment, to be married off.

Educating boys and girls together until puberty, as the Greeks did, had appeared to be a hugely successful experiment in producing future Ottoman leaders. But seeing a free and educated girl suddenly thrust into a life with no future until she was rescued by marriage now loomed as a serious challenge to her doting guardian.

A pious woman, Lady Hafsa visited the mosque to enlist Allah's help in solving her dilemma. Two days later—whether by divine intervention or sheer chance—the help she needed presented itself in the form of the Sultan's concubine, Hürrem, who had begun her life at court as a gift from the Grand Vizier to the Sultan, purchased by him at the Istanbul slave market. She now had risen to the status of Second *Kadin,* a Mother of Princes, by providing the Sultan with a son. The First *Kadin,* Rose of Spring, mother of the Sultan's first-born male, Prince Mustafa, had failed to produce a second male heir to guarantee the succession. Given the high rate of child mortality, Hürrem's boy was wildly celebrated as a savior of the Ottoman dynasty and earned her the title of Second *Kadin.*

So when Hürrem appeared at the Valide's door tearful and in need of solace in the days following the circumcision of her older son, the concubine was greeted warmly by Lady Hafsa. This was not the first time the Second *Kadin* had sought counsel from the Valide. Soon after the birth of her son Mehmet, she had begun to cultivate the boy's grandmother. Never aggressively, always respectful of protocol, always careful to request an appointment before she crossed the long hallway that divided the Valide Sultan's suite from the rest of the harem. And always bearing gifts—a special cream to whiten the aging skin, a sleeping draught to bring sweet dreams to the Valide's sleepless nights. Full of news of the great world, Hürrem was sure to bring along gossip collected from the Jewish peddler women from whom she bought her laces and ribbons and lotions and potions.

At first Saida resented the interloper. Since childhood, her grandmother's attention had been fixed on her. Now she had to share it. But as time went on, she began to look forward to Hürrem's visits. She even began to ask Hürrem to beg small favors for her from her father, the Sultan. Not that she was afraid of him. But, as Hürrem so often reminded the Lady Hafsa and Saida, bearing the weight of the world on his shoulders, the beloved Sultan ought not to be burdened with their small concerns, least of all by the ones who loved him most.

"Allow me to see what I can do," Hürrem would say, "before we trouble the great Padishah. Poor man, he carries such a heavy weight." Their duty, after all, was to lighten his load, he being the source of light in their lives and in the whole world. Even the Valide Sultan, the mother he revered, bowed and kissed his hand when he entered her rooms. And she addressed him as "my lion."

Their mutual adoration of this man had bound the three women together. Over time, Saida lost most of the jealousy she bore her father's favorite *Kadin*; and the Valide Sultan gave up some of her pride of place. Lady Hürrem had managed to smile her way into their hearts, a very shrewd preparation for the day when she might need the help of one or both of them.

Today being such a day, Hürrem was now familiar enough to make a direct appeal to the Valide Sultan. Ever respectful of protocol, she first apologized profusely for disturbing the lady and made certain to assure the Valide that what she was seeking was simply the advice of a wise woman. Then she got to the point: a rumor she had picked up while bathing in the *hamam*. Only a whiff of scandal. Nevertheless, most disturbing. By now, she had their undivided attention.

"I have heard a story." She leaned forward and lowered her voice to a whisper. "Perhaps it is not true. But if it is..."

The Valide, a woman not given to touching any being less exalted than herself, reached out to pat the other woman on the shoulder.

"What is this rumor, Hürrem?" she asked gently.

Silence. A sigh.

"We cannot help you if you do not tell us."

"Oh, Lady, I am so ashamed. I fear it is all my fault for being so slow to learn. Although I do try..."

"To learn?"

"To learn my letters so that I can write to my exalted lord in my own hand and read the letters he sends to me. As it is, I must trust the scribe who writes my words down and who reads the Padishah's letters to me. I cannot believe this scribe would betray me, and yet there is this rumor..." She dabbed at her eyes with a gold-embroidered handkerchief. "I am told that my letters are being hawked in the bazaar."

"Sold? For money?" Even the imperturbable Valide was perturbed.

"Copies of them."

"But who would do such a thing?"

"Who indeed?" Hürrem echoed. "My scribe came to me from the Grand Vizier's school. He was handpicked. It cannot be him. But if not..." Her voice trailed off. Then, suddenly, she turned and focused her gaze directly on Saida. "Is there no one I can trust?"

At that moment the solution to all of Hürrem's problems became clear to the Valide.

"Saida will help you," she announced, pleased with herself, turning to the girl. "Did I not tell you that your studies would find good use someday, my darling child?" Then, back to Hürrem, "Some members of the court were against training a girl in anything except embroidery and sherbet-making. But I prevailed on my son, my lion, to allow Saida to join her brothers in their studies. To her credit, she is today the most literate princess in the world and has memorized most of the Koran, which brings her father great joy. Now she is able to do him another service, to save him from the breath of scandal. As you know, she often helps me to write my letters, and now she will help you."

So it was settled. Henceforth Saida would pay a daily visit to Hürrem's quarters to read aloud the letters the Sultan wrote to her when he was on campaign and to transcribe Hürrem's answers. She would also translate the poems the Sultan dedicated to his Second *Kadin*, written under the pseudonym *Muhabbi* or *He Who Loves*, which he composed in Persian—his choice of language for poetizing. A happy arrangement for all. A scandal avoided. The beloved Padishah protected; Hürrem rescued. The wise grandmother had saved the day.

Yet several months later Saida was beginning to sense something too easy in the Valide's solution. A practiced survivor by the age of twelve, the princess had cultivated a nose for intrigue. Experience in the harem had taught her that life did not unfold with the ease of her entree into Hürrem's household service unless someone behind the scenes was pulling the strings. Yet months of daily attendance had revealed to Saida no hidden reason for her inclusion in Hürrem's retinue, except the Second *Kadin*'s immediate need for a trustworthy secretary. Nothing more.

When the princess arrived at Hürrem's suite, she was always greeted warmly and respectfully. Her accomplishments were highly praised. And she was thanked often and promised rewards for service in the future. Saida, the Second *Kadin* said, had saved her from a very serious threat to the happiness she shared with her adored Padishah, whom she treasured more than her own life. As the lady put it, "His letters keep me alive. Without the reminder that he will return to me, I would expire of grief."

Through her letters as well as her conversation, Saida had come to know Hürrem as a natural hyperbolizer—guilty of the odd lapse of taste, perhaps, but that was hardly proof of insincerity, the girl told herself. Besides, there were certain advantages to the princess's new status as a confidante of the favorite: the opportunities to witness momentous events such as her father's triumphal procession when he returned from his annual campaign. Outings through the streets that the cloistered women of the harem were never offered. And Hürrem's constant assurance that the orphan girl now not only had a grandmother to look out for her, but had found a second mother—herself, the Second *Kadin. At least*, Saida thought, *until Hürrem's own daughter, Mihrimah, is old enough to do for her what I now do.*

But Saida had schooled herself to accept each day's bounty without too much thought for what the future might bring. Even if it was not her nature, her faith told her that her fate lay in Allah's hands. And much as she longed for the old days of wild horse rides and secret meetings on the island of Kinali, she was resigned to making the best of her new life.

As for the boys, Danilo was not the only one in the room to feel a chill when the *Kapi* informed the students that this would be their final class in the Harem School. Like him, most of the students had not, until that moment, given much thought to their future. Some day, of course, they would grow up and leave the harem. Some day. But tomorrow? Danilo turned for reassurance as he often did to his seat mate, Princess Saida. But in vain. For the first time he was met with hooded lids and a turning away of the head.

That gesture told him better than words that she was no longer his royal playmate, that she was as lost to him as any legendary princess locked up in any tower.

Danilo was no stranger to loss. He had learned to keep his grief at bay by filling his days with activities. But he had no defense against thrusts of memory that came upon him unexpectedly and left him feeling that a piece of himself was missing. The doors of childhood were closing on him, and the future loomed up dark, lonely, and hopeless.

As he stood at the harem gates, waiting for his groom to take him home from school to the Doctor's House for the last time, thinking he had never been so miserable in his entire life, who should emerge to bid him farewell but Prince Mehmet. The little prince had come to say goodbye since they were unlikely to meet again soon. Mehmet himself had given up all hope of graduating from the Harem School with the current crop.

"My marksmanship, my mastery of language, my deportment, even the fact that I did not cry out at my circumcision — of all those things that I thought would recommend me for the Sultan's School for Pages — none of them avail against my young age," he reported sadly. "I am to be left behind. I am not old enough and must wait for the next cohort, unlike you, Danilo, who will certainly be selected as a page in one of the Sultan's schools, maybe in the Sultan's own school in Topkapi Palace."

It was a thought, much less a hope, that Danilo had not allowed himself. Under the Sultan's eye in his School for Pages, a limitless future awaited those who could earn it. Judged strictly on the basis of their ability, students who survived a severe weeding-out process would end up finally in the highest class, the Fourth *Oda*, whose members served the Sultan personally: dressing and barbering him, guarding him, and sleeping in his private quarters. They were also put in the way of his notice, his favor, and, not the least consideration for Danilo, his horses and his stables.

But Mehmet had it all wrong.

"Believe it or not, Mehmet," Danilo explained, "it's even more hopeless for me than for you. You may be held back this year, but you will eventually have your chance. Whereas I will never be chosen for the Palace School because I am a Jew. Despite the Sultan's favors to my race, no Jew has ever gained acceptance to his school."

"But think of this, Danilo: the personal intervention of the Sultan surmounts all barriers."

When Danilo looked askance at this smart response, Mehmet

added, "Remember, the Sultan's physician has the Sultan's ear. Talk to your father. But be quick. I hear most of the places in the First *Oda* have already been filled."

With that slight encouragement, Prince Mehmet brought a ray of light to the dismal landscape of Danilo's hopes. Perhaps he did have a slim chance. According to Ottoman law, the Sultan's will did prevail over custom. His father did have the Sultan's ear. And the Sultan did have the power to secure a place for him in the School for Pages... if he would.

But Judah del Medigo had other plans for his son. He had already approached a Sephardic family in Balat with whom Danilo could complete the preparation for his bar mitzvah while his father was off on campaign. During the winter when there was no military action, Danilo would remain at home in the Doctor's House being tutored by his father in mathematics, astronomy, Latin, and Greek. This would prepare him for a European university, preferably his father's alma mater, the renowned university at Padua.

For Danilo, his father's plan had serious drawbacks. No horses in Balat, no playing fields, no gerit contests; at best, the odd game of tennis on the Princes' Islands where a few well-to-do Jews kept European-style villas. He had already abandoned all hope of seeing his princess again. Must he lose everything?

The quarrel that erupted over this issue burst upon both father and son like a summer storm—one minute, blue sky; the next, icy sheets of venom and forked lightning. They quarreled awkwardly, not being used to quarreling—long silences punctuated by spurts of angry dialogue.

"I never should have allowed you to become involved in the life of the palace," Judah sighed. "It has given you a false idea of who you are."

"And who would that be, sir?"

"You are a fourteen-year-old boy brought up in the Jewish faith, consecrated to the Jewish God."

"But you don't understand, Papa. I am not you. I have goals."

"Goals! What goals? To gallop around on the back of a horse

like a ruffian until you fall and break your neck? Or to serve the Sultan as a *sipahi* and get yourself killed in a jihad? You are not one of them. We Jews are not fighters."

"Joshua was. And David."

"Spare me the Torah lesson. You know perfectly well what I mean."

"Yes, sir, I do. You mean that you want to make me into an image of yourself, a man of the book, wrapped up in books, away from the world."

"And is that so terrible?"

"No, sir. For you it is the ideal life. But I am not you. I am not..." The boy hesitated.

"You are not Jewish?"

The boy took a deep breath, then spat it out. "I have the blood of a warrior in my veins."

There it was. Out of the box. The forbidden subject.

Silence.

"I apologize, Papa. I didn't mean to say that."

"Why not? It is true. I am not your blood father. We know that. But since you were born to my beloved Grazia, I have always thought of you as my son. Your mother's son, of course. But my son, too."

"And that is how I think of you, Papa, as the father who has cared for me all my life. And whom I love. But, sir, does that mean I must deny my blood heritage? I am your son, but I am also the son of Lord Pirro Gonzaga, even though he does not acknowledge me." The boy bit his lip. Could that be a hint of moisture at the corner of his eye?

Inured as he was to human suffering, the doctor could not bear the palpable signs of his own son's misery. He held out his arms. "Oh, my dear boy, my son." He gathered the boy up in a long embrace, and there they stood in the middle of the room, clinging to each other.

At length, Judah cleared his throat and spoke. "Of course, I cannot force you to go against your nature. Blood or no blood, a parent should not impose that burden on a child. I admit to you that I am mystified by your passion for this wild jousting sport that I find suicidal. It is not a trait I hoped to find in my son."

"But, sir, I am also my mother's son, my mother who told me stories of racing against her brothers in the Mantovan hills, about the touch of her pony's soft nose on her cheek, the pleasure of brushing his coat until it shone like satin."

"Your mother was a scholar and a scribe who —"

"Who gave up much that she loved for you, sir," the boy interrupted. "I never saw her gallop a horse or risk a jump. I only heard her talk about it, longingly, and now you are asking me to make the same sacrifice."

"No, not true. I want to prepare you for the life of a civilized man."

"And do not the Islamic sciences that I will study at the Palace School accomplish that, sir? You yourself admit that you learned the most part of your doctoring from studying Arabic medicine."

"Greek medicine, yes," Judah corrected him.

"But who preserved the Greek texts, Father? The Islamic caliphate. I will get a good education in the Palace School, sir. You know that. Better than from some callow tutor to the sons of a rich merchant in Balat."

This was an argument that Judah could not refute. He retreated into silence, then summoned a servant.

"Tea?" he asked as if entertaining a stranger.

The boy nodded. A brazier was brought and a chaste silver teapot. They drank in silence.

The boy cleared his throat, then spoke, unable to meet his father's eyes. "If I am selected for the Palace School and you force me to live with some family in Balat instead, I will take the first opportunity to run away."

"Is that a threat?"

"No, sir. A warning."

"What about your Jewish studies?"

"I will continue to read with the Ahrida congregation in Balat on Fridays and Saturdays as I always have. And I will be ready for my bar mitzvah when you return from campaign."

"And on the other five days, how will you pray? What will you eat? Pig?"

This was foolishness. Both knew well that pork was forbidden to Muslims as well as Jews. But Danilo refused the bait and took the high ground.

"I will live proudly as a Jew, sir," the boy replied. "You have my word on it."

Judah lowered his eyes, cowed by the shining sincerity of the response. He had cut the ground from under himself with bullying and bombast.

"Of course you will not eat pig. No respectable Muslim school would serve you pig. No more quarreling." He extended his hand, looking for a truce. "Since the Sultan's School for Pages seems to be your heart's desire, I will speak to him. With your fine record in the Harem School, I have no doubt you will get your wish."

"Thank you, Papa."

The rift was healed. The doctor had capitulated. But he had not given up the fight. It seemed to him that he was battling for nothing less than his son's very soul. And that this was only a skirmish in what promised to be a long war.

Danilo had no such cosmic view. For him the Palace School simply represented the best that life had to offer him at the time. He had no doubt that someday in the distant future, he would set off to follow in the doctor's footsteps to the university at Padua. But at that moment, his life's ambition was to ride a horse of his own into the oval at the hippodrome, his *gerit* poised for the joust, and end up being crowned with an olive wreath as the crowd roared.

5

BE CAREFUL WHAT
YOU WISH FOR

WITH ITS PROMISE OF THE BEST HORSES, THE BEST teachers, a fine wardrobe, generous pocket money, and a guarantee that he would be judged only on his own merits, the chance to gain a place in the Sultan's School for Pages instantly became the focus of Danilo's life. As his father had foreseen, the excellent record of his two years in the Harem School spared him the preliminary screening process and he was immediately placed in a select group, out of which a fortune-favored twenty would be chosen for admission to the First *Oda* at the Sultan's school in Topkapi Palace. The less fortunate applicants would receive their training at one of the other two pages' schools — one situated in the Sultan's summer palace at Edirne, the other in the Grand Vizier's palace on the hippodrome.

As was customary with the Ottomans, the sole criterion in making assignments was merit, except, of course, for the princes of the royal family, whose places were automatically reserved. Each year examinations for the twenty cherished places were held in the Harem School during its annual recess. The tests covered a wide range of subjects — horsemanship, personal cleanliness, Turkish history, arithmetic, and most important the three languages required of every Ottoman courtier: Persian (the language of poetry), Arabic (the language of the Koran), and Turkish (the language of everyday life).

Not many weeks before, Danilo had sat in these classrooms studying these same subjects. And he had done well. But seated in the same room facing the entrance exams, he found himself increasingly distracted by a coterie of ghosts that settled down in his company. The elusive presence of his princess, his playmates, and his teachers hovered over him. No matter what test he was trying, these mournful grey wraiths were there; twisting reminders of everything he had lost.

Day after day, the other aspiring pages strutted out of the examination rooms whooping and hollering while Danilo sank lower and lower in his own estimation. At the end of the examination week, he emerged from the ordeal stripped of his confidence and convinced that every other aspirant had done better than he had. Even his father's reassurance that the Sultan favored his application did not lift his spirits. From his window at the back of the Doctor's House, he could look directly across at the entrance to the Palace School, a pair of massive carved wooden doors framed by two fat porphyry columns. Would he be invited to cross that threshold?

He feared to leave the house lest a message arrive announcing his fate. Not that he had any place to go. Since he first arrived in Istanbul, the Harem School had been the center of his life — a place for learning, of course, but even more for good times and companionship where he had come to be treated as part of the royal family. For the princely boys, the harem would remain their home until they were dispersed among the pages' schools to continue their education. But with his cohort disbanded, Danilo was left literally friendless and rootless.

As the days passed his natural zest for life began to evaporate. He took to spending his evenings on the rock ledge at Palace Point, straining for a glimpse of the Mediterranean and dreaming of Italy as he had done when he first came to live with his father. And it was there that he was sought out by a gorgeously arrayed page whose only comment on finding him was, "You're lucky it was I who found you and not one of the guards. Do you know whose preserve you've invaded?" Without waiting for an answer the stranger dug into his jeweled sash and produced a small scroll, tied with a satin ribbon and sealed with the Sultan's *tugra*. "Read this," he ordered.

Although he spoke quietly, his manner was so assured that Danilo found himself obediently breaking the seal and reading, in beautiful calligraphic script, that he had been accepted into the First *Oda* of the Palace School for Pages. The messenger, a tall, strikingly handsome young man who appeared to be about twenty years old, told Danilo that he himself was currently a page in the Third *Oda* and a member of the Sultan's *gerit* team.

His name was Murad and he had drawn the assignment of mentor to the new recruit.

"On your feet now. Let's get the hell out of here before we're both thrown in the dungeons." As he held out a helping hand, he added, "I'll say this for you, del Medigo, you've got nerve setting yourself up on the Grand Vizier's dock."

In addition to the document, Murad had also brought with him a complete suit of clothing and a set of verbal instructions, brief and precise. The page Danilo del Medigo was to be ready to move into his *oda* at two hours after the first prayer the next morning.

"I will be at the door to collect you. Be ready. And bring nothing with you," he instructed.

"Nothing?"

"Nothing. From now on, everything you need will be provided for."

"Everything?"

"Including your toothbrush," was the answer. "Now try on these," he said, holding out a pair of yellow leather boots soft as butter. "We measured them from your riding boots, but mistakes happen. I have left your new wardrobe with your father's manservant. Be sure to wear everything in the box when you get dressed tomorrow morning. Those clothes will tell everyone that you are a student page—an *ich-oghlanlar*—not an apprentice. Understand?"

Danilo shook his head, uncomprehending.

"We have two types of pages in each of the Sultan's schools: the student pages like ourselves, and the apprentice pages called *ajemi-oghlanlar*. They will become gardeners and gatekeepers and halberdiers and hangmen. Whereas we"—he paused for emphasis—"we will go on to rule the world."

With that, Murad was gone, leaving Danilo sitting on his rock, not quite able to believe what had just happened. And there he remained, uncertain of his next move until, taken by some errant impulse, he made his way back to the Doctor's House and headed straight for his father's *studiolo*. There on the wall hung a Gregorian calendar, a relic of his father's Italian life. He reached over for a quill, dipped it in the inkstand, and carefully circled the day's date: August 28 in the year 1530. *This*, he told himself, *is the happiest day of my life.*

It was not until nightfall, when he drew his bed curtains aside, that he fully realized that this would be his last night under the familiar silken coverlet. It had been his comfort since the first night he slept in his father's house, and he felt a powerful urge to wrap it around himself one more time. Instead, he turned away from the bed toward the box of clothes that Murad had left for him. When he opened it, there lay his new life, neatly folded. One by one, he began to shed his familiar garments and substitute each one with its replacement.

First came the new undergarments, not so different from the ones he was wearing but laundered to a whiteness never achieved in his father's laundry. Then the *shalvars*, perhaps a little more shapely than his regular trousers, but of a linen similar to what his father bought for him. The girdle was quite another matter. Made from cloth of gold and fastened with a golden clasp, it was the finest thing that he had ever worn in his life. After that came a shiny satin vest and a linen pocket handkerchief. All in all, a most generous gift. But Murad had saved the best for last.

At the bottom of the box lay a brocaded caftan wrapped in a linen bag. Danilo unwrapped it carefully and held it up against his body, dazzled by the richness of the fabric. Even his father did not own a caftan of such quality. Slipping into it was like stepping into another world. As he fastened the jeweled buttons, he began slowly to glide around the room, brocaded and bejeweled, bowing and murmuring greetings to unseen guests, as he had observed members of the Sultan's entourage doing.

Only once did it occur to him to wonder how his father would have viewed these trappings of Oriental decadence. And the moment the thought came, he banished it from his mind. Luckily, Judah was absent on an herb-buying jaunt to Venice and was not there to cluck his disapproval.

The next morning, just as the *muezzin* announced his second prayer of the day, Murad appeared as promised and, after a quick wardrobe inspection, led his charge across the Third Court past the massive columns and into the Palace School. There, poised at the giant doors of the Great Hall, the senior page paused to remove his boots, an example that Danilo quickly followed. When he looked up, what lay before his eyes almost took his breath away—a vast space paved in a black and white marble pattern, bordered by massive marble pillars, and topped by a painted dome smothered in azure and gold flowers. It presented a stunning contrast to the cozy Harem School. What made it seem even grander in Danilo's eyes was that the hall was almost completely empty at this hour except for the few pages who flitted back and forth like shadows without making a sound. In these precincts, Murad explained, silence was enforced out of respect for the Sultan, should he happen to honor them with a visit.

From the Great Hall, they proceeded through a labyrinth of marbled corridors until they reached a wide portal carved with a single motto, a warning to all on the premises that God ruled: *La Ilaha' Illa Allah Mohamed Rasoul Allah*. There is only one God and Mohamed is his prophet.

"And now we come to what will be your residence, the Hall of the First *Oda*," Murad announced as he ushered Danilo through the portal of his future home.

Perhaps the grandeur of the entrance hall had led him to expect too much. Whatever the reason, Danilo could hardly contain his disappointment at the meagerness of the dormitory. The room was big, God knows, but crowded from end to end with rows of tiny cubicles and hemmed in by a gallery halfway up the wall from which the entire room could be observed. In the Doctor's House, his father had provided him with a spacious, sunny private room, a soft bed, and a carved desk. Here, he was presented with a cell not much larger than his old bed, featuring a thin pallet, a lumpy kind of quilt, and a small storage chest, which, Murad explained, would do double duty as a desk.

Although Danilo tried his best, he could not conceal his disappointment from his sharp-eyed mentor.

"You'll be out of here before you know it," Murad assured him. "The competition for places on the *gerit* team begins tomorrow, and if you land a place on the team—which I hear is more than possible—you'll move right in with us, into the Third *Oda*. But first you need a haircut." With that, he led the way through the dormitory to an adjoining suite of rooms, the *hamam*.

Being still young and of fair complexion, Danilo had not much to show in the way of a beard and therefore not much to lose when it was summarily shaved off. But he had continued to keep his blond hair at shoulder length in the Italian style throughout his years in the Harem School. In a way, that cap of golden curls was his badge of identity. Now the curled locks lay all around him on the floor, except for one tress in front of each ear carefully trimmed to line up with the tip of his nose. He left the barber's chair feeling naked. The loss of his privacy, he could tolerate. But his hair...More than any other thing, that first haircut brought Danilo a glimmering of what it meant to be the Sultan's personal property, to be done with as his master wished.

Murad hurried him along to the first meal of the day, then being served. On this day, the new page was given special permission to take his meals with Murad and other members of the *gerit* team in the Hall of the Commissariat, all of them handsome, all good-spirited, all hungry like himself, and all ready to welcome a fellow athlete whose reputation for prowess with the *gerit* had preceded him. Just as Murad had planned it, this glimpse of what his life in the Palace School could become restored Danilo's will to make the team, or die trying.

Mind you, in living memory, no member of the First *Oda* had ever made the leap straight to the *gerit* team in the first try. But then, no Jew had ever been accepted to the Palace School either. And Danilo gathered from the hints he got at the commissary table that his value to the team had been the deciding factor in his acceptance to the school. Tidbits of conversation such as, "the team has been in need of some younger blood" and "we're looking forward to riding with you" and "it's time that every *oda* was represented on the team," suggested that his masters would likely want to make quick use of the talent they had selected him for.

That night, at the end of his first day and second meal, Murad brought his charge back to his dormitory, not as unabashedly happy as he had been before the haircut but fairly optimistic about his possibilities. After showing him how to unroll his blanket and how to hang it up the next morning, and teaching him the pages' main prayer for the Sultan—for the repose of the souls of dead sultans and for the guidance of the priests of the *Ulema*—it was time for Murad to say goodbye.

But wait. Just one more thing. As soon as Danilo received his first pocket money, he would be free to buy his own clothes. "But be sure," Murad warned, "to dress in a manly fashion. Especially do not choose feminine colors."

"Such as?"

"Oh, you know. Fuchsia or lavender. No black. And remember, you are the Sultan's page. People are watching you. Always have your clothes pressed and your caftan buttoned; underwear clean and—important—a fresh pocket handkerchief every day." This was the third time that day he had heard about the pocket handkerchief. It had been a long day. He had been shorn of his hair, like Samson, and pummeled and harangued and ordered around from sun-up to sunset. He had had enough.

But Murad, concerned lest he fail in his tutorial duties, plunged on. "Pay attention to what I tell you. You must be sure to take a bath at least once a week. And get a weekly manicure and pedicure. And shave at least twice a week. And have a hair-cut once a month."

Danilo was quite certain he had been given these instructions in full at the *hamam* that morning, but it seemed rude to interrupt so he nodded his understanding and let the lecture continue to roll over him. And roll on it did.

"It is anathema to manicure in public or to splash water on others in the *hamam*. And, in the dining hall, don't forget, never begin to eat until your superiors have been served and do not gobble up the food with your eyes no matter how hungry you are. Or eat in haste or talk with your mouth full. Above every-thing else, Allah forbid should you belch or hiccough during a meal." Had he not been so tired, Danilo would have become resentful by now. But he nodded agreeably, anything to get rid of his new *lala*.

"Last thing. In the street, no yawning, no stretching, no scratching, and no hunting for fleas."

Again, Danilo nodded obediently and was rewarded with a sudden curt, "I bid you good night." At last.

But as he was drifting off he heard, as if from a far-off dis-tance, the voice of Murad droning on in his head. "Something I need to tell you..."

This voice was not in his head. This voice was beside his ear on the pillow. This voice belonged to a hand that was shaking him awake. "This is important. Wake up and listen."

Wearily, Danilo opened his eyes.

"I forgot to impart to you the advice I received from my men-tor when I entered the school." Would this endless tutelage never stop?

"Tomorrow?" Danilo asked hopefully.

"'Tonight. There is paper and ink in your cask. Write this down. That way you will not forget." And there he stood, implacable, a sterner enforcer than any teacher Danilo had ever had, including his Albanian riding instructor.

"Now write."

Danilo dipped the pen into the ink and wrote, "A page must keep silent as a woodcutter in a Russian peasant's house. He must comport himself as if honey were on his tongue and oil of almonds on his back. At times he must be blinder than a mole, deafer than a heathcock, more insensible than a polypus. But, at other times, he must have the eyes of a lynx and the ears of a Pomeranian wolf-dog. He must learn to turn his eyes always upon the ground (as if Danilo was too stupid not to have noticed that all the pages kept their eyes on the ground) and to keep his arms always crossed over his breast. (That too!) As he approaches manhood, he must become more circumspect, trust no one, expect the worst. Mankind is wicked. Self-interest is the mainspring of action. And virtue is mere hypocrisy. Remember this," he concluded. "You know nothing of the world. How are old you? Fifteen?"

"Fourteen," Danilo acknowledged.

"As I said, a boy. That school in the harem is a nursery. This school will make you a man of the world. Someday you will thank me for this advice, even if tonight you hate me for disturbing your sleep. So, good night." This time, his mentor was gone for good. Left alone at last but now beyond fatigue, Danilo wondered if he was capable of remembering the catechism of instructions, which led him directly into questioning if he really wanted to. *Papa was right*, he thought. *This is no place for me. Rules, rules, rules. And a hard bed and bad food. Maybe I should give it up.*

Even a visit to the stables to register for the *gerit* contest the next morning did little to rekindle his enthusiasm. As he trundled his heavy gear to the practice field, he found himself wondering why he was there. Only a few steps away lay the comfort and freedom of his father's house. Why not just chuck the whole idea? Everybody knew that no page from the First *Oda* had a chance to play on the Sultan's *gerit* team. And the thought of spending an entire year in the First *Oda* being watched and measured and found wanting loomed up gloomy, bleak, and dismal.

That was his mood when he entered the lists for the hurling contest the next morning. Of course he won the first round against the boys of the lower *odas*. But what did that signify? Only that he was the best of the worst. And when the older contenders stepped up, his score was no better than their best. But in the riding ring, his mood began to change. It was one of those days when he could do nothing wrong. Riding backward toward the target, he fired off a stream of arrows and hit the target in the center every time. Galloping across the ring, he leaned down and retrieved a ball from the ground without slackening his pace for a moment. The entire afternoon went like that. And when he looked over at the judges' stand just before the final test, whom should he see but his riding master from the Harem School motioning at him with both thumbs up. A very good sign.

The final round was a jump, the highest he had ever attempted. He cleared it with room to spare and cantered off the field, still far from confident that he had passed the test but pleased with himself for having done his best. Whether that was good enough, only time would tell.

He had not long to wait. The final selections were announced in the dining hall that evening, and Danilo del Medigo, the freshman Jew, headed the list of those chosen to join the Sultan's *gerit* team that year.

Did he have a momentary longing for someone to share his good news with? Yes. Did he think wistfully of Princess Saida, his confidante and friend? Yes. But she was lost to him now, beyond reach. And his new teammates were beckoning.

Being younger than all the rest, he quickly became a kind of mascot to them, the frequent butt of rude jokes but at the same time the subject of real affection. And he had his horse for companionship, his own horse — a gift the Sultan gave to each member of his team—which Danilo named Bucephalus. And he had the rights to his own stall in the Sultan's stable, where he spent his evening hours combing and grooming the animal's coat until it shone, as he recalled his mother having told him she did as a girl. Buoyed by this double dose of good fortune, he barely had time to notice the darker side of his newly charmed life. And the news he sent to his father, who was away on campaign in the field, was all good.

Dear Papa:

Today in the ring, I un-saddled myself and re-saddled myself at full gallop. This is one of the four basic turns we must master in this first year. The last of the four is when we gallop two by two and switch horses in mid-gallop. I tried that once in the Harem School with Prince Mustafa as my partner, and we both ended up in the ditch with skinned knees. But here I know that I will master the move because my partners are all such excellent riders and we practice every day, rain or shine. I know that you view the *gerit* as a hazardous sport, but, Papa, a man can be trampled in the street by a runaway camel. And here, we learn slowly, step-by-step, always very carefully watched and constantly warned to take no unnecessary chances.

I hope this will allay your fears for my safety. Believe it or not, I am most secure when I am on the back of my horse. And, Papa, where else would I get to ride every day with my friends, on my own horse? And Bucephalus keeps me company in the evenings when the others are at the mosque. And, yes, I take my Torah

with me to the stables and read to him. I do not believe
it matters to God where or with whom we do our study.
Do you have thoughts on this?

Your most respectful son,
Danilo del Medigo

P.S. As you warned me, the discipline is strict, even
harsh. But there are no picky quarrels or tattle-telling
between us in this school, only friendship and loyalty,
because we stand or fall as a team.

I thank you every day for allowing me to be here
and I thank God every day for bestowing on me such
good fortune.

6

A WISH COME TRUE

STRICT? HARSH? IN WRITING ABOUT THE SCHOOL FOR Pages to his masters in the Venetian Senate, their *bailo* reported that discipline was enforced with an austerity and a relentlessness that rivaled a Capuchin monastery. For Danilo del Medigo, it represented a way of life unlike any other he had ever known. Having lived through the sack of Rome, he was no stranger to violence and cruelty. And certainly his residence in Topkapi, where every event unfolded with scrupulous obedience to protocol, had acquainted him with the formality of the Oriental style. But the impersonal, calculated punishment meted out by the school's eunuch overseers stationed night and day on the balcony overlooking his dormitory was something new in his experience. Monitored by the eunuchs for their behavior, by teachers for their academic performance, and by a *mullah* for their religious observance, the young pages were constantly subject to severe punishments for the slightest infringement—lateness, dirty shoes, a misspelled word, a whisper during prayers.

One hour before dawn, the sleeping pages were summoned by three strikes of a gong suspended from the ceiling of their dormitory. Half an hour later the Chief Aga came around to inspect their beds. Any page discovered still in his bed was pulled out and scolded. Always an early riser, Danilo did not find this onerous. But when one of his mates overslept for the third time and was punished with ten strokes of the bastinado that crippled him for a week, the screams of the offender when the cane cut into the soles of his feet seemed to bite into Danilo's own flesh as well.

The routine was unvarying. Lessons began at sun-up. At four hours after sunrise, the first meal was served, consisting of boiled mutton without sauce, a thin loaf of bread and a bowl of cheese, lentil or cream soup thickened with rice, honey, and saffron or currants. No salad, no sherbet, no melons, and no variation except for the currants.

Next came school work and athletic training followed by the second meal—the same monotonous repast as the first, day after day. With his already healthy appetite stimulated by daily bouts of physical exercise, Danilo would have been ready to gobble down the thinnest shepherd's gruel had it been the only dish on offer. But most of the pages—some more picky, others hungrier—complained bitterly about the food.

At sunset, prayers were attended in the mosque—from which the Jewish page was excused—followed by a quiet hour of Koran study and ablutions. The presiding eunuch announced bedtime by striking a cane on the floor. Lights out. No talking. In the morning while the pages were at the mosque, the caregivers searched through their trunks for groceries and love letters.

This regimen was followed six days a week, punctuated by the mandatory five prayer breaks each day. The only deviation was a serving of pilaf at the second meal every Thursday.

But twice a year two official *Bayram* festivals were celebrated: the *Bayram* of sacrifice that marks the sacrifice of Isaac and the *Bayram* of sweets at the end of Ramadan. On these two occasions, the pages dressed up in their finest clothes and attended a *baisemain* held by the Sultan where they kissed the hem of his garment and, with his blessing, received his permission to spend the next four days pleasuring themselves day and night.

Uninhibited by any thought of rules or punishment during these respites, they were permitted to leave the confines of their dormitory and cross the waterway, awash with caiques and barges loaded with revelers. Once landed, they were free to roam the streets of the capital unhindered and unfettered.

Other than the *Bayram* reprieves, it was all work and very little play for the Sultan's pages. Seen through the eyes of someone like the Venetian *bailo*, the investment of thought, time, energy, and money needed to keep this training school running seemed excessive. But to the Ottoman sultans, this school was the bedrock of what foreigners called the Ruling Institution and what their subjects simply called the Sultan's *cul*, a governing caste of slaves who owed allegiance strictly to him. This *cul* was the unique invention that had enabled an obscure mongrel nomadic tribe to conquer, hold, and expand a sphere of influence exceeding the Roman Empire in less than one hundred years.

The speed of that transformation boggled the European imagination. Observing it from the west, it seemed as if one day the Osman tribe was a ragged band of *ghazi* march warriors and overnight became the scourge of Christian Europe. Having converted early on to Islam and changed their name from Osman to Ottoman, they attributed their remarkable rise to the beneficence of Allah. They saw their mission as a *jihad* against infidels. But they went at it with a stony pragmatism that owed more to Sun Tzu than to Mohammed. And like their Oriental forbears they seemed to have a gift for recognizing problems early and solving them without delay, often using methods borrowed from others, in particular their enemies.

When, in the middle of the fourteenth century, the first Ottoman gave up being a march warrior in the style of Ghengis Khan, took on the title of Sultan, and set about to create an empire, he wasted no tears on the demise of his traditional tribal council. Clearly that instrument of clan life was inadequate to the tribe's new ambitions. In what became a hallmark of Ottoman style, the new Sultan and his advisors began to look around—not only in Asia but in Europe as well—for models of how other great powers protected, maintained, and managed their greatness.

To the west, the rapacious barons and rebellious dukes of Europe offered ample evidence that aristocracies of blood were breeding grounds for corruption and insurrection. So there would be nothing like a hereditary caste of nobles in the new Ottoman Empire, except for the heirs of the Sultan, the new title adopted for the former tribal chief.

The very idea of a republic was completely alien to their tribal tradition. But Egypt provided a useful exemplar. The Egyptians had bought themselves an entire army in the slave markets of the Mediterranean, had trained them to the highest levels, and had gone on to win battles with them. Why not take this practice a step further? Why not expand the role of the slave caste beyond the military to cover service in the civil arm of government as well?

Of course, certain small adjustments became necessary. The slave markets could and did supply soldiers and gardeners and grooms and hangmen, but they did not offer the superior types—boys of the highest intelligence and ability—who could be trained to run a world empire. For those candidates, the Ottoman Empire builders needed to cast their nets wider than the slave markets. As observant Muslims, they were prohibited from enslaving other Muslims. But the Koran had nothing to say about enslaving infidels.

Tax levies are as old as time. All over the world, farmers give up a portion of their crops as fiefs. The church exacts tithes from its followers. It is an old idea. But the Ottomans bent it in a new direction. Their ingenious invention, the *devshirme,* was an impost not of taxes or crops but of manpower, specifically a levy of one son out of every thirty born to the conquered Christian families in the Ottoman Empire. Of the judges sent abroad to harvest this human crop, it was said that they were more skilled in judging boys than trained horse dealers were in judging colts.

Out of each draft of the *devshirme*, the most physically perfect, the most intelligent, and the most promising boys in every respect were set aside for the Sultan's personal service. They became members of his *cul*. Once selected, these "tribute boys" were immediately converted to Islam. But these slaves rarely severed their Christian roots completely. Deep inside them, there often ran a tendency toward drunkenness and whoring (for which, with typical Ottoman bureaucratic efficiency, a provision had been made in the form of the semi-annual *Bayram* outings during which all rules of behavior were suspended).

Once they were certified as loyal Muslims, the pages of the *cul* were assigned to one of the Sultan's personally supervised schools, which also served as training grounds for his sons and nephews. There the brainiest became bureaucrats, the brawniest became officers, and from them all the highest posts in the land were commissioned. Once selected, all were treated equally — prince or slave, it made no difference.

Not surprisingly the Europeans were shocked when they discovered that this formidable new Turkish Empire was not actually ruled by the Turks themselves but by a Christian-born slave caste. It cut clean across the hereditary principle they held so dear. Equally incredible were the reports that in many poor areas, Christian families vied for the chance to send their sons into Muslim slavery, seeing opportunity where any right-thinking Christian could see only shame. But some perceptive European observers were impressed by the invention of the *devshirme*. One of them, Ogier Ghiselin de Busbucq, the Flemish ambassador to Istanbul, described the *cul* system as a "ruthless meritocracy."

"Their ideas are not our ideas," he wrote. "They care for men as we care for our horses," he explained to his masters. "With us birth is the standard for everything. There is no opening left for merit. The prestige of birth is the sole key to advancement in the public service, whereas among the Turks no distinction is attached to birth. Each man in Turkey carries in his own hand his ancestry and his position in life, to make or mar as he will.

Those so-called slaves who receive the highest offices from the Sultan are most often the sons of shepherds and herdsmen, and far from being ashamed of their parentage they actually glory in it. Nor do they believe that high qualities are either natural or hereditary but, rather, the result of good training, great industry, and unwearied zeal. So honors, high posts, and judgeships are the rewards of great ability and good service. And if a man be dishonest or lazy or careless, he remains at the bottom of the ladder."

In the pages' schools continuous thought and care were devoted to training worthy boys for leadership. As the ever-astute Busbecq pointed out to his civilized Belgian patrons, with no little irony, "In Europe, if we find a good dog or hawk or horse we spare nothing to bring it to the greatest perfection of its kind. But if a young man happens to possess an extraordinary disposition, we do not take like pains. And we receive much pleasure and many kinds of service from the well-trained dog, horse, and hawk, but the Turks receive much more from a well-educated man."

Nowhere was the painstaking care that Busbecq noticed more lavish than in the Sultan's own Palace School. There, not only were the pages guided carefully through their curriculum of study and sport, they were also monitored in the more mundane aspects of their daily lives — deportment, posture, diet, grooming, hygiene, to mention a few.

Nothing was left to chance. In setting up a schedule for the boys, care had been taken to calculate the exact point at which a group of constantly monitored, tightly controlled young men of high spirits and good health would need a release from discipline. How often should they be given a refreshing break from their rigid routine? Once a year? Twice a year? Twice a year seemed about right. That was the point at which it must have occurred to some long-dead vizier that, by a happy coincidence, the widely celebrated *Bayram* festivals could serve a useful, double purpose since they too occurred twice a year. And ever since, the Palace School dedicated each *Bayram* to both religious observance and pleasure. So it was that twice a year the pages were set free, as it were, to loosen up their tight muscles, soothe their raw nerves, and banish anxious thoughts from their minds.

Perhaps it was the ultimate measure of the control exercised over these boys that even their freedom was doled out in measured doses at regular intervals like medicine. And, just in case twice a year was not quite enough of a tonic to restore good humor and willing obedience, the Sultan by decree proclaimed his own festivals to celebrate royal weddings, circumcisions, and military victories — additional opportunities for the pages to run wild for four days.

By the time his first *Bayram* rolled around, Danilo del Medigo was more than ready for it. He was already beginning to chafe at the unvarying routine and the constant surveillance. But unlike his fellow pages, who talked longingly of getting drunk and raising hell in Galata, he found himself nursing thoughts of stretching out on the rock ledge at Palace Point looking seaward to what his mother called "the wine-dark sea." Many nights he dreamed of being carried over the waves back to Italy in a sleek, black caique, often waking up with traces of tears on his face.

Even the new horse that he had renamed Bucephalus didn't bring him much in the way of comfort. He knew he ought to be happy. He had everything he always wanted. His wishes had been granted. And his father's oft-quoted warning often came to mind. "Be careful what you wish for. You may get your wish."

In his Book of Pages, the Chief White Eunuch had recorded only one black mark against the name Danilo del Medigo in his first quarter. The offense noted was Occasional Inattention. Not General Inattention, simply Occasional Inattention. The Aga had recorded that during lessons the doctor's son showed a tendency to drift off as if to another country and needed to be jarred back to attention with a stick.

The Aga further reported that the page was observed adrift in this strange mental state during the reading of one of the Sultan's own poems. (Suleiman, a great admirer of many Persian things, wrote poems in that tongue under the pseudonym *Muhabbi* or He Who Loves.)

It was the opinion of his teacher that abstraction eluded del Medigo. The boy had a mind only for the practical, such as the calculation a *gerit* player must make, weighing speed against balance, to choose the precise moment for the thrust. His body, the teacher wrote, was more intelligent than his mind. But it is worth noting that this teacher was himself a Persian poet and thus inclined to value poetry over horsemanship.

The page's riding instructor, an Albanian who therefore took horses seriously, had awarded del Medigo the highest mark in horsemanship. This page was destined to engage in a tournament at the hippodrome, he reported. Pleading the case of his star student, the Albanian pointed out to his fellow *lalas* that the boy was the youngest member of the Sultan's team and that, while he was a pupil in the Harem School, he became accustomed to living at home. Dormitory life was a big change for him. Further, because the annual military campaign got a late start that year, the page's father, the Sultan's Chief Body Physician, had not yet returned home for the winter. Perhaps the page missed his father. He was, after all, a motherless boy far from his homeland. Maybe that was where his mind wandered—to far-off Italy or to his mother who had perished at sea while bringing him to Istanbul. Then, because no human being, no matter how understanding, is not completely lacking in prejudice, he added, "The boy is, after all, a Jew. A special case."

Although he did not acknowledge it to his colleagues, the Albanian riding master was beginning to have his own reservations about his protégé. Of late, del Medigo had become careless in the riding ring, rushing the jumps, his balance slightly off. He seemed almost to be courting danger for its own sake, a serious shortcoming in a young rider. But there was one point on which all the teachers agreed: if anything could cure del Medigo of his malaise, it was the coming *Bayram* break. A few nights in the fleshpots of Galata were all he needed to bring him back to his old self.

And indeed, when Danilo returned to his class after his first taste of *Bayram*, he was a changed person: attentive in his classes, meticulous in his riding style, convivial with his mates. *Bayram* had done the trick. But not for the reasons that his teachers thought.

Danilo did not go off to Galata with his teammates on the eve of his first *Bayram* break. After attending the Sultan's *baise-main* with them, he excused himself with a lame explanation about some Jewish obligation. Hell-bent on reaching the inns of Galata before dark, his mates left him to his own devices and he set off at sundown for the rocky ledge overlooking the Grand Vizier's dock. There, he spent two hours shivering from cold and nerves, reaching into his sash every so often for the note, by now well-thumbed, that he had found tucked into his blanket that morning.

Written in red chalk, wrapped around a cinnamon stick, and tied with a silken ribbon, it read, "If you are still my paladin, be on the ledge above the water after the last prayer. Fortune favors the bold. Burn this." At the bottom, two dots and two dashes. No signature. No need for one.

Of course he did not burn the note. He had kept it nestled under his sash, next to his skin throughout the day, except for the times he took it out and rubbed it between his fingers in anticipation. As he wiled away the hours waiting on the ledge, the feel of it in his hands warmed his fingers. But, at the same time, the message itself chilled his heart.

During their days in the Harem School, he and his princess had been seen as children and their escapades in the woods of Kinali as pranks. But now, Princess Saida was officially the Sultan's marriageable daughter. And Danilo del Medigo was one of the Sultan's chosen pages for whom a hint of betrayal such as a dalliance with the Sultan's daughter meant instant death. Hence the shiver that came over him when he reached into his sash to touch the note that was left under his pillow that morning.

When the shadow of the Sultan's caique finally appeared around the cove, he hardly dared peer out. Then he heard a whistle that seemed to issue from the caique—two long, two short. Gathering his courage, he placed his fingers on his lips and imitated the code. All this whistling was bound to attract attention. But wasn't that the idea?

Footsteps. Too late now to make a run for it. If this meeting had been found out, if these were the Sultan's men coming to get him, he was as good as dead anyhow. He straightened his shoulders and walked out into the darkness to meet his fate, a fate that presented itself in the shape of a fat, black eunuch looming up in the darkness and beckoning him silently onto the craft moored at the dock. It was a sleek skiff resembling a Venetian gondola with an upturned prow painted white with gold markings and a green border along its length. In the center there was a canopied seat spread with embroidered velvet cushions. Behind it a flag emblazoned with the Sultan's personal *tugra* fluttered in the breeze.

The trip to the island of Kinali was made in perfect silence. Coming ashore for the first time since he left the Princes School, Danilo hardly recognized the little island that served as a childhood playground for him and his princess. Months had passed since he said goodbye to everything it symbolized. But, once ashore, his feet found their way through the underbrush to the familiar clearing and there stood the ruined mosque, roofless but with its walls still intact, the rusty portal, the half-hinged gate.

"Is that my paladin returned from the foreign wars and come to rescue me from this cave?" a sweet voice crooned in the dark.

He pushed through the gate into the moonlit mosque and found his princess reclining on a bed of dried leaves, supported all around by pillows; her long, black hair loose, her eyes blazing, an ethereal vision in some diaphanous stuff that made her seem suspended in a cloud. This was a side of his princess he had never seen before.

"Are you still my paladin?" Her voice emerged low and husky from the cloud.

"I am, Princess." He slid easily into the old familiar game.

"And will you love me faithfully as long as we live?"

"I will, Princess."

Then, in a move quite new to the game, she emerged from her bed of leaves like one of Raphaello's angels rising up to heaven, held out her arms, and commanded him, "Embrace me."

The *coup de foudre* struck them both at once with the suddenness of a thunderbolt on a cloudless summer day, and they clung to each other with an intensity that surprised them both. At that moment, Danilo was not quite sure whether he was the Sultan's page embracing the Princess Saida or Zerbino embracing Princess Isabella.

Hours later, in the deep night when he was lying in his own bed, he tried to recapture the evening in memory. But it eluded him like a half-remembered dream. No, not a dream. More as if Aphrodite had descended from on high, clad in her magic girdle, and bestowed on him a gift from the gods. None of it was anything like his experience with the generous whore at Ostia who had promised to take him on a trip to heaven. Making love to a princess whose virginity was inviolate turned out to be quite different from making love to a whore.

His night with the whore—appreciated and never to be forgotten—had been an adventure of the senses: arousal and satisfaction. With the princess, there was never a question in his mind that he would satisfy himself at the expense of her virginity. In the Sultan's eyes, his daughter's hymen was his jewel, to be bestowed by him on a husband of his choosing. And any man who aimed to take possession of that jewel was a dead man. But, his own pleasure aside, Danilo would never have allowed himself to expose Saida to the risk of punishment that was bound to fall on her if she were to dishonor her father by losing her virginity before marriage. Nevertheless, when he cupped her naked breasts he felt he had the world in his hands. For that reward, holding himself back from the act of possession was a small price to pay.

By the time the next *Bayram* holiday rolled around he was prepared for the black eunuch on the Sultan's caique. And the princess's explanation that Narcissus (the name given to the eunuch slave when he was cut) was her grandmother's steward and acted with the Valide's authority, went a long way toward explaining how a black slave was able, in defiance of both law and custom, to transport a princess and a page in one of the Sultan's own fleet of caiques to a tryst on the Princes' Islands. If the Valide's factotum made a request in her name, only a fool would question it, much less refuse to honor it. As to how the princess had managed to slip in and out of the Sultan's harem after dark—it being the second-most carefully guarded enclave in the entire empire (the Sultan's *selamlik* was, of course, the first)—Danilo had only a single clue: a request the princess made of him casually when their first rendezvous came to a close. How difficult would it be, she inquired, for him to come by a medicine from his father's pharmacy without the doctor's knowledge?

"Not at all difficult," he allowed. "Name your poison."

She shuddered. "No, not a poison. What I need is a strong sleeping draft that can be brewed in a pot of tea and will keep the person who drinks it fast asleep all night long. But not," she quickly added, "something that would do the person any harm."

He arrived at their next meeting bearing a flacon which, he assured her, contained enough calming medicine to put an entire army to sleep, doled out at the rate of five drops per cup. She thanked him prettily with a curtsy as if he had presented her with a bouquet of posies, and the matter was never discussed between them again.

After that first rendezvous they met secretly every *Bayram*, and whatever festivals cropped up in between, on the little island of Kinali and made love—chaste love. For Danilo, the magic of her never went away. The sweetness of her breath, the taste of her skin, never lost their savor, spiced as they were by the risk, the danger, and even by the very infrequency of their meetings. And, as one *Bayram* followed another, those meetings became more and more like journeys to a different country, in a time out of mind.

Can children fall in love? Yes, if the blood is hot enough and the stakes are high enough. To Danilo, a boy who had always lived in his body, the princess was round and soft like a girl and she kissed like a girl, but she rode and punched like a boy. To the Sultan's daughter, he was the farthest thing in the world from the old, fat Vizier with greasy black hair and beady eyes that she was destined to marry. What they had stumbled into was so perilous that it was bound to become irresistible to a boy chafing at the iron bonds of school discipline, and a girl no less bound by the silken cords of the harem, which grew tighter with each passing day. Perhaps the question was not how could such a thing have happened, but how could it not?

7

PALADIN REDUX

NEARLY TWO YEARS HAD PASSED SINCE THE
princess and the paladin graduated from the Harem
School. By now they had mastered the stealth, the
logistics, and the rules of their game. Most important, both
had the nerve for this dangerous escapade, and the talent. On
the little island of Kinali they found their ideal venue. And,
surprisingly, between the two of them, they had been able
to summon up enough patience to keep their fragile creation
afloat through four *Bayrams,* plus a festival to mark the birth of
a third son to Hürrem (a hunchback, true, but still a boy), and
a celebration of Sultan Suleiman's conquest of Budapest. Only
six meetings, none longer than a few brief hours, but each long
enough to fan the flame and keep it alive.

Since Danilo's unfortunate lapse during his reading of the
Sultan's poem, he had managed to avoid any further black
marks against his name in the Chief Eunuch's Book of Pages.
He had also made his father proud by learning and performing
the ancient Hebrew ritual that earns a Jewish boy a place among
Jewish men. And the day after the Sultan's homecoming from
Austria, he was to make his debut at the hippodrome as a

member of the Sultan's *gerit* team in the games dedicated to the current victory at Guns.

There had been times during the last two years that the tight bounds of a page's life seemed to Danilo too high a price to pay for its rewards, times when he was tempted to give it up, cry, "Enough!" and retreat to the safety and comfort of his father's house. But just when the rigid, cloistered routine seemed more than he could bear, along came Narcissus bearing a silk-wrapped summons to rescue him. Somehow the prospect of those nocturnal escapes, as well as their pleasure, managed to supply whatever mysterious glue holds lovers together. Only once since their first rendezvous at Kinali had the fragile idyll threatened to collapse.

It was on the eve of their third *Bayram* together as they were about to part. By unspoken agreement, they never said good-bye to each other. But this time, Danilo, overtaken by a sudden stab of misgiving, blurted out, "How do I know if I will ever see you again?"

Suddenly rigid in his arms, the princess glared at him. "We don't know. That is how things are between us."

What had he done to turn her so cold?

"You don't understand. Let me explain. Have you never wondered why I am still an unmarried virgin at close to fifteen years old? A year and a half out of the Harem School and not a husband in sight?"

He had not. "But I have often wondered how you manage to commandeer your father's caique," he told her. "And how you get Narcissus to risk his life for you."

"Narcissus is a separate matter," she replied, brushing his question aside. "Only one person counts in my life. My grandmother. It is she who holds my happiness in her hands. In her name, anything can be done. She is the Valide Sultan. No one disobeys her orders or any orders given by her steward in her name."

"Are you telling me she approves of"—he gestured around him—"us?"

"Of course not. But she wants me to stay at her side until she dies, which means that I will not marry as long as she lives. Which means I am free to do as I please...for now," she said, leaning heavily on the now. "But my grandmother is not well. She gets weaker every day. One of these days, she will die."

"And then?"

"I will be married off to some fat, old, toothless pasha or vizier. Have you ever thought of that?"

"Is there no way out?" he asked gently.

"None."

After that flat, final word there seemed to be nothing more to say. But, in the silence that followed, a thought occurred to him. "What about me?" he asked.

"You? You will be fine. You will marry a pretty girl of your own faith and be happy with her. I am the one who will spend her nights in hell."

"I didn't mean what would happen to me. I meant me for a husband. I could marry you."

"A man of no fortune or future and a Jew to boot? You marry an Ottoman princess? Ha!"

The laugh that accompanied this blunt assessment seemed so cold, so calculating, that he turned away from her.

"Now you mustn't get sticky about it. You will make me cry and spoil everything." Then, without warning, she leaned close, took his face in her hands, and looking deep into his eyes continued with a tenderness he had never seen in her before. "What we have is a miracle. Somehow the gods were looking the other way and let it happen. But it wasn't meant to be and it can't last. You once told me that we inhabited the same world. And yes, here in Kinali, we do. But out there"—she gestured toward the towering landscape of the city behind them—"out there, we do not. You come from a place where anything is possible. I belong to a world where everything is foreordained. My faith tells me that I have a destiny to fulfill and it has given me the strength to perform my duty. I will marry and you will go back to Europe where you belong. For us, there is no tomorrow. That is our fate. But I will die knowing that at least I have had a taste of true love. That is all there is for me. And, if my grandmother lives on, maybe a tomorrow or two. So let us enjoy it.

"Think of me." She pressed his hands in hers urgently. "I am the one who is going to marry some smelly old reprobate and bear his children."

"I don't like to think about it," he admitted.

"Nor do I," she said. "So let us not. Let us never mention the future again. Let us not even allow it into our dreams. Agreed?"

"Agreed."

"Promise on your honor?"

"I promise."

Since then, two *Bayrams* came and went, and their vow had been honored scrupulously. The moment that the Sultan's sleek black caique bearing the Sultan's *tugra* pulled up on the silver sands of Kinali, time stopped. And only when the craft returned to collect him did the clock start to tick again.

By now, Zerbino and Isabella had left center stage. Danilo and Saida didn't talk much but, when they did, they spoke as themselves, in their own voices, telling each other tales of things that had happened to them in their younger years. They rarely talked about events in the present. Somehow, the present edged too close to the future.

Most of the time, they rolled around in the leaves exchanging passionate kisses. Sometimes they played the games of childhood. Perhaps because she was younger, Saida cherished a fancy for tag and blind man's bluff, flitting from tree to tree like a naughty nymph while Danilo staggered around blindfolded trying to catch her. He could never understand how someone so silly could muster such a resolute will. Still, a part of him loved her fancies and her contradictions and her dress-ups.

What will it be this time? he wondered as he waited on the rock ledge for his transport to Kinali. The last time they were together, on the eve of the *Bayram* of Sweets, she had greeted him with a bowl of iced sherbet that she swore she had made with her own hands. The time before that, she had brought along a mysterious dream powder for them to sniff that made him sleepy all the next day. It certainly made for a sweet *Bayram,* but with his *gerit* debut only a day away, it wouldn't do for tonight. Definitely, he thought, if she turned up with some new potion, he must regretfully decline.

But when he reached the little green glade, she was not there. Instead, he was met at the rusty gate by a lone horse tethered to the iron railing, switching its tail and nibbling contentedly on the vines twined around the gateway.

An avid reader of Fuyuzi's *Book of Equines*, he could not resist the urge to give the animal a quick appraisal — teeth, nose, withers, haunches — at which point he was interrupted by the familiar lilting voice.

"Is that my paladin come to rescue me?"

He pushed through the gate into the moonlit mosque and there she was, not reclining but sitting upright, a far cry from the harem odalisque who had first appeared at Kinali with kohl-blackened eyes swathed in diaphanous scarves. This girl, gotten up as a horse trader in a fringed leather vest and a pair of pointy, studded riding boots.

"What do you think of my horse?" she inquired, narrowing her eyes in the manner of a wily bargainer. "How much would you give me for him?"

"How much are you asking?" he drawled, trying to make his eyes even shiftier than hers. He knew she could never sell the horse even if she wanted to. Everything she owned belonged ultimately to her father.

"I might take nineteen hundred," she teased.

"That's robbery. His teeth are black. His ears are too close together. He's long-waisted, his n\ose is too big and his back has a curve in it." Danilo had learned a thing or two from Fuyuzi.

"It doesn't matter." She shrugged. "I've changed my mind about selling him."

"Why?"

"Because I'm fond of him. I've named him after your father."

"You what?"

"He's the best horse I ever had so I named him after your father."

"You named him Judah?"

"Not the doctor. Your blood father, Lord Birro, the knight beyond fear or reproach. I did it for you." He was not as pleased as she expected he would be. "We Ottomans are not too proud to name our horses after the people we love," she advised him haughtily.

He smiled, amused at her prickly pride. "Don't try to use that 'we Ottomans' line on me, Princess. You forget, I know that you are more like half-Mongol, half-Turkoman on your father's side and your mother was a Seljuk."

"A Seljuk princess," she corrected him.

"And my blood father is indeed a Christian knight. But," he corrected her, "his name is not Birro. It is Pirro. Lord Pirro Gonzaga."

"Well, it's too late to change the horse's name now," she told him, tossing the subject aside with a wave of the hand. "He's registered at the stud."

That settled that point. "But where did you tell your father you got that name?" he asked.

"I told him Birro was an Egyptian warrior at the time of Ramses the Second."

"And he believed it?"

"My father knows nothing about ancient Egypt," she sniffed.

He shook his head, overcome by the combination of her duplicity and her candor. "Do me a good turn, will you, Princess? If you ever stop being my friend, let me know. Because I wouldn't have a chance against you as an enemy."

The very word wiped the mischief off her face. Her eyes widened. Her tone softened. "But I could never be your enemy. You are the love of my life." She said this quietly, without touching him and yet with a piercing gaze that fixed the words in his heart more securely than an embrace.

These times on Kinali had a strange quality. Short though they were—a few hours at best—there was no haste about them, no pressure to snatch at each moment as if it might be their last. They simply took up where they had left off months before as if only days or hours had gone by; as if theirs was one long, unbroken courtship; as if each kiss, each touch only reached farther into their hearts to reveal a new depth of passion. And, when time crept up on them, no matter how many hours they had managed to steal, it always seemed as if hardly a moment had passed.

A shrill signal from the Kinali shore announced the arrival of the Sultan's caique. Their time was up.

Still, she did not release him from her gaze but put her hands on his shoulders to draw them closer together. "I would give all my treasure to see you ride at the hippodrome," she told him. "But since I cannot, this will watch over you in my stead and keep you from harm." In one swift move, she looped a chain around his neck and dropped something small and cold on his chest. Then she was gone, and he was left to make his way to the waiting caique that would ferry him back to the Grand Vizier's dock.

All the way home he was conscious of the disk pressing against his naked chest but something in him resisted taking it out and looking at it. Not until he was in bed in his dormitory did he finally reach under his quilt and hold it up to the light. It was a deep blue eyeball embedded in a white orb—the traditional talisman against evil that hung in every Turkish household. But, unlike those common amulets, this one had a clear, bright blue sapphire gem mounted at its center.

As he peered into the crystalline depths of the jewel, thoughts of the future invaded his mind. *How long can I have her? How long before we get caught? You promised,* he reminded himself, *never to think of the future. Not even in dreams. If you must dream,* he told himself, *dream of the gerit. The gerit... Bucephalus...*

Now, for the first time in this long night, he remembered that, in his haste to obey Narcissus's summons, he had failed to make his nightly visit to the stables. Tossing aside his covers, he threw on a cloak and made his way in the dawning light to the Sultan's stables in the Second Court. To be sure, Bucephalus was awake, waiting patiently for his master's good-night caress.

"You waited up for me. You are a good old horse." He took the horse's majestic head in his hands and looked into the soft, sleepy eyes. "The truth is, once I got her note, I lost my senses. That's how it is with women. They're not like we are. They beguile you."

Absentmindedly, he reached over for a handful of feed and held it out. And Bucephalus, either because he had a forgiving nature or because he was feeling peckish, accepted the peace offering, then lay down on his bed of hay and was soon fast asleep.

By now, the sun was up. A weary Danilo trudged back to his bed vowing to put all other thoughts out of his mind and concentrate on preparing himself for the upcoming contest. The empty pallets all around him gave evidence that most of the pages in his *oda* were still out carousing the stews of Galata. Very well for them. But he was a member of the Sultan's first team. Twenty-four hours from now, he would be riding into the oval of the hippodrome as thousands cheered. His coaches had placed their faith in him. His teammates depended on him.

Inshallah, he repeated aloud, trying to evoke in himself some sense of being in the hands of a higher power. But the words that seemed to bolster up his teammates didn't work for him. His god did not interfere in horse races. If he did well in tomorrow's *gerit*, it would not be because Allah had willed it but because he, Danilo del Medigo, had proven himself worthy. This night had been a mistake. He ought to have spent it resting his mind and body. But it was not in his nature to regret things done that could not be undone. What he needed now was a day to restore his tired muscles and clear his mind of any impediment that might cloud his judgment on the field. Sleep.

He was about to fall on his pallet fully clothed when he caught sight of a sheet of vellum pinned to the quilt, handwritten and stamped with the Sultan's *tugra*. It was a *firman* entitling the bearer to a place in Divan Square, where a select group of courtiers would gather that afternoon to welcome the Padishah home from his Austrian wars. An invitation from the Sultan was tantamount to a summons. But mostly the boy was thinking of his father, who would be searching the crowd eagerly for the sight of him. He must be there, behind the velvet rope, when his father rode by in Suleiman's train. There would be no long day of rest for him. *Better sleep fast*, he told himself as he closed his weary eyes.

8

ON THE EVE

EVERY YEAR ON AN APRIL DAY AFTER RAMADAN, THE vast conglomeration of men, animals, weapons, and baggage trains that constitute the Ottoman war machine gathered in a field north of Istanbul. They came together, the British consul reported to his masters, as though they had been invited to a wedding. War was a season to them, he observed, like winter.

The previous spring, on a day sanctioned by the court astrologer as most auspicious, the Ottoman army led by the Sultan had set off on campaign to Austria. Their goal: plunder territory to add to an expanding empire that had already yielded them more land than the Romans controlled at the height of their power. Today, after a long, hard campaign that took him halfway across Europe to the gates of Vienna, Suleiman the Magnificent was coming home.

To prepare the crowds gathered on the streets of Istanbul to greet him, heralds had spent the evening trumpeting news of his capture of the Austrian town of Guns on the return journey. No one dared to question how it was that the Sultan failed to take Vienna and was forced by the onset of winter to raise his siege of the Austrian capital and return home. That detail of the campaign was not spoken of. Not in his palace. Not in the streets. Not even in that breeding ground of gossip and rumor, the Grand Bazaar of Istanbul. What would be celebrated today was that, once again, the campaign season had ended in a glorious victory for their Padishah, Defender of Islam and the Shadow of God on Earth. The Austrian stronghold of Guns had been captured. No mention of Vienna.

The Padishah's welcome promised to be tumultuous. The Turks were proud of their victorious sultans. And the sultans in their turn took care to provide a celebration, lasting at least a week, of parades and games and music and dancing and free food.

The heralds had not yet announced the exact hour of the Sultan's arrival on the streets of the city from his staging area across the Bosphorus. But, in spite of strenuous efforts to keep it secret, news of his imminent appearance had somehow filtered across the waterway, floated down into the Grand Bazaar, and was rapidly spreading through the streets of Istanbul.

"Have you heard? The Padishah will arrive today."

"They say he has already decamped at Üsküdar."

"I have it from a reliable source at the palace. He will not be home until tomorrow morning."

As he trudged across town the black eunuch named Narcissus paid no attention to the whispers. In his position as chief steward to the Sultan's mother, the Valide Sultan, he was party to every detail of the monarch's itinerary, both at home and abroad. Suleiman kept in daily contact with his mother. When he was on campaign, he wrote to her every day. When he was in residence at his walled domain in Topkapi Palace, he visited her daily at the Old Palace where she ruled his harem. During his long absences on campaign, he appointed her his Regent. And because Narcissus had this great lady's complete confidence, the black slave knew everything she knew, every intimate detail of her life including the precise hour at which her son would cross over the Bosphorus from the staging area at Üsküdar to parade through the streets of the city.

Like all eunuchs, Narcissus tended toward obesity. It was a long, hot climb for him from the harem to Topkapi Palace. But Narcissus soared above the buzz of the streets, buoyed by the vast sea of rumor and gossip that surrounded him. As he climbed the steep winding road to Palace Point, rivulets of perspiration ran down his plump face. Partly it was the unseasonable heat of the autumn day that made him sweat, partly nerves. Periodically he would reach down to pat into place the small pouch that hung from his girdle. That silken sheath contained an item that, should it be discovered, could cause great distress to the sender. As for the effect of such a discovery on the messenger, Narcissus shuddered at the thought of the beating he would suffer if the pouch at his waist were to fall into the hands of some officious palace guard. He could feel the sting of the *bastinado* on the soles of his feet just thinking of it.

Once he had reached the summit, the overheated slave took a moment to wipe his brow, plan his next move, and survey the scene that stretched out before him. Many years ago when this summit was captured from the Byzantines by the Ottoman conqueror, the peak had been flattened to accommodate a citadel — the last stand, if need be, for the defense of the city. But seven decades of Ottoman rule had slowly erased all evidence of its military past, and now, viewed from its towering Imperial Gate, Topkapi Saray stretched ahead in an adjoining series of three enclosed courtyards, each separated from the other by a gated wall. Behind the massive ramparts that enclosed the entire *saray* there was no single structure to house the monarch. Instead each court contained a scattering of airy kiosks and pavilions dotted about like stone tents, giving the whole place a closer resemblance to a nomadic encampment than to a European-style palace.

Narcissus encountered no difficulty passing through the Imperial Gate into the first of the palace's three courts, a huge rectangle that extended for a thousand feet called the Procession Court. Traditionally every citizen of the Ottoman Empire — slave or free — had the right to petition the Sultan in his palace.

As a consequence, the Procession Court was always packed with a generous sampling of the palace clientele: petitioners on foot, ambassadors bearing gifts, carts loaded with twittering Circassian virgins, and hundreds of palace personnel scurrying about like a colony of ants, all weaving their way between horses and groups of swaggering Janissaries in white turbans and yellow boots.

A keen eye could also spot the occasional ghostly figure of one of the Sultan's security guards, who went by the name Men in Black because they did double duty as hangmen and executioners, hangings and executions being a routine part of life in the First Court. What was missing from the scene on this day was the fairly common sight of a severed head on an iron spit, thrusting up out of the conical top of one of the towers of the medieval gate, left there to blacken in the sun as a warning to anyone who incurred the Sultan's displeasure.

In this mélange, one single, fat, black eunuch hardly merited attention. But at the next gate, the so-called Gate of Welcome at the far end of the Procession Court, two tall crenelated towers silently proclaimed the end of public access and the beginning of extreme vigilance. At the Gate of Welcome (who among the sober Ottomans could have chosen this ironic designation for the site where the occasional human head is mounted on a pike?), all must dismount except the Sultan himself and, of course, his mother, the Valide Sultan. Even the Grand Vizier dismounted at the Gate of Welcome and walked into the Second Court in his stockings.

Although the Gate of Welcome presented a direct entry to his destination, Narcissus had no intention of risking an encounter with its notoriously unwelcoming guardians. Instead, once through the gate he veered sharply left toward the old Christian Church of Irene, which was currently enjoying a Muslim incarnation as an armory. Smooth as an eel, he slithered in and out among a number of small kiosks toward the outer wall of the palace beyond the church.

A devotee of beauty, the pleasure-loving Narcissus was

sorely tempted to linger a moment and enjoy the gardens, scattered with flowers, shaded by casual groupings of orange trees, bisected by winding paths, spicy with the scent of jasmine, and soft to the foot. These were the touches that gave the palace its cognomen, the Abode of Bliss.

But Narcissus had no time for bliss. He headed straight for a small opening in the outer wall known as the Boot Gate, which he had been told was likely to be unguarded this day. Everyone in the Sultan's service had been conscripted to help prepare the capital for the victory parade. With a good part of the palace staff thus seconded to the procession route, it was all but certain that he would find an unimportant post like the Boot Gate neglected. And, to be sure, when Narcissus pushed aside the vines that concealed the little arch, he found it completely unmanned and was able to stroll unhindered into the wild moraine beyond the walls.

Here, in stark contrast to the manicured palace grounds within, the terrain had reverted to its true nature: a rock-strewn, prickly undergrowth with only the occasional neglected orchard to recall the days when the early Ottoman sultans raised fruit for their tables in their own backyard. In this virtual wilderness, Narcissus could traverse the full length of the palace grounds outside the walls, unimpeded by the guardians of either the Gate of Welcome or the last of the three gates, the Gate of Felicity. There, at the end of the summit, he only had to scale the wall to regain access to the Sultan's private grounds undetected.

Narcissus was well acquainted with the dense thicket that surrounded the citadel and quickly located the outer pathway known to its familiars as the Eunuch's Path, so-called because it was customarily used by palace slaves bent on errands of dubious legitimacy. When they spoke among themselves of this walkway, the students in the dormitories of the School for Pages located in the Third Court told tales of sneaking along the Eunuch's Path in the dark night and being tripped, pricked with thistles, and beaten bloody by the evil jinn who hide out in tree trunks.

Narcissus was not put off by such tales. As he zigzagged between patches of light where the sun slanted down through breaks in the foliage, he was secure in his knowledge that jinn never operate by daylight, only by night. What did frighten him were the Janissaries who stood guard over the Third Court and would as soon kill an intruder as look at him.

An even more immediate concern was how he would scale the wall to get back into the palace grounds. Would it still be there, that ancient, creaky fruit ladder that had served him and so many before him?

Narcissus sank to his knees and uttered a short prayer: *Please let the ladder be in its place.* Having been raised a Christian, he had never fully espoused the religion to which he was converted by the circumcision knife. He did not read the Koran, did not pray five times a day, had never been to Mecca and did not plan to go. But he did ask the Prophet for help when he needed it. And today the Prophet, in his mercy, obliged. There, propped up against the stump of a dead pear tree, stood the old ladder. The poor thing was so ancient that no one had ever judged it worth removing.

Taking care to move silently, Narcissus carried the ladder to the wall, making certain he was not within sight of the guards in the wheeled kiosk that patroled the hillside. Then he mounted the creaky ladder step by careful step, pulled the ladder up behind him, and repositioned it on the inside of the wall. When the pages of the Sultan's school executed this part of the manoeuver they simply jumped from the top of the wall to the soft ground below. But Narcissus was no athlete, and he had to go carefully so as not to soil or damage his caftan, a gift from the Valide Sultan.

Mind you, Narcissus had not decked himself out in his best finery today out of vanity. His costume was a stratagem. If by chance he should be stopped by one of the Third Court vigilantes and called to account for his presence in that oh-so-private enclave, the gold-embroidered caftan might be his best protection against harassment. The relationship between the white eunuchs of the palace and the black eunuchs of the harem was touchy at best.

The white slaves felt superior because the Sultan had chosen them to watch over his person. The blacks claimed higher status because the Sultan had chosen them to watch over his most prized possessions—his women. An expensive caftan that marked the wearer as a highly placed personage in the harem would put him several moves ahead in any confrontation that might develop with the Sultan's Janissary guards. So it was not as an adornment but rather as a piece of interpersonal armor that Narcissus had donned his priceless caftan today.

When he dropped safely to earth inside the grounds, the way was quite clear for him to advance directly to his destination, the School for Pages, a structure built up against the Gate of Felicity. The Sultan took a deep, personal interest in his pages. Like his treasure, his doctor, and his holy relics, he liked to keep them close at hand. Hence the presence of the School for Pages, the Treasury, the Doctor's House, the Pavilion of the Blessed Mantle, all within calling distance of his *selamlik* in the Third Court.

A quick glance at one of the sundials that decorated the grounds told Narcissus he was on schedule. Excellent. The Sultan's *gerit* team practiced hurling in the athletic field behind their dormitory every day before the last prayer. "You are sure to find Danilo del Medigo there if you don't dawdle on the way," he was told before leaving the harem. And indeed, when Narcissus rounded the corner, there stood before him a row of twelve handsome young men lined up facing a battery of dummies, each page bearing a long pole with a sharp point—the Turkish lance known as the *gerit*. Among them, Danilo del Medigo was easily identified by his mop of yellow hair, which stood out in stark contrast to the dark locks of his teammates.

In *gerit* training, hurling was practiced separately from horsemanship. When the team competed in a true *gerit* contest, the players were mounted on fine horses and hurled their *gerits* at flesh and blood adversaries while in full gallop. Even here on the practice field, advancing on a cadre of straw-filled opponents, they were an impressive bunch—tall, muscled, each one with a finely chiseled physiognomy. Candidates for the Sultan's School for Pages in Topkapi Palace were carefully screened for the slightest imperfection. Suleiman took seriously the Koranic precept that outer beauty was what Allah bestowed on inner virtue.

On command, the players rushed forward in a row, weapons poised. When the Master of the Gerit deemed that they had reached the ideal range, he shot a volley with a pistol and in tandem they hurled their weapons at the dummies facing them with all the force they could muster. A veritable rain of *gerits* poured down on the dummy targets. Each tip was stained with a different color of dye to mark precisely which part of his target the marksman hit. Points were allotted by the Master: five for the heart, four for the skull, and so on. Then the whole drill began again. Almost never did a hurler fail to hit the target altogether. These were, after all, members of the Sultan's own *gerit* team.

Narcissus managed to edge quite close to the practice field without attracting notice. And when the Master of the Gerit called for a water break, the eunuch quite naturally approached the blond page, del Medigo, with an offering of spring water he had poured from a spigot for the purpose. (A fresh supply of spring water was brought down from Mount Ulu to the practice field every afternoon. Nothing was too good for the members of the Sultan's *gerit* team.)

The eunuch's task was well begun. Contact had been made. Now he could allow himself the indulgence of enjoying the pleasures of the scene, not least the balletic grace of the hurlers. But when the practice ended, he was once again all business. Edging forward as the team of beautiful young men trooped off the field to wash up in the *hamam*, Narcissus placed himself unobtrusively but visibly close to the edge of the path, the very spot where Danilo del Medigo stopped to investigate a stone in his boot. As the blond page took off the boot and shook it, a roll of papyrus was thrust into his hands and stripped from his hands into his boot in a single fluid motion. Not a word was exchanged.

Moments later, in the *hamam*, Danilo del Medigo was trading jokes with his teammates while they were being pummeled by the masseur and scrubbed and scraped in hot water and cold by the scalpers, those experts with the sharpened mussel shell from which no vagrant hair escaped. He even stayed behind to have his nails pared since he was in no hurry. He had already made apologies for not accompanying his teammates on their quasi-illegal outing beyond the walls that evening. Were it not for his proven prowess with the *gerit*, young del Medigo's reluctance to carouse with his teammates on their free days might well have subjected him to a brutal hazing. But the boy was, after all, the youngest member of the team, and his fellow pages made allowances for his reluctance, assuring each other that next year he would be out drinking and whoring with them like a man. For now, all he had to suffer was a little mild teasing before they bundled themselves off to the fleshpots of Galata via the Eunuch's Path and left him free to investigate the contents of his boot.

Inside he found a single sheet of paper that looked as if it had been torn out of a book. When he broke the wax seal that held it together, out tumbled a fresh red rosebud anchored in a single stick of cinnamon. He smiled broadly and tucked the little tokens into his girdle, then turned his attention to the paper in which they were wrapped.

Unfolded, it revealed a sketchy landscape in red chalk featuring a black caique of the sort that plied the waters of the Bosphorus. The sleek craft was tethered to a small dock. The sky above was empty except for a perfect half-moon hanging low in the west sky, which cast a shower of moon rays onto a small banner flying from the prow of the caique emblazoned with a single word: *Tonight*. The message that Narcissus was sent to deliver had been deciphered and perfectly understood.

9

FORTUNE FAVORS
THE BOLD

I N THE STAGING AREA AT ÜSKÜDAR, THE ADVANCE units of Suleiman's returning army were preparing the city of tents that was erected wherever he spent the night on campaign, be it for a month, a week, or a day. Fully assembled, his private quarters in the field became a replica of his *selamlik* at Topkapi Palace. There was a sleeping tent, a bathing tent, an audience tent, a wardrobe tent, a cooking tent, his doctor's tent, and the vast portable shed that enclosed his treasury. When the Sultan traveled, all the gold he owned traveled with him.

On campaign, his governing council, the *divan*, had continued to meet four times a week as it did at Topkapi, assembling in a huge meeting tent capacious enough to accommodate its entire membership—viziers, judges, and men of religion, the *Ulema*. The sleeping tents for his councillors and their attendants clustered around their portable council chamber, setting this distinguished group off from the tents that housed the hundreds of servants, clerks, and pages who together enabled the Sultan's private quarters to function in their accustomed way as both a residence and the seat of imperial power.

The campaign caravan also included a bazaar that was set

up each time the march came to a halt—stall after stall of merchants and tailors and shoemakers and blacksmiths and their camp followers, all of whom had to be tented and fed. Plus the many portable mosques required to accommodate the spiritual needs of this vast population, together with their attendants. And we have not yet begun to consider the actual fighting force—the Ottoman army proper—with all of its branches and auxiliaries. No wonder that, fully mustered, Suleiman's army on the march numbered upwards of three hundred thousand souls. And animals too numerous to count.

This, then, was the small city that was assembling on the banks of the Bosphorus the eve of October 23, for a single night only.

Why bother to unpack and repack this vast encampment for only one night? Why not disperse the various units into the city once they reached the Bosphorus and save time, trouble, and expense? Because Suleiman the Magnificent was no mere general or head of state returning home from the wars. He was also the King of Kings, the Unique Arbiter of the World's Destinies, Padishah, Sovereign of East and West, Master of Two Continents and Three Seas, Caliph of the World, Defender of Islam, the Shadow of God on Earth, and on a less-exalted plane absolute ruler of the largest empire the world had ever seen. Such a man must enter his capital like a god descending from heaven.

By sunset, when the Sultan and his entourage galloped into Üsküdar, the waters of the Bosphorus were already churned up from the barges bearing all the paraphernalia needed for the next day's victory parade—huge boxes of banners and shiny medallions, trunks full of saddles and bridles, complete sets of polished musical instruments already tuned, hundreds of parade horses to replace the dusty cavalry of war. Even now, a fresh crop of equestrian mounts was waiting to be caparisoned in their gold-edged, gem-studded parade blankets. One entire barge had already crossed the Bosphorus loaded with barrels of scented rose petals to be scattered from the rooftops, Roman style. Overnight the ragged, battle-scarred force that had arrived from Austria would be transformed into a fantasy cortege out of Caesar's Gallic wars.

Amid this furious activity, the Sultan was quietly enjoying a hot bath before he retired for the night behind his gold-embroidered tent flap. The rigors of tomorrow's long, slow ride through the streets of his capital demanded that he be well-rested.

Meanwhile, across the water in the city, the air resounded with the clatter of hammers and the grunts and groans of workmen. A thousand torches lit their labors. With only a night and a morning to prepare, the palace Janissaries were already climbing poles all over town to string up victory banners. Palace launderers had been pulled from their tubs, guards from their gates, and armorers from their forges to construct kiosks on stilts at every main intersection. From these platforms, an avalanche of coins and sweetmeats would rain down on tomorrow's crowds.

At the hippodrome, a hundred palace gardeners, who normally practice their carpentry skills constructing delicate trellises and airy pergolas, were throwing together row upon row of temporary stands for the games and circuses that would enliven the week-long celebration. And this entire makeshift workforce would stay at their task throughout the night if necessary to transform the capital into a Roman carnival. The Ottomans were experienced looters. They had appropriated their poetry from the Persians and their protocol from the Byzantines. To master the art of celebrating great occasions, they sought mentors even farther afield and studied the world's greatest crowd-pleasers, the Romans, who taught them that bread and circuses went a long way toward filling empty stomachs and empty purses that had been drained by war.

In contrast with the city streets, life behind the walls of Topkapi Palace remained untouched by this tumult. In the First and Second Courts tranquility prevailed. And in the Third Court total silence reigned as always. Not yet back in residence, the Padishah was already enforcing his will from the staging area across the water.

Suleiman valued silence. He was the sultan who introduced the teaching of sign language to his servants so as to limit the number of words they would need to utter aloud. Whoever walked in his *selamlik* walked shoeless. The tap of heels on the cobblestones irritated the Padishah. Even the corps who guarded this most private domain walked their patrols barefoot. They knew by sight every one of the Sultan's attendants and every soul who had regular business in the Third Court. And God help anyone who wandered into these precincts accidentally.

Of course, Danilo del Medigo ran no such risk as he made his way from his dormitory in the School for Pages to the Doctor's House. His father, Judah del Medigo, was one of the small number of attendants the Sultan held close. On the first day of his service as Suleiman's Chief Body Physician, the doctor was given this house in the Third Court of Topkapi Palace to use as both his residence and his pharmacy. (Perhaps "loaned" would be a better word than "given," since any gift from the Sultan to a retainer or slave was presumed ultimately to belong to the Sultanate and must be returned on the death of the recipient.) But as long as Judah continued to be the Sultan's Chief Body Physician, the Doctor's House remained his son's home.

He still returned to his father's house every Friday—by special permission from the Sultan—to celebrate the Jewish Sabbath. This dispensation had no precedent. But the Sultan valued his Jewish physician highly and, being a devout Muslim, understood the value a father places on his son's religious education.

What made the arrangement most convenient was that, since the Sultan's school was conceived from its beginnings as a training ground for the elite few who might be expected to enter his service, it was built across the court from the Sultan's *selamlik*. This proximity made it easy for Danilo del Medigo to live up to the obligation imposed by his father—with the Sultan's assent—to leave the School for Pages at dusk each Friday and prepare himself for Sabbath services. Even when the doctor was off campaigning with the Sultan, the son was still excused to attend *Shabbat* services in a synagogue outside the walls every Friday evening and Saturday.

After three years of this singular arrangement, the novelty having long worn off, the sight of the fair Jewish page trudging back and forth from his dormitory in the School for Pages to his father's house raised no questions in the wheeled guardhouse that moved constantly back and forth between the Gate of Felicity and the rear wall of the palace. But should the boy venture beyond his accustomed route, he would fall under as much suspicion as any other errant page.

So it was that when Danilo made his way at sundown from his dormitory to his father's house as usual, he navigated among the grazing gazelles and the sundials and the pretty fountains as nonchalantly as any practiced Argonaut. But later that night, when he emerged into the darkness through the rear door of his father's house with a stout rope looped over his shoulder, he crept along under the eaves warily, like a miscreant.

Phoebe, the moon goddess, had provided him with half a moon's worth of illumination filtered by a mantel of fluffy clouds, just as it appeared in the sketch still folded in his boot. The rear wall of the palace was a short dash from the back of the Doctor's House. For a champion hurler like Danilo, it took only one toss of the looped rope to anchor it on a spike protruding from the top of the wall. Agile as a monkey, he scaled the stone face of the wall and jumped down on the other side, trailing the rope behind him. He then curled the rope up neatly and secreted it in the stump of the ancient pear tree behind the rickety ladder casually balanced against the trunk. From here it was but a few feet to the Eunuch's Path and freedom.

But tonight Danilo del Medigo was not bound for the forbidden pleasures of Galata. Instead, he crossed over the Eunuch's Path and headed downhill through the sloping thicket toward a small dock below, picking his way delicately between openings in the underbrush, invisible in the darkness but familiar to him from many previous rambles.

The descent was not long, but it was steep and somewhat perilous. When this palace was built by Mehmet the Conqueror, he not only had the peak leveled but also its entire surround pitted with potholes and barbed wire to repel invaders. Since then no one had summoned up the nerve to sail through the Dardanelles and lay siege to old Constantinople. Nowadays, the sea side of Palace Point was a quiet cove most notable for the little pier at the foot of the slope commonly known as the Grand Vizier's dock (although its true purpose was to serve as anchorage for the Sultan's personal fleet of caiques). This jetty also functioned as the ideal embarkation point for Suleiman's not-infrequent, incognito jaunts into the bazaars and inns of the Galata district and for his discreet moonlit outings on the Bosphorus.

Given the extremely private use to which the little dock was put, it need hardly be said that anyone foolish or careless enough to be caught in these environs at night could count on finding himself at the bottom of the Bosphorus by morning. But the lure of the forbidden—the risk—was indeed the very thing that had enticed Danilo as a young boy to sneak out over the wall after his father was asleep, and make his way to a narrow rock shelf overlooking the jetty, where he spent many moonlit hours gazing down at caiques and skiffs and lighters slicing through the rippling waters of the Marmara Sea toward the Mediterranean and Italy. It was the most peaceful spot in the boy's world, as well as the most perilous. Nestled in the rocks among the rest of the flotsam and jetsam he felt strangely at home. And in the early years of his life in Topkapi, it was the place where, splayed out on the ledge gazing westward, he allowed himself to dream of the day he would see his homeland again.

But Danilo had long since given up yearning for the past, and as befits a healthy boy on the cusp of manhood, he was fully engaged in enjoying whatever pleasures Fortuna chose to bestow on him in the here and now. At the same time, tonight's escapade was a kind of extension of those boyhood junkets, although the game was now much more complex and the penalty for discovery even greater than what might have been meted out to a boy who simply wandered inadvertently into the Sultan's private preserve.

Tonight he crawled down the side of the hill with the assurance of one who had long since mastered the terrain, making certain not to create a sound. It was slow going, but he arrived unscathed and unobserved at the familiar rock shelf. From this vantage point overlooking the confluence of the Bosphorus and the Marmara Sea, he could safely observe the Grand Vizier's dock without being seen by any caique that might be coming or going on the Sultan's business.

The scene below bore an unmistakable resemblance to the chalk drawing tucked in his boot, up to and including the sleek craft that soon heaved into view. It was rather small as caiques go, powered by only four oarsmen but marked indelibly as a part of the Sultan's fleet by his *tugra* — the calligraphic emblem that graced all his possessions — imprinted on the prow.

Once the caique entered the cove, Danilo covered the distance to the jetty in a series of hurdles and clambers aboard the craft, not waiting to be handed in. Without causing so much as a ripple, the caique shot out into the open waters of the harbor. Directly ahead lay the entrance to the Golden Horn. The oarsmen steered clear of it, thrusting the nose of the craft into the rougher waters of the Sea of Marmara. Seated with his back to the oarsmen — the less they saw, the less they would remember — Danilo watched the minarets and rainbow domes of Istanbul soften and fade into the blue-black night.

Just then, as if to signify her approval of the venture, the moon goddess parted the clouds to reveal the fringe of silver sand that circled the Marmara seacoast. The boy took a moment to thank the goddess for her favor. Then he leaned back, drew a deep breath of the briny air, and for the first time that day allowed himself to anticipate what lay in wait for him on the little island of Kinali.

He had not long to dream. The Sultan's oarsmen were the strongest and quickest in the Ottoman navy. They kept the narrow craft cutting through the waves at a stiff pace, and in what seemed like no time they were lifting their paddles out of the water to manoeuver their way to the shore. No jetty here.

These days, the island of Kinali was long abandoned, too unimportant to rate even a small dock. It was assumed that no one had bothered to come here since the days when the Byzantines used the Princes' Islands as places of exile for their most troublesome family members.

Wordlessly, Narcissus held out a hand to assist his passenger ashore. The caique pushed off, and for a short moment the blond head could be seen bobbing up and down on the beach. Then it disappeared into the woods.

Danilo had not far to go. Kinali was small, one of the lesser of the Princes' Islands. But the pathway through the woods was overgrown and his progress was slow. In Byzantine times each of the smaller islands had its monastery and its purpose. When a new emperor succeeded to the throne, he customarily banished to these little islets the patriarchs and princes who might conceivably threaten his hold on imperial power. There they were committed to the care of various monasteries — after they had been sapped of their will to escape by being blinded or otherwise mutilated.

Danilo knew these stories, but tonight, as he made his way through the dense little woods, his thoughts were far from the excesses of the Greek Orthodox Christians. *Damn thistles*, he cursed under his breath. It had been so long since the last time that he had forgotten to wear gloves. Every time he set foot on this path, the thicket got thicker and the thorns got sharper. Pretty soon he would have to bring an axe.

He lifted his hand to lick the blood off his fingers. Then, placing them against his teeth, he broke the silence with a piercing whistle.

His whistle elicited a human response. "Is that my prince come to rescue me?"

The sirens calling out to Odysseus must have sounded like this. But Danilo del Medigo was no war-weary veteran pining for a distant wife. He had yet to face his Troy. For him, the risk only enhanced the appeal of the venture.

A thick leafy branch barred his way. He stepped back to get

some purchase on the slippery forest floor, took two quick steps, and aimed a high kick at the offending barrier. It broke off at the crotch, creating a gap in the greenery and revealing a grassy circle open to the air and the moonlight. In the center of this glade, looking as if it had been painted there, stood a ruined mosque, roofless but with its walls intact, a forlorn relic protected only by a rusted portal that could barely support its half-hinged gate.

"Tell me this, Sir Knight"—he still could not see her, but just as the poet tells it, each of her words was a purling note like honey—"how will you reach me, locked away as I am behind an iron gate?"

He stepped up to the gate. "I have the password, lady. *Audentes fortuna juvat*." Pliny's final words before the poet leapt into the fiery furnace of Vesuvius. Fortune favors the bold.

"Fortune favors the bold," Danilo repeated with a rhetorical flourish as he bound into the grassy circle.

IO

TWO WOMEN

I N 1453, THE OTTOMAN SULTAN MEHMET THE
Conqueror sailed up the Dardanelles and captured the
fabled city known to the Greeks as Byzantium, to the
Romans as Constantinople, and to the Turks as Istanbul. It
was a city soaked in history, suspended in a mist of Roman law,
Greek literature, and Christian theology—an inspired choice
for an upstart whose ancestor had burst forth from Central
Asia less than a century earlier, unknown and unheralded,
and who was now in need of a well-positioned capital for his
emerging empire.

With full command of the Bosphorus, that great waterway
between the Mediterranean and the Black Sea, the old fort Constantinople offered immense scope for the European–Asian
commerce that was already the life-blood of the new Ottoman Empire. The peak, Palace Point, also possessed the natural topography of a citadel, surrounded as it was by the waters
of the Bosphorus, the Sea of Marmora, and the Dardanelles,
which combined to form a huge natural moat.

Did Mehmet, a poet as well as a warrior, hear the echo of the
Persian military airs that the Ottomans had adopted for their

own as he wound his way up to the old Roman acropolis at the summit? Was this the moment he decided to build a new royal palace for himself at the apex of the summit? Did he perhaps foresee a future procession with banners waving and an adoring populace on their knees all along the rocky route honoring a new king of the world—if not himself, then one of his successors? Did this vision of empire come to him as he stood on the acropolis, flanked by his own *tugra* fluttering in the breeze at his right hand and the Prophet's banner at his left?

Mehmet was a visionary. He must have sensed the potential power of those twin standards: a military force equal to that of ancient Rome driven on by a deep faith in the holy purpose of the *jihad*.

Mehmet the Conqueror did not live to see such a procession. Nor did his son, nor his son's son. But less than one hundred years after he captured Constantinople, his great-grandson, Suleiman, had already taken part more than once in just such a procession, filling not only the streets of Constantinople but the roofs and windows, as well, with adoring subjects shouting, *"Al Hamdulillah*, the blessing of God upon thee, O *Ghazi!"*

Last year, Suleiman had returned victorious from Hungary. This year, he returned victorious from Austria. Looking down from his perch in paradise, where all great *ghazi* warriors go when they die, Mehmet must have taken great pride in the fruit of his loins whose accomplishments already rivaled his own.

Although the Sultan's victory procession was not scheduled to begin until afternoon, the crowds were already beginning to gather in the early-morning sun. It was a remarkably well-behaved assemblage—the Ottomans were the world's experts at crowd control—a buzzing swarm that separated like the Red Sea for the Sultan's golden coach as it made its way from the harem in the old palace to Topkapi Palace.

The coach had moved slowly but steadily though the seething mass of worshipful humanity that thronged the streets. However, when it began the ascent to Palace Point, the two women inside found themselves buffeted from side to side as if by a turbulent sea. Not for nothing was this road known as the Path That Made the Camel Scream. The women took it in good spirit. The younger of the two, Princess Saida, although somewhat fatigued, always welcomed an opportunity to escape her grandmother's perfumed cloister. Beside her, Lady Hürrem, the Sultan's Second *Kadin*, inhaled the excitement of the crowd like a heady perfume.

"Thrilling, isn't it?" she inquired.

The young woman agreed. The hero of the day was her father. Never before had she felt so close to him. Or so distant.

"I am pleased to have brought you along, Saida," said the Second *Kadin*. "It is not right for a young girl to be locked up in the harem, especially not a royal princess. How long is it since you've been outside the gates of the Old Palace?"

The girl considered before she answered. In that shark pool of envy and ambition that was the harem, a motherless girl learned early to watch her tongue.

"I believe it was two years ago that my grandmother took me with her to a celebration at the hippodrome," Saida answered after a pause. "When my brothers were circumcised."

"And before that?"

"I remember some picnics on an island in the Sea of Marmara—I believe it is called Kinali—when I was a little girl."

"Well," said Hürrem, "you are not a little girl anymore. You are a woman, Saida, a princess of the royal blood. You must begin to get used to the world you will live in when you marry."

The girl stiffened. "Marry?"

"Of course, marry," Hürrem continued, heedless of the girl's discomfort. "Don't tell me you have never thought of it. Every young girl thinks of marriage. Why are you shaking? Does the thought of marriage disturb you?"

Yes, it does, lady. The girl bit her tongue to keep the words from coming out.

"What upsets you? Leaving the harem?"

Yes!

"Leaving your grandmother?"

Yes!

"I do wish you would answer me. You are a clever girl. Surely you must realize that, much as she loves you, your grandmother cannot hold you close forever."

Yes, she can.

"Will you always love me, grandmother?"

"Always." Her grandmother's voice echoed in her memory.

"Say you will never send me away from you."

"As long as there is breath in my body, I will never send you away."

Everyone in the harem knew that the Valide Sultan and her son, the Sultan, doted on the motherless princess. So everyone had left Saida to her grandmother's tender care. At least they did until the Russian *Kadin* Hürrem began to cultivate the old lady and offered herself as a second mother to the Princess Saida — in her own words, "to add some joy to her life."

"If you look through the slit in the curtains you will see the twin towers of the Gate of Salutation," she instructed. "Over to the right, in front of the Hagia Sofia."

Obediently, Saida peered out through the curtains.

"Do you see them? Are they not majestic? Oh, I do love this palace. The views. The gardens. So much more amenable than that dilapidated old wreck where we live. And so much closer to your father. Have you ever thought what it would be like to live in Topkapi Palace with him?"

A month ago, the question, coming at the girl unexpectedly, would have thrown her. And although this was their first time out together, she had had several weeks to get used to her stepmother's abrupt twists and turns of mind. In truth, Saida had never given a thought to living anywhere but in the Old Palace where she was brought up. *Why would she expect me to think about living in Topkapi?* she wondered.

Unable to find a quick explanation, she neatly turned the question back on the questioner. "Have you ever thought about it?" she inquired sweetly.

"Oh, yes," came the answer. "I dream about it. Every time your father invites me to join him there, I cannot help but think how wonderful it would be not to have to go back to the Old Palace at the end of the visit but just stay there, close to him. It is my heart's desire. But I am fated to live out my days surrounded by women and gossip, with a city between us."

The lady sighed and then shrugged. "Of course, it is very different for a princess. You will leave the harem when you marry. You will have a palace of your own with slaves to do your bidding and an obedient husband—he had better be or your father will have his head on a pike. Not like me, who will always be a slave."

"But you are a *kadin*, a mother of princes."

"Second *Kadin*," Hürrem corrected her.

"But my father loves you beyond all women. I know that from his letters to you, the poems he writes to you, and the jewels he sends you."

"I would give them all to be a simple wife, to live with the man I love as free women do, together with our children." Hürrem's face softened into dreaminess. "A royal family like the Osman clan was in the old days. Then you would be a true daughter to me." She caught herself. "Of course you are like a daughter to me now, a beautiful daughter, but I see you do not share my dream. Perhaps I have underestimated your love for your father."

"Oh, no, Lady Hürrem. He is the sun and moon to me." This time Saida spoke without hesitation.

"Spoken like a royal princess." The Second *Kadin* nodded her approval. "Your grandmother has raised you well. But I fear she has hidden you away in the harem too long. Perhaps it is time for a move."

"Oh, no, I could never leave my grandmother. She has watched over me from the day my mother died. And, now that she is old and failing, it is my duty to stay by her side."

"And she feels the same love for you. We have often spoken of you."

"You have?"

"We two are of a mind, the Valide Sultan and I. She loves me because I have given her son two sons of his own to carry on the line should a calamity strike Prince Mustafa, Allah forbid. Your grandmother is a wise woman. She understands Ottoman ways. The First *Kadin* gave the Sultan only one living son. All the rest have died in the womb. I believe there is something wrong with her insides. With me, he now has three more sons and the succession is assured."

"But my brother Mustafa..." Saida had lost her poise in the labyrinth of this conversation.

"Your half-brother Mustafa is the Crown Prince. The heir. And if it is the will of Allah, he will succeed his father when our beloved Sultan is... I cannot bring myself to say the words."

"May God grant him many more years of health and strength," Saida finished her sentence for her. But the princess's mind was flooded with questions she dared not ask. There had been no mention of the other *kadins*. Or of the Valide Sultan. "What will happen to the harem?" she blurted out.

It was Hürrem's turn to be confused. "The harem? Nothing will happen to the harem," she replied. "It will remain in the Old Palace. All I'm thinking of is a special place for our family here in Topkapi Palace. And, by the way, if you are concerned about tradition, I must tell you that until a few decades ago, there were always women in Topkapi Palace. Did you know that?"

Indeed, Saida did not. And Hürrem was only too pleased to enlighten her. The Russian might not be literate, but she had made it her business to acquaint herself with the customs of her sultan's people.

"You seem to think that my plan is some dangerous innovation. But in fact it is the revival of a tradition almost one hundred years old. Understand this," she continued with a wag of the finger. "From the day your honorable ancestor, Mehmet, completed his palace—from the very first day—rooms were set aside for particular women that the Conqueror wished to keep close to him.

Believe me, Princess, I know my history. You have my word on it. There have always been women in Topkapi Palace."

II

IN THE COACH

THE SECOND *KADIN'S* RESEARCH WAS FAULTLESS. There had always been women in Topkapi: unacknowledged, unofficial, but ever present. On the day that Mehmet, the Conqueror of Constantinople, decamped from his old palace in the middle of the city and removed himself to Palace Point, rooms were quietly set aside in his new palace for visits from his girls. He took with him to Topkapi his kitchens and his stables and his treasury and the school for his pages and his Great Council, the *divan*, and his cooks and his grooms and his household troops and his wardrobe and his dressers and his tasters and his barbers and his kennels and his hospital and, of course, his doctors. But his harem, the dwelling place of his women and children, he pointedly left behind in the Old Palace under the watchful eye of his mother, the Valide Sultan.

The Prophet himself declared, *Heaven lies beneath the feet of thy mother.* A man could have many wives and many slaves. He could cast off the unwanted ones and take others at will. But he could have only one mother. She occupied a unique place that nothing could alter save death. Who, then, could better be entrusted with his most valued personal possession—his women? Under the watchful eyes of a succession of Valides, girls from all corners of Asia, Europe, and the Ottoman Empire— taken as booty or sold into slavery by their parents or bestowed on the Sultan as gifts—were selected, groomed, educated, and finally presented to the Sultan by his mother for his approval. His selection having been made for him, he would then pay a visit to his harem for an afternoon dalliance.

But no man, least of all the Shadow of God on Earth and Master of Two Seas and Three Continents, relished being forced to mount a horse and ride halfway across a city just to spend an hour or two of pleasure. Or to announce the visit twenty-four hours in advance as protocol proscribed. Or to go through the elaborate ritual that these visits entailed: the girls lined up to greet him, to sing and dance for him, to joke with him, to serve him sherbets made with their own hands—much as he might love sherbet.

Then came the business of having to choose one girl over the rest and, after that, the interminable wait while the chosen one was washed and oiled, her body scraped free of every trace of hair with a sharpened mussel shell, her nails dyed, her under-arms hennaed to ward off any sweat that might be generated by the act to come, Allah forbid. In spite of the Sultan's exalted sta-tus as the Unique Arbiter of the World's Destiny, the harem had its customs and there was nothing the Sultan could do to speed up the process but sit patiently sipping sherbet with his mother.

Before the reign of the Conqueror, things were different. The first Turkoman tribes who filtered down from Mongolia over the steppes of Central Asia were simple nomadic people seeking pasture land for their flocks. While searching for fresh fodder, they became aware of the riches passing along the Ana-tolian trade routes—silks, spices, and furs. Almost at once, the welfare of their herds began to take second place to the rich rewards of raiding for plunder. To these so-called march war-riors, raiding soon became the business of life and booty, the prize. For them, home was now more often the saddle than the tent. In this uncertain world, the harem evolved as a haven where tribes of march warriors could sequester their women safely during their long absences.

In those early days, the Osmans were one of many tribes allied in a loose Turkic brotherhood ideally suited to casual brigandage. But the push westward soon had them nibbling at the boundaries of the Seljuk Empire, a vast territory that stretched from the mountains of Central Asia to the ancient ports of the Aegean Sea. Gathering around them a makeshift army composed of raiders, landless peasants, shepherds in arms, Sufis, and misfits, the Osman tribe began a westward trek that swept aside everything in its path. And somewhere on the long trek from the Caucasus to the Aegean, the Osman *beys* renounced their shamanism and became *ghazis*, fighters for the glory of Islam.

They were chewing up the old Roman Empire as if at a feast. Then down from his Asian stronghold galloped their fellow-Mongol, the dreaded Tamerlane. Like a thunderbolt, he decimated the Osman army, executed their sultan, and turned his sultana into a slave. By everyone's measure, this ignominious defeat spelled the certain destruction of all Osman hopes. Yet in an astonishing show of resilience, a new Osman leader, Mehmet, arose from the ashes to repel the Mongol hordes. Then poised on the far western edge of Asia, Mehmet brought his army face to face with Christian Europe at its eastern extremity: Byzantium.

The outcome was inevitable. Constantinople had never recovered from its brutal sack by the marauding armies of the Fourth Crusade. Weakened to the point of paralysis by their Christian brethren, the Byzantines proved no match for the hungry Turkomen. Converging on the capital from north, south, east, and west, the battle-hardened central Asians drove from the field the last viable military remains of the once mighty Eastern Roman Empire. A pitiful remnant withdrew to the safety of their capital, Constantinople, to await the coup de grâce. On Tuesday, May 29 of the year 1453, Mehmet the Second captured the ancient city of Constantinople, renaming it Istanbul and erasing the last trace of a Christian presence in Asia.

Now the Osmans were indeed *ghazis*, not only in name but in fact. The nomadic Mongrel chieftain had emerged as truly a killer of infidels, a holy warrior, a *Ghazi* Sultan. Mehmet the Conqueror renamed the Osman family Ottoman and, seduced by dreams of empire, took on the additional title of Padishah — the Persian word for "emperor."

Gradually the Osmans' nomad tents gave way to palaces; their horses began to share primacy with gunpowder; their dervishes were folded into traditional Islam, now the official religion of the empire. And, since empires cry out for dynasties, the harem — that safe haven for warriors' wives — took on a new shape as a hothouse in which to procreate male heirs to the Ottoman dynasty.

In this new imperial harem, each time the Sultan bedded a girl the event was entered in a velvet-bound couching book, a diary kept by the Chief Treasurer to establish beyond doubt the birth and legitimacy of the Sultan's children. The name of the concubine and the precise day and hour of the encounter were meticulously recorded by the palace scribe and countersigned by the Sultan. There could be no margin for error when, any time the Sultan couched one of his harem concubines, the result might well be the birth of the next heir to the largest and richest empire in the world since Roman times.

Such a momentous outcome could not be left to the vagaries of passion. Or fancy. Or even pleasure. By the time the Conqueror's great-great-grandson Suleiman became Sultan, copulation in the harem had long since been wrung dry of delight by the grinding machinery of protocol — officially. But unofficially, there were and always had been women in and out of Topkapi Palace.

This arrangement suited the Ottomans, as dedicated to Oriental formality as the Byzantines but also adroit at accommodating human frailty. Suleiman, as well as being the Shadow of God on Earth, was also flesh and blood. In emulation of his forefathers, he tended to avoid direct defiance of tradition. Instead, like his sires, he simply took what he wanted when he wanted it, leaving his courtiers to clean up whatever mess ensued. And, as long as he did not indulge himself too frequently or too blatantly, all eyes turned away, including the eyes of his mother, the Valide Sultan.

This style of accommodation also appealed to the Sultan's subjects, a people at the same time hot-blooded and coldly formal, who had no difficulty rearranging the geographic boundaries of two continents, but who would resist to the death an alteration in the way a turban was wound. For the Turks and for the Sultan himself—who was, after all, one of them—there was no incongruence between the formal bedding practiced in the harem and the casual couplings in his private quarters in Topkapi Palace. A cart could be dispatched discreetly to pick up a small party of visitors (or, if the Sultan so directed, a single visitor) and bring the guests to his *selamlik*. Removed from harem protocol, what happened there need not be recorded in any book. If an inconvenient pregnancy were to occur, it would be neatly terminated by the court abortionist.

At the outset, when the Ottomans were still Osmans, they had contracted dynastic marriages with other ruling tribes. But by the reign of Mehmet, the Ottomans no longer had need of military allies, so they ceased to marry princesses and turned to concubines to produce their heirs. These girls, being slaves, came unencumbered by powerful and protective fathers and brothers.

And for one hundred years the Ottoman sultans lived two separate lives—the official one of the harem and the unacknowledged one of the Sultan's *selamlik*—untroubled by interfering in-laws. Everyone knew who occupied the heavily curtained wagons that traversed the city streets from the Old Palace to Topkapi and back in the dark. But by common consent the identity of the occupants of the anonymous vehicles, indeed the ownership of the vehicles themselves, was not a subject for speculation. Not even thought of. Simply a fact of life.

But now, after more than a century of discretion, an intruder had disturbed the established order. A red-headed vixen not even beautiful, say those who saw her being sold in the slave market where the Grand Vizier bought her as a gift for his master. Somewhat skinny, more like a boy than a girl, they said. And with an unseemly air of flamboyance — almost defiance. Unlike the Circassian virgins traditionally favored by Ottoman Sultans ever since they began to beget children with slave girls instead of wives, this one was a Russian. With green eyes. She was called Hürrem, the Laughing One. Modest girls did not laugh.

In the streets and bazaars, heads shook at the mention of Hürrem — one day, a piece of bought meat, the next, a *kadin*, a Mother of Princes. Some say she bought filters and potions from Jewish peddlers that she placed in the Sultan's mouth when she kissed him. And in the stews down at the port, where gossip was served and consumed faster than wine, they said she was a witch.

Of course a good Muslim did not believe in black magic. But, if not from spells and incantations, where did this Hürrem get her power over the Sultan? If not through witchery, how did she get his permission to show herself at the celebration of the circumcision of their sons (as no *kadin* in memory had ever done), where she sat enthroned on the balcony of the Grand Vizier's palace while the crowd below gawked? True, she was veiled. Even so...

If the First *Kadin*, Rose of Spring, or any other Mother of Princes had taken such a liberty, she would have been tied in a sack full of stones and dumped into the Bosphorus. But for this Russian, it was not enough to be a *kadin*, the Mother of Princes. Although she had managed in short order to produce two sons, with another, by Allah's grace, on the way, she still must take her place in line behind the mother of the Sultan's first son and heir, Prince Mustafa. Like it or not, she was the Second *Kadin*. Yet she acted as if she were the First. And today she was taking a liberty that not even the Valide Sultan would dare. She had commandeered the Sultan's gilded coach!

Without even a *tugra* to mark its owner as the Sultan, this vehicle had no need of identification. There was no other like it in the city. Nor, for that matter, anywhere in the Ottoman Empire. There was only one other in the world, owned by an Italian Marchesana named Isabella D'Este who captivated all Rome dashing about in it until, alas, the city was sacked by the Christian king of Spain and she was forced to flee for her life, sans coach. What the imperial mercenaries did with it during the sack of Rome, God only knows. Probably melted it down for the gold in the fittings. But years before the sack of Rome, Sultan Suleiman in connivance with his good friend, the Venetian *bailo* (they had since fallen out), arranged to have Isabella D'Este's coach duplicated in the workrooms of Murano: a perfect miniature room on wheels with glass windows set into its gilded doors. Venetians could accomplish miracles if the price was right.

Somehow the *bailo* had managed to smuggle a pair of engineers into the Colonna Palace where the Marchesana was living to take the measurements of her coach. (Apparently, the Marchesana Isabella was not living in her own palace but was renting a palace from the noble Roman Colonna family. Imagine it! Renting out their palace like common innkeepers. The Sultan would never understand these Europeans.) And now Suleiman had his own golden coach, reserved solely for his use on those days when his gout was bothering him or when he simply chose not to ride his horse.

It was this conveyance that the Second *Kadin* had chosen to commandeer for her ride across town this morning to welcome the Sultan back from his Austrian triumph. And there were few in the crowds witnessing her ride who did not curse the upstart bitch for rubbing it in their eyes that in his absence, she ruled.

Inside the carriage the Lady Hürrem could not help but hear the hisses of the passersby as she rode through the streets. Did she care that she was hated? Had she no fear? No shame?

The answer was very little, if any, of either. She was a Russian, after all, and Russian women were bold. And canny. They said she wrote to the Sultan every day when he was campaigning in Austria. Not herself, of course. She could not write in

Turkish. But some of her letters had been copied and sold in the bazaar. Do not ask by whom. That scribe's head would be mounted on a pike in the First Court if his name were even whispered.

Unhappy, Hürrem longed for her adored Padishah, she wrote. She sighed for him. His children cried for him. They could not wait for the sight of his beloved face. How sad it was, she wrote, that the route of his victory parade did not take his procession past the Old Palace so that his children could see with their own eyes their father, the greatest king in the world, make a triumphant entry into his capital. An old woman in the Valide Sultan's household had told her that in the days of the first Osman *ghazis*, their wives came out into the streets to welcome them home from their victories. Of course Hürrem was not a wife, only a poor slave. But even a slave could dream.

She went on to write of her longing to be granted a place among the multitude of the Sultan's lesser subjects who were permitted to witness his triumphant return. How long must she wait, behind the distant walls of the harem in the Old Palace, for sight of him? What she would give to see him pass through the Imperial Gate, victorious once again over that European upstart, the so-called emperor! As if there could be any emperor but her own adored one.

That was how she addressed him in her letters. Mountains of flattery so high that even a sultan could not see over the top. And the result? Today she was riding up to Palace Point in his golden coach, now approaching the Imperial Gate of Topkapi Palace.

"Halt the carriage!" The captain of the Palace Guard stepped directly in the way of the vehicle. "Identify yourself. Who rides within?"

A Janissary captain was a formidable force. But the Second *Kadin* was not easily intimidated.

"Show him the document," she instructed her companion, the princess Saida. "Wait. You must pull your sleeves down over your hands." Allah forbid should the Janissary glimpse so much as an inch of the princess's flesh. The girl had a lot to learn. "Now pass the paper through the slit in the curtain and make sure he doesn't touch you."

The captain of the Guard, well schooled in these matters, took the rolled-up scroll that was being handed to him, making certain to avert his eyes. Then, stepping back, he untied the satin ribbon and read for the benefit of his sergeant:

To the Chief of the Palace Guards,

Greetings from your Commander and Sultan! The esteemed Lady Hürrem, Second *Kadin* of the harem (inside the carriage, Hürrem winced at the word "second") will arrive at the Imperial Gate on the day of my return from Austria. She is to be welcomed and conducted to the Diwan Tower, there to be made comfortable in my rooms at the top of the tower together with any ladies in her train.

Sealed with the Sultan's *tugra*.

The Janissary captain waved the coach through the Imperial gate and into the First Court.

"That was the Bosphor *Kadin*," he informed his sergeant once the coach was out of earshot. "Smell this." He waved the document back and forth under the other's nose. "That's her scent. I'll bet you it cost our Sultan more for a drop of that stuff than he pays us in a month."

Hürrem was not popular with the Janissaries. They were the ones who named her the Bosphor *Kadin*—the Sewer *Kadin*.

12

THE DIWAN TOWER

THE KEEPER OF THE DIWAN TOWER WAS AN OLD MAN without malice. But he was a Turk. He was not comfortable with change. So when an unfamiliar clatter on the stairs told him that today's visitors were women, his foot began to jiggle irritably. His orders spoke only of visitors. He assumed, as would anyone who understood the customs of Topkapi, that the Diwan Tower was off limits to all but a chosen few—each one of them, a man.

When he was in residence, the Padishah tended to make his appearances at the tower unannounced, looming up out of the darkness, sometimes accompanied by only one page. He would stand at the edge peering through the lozenge-shaped slits in the balustrade looking for...what? Enemies approaching through the Dardanelles? His own fleet tucked neatly into the Golden Horn? The caiques and barges plying their way back and forth across the Bosphorus?

Sometimes when the keeper was alone, he walked over to the balustrade and placed himself just as the Sultan did, gazing south toward the Sea of Marmara, trying to imagine the Dardanelles, the Mediterranean, Egypt, and beyond to the far western limits of the Ottoman Empire, Algeria, and Tunis. Then he pivoted eastward, just as the Sultan did, toward Syria, Azerbaijan, and Armenia. Then a half-turn toward Üsküdar, and farther to Bosnia, Wallachia, and Hungary, the Magnificent Suleiman's most recent conquest.

What does the Sultan think about, the old man wondered, as he made his three-hundred-and-sixty-degree turn, *when whatever direction he looks in, everything belongs to him? Does he give silent thanks to Allah for the gift of this vast empire? Does he plan further conquests? Or does he think about women? Or his gout?* The guard hardly dared to speculate. He knew his duty: to remain at his post, to defend it to the death, to keep the loggia ship-shape at all times, and, if his master should come upon him unexpectedly, to get out of the way as quickly as he could, always making sure not to turn his back on the Padishah. Even foreign ambassadors took care to back out of the Sultan's presence at all times.

Very rarely, on a hot night, the Grand Vizier would also climb the winding staircase of the Diwan Tower to catch a cool breeze. And on one never-to-be-forgotten occasion, the Venetian ambassador was invited up. That was before the Ottomans went to war with Venice. But women? No woman in living memory had ever climbed these stairs. Yet here they were, one of the *kadins* and her companion, both wrapped up from head to toe — and finger — in their *feraces.* As long as a man was present, the women had to remain covered. The afternoon sun was beating down. They were suffocating in their protective cloaks, but the Keeper of the Tower had not been relieved of his post. The penalty for desertion was beheading. What was he to do?

Fortunately the old man was soon released from his dilemma by the arrival of one of the black eunuchs of the harem, an arrogant beggar who waved him away contemptuously. *Hairless, fat, and impotent, who are these creatures to treat a soldier with thirty years of service so disrespectfully?* the guard thought.

The guard had a good mind to challenge the eunuch's right to give him orders. But a quick survey of the jewel-encrusted scimitar that hung from the eunuch's belt told him that this black beauty had climbed to a great height on the Sultan's ladder. For all the guard knew, this silk-clad jackanapes might be the head black eunuch of the harem, the *Kizlar Agasi* himself. Prudence prevailed. The old soldier obediently made his exit, taking care not to show his back to the black man, just in case.

The moment he was out of the way, the Second *Kadin* initiated the process of settling in. Off came her headgear, the Constantinople-style *yashmak*; first the hair-covering, which she tossed aside with a sigh of relief, next the nose piece, with which she needed help since it was pinned behind her head with a diamond clasp. The princess obliged.

Lady Hürrem set about in a comradely spirit to do reciprocal maid service for Princess Saida. "Now you." When she was done, she pitched all the head coverings into a corner where, presumably, someone would come along to retrieve them.

Next, the cloaks. Saida's was a delicate pink silk, suitable for a young girl. For the matron, diaphanous lavender scattered with gold flowers. These priceless embroidered garments were also flung into a corner. Given her way, Saida would have folded them up neatly. Trained to a high standard of rectitude by her grandmother, she was offended by the Second *Kadin's* careless habits. But in spite of herself, she was also fascinated by the wanton extravagance of her father's favorite.

Now shed of their outer garments, the two women sat companionably on a divan, each one still wrapped in enough layers of luxury to protect her dignity. Over their soft muslin underpants, both wore *shalvars* of Bursa brocade, embroidered in silver and gold thread so that when the sun's rays filtered in through the slits in the balustrade the embroidered pantaloons glisten. On their feet, pointed yellow Moroccan shoes. On each head, a little cap, Hürrem's made of gold velvet with a gold tassel, Saida's blue. Both *takkes* were edged with pearls, but the *Kadin's* was encrusted with diamonds as well. And to complete the costume, each woman wore a silk waistcoat, buttoned in Hürrem's case with diamonds and in Saida's with pearls. The whole outfit was held together at the waist by a bejeweled girdle, Hürrem's double width to accommodate twice as many gems. Highly placed Turkish women generally swathed their waists with embroidered fabric belts. But to the harem women, the bejeweled girdle was a particular badge of honor.

"Sit here beside me." Hürrem pat the brocaded sofa hospitably. And to the eunuch, in a much harsher tone, "We need more pillows." Then to the girl, "This place is sadly lacking in a woman's touch. And sherbet." She shouted after the eunuch who had taken off after the pillows, "And some sweets. And melons!" Hürrem turned to Saida. "We may be in for a long wait. With all the crowds in the streets, the procession will have to move slowly. Meanwhile, we can continue our chat." And, without a pause, "We are agreed, are we not, that here in Topkapi Palace is where we should live?"

Although Saida was certain that she had voiced no such agreement, the boldness of Hürrem's assertion left the girl at a loss for a way to deny her assent without seeming rude. And Hürrem, who was quite unaccustomed to even the slightest sign of opposition, took the silence as agreement.

"You are a good daughter. You understand how necessary it is for us to be at the great man's side, not buried halfway across the city." She squeezed the girl's hand affectionately. "It is long past time for you to marry and take your place in the dynasty. Your father needs you to support him with a powerful husband bound to him by marriage. An admiral perhaps. When we are in the palace, your father will be close at hand to guide us in the selection of your *damat*. Think of how much easier it will be for him to find the best *damat* and plan your marriage once we are living side by side at Topkapi."

Saida was not unaware of Hürrem's plans to marry her off once her grandmother was gone, but suddenly what had been a prospect in the dim future was now looming straight ahead.

"But there is no space in Topkapi for the harem," she protested.

For Hürrem obstacles were made to be battered down. "Rooms can be built, my child," she assured the girl.

"What about my grandmother?"

"The Valide will remain in the harem to supervise the concubines just as she is." Hürrem had thought of everything. "Don't look so sad," she cajoled, for the first time noticing the girl's distress. "Your retirement in the harem has made you ignorant in the ways of the world. As your second mother I take it as my duty to help you grow up." She tilted her head to one side. "Do this small thing for me," she coaxed. "When your father rides up to the Imperial Gate today, ask yourself: can it be beyond the powers of this man, the Shadow of God on Earth and Father of all the Sovereigns of the Earth, to make a small place close to him for his own family if he wishes to?"

Before Saida could muster an answer, a distant blast of trumpets announced that the Sultan's victory procession was approaching the palace grounds. As one, the two women rose from the couch and moved to the balustrade to press their eyes against the lozenge-shaped holes in the brickwork. They were just high enough on the balcony to see below them in the court the arrival at the Imperial Gate of the Sultan's military band, and to hear the blasting battle music that struck terror into the hearts of enemy soldiers from Belgrade to Aleppo.

"*Sipahis* come first," Hürrem advised the princess. "The cavalry always heads up the procession. Watch for the horses."

And to be sure, as she spoke, the *sipahis* rode into view, each horseman with a wild-animal skin thrown over his shoulder like the Greek heroes of old. Fascinated, the women watched as the horses pranced, then leapt, forelegs raised together. Then, forelegs still in the air, they raised their hind legs with a spring before the forelegs hit the ground.

"That," Hürrem informed Saida, "is a curvet. No other horsemen in the world do it as neatly as ours."

Once the *sipahis* had astonished the crowd outside the palace gates, they filed into the First Court and took up positions along the north side, opposite the Sultan's guests behind the velvet rope. There was just time for one last manoeuver before they disbanded for the season.

Next came the command, and in rows of six from a standing

start they galloped toward a brass ball suspended in the center of the First Court, swiveling in their saddles to fire showers of arrows at the swaying target. Not one arrow had missed its mark.

Up in the loggia, the princess clapped her hands and shouted, "Bravo!"

Beside her, Hürrem cracked a wide smile. "This is the world I want to introduce you to. What a shame it is that we must go back to the Old Palace tonight. Tomorrow comes the *gerit* contest between the pages of the Sultan's school and the pages of the Grand Vizier's school."

At the mention of the Sultan's *gerit* team, Saida jerked to attention and her eyes widened expectantly, a transformation unnoticed by Hürrem, who was completely absorbed in her own monologue.

"You know, of course, that your father takes a great interest in his pages. Or perhaps you don't. I sometimes wonder how much you do know about his life."

"He has spoken to me of the pride he takes in his pages," the princess replied. "And I know of his fancy for the *gerit*."

"But you have never actually seen a contest?"

"Only as a child in riding school. They allowed the boys to play the *gerit* on their ponies with cut-off lances."

"How would you like to see them play with sharpened lances on full-grown horses?"

"Madame, I would love it more than anything." Although she was trying to keep her composure, Saida could not hide her rising excitement.

This was the kind of enthusiasm Hürrem had hoped to kindle. "Perhaps it can be arranged." She smiled the slow, sleepy smile of the cat that has cornered the mouse. "Tonight, I am invited to dine with my adored Padishah in the *selamlik*. What if I were to entreat him to find a small suite of rooms tucked away somewhere in this vast palace, where we two could bed over until tomorrow?" She paused to let the idea sink in. "In the evening, there will be beautiful fireworks and the whole city will be dancing. Would you not like to sit next to your adored father in a balcony of the Grand Vizier's palace tomorrow and watch the *gerit* match?"

"More than anything," the girl admitted. "But my grand-mother expects me to see her to bed tonight."

"I will send one of the palace eunuchs over with a message that your father wishes it so."

"But does he? Will he?" Was it really that simple?

"After a triumphant day like today," Hürrem reported, as if issuing a bulletin on the state of the weather, "he will surely be pleased with the world and inclined to grant favors. It is a propitious moment to present a small request from his loving and most favored daughter."

"Dare I?" Saida asked, almost to herself.

"You need do nothing. I will deliver the message for you this time. But you must learn to value yourself and your own wishes. Your modesty becomes you well, daughter. However, there is such a thing as an excess of modesty. No man likes a woman to lick his boots like a dog. Not even a sultan."

Below them in the courtyard, the band struck up the rousing chords of "The Sultan's March." Then Hürrem took a deep breath and pulled herself up to her full height.

"You are a princess of the royal blood," she pronounced. "It is unseemly for you to be traipsing back and forth across town like a gypsy."

13

THE DOCTOR ARRIVES

FOR THE SULTAN'S CHIEF BODY PHYSICIAN, EVERY moment of the procession into Istanbul was agony, even though he was being carried on a cushioned litter by four handpicked bearers. Last night when Suleiman's army had arrived in Üsküdar, the doctor had begged to be excused from the victory march into Istanbul and be allowed to steal across the Bosphorus in an unobtrusive caique to his home. Like a sick dog, he longed to come to ground and lick his wounds.

The Austrian campaign had not been kind to Judah del Medigo. All through the long march home he had felt himself weakening from the suppurating wound he suffered at Guns when his arm was grazed by a stray Austrian bullet and then became infected. In the field of mud that the rain made of the Turkish camp at Vienna, where more men died of bad water than bullets, he ought to have had himself invalided out. Instead, he kept on doctoring the Sultan and was rewarded with an intermittent fever that no physic in his cabinet could put down. As they say, a physician who treats himself has a fool for a patient.

More than anything, the doctor missed his bed. After years

of service to kings and popes and sultans, he was still not at his ease in military camps. Nor was he secure on the back of a horse. Judah del Medigo was a scholar and a healer. To him, the killing field had always been alien. Yet, with the single exception of a wonderfully sedentary general in Venice, every one of his celebrated masters had insisted that he accompany them on campaign. Understandable. The battlefield was, after all, the place of greatest peril for the leader, the place where he most needed his body physician.

Now Judah del Medigo's lifelong ordeal was over. He had the Sultan's word on it. When, after a hellish thirty-day siege, the Ottomans finally defeated a stray remnant of the Austrian army at Guns, the Sultan asked his physician to name his reward for service rendered beyond the call of duty. *Send me home*, Judah longed to ask. But his pride wouldn't allow it. Instead, he simply requested relief from field duty in all future campaigns. This was the second time he had been engaged at the Sultan's side in a lengthy, unsuccessful siege of Vienna, and he honestly believed that one more rain-soaked summer campaign besieging the emperor's capital would kill him.

Anyone with eyes could tell at a glance that over the past three months, the doctor had deteriorated from a vigorous specimen—remarkably robust for a man in his sixties—to a pale shade with cloudy eyes, hanging flesh, and a tremor in the limbs. *He is an old man*, the Sultan thought. *And sick*. It was a rare moment of recognition for that remote being who tended to regard those close to him purely as extensions of himself.

The doctor's request was granted. Questions of compassion and gratitude aside, Judah del Medigo's dilapidated state suggested that the time had come for the Padishah's Chief Body Physician to make way for a younger man. So the long trek home along the Danube was Judah's last campaign march. From now on, he would remain in residence in the house the Sultan had given him in the Third Court. But today, the Sultan insisted that his physician must take his place in the triumphal procession from Üsküdar into the capital. Suleiman had been groomed for high heroism. He knew that a true hero enhanced his glory by sharing it.

"Your son will be so proud of you," he assured the doctor. "To see you enter the city borne on a litter in my train like a prince, that is a sight he will cherish all his life."

And what about the sight of his aging and aching parent dying on his own doorstep? Judah asked silently. But he was well enough acquainted with his master to know when the man had made up his mind. So here he was, being bounced up and down on the cobblestones, his back crying out for relief, as he fulfilled the demands of royal honor. By now, both sides of the parade route were packed with the Sultan's subjects, four or even sometimes five deep. In this crush, the bearers of the doctor's litter were forced to swerve one way, then another, to avoid harming the bodies pressing against the litter on both sides.

Seen through Judah's fevered eyes, the crowd took on the aspect of a pack of howling wolves. It was a hallucination. This was not an unruly mob. Not even a boisterous one. But with many thousands of pairs of feet milling in the narrow streets, there was bound to be the odd jostle or collision. And much more noise than was usually tolerated in this strictly regulated city. Because today, every citizen of the capital who was not lame or at death's door had turned out to celebrate the Sultan's victory at Guns over the king of Spain, acknowledged in Europe as Charles the Fifth, the Holy Roman emperor.

Of course, the Turks never referred to Charles the Fifth as the emperor. For them, there was only one emperor, one Padishah, their Padishah, known to the world as Suleiman the Magnificent. And today he would appear before them in his most traditional and exalted role: the Warrior of God against the Infidel, the *Ghazi*, Son of *Ghazis*, and Sultan of *Ghazis*.

It was in defense of the faith that the *Ghazi* Sultan set out every spring on campaign, as his forefathers did. That he returned laden with booty and prisoners and conquered ever more territory on three continents was proof that Allah smiled on his endeavors. So the intoxication of the citizens was tempered by their awe at Allah's beneficence. And the doctor's pain was tempered by knowing that at every crossing, he was that much closer to his home, to his bed and to his son, Danilo.

The Sultan had sent word ahead that the doctor's son was to be given a place behind a velvet rope in the First Court of Top-kapi Palace, a place where the page should get an excellent view of his father being borne into the palace in the Sultan's train. But when the long procession began its ascent of Palace Point, Danilo del Medigo was not on his way to take his place behind the velvet rope in the First Court of Topkapi Palace. He had not bathed. He was not shaved. He was nowhere near the First Court. He was, in fact, stretched out beside his horse in a stall in the Sultan's private stables, fast asleep.

14

IN THE STABLE

STILL ADRIFT IN THAT BLURRED TERRAIN BETWEEN sleeping and waking, Danilo heard at a distance the strains of "The Sultan's March" played by a military band. Drowsy, more asleep than awake, he set it aside as part of his dream, a terrible, foul-smelling dream of dodging a snorting, bucking horse that kept kicking out at him. He felt his nose twitch and instinctively raised his hand to remove the source of the tickle—a straw. Then came a familiar odor—horse manure—but mixed with something else, something less familiar. Something fetid, rank, and evil-smelling.

Still clinging to the last vestiges of sleep, he rolled over to one side, closer to the bad smell, sniffing. All at once he was fully alert. Before he even opened his eyes, he knew where he was. He was in the stall of his horse, Bucephalus.

The sound of the animal's labored breathing brought back his memory of the previous night. Of being wakened in his dormitory bed by Abdul, the stable boy.

"Wake up, sir, you must come to the stable. Your horse is sick. Very sick."

"Bucephalus? Sick?" The horse had been in perfect health

when he left him a few hours earlier.

"He cries. He moans. And now, his belly swells."

"Did you call the horse doctor?" Danilo asked, throwing on some clothes haphazardly.

"The Master of the Horse is in Üsküdar with the parade horses, sir." Of course, the Sultan's horse doctor would be in Üsküdar preparing the Sultan's horses to appear in the procession.

One last yank at his girdle and Danilo was off, followed by the stable boy, both barefooted, dashing past the long hall of the School for Pages, ducking into a small corridor, skirting the big barn, now empty, and finally reaching the stall of his ailing horse Bucephalus, his pride, his joy, the love of his life, the Sultan's gift to him. *Oh, God, don't let it be the colic,* he thought.

Even before Abdul swung open the gate of the paddock, they could hear the mournful neighing of the suffering horse. In the stall, the animal lay cramped, the way he lay in his mother's womb, head rolling from side to side. Unmindful of the muck, Danilo threw himself onto the straw beside the horse, stroking the sweaty brow, heedless of the foul breath issuing from the open mouth.

"Danilo is here, Bucephalus. Danilo will make you better," he whispered. In fact, Danilo had no idea how to cure a sick horse.

"Abdul, you must get to the staging area." He reached for the pouch that hung from his girdle. "Take this money." He held out a handful of coins. "Run to the harbor. Get one of those louts to ferry you across the Bosphorus. Pay him what he asks. Find the horse doctor. Tell him he must come. Bucephalus is very sick."

And the groom was gone, leaving Danilo and his horse to weather what was left of the night together.

In the hour before sunrise the muezzin's voice was heard, calling the faithful to the first of the day's prayers. As if in response, Bucephalus shook himself to his feet, sweat pouring down into his blood-red eyes, stood still for a moment, and then expelled a huge bubble of gas. Then he began to thrash wildly, kicking out against the paneled wall of the stall. Blind instinct led his terrified master to a guide rope hanging on the wall. Bobbing and weaving to avoid being butted by the pain-maddened animal, he looped the rope and made a desperate attempt to throw it over the horse's head.

With great patience, he tugged the animal out of the stall, coaxing, pulling, smacking, anything to prevent the poor beast from laming himself as he kicked at the paddock wall. Of course, there was no contest between a man and a horse eight times his weight. But somewhere beneath the fever, the much loved animal responded to his master's will and was slowly eased out of the stall.

Not knowing what else to do, Danilo began to walk the sweaty horse back and forth along the length of the stable, the way he had done so often, cooling him down after a race. Up and back, over and over, always keeping a firm hand on the rope that the poor beast continued to yank at every so often, as if in a spasm.

Finally, by the first light of dawn, the loud neighing subsided into a soft moan and Bucephalus, after emitting a terrifying series of loud, smelly farts, walked back into his stall of his own accord and lay down in the straw. *Is my horse*—Danilo could not bring himself even to think the word—*dying?*

He reached for a sponge and proceeded to wipe the sweat very gently from the horse's head. Then, settling himself down on the straw, he whispered into the velvety ear, "Live, Bucephalus. Live. Please don't die."

And there they lay, face to face, master and horse, the master weeping unashamedly, his tears mixed with the sweat of the horse. Now, for the first time, the thought came to him that a rider without a mount cannot compete in the *gerit*. The thought was too painful to face. He closed his eyes to shut out the world and allowed himself to drift into a nap. *Only for a few minutes*, he told himself. *Just until Abdul comes back from Üsküdar with the Master of the Horse.*

But when he awakened, the sun was shining bright through the slots of the stall and there was no horse doctor. And no groom.

"Abdul!" he shouted. "Abdul!"

After three shouts, the groom came limping in from the barn, carrying a pail and favoring his right leg as he tended to do when feeling put-upon or ill-used.

"Where have you been? Where is the horse doctor?"

"He would not come, master."

"Did you tell him that Bucephalus was very sick?"

"He was attending to the Sultan's own horse. The white horse; the stallion that the horse doctor himself chose to lead the procession."

The procession. Oh, God. Did I miss it?

"What time is it?" Realizing as he asked that the groom had no way of knowing the time, he rephrased the question. "Has the muezzin called out the third prayer?"

The groom could not remember. His religion did not demand that he keep track of the daily prayer schedule. The muezzin did that with his call to prayer. All the boy had to do was fall to his knees five times a day, face Mecca, touch his forehead to the ground, and intone, *Allahu Akbar.*

"What about the music? Have you heard the music for the third prayer?" Danilo pressed.

"I think I heard the muezzin on the way to Üsküdar." Abdul wrinkled his forehead in an effort to remember the events of a few hours ago. "Yes, I think so. How else did I get my knees wet?" He smiled, pleased by his own cleverness. "Yes, I knelt down on the deck on the way to Üsküdar." A pause. "Or was it on the way back that I prayed?"

Hopeless. But Danilo gave it one last try. "Tell me what happened at Üsküdar. Did you see the parade horses leave the camp on a barge?"

"Oh, yes, I crossed with them. Otherwise I would still be back in Üsküdar. You didn't give me enough money. I had to pay it all to the boatman on the way over. And even so, I had to walk to the camp from the dock. You should have given me more money, master. My feet are very sore."

"Sorry." Danilo knew when he was beaten. "I will make it up.

Now, tell me, had the procession begun when you landed back in the city? Did you see the *sipahis*? The Janissaries?"

"*Sipahis*, yes. Janissaries, no. Lucky for me. You know what they're like on a feast day."

"Thank you, Abdul." *May you rot in hell, Abdul.* As this curse rose in him, he heard again the strains of "The Sultan's March," louder this time, unmistakably real. So the music was not a dream, simply far off, which meant that the procession was at the very beginning of the long climb up to Palace Point. If he ran all the way, he might still be able to take his place behind the velvet rope in time. For him not to appear after receiving a personal invitation from the Sultan would be unforgivably disloyal. In the crowd of hundreds he would be the only one present to honor the doctor, a widower with no other living relatives than his only son. Absentmindedly, Danilo picked at the wisps of straw clinging to his caftan. *What's this?* A lump of manure was stuck to his girdle. He couldn't possibly appear behind the velvet rope in the state he was in. To appear dirty and disheveled would bring shame on the Sultan.

What a mess. He would never get out of this scrape. His father would never forgive him. His horse would never be well. He would never compete in the *gerit* at the hippodrome. Any bad thing he had ever lived through paled in significance beside the events of this cursed day.

But whatever black marks Danilo had picked up in the Aga's grading book, nowhere had anyone marked him as fainthearted. Stubborn, yes. Stiff-necked, yes. But all agreed that Danilo del Medigo was one who, as the Albanian riding master put it, always got back on the horse. He had one dim hope left: forget the velvet rope and simply be at the door of his father's house to greet the doctor when he arrived home.

As the faint music of the procession got louder, the boy's backbone began to stiffen. By the time he was on his feet he had begun to concoct a scenario to account for missing the procession. A sudden earache...toothache...headache. But by the time he had brushed himself off and called for Abdul, he had discarded these ideas as feeble. No matter. Something better would occur to him. Meanwhile, his immediate task was to beat the doctor home to his own door.

"Here is what I want you to do, Abdul. I want you to stay with Bucephalus. I am going to my father's house to make my peace with him. Don't leave the horse for any reason. And don't feed him. Or water him." These were tips he had picked up from frequenting stables. "If the horse doctor comes..."

No time for ifs. He was off at a run. The fastest route would be to take the Eunuch's Path to the Third Court. As he was running, he reviewed in his mind what he would say to pacify his father. He knew himself to be an atrocious liar, sure to give himself away by stammering or blushing. Better to tell the truth. That he stayed up all night waiting for the Master of the Horse and then fell asleep. *A lame excuse*, he thought. *A lame horse made for a lame excuse.* Bad joke. But having thought it cheered him up nevertheless.

Now, he was back in his dormitory where this miserable day began. From here on, everything depended on Fortuna. There was a back door past the classrooms, which was often kept slightly ajar by a small, triangular piece of wood. If he was in luck, one of the pages would have put it in place today for the holiday outing, and Danilo could make the dash around the entire circumference of the palace without being questioned or held up—if his luck held. Thank God for the Eunuch's Path. Thank God for the old fruit ladder. Pray God that the last user had the decency to replace it against the dead tree trunk outside the wall. He spat on his forefingers and rubbed them on his forehead, muttering some fragment of a prayer in Hebrew and, for extra protection, adding a plea to the goddess Fortuna. A born and bred Italian, Danilo continued to turn to the old pagan dame for help when he was in serious trouble, on the off chance that she was still doling out her whimsical favors.

15

THE SULTAN ARRIVES

I T HAD BEEN A LONG, HOT WAIT FOR THE LADIES AT the top of the Diwan Tower. Noon had come and gone. After the climb up the tight little staircase of the tower came hours of pomp and spectacle. But still no sign of the Sultan on his white horse. And sherbets and cakes and melons and soft pillows and cooling poultices for the eyes could only assuage so much discomfort.

By now, Princess Saida was beginning to wilt in the unseasonable heat. The hours in the tower had reduced her perception of the event to a whirling blur of banners and animals and uniforms and weaponry. She had been exhorted by the Lady Hürrem to applaud the Sultan's cavalry, to revere his cadre of Islamic judges, to cheer his hundreds of camels and thousands of caparisoned horses, and to wonder at a weird gaggle of muffled Bedouins atop the battle wagons that hauled the celebrated Ottoman cannons along the parade route.

No doubt about it, the procession provided a prodigious feast for the eyes, which was not to say that the other senses had been neglected. Between courses, the spectators were served up a series of auditory delights, such as was provided this afternoon by the Anatolian Seljuks, each of these mini-parades accompanied by its own band. And all of this accompanied by a constant unrelieved cacophony of cheering, shouting, and blaring horns.

Attuned to the serenity of the harem, where the loudest sound to be heard was the twittering of birds, Princess Saida was overwhelmed by the bombardment of sights and sounds. In the two years since her brothers had left the Harem School, her life had slowed down to the daily pace of the harem, where a visit to the *hamam* baths could take an entire afternoon and a complete depilation (undertaken at the first sign of a hair anywhere on the body or in its crevices) easily occupied the better part of several hours. It was not surprising the headache that had begun early in the day now held her temples in a vise-like grip. Even the shining prospect of witnessing tomorrow's *gerit* match at the hippodrome dimmed under the barrage of heat and noise. Barely fifteen years old, the princess was no match for the Second *Kadin*, whose early years as a peasant girl in Russia had given her the staying power of an ox. At heart, Lady Hürrem was still a farm girl, as awed by the trappings of royalty as any other peasant, and so captivated by the pageantry unfolding below them that she barely noticed the discomfort, much less the exhaustion of the girl beside her.

"Is it not thrilling?" she asked for what seemed to Saida the tenth time. "And soon..."

Soon it will be over, the girl thought wishfully.

She longed for the serenity of the *hamam*, where any inclination toward rapid movement was inhibited by the high, stilted wooden clogs that the harem beauties wore to preserve their tender feet from hot marble tiles and to prevent them from slipping on the wet floors. These pattens also served to slow the women down and to train them, as ponies are trained in the show ring, to move through life in an even, mincing gait. It also helped to habituate the harem girls to a way of life in which the most strenuous sport was a game of "Istanbul Gentleman," where one of the girls—dressed as a man, her eyebrows thickened with *kohl* and with a pumpkin on her head—sat backward on a donkey clutching the animal's tail, while the other girls tried to knock her off. The game was, at the very least, a highly domesticated version of the *gerit* match and certainly a far cry from Saida's early years in the Harem School, when she romped in the meadows playing kick-ball with her brothers and male cousins.

But now, two years of the soft life of the harem had taken their toll on her. Halfway through the day she was already done in, whereas Lady Hürrem couldn't wait for more.

"And soon you will see your father again after...how many months? It seems to me like an eternity." Hürrem reached for a sweet cake to ease her anguish but stopped, holding the pastry in mid-air. "Do you hear it?"

"Hear what, lady?"

"The tune. It's 'The Sultan's March.'"

And to be sure, the sound of fifes and drums, the clash of cymbals and the jangle of tambourines were discernible at a distance.

"Be still my heart." Hürrem clutched her bosom. "Listen!"

Happy to have something to contribute to what had been a long-running monologue, Saida responded, "The philosopher Plato says that music gives a soul to the universe, wings to the mind, and life to everything."

"Where did you learn that?" Suddenly, Hürrem's sentiment was replaced by suspicion. "Surely they did not teach you such heresies in the Harem School."

It was Saida's moment and she savored it briefly before she replied, "I believe I heard it from my honorable father, the Sultan," which brought the conversation to a full stop and enabled the princess to retreat to a sofa to enjoy a moment of quiet. But not for long. Soon, a loud blast announced the arrival of a fresh novelty below.

"Come here," the lady beckoned the princess. "Come to the balustrade. Look down. Don't be afraid. You must see the Janissaries."

Wearily, Saida made her way back to join the lady at the parapet and leaned her throbbing forehead against the cool bricks. *When will it be over?* she thought.

"Any minute now he will appear," Hürrem advised her, "just as soon as the Grand Vizier condescends to move himself from his master's path."

Indeed, it did appear that Ibrahim Pasha was prolonging his moment of adulation far longer than need be, stopping constantly to lower his jeweled turban to the crowd.

"You would think to watch him that *he* had won the war," Hürrem sniffed. It was no secret in the harem that she loathed the Sultan's chief councillor and constant companion.

But ("At last," Hürrem sighed) the Grand Vizier and his train disappeared through the Gate of Felicity, and their place was filled by the Sultan's hand-picked Janissary corps, unmistakable in their handkerchief-shaped white turbans and purple silks.

"The Padishah's most trusted men," Hürrem explained. "They are prepared to die rather than face defeat."

These elite of the elite presented quite a different aspect than any of the troops that had gone before. Most striking, they were not in battle order but marched out of line in a dense pack, swaying like sailors and carrying almost no defensive armaments, each one bearing only a single harquebus or scimitar and every one with a little hatchet or spade hanging from his waist.

To make up for their lack of firepower, each of their turbans was festooned by a prodigious plume of bird of paradise feathers that fell in a curve down each back almost to the knees.

This odd contingent did indeed quicken Saida's jaded senses. "So these are the famous Janissaries who put the fear of Allah into the armies of two continents. They look more like diggers than soldiers to me," she commented.

"Do not be fooled by appearances, my girl," Hürrem admonished her. "It was with just such weapons that the Ottoman army took from the Europeans the strongholds of Rhodes, Belgrade, and Budapest. When there are a hundred thousand men all working together with shovels and spades under the walls of a fortress, no amount of defenders can hold up a wall."

"How do you know these things?" Saida asked, curious in spite of herself.

"Because I set myself to learn them as I want you to do. Believe me, a woman's charm can go only so far with a man. Sooner or later, your husband will want a companion, somebody to talk to. And to joke with as well."

A subtler woman might have noticed that, at the mention of the subject of marriage, she seemed to have lost her listener's close attention. But Hürrem was a woman who considered it worth her while to observe nuances only in her dealings with men. With slaves, children, and other women, she found it less troublesome simply to pursue her own ends directly. So she went on chattering about marriage — a subject close to her heart — as Saida sank slowly back into lethargy.

"Saida, you are not listening."

Reluctantly the princess managed to summon a somewhat half-hearted enthusiasm for the marvelous Janissaries even though she could not quite believe in their invincibility. They looked so . . . sloppy.

Once emptied of the rowdy Janissaries, the great square of the Second Court went silent. The first one to notice the black banner unfurled behind the two octagonal towers of the Middle Gate was Saida, and she did not need to be told what this portended. She stood up and lowered her head as a single member of the Ulema, honored above all the priests of Islam this day, walked solemnly into the Second Court, his eyes focused on the book in his hands. He began to read from the forty-eighth chapter of the Koran, the sura of Victory. He was followed by three other clerics who together slowly raised the tattered black flag to its full height. This was the Prophet's Banner, one of the holy relics of Islam, which, along with the Prophet's Mantle and his sword and a hair of his beard, the Ottomans considered their greatest treasure.

The first time Suleiman had set out to settle the fate of Vienna, this misshapen piece of black wool was taken from its pure gold cask, wrapped in forty silk coverings, and carried reverently all the way to Austria and back. During the terrible weeks of the siege of Vienna, it waved over the Ottoman encampment under the walls of the city, wordlessly exhorting the followers of Mohammed to fight for the faith, promising them that he who gave his life under its aegis would go straight to Paradise. This season it waved over the defeated ruins of Guns. Next season it would lead the way to Baghdad, *Inshallah*.

Directly below the tower, officials lined the path decorated like human icons in their jeweled turbans and gold-embroidered caftans. As the banner passed, they threw themselves face-down, careless of their finery, sobbing and calling the name of Allah. And there they remained, prostrate in the dust, until the banner was placed upright just outside the Gate of Felicity in a deep depression in the stone, carved out for the purpose in the days of Mehmet the Conqueror.

Up on the loggia, Saida joined those in the crowd able to repeat the Koranic reading from memory and, along with the rest, fell to her knees when the banner was raised, reiterating, "God is Great." Beside her, Hürrem, in no hurry to soil her finery, simply bowed and smiled approvingly at her stepdaughter. The girl had all the instincts of a true princess and was also quick to learn. She would make a valuable addition to Hürrem's entourage if and when the Second *Kadin* had need of her.

With the Prophet's Banner safely moored and the Sultan's return duly sanctified by the reading of the sura of Victory, the stage was set for the hero of the day to take his place on the gold throne set out for him under the eaves of the Gate of Felicity. But instead of her father astride his mount, Saida saw coming through the gates a most curious conveyance: a litter, magnificently decorated for the occasion, held aloft by four sturdy bearers, its curtains pulled back by gold cords to reveal an aging man, perhaps once strong and hardy but now pale and shaking. In complete contrast to every other participant in the procession, he was dressed in a plain black cloak. And, to mark him off even further from the Emirs and the Agas and the Viziers, this poor fellow, hunched over and grimacing, seemed not to appreciate — not even to be aware of — his place of honor.

"Who is that man looking so foolish and dressed all in black?

Why does he not wear a fine caftan like the others?" Saida asked Hürrem.

"That is the Padishah's physician, Judah del Medigo."

"And why does he dress all in black?"

"Because he is a Jew who does not follow our ways."

"And why does he ride so close to my father?"

"Because he is a miracle worker. Twice he has saved your father's life, once at Mohacs and once in Belgrade."

"You don't mean literally 'saved my father's life,' do you?" the girl asked over her shoulder, her eyes on the slight, hunched figure below.

"Yes. Saved his life."

The girl rose to her feet and pressed her eye to the lozenge-shaped slit in the brickwork. "He hardly looks capable of saving his own life."

"That is because he was laid low by a fever at Guns. But during the first Austrian campaign, this Jew risked his life to save the Padishah from drowning."

The girl turned away from the scene below to give Hürrem her full attention. "Tell me about this heroic act."

The lady was only too pleased to oblige. Not without cause was Hürrem known as the Scheherazade of the harem.

"The route back to Buda lay across the Danube," she began. "Men and horses and weapons had to be carried over the wild river on pontoons that they made right there on the riverbank out of skins. Of course, our Padishah was the first to brave the raging waters."

The girl nodded. Of course he would be. "But what about the doctor?" she asked.

Suddenly suspicious, the woman turned to look at her. "Why are you so interested in the Jewish doctor?"

Saida answered without a beat, "If this doctor has saved my father's life, he is a hero to me and I am ever in his debt."

Hürrem nodded, satisfied.

"Now tell me, how did he save my father's life?" Saida asked, more casually this time.

"The Padishah's pontoon capsized in the river. He slid into

the torrent, and before anyone realized what had happened, the doctor jumped in after and held him aloft until the Janissaries pulled them both out."

"Bravo."

"Bravo, indeed."

Then, being a woman who did not care overmuch for the role of the echo, Hürrem added, "Now you understand why I told you to salute the old man. But enough of him. Come." She beckoned the girl back to the sofa. "I feel the need of refreshment." At the snap of her fingers, the eunuch produced a gilded tray decorated with diamonds and loaded with sweets. "Taste this *rahat lokum*. It will give rest to your throat. The Europeans call it Turkish Delight."

"But you aren't having any yourself."

"The truth is that the moment I heard the Sultan's music, my stomach went into a convulsion. It has been so long. And the world beyond is full of women." Reaching for Saida's hand, she grasped it tightly. "Will he still find me pleasing?" Her touch was icy cold.

Embarrassed by the unexpected confidence, Saida cast about for a change of subject. "The doctor's son was a pupil in the Harem School," she heard herself saying. "I knew him when he was a boy."

Hürrem picked up bits of information the way a beach walker collects stones. "You knew him in school?"

"A little. He was a pupil there before he became a page."

"What's his name?"

"It's Italian. Danolo, I think. Maybe Danilo. I don't remember."

"Well, your school chum has come a long way from the Harem School. He's now a champion at the *gerit*. I have heard about him from my son" — she stopped to correct herself — "from your brother, Mehmet, who thinks very highly of him."

Saida waited for more, but Hürrem had a new distraction. The Sultan's band had entered the Imperial Gate.

"Do you know the air they are playing?" Hürrem asked. "You should. If you had spent more time here in the palace — if we lived here — you would know such things. Now that the Sultan is back in residence, they will play every afternoon at the time of the *ikindi*. And everyone in the palace, from the great Padishah to the lowest toilet cleaner, will stop his work and make his third prayer to Allah. Oh, he is such a wonder!"

There was no time to clarify whether the wonder she referred to was the Sultan or Allah himself, for at this moment a quartet of mounted heralds was coming through the Imperial Gate, calling out, "Stand back, the Sultan comes!" And, as if a wand had passed over them, the entire assemblage held its collective breath and fell into a dead silence.

By retreating to the rear of the loggia and craning their necks, the two women in the tower were just able to see the victorious Sultan emerge. A tall, slender figure straight as a pike and deadly pale, he rode resplendent on a milk-white Nogai steed, wearing a triple aigrette stuck into his turban sideways in the Persian fashion.

As always in his public appearances, the Padishah proceeded slowly. His subjects needed time to capture the moment for retelling to their grandchildren. Besides, it would hardly do to have the exalted *ghazi* rip through the crowd shooting arrows in all directions like a wild *sipahi*. What was needed here was gravitas. And to assure that the Sultan's mount would play its part in that spirit, the horse had spent the previous night — as he always did before a procession — suspended by straps to ensure that he walked with halting gravity.

Slowly, Sultan Suleiman made his way through the First Court, inclining his long neck first to the right, then to the left, acknowledging each individual bowed down before him. He disappeared briefly from view behind the twin towers of the Gate of Salutation and then reappeared in the Second Court followed by seven Arab horses in embroidered trappings set with jewels, led by seven pages as resplendently attired as the horses they led. But, gilded as they might be, they were no match for the Padishah — the *ghazi* himself — who held his victory out to his subjects like a lion holding his quarry in his paws, inviting them to share it.

The moment he came through the gate, Hürrem, now oblivious of her companion, walked slowly to the balustrade, straight-backed like a sleepwalker. Never taking her eyes off the slim, elegant figure on the white horse below, she reached into a small pouch that hung from her diamond girdle and withdrew from it a fine white silk handkerchief embroidered in white flowers by her own hand. And there she stood—a statue—as the Sultan made his progress through his people.

It took some time, but at last he emerged directly in front of the Diwan Tower. There he brought his mount to a halt. What followed unfolded like a tableau, the players coordinating their movements in a smooth arc as if rehearsed.

Dead-still on his mount, the Sultan slowly raised his eyes to the top of the tower. Up on the loggia, a hand lifted a delicate silk handkerchief and thrust it out through the octagonal slit in the brickwork. The Sultan's gaze was fixed on the small white square waving languidly back and forth in the breeze. Then, with a gasp, Hürrem sank to the ground, the handkerchief waving a forlorn farewell as she pulled away from the balustrade. She had collapsed into a faint, incontrovertible evidence of overwhelming passion.

Having accidentally encountered the world of the French *romans* at an impressionable age, Saida was something of an aficionado of romance. There was always a possibility that the faint might have been calculated. But the princess remained a confirmed believer in knights-errant, princesses in towers, and the primacy of true love over all. Besides, the look that transfixed the Second *Kadin's* face when she first caught sight of her Sultan-lover could not have been dissembled, not even by the finest actor in the empire.

16

THE DOCTOR'S HOUSE

MID-AFTERNOON AND NOT A CLOUD IN THE SKY. A good augury for the next day's *gerit* contest in which, Danilo reminded himself as he pegged along the Eunuch's Path, he may now never take part. Still, he kept up his pace, determined to salvage what he could of a disastrous day. And he did manage to circumnavigate the old palace walls in record time. But would he make it to the Doctor's House before his father? To miss the public ceremonies in the Second Court might just be excused. To fail to meet his father at his own door after a long absence might never be forgiven. Around the turn of the path, the Doctor's House came into view, easily identified by the heraldic flag bearing the sacred snakes of Asclepius that fluttered from the roof. (The ancient god of healing was another pagan hero whom Judah had no difficulty accommodating in his pantheon.)

To reach the house, Danilo still had to surmount the exterior palace wall. If the old fruit ladder had been carelessly left behind on the palace side, he would have to scale the wall. Definitely possible (he had done it more than once) but a time-consuming climb. However, for the first time that day, Fortuna had smiled on him. There the ladder stood, propped up against the stump of the dead pear tree.

With a brief thank-you to the gods, Danilo disengaged it from its perch and carried it to the wall.

As might be expected, the soldiery assigned to the kiosk that overlooked the hillside had been given the afternoon off to attend the parade. But Danilo was taking no chances. His ears pricked for the sound of a patrol, he mounted the creaking ladder step by careful step, then with an athlete's grace leapt to a safe landing on the soft grass that lined the inner edge of the Third Court. As he made his way across the garden to his father's house, he could not help but smile at the memory of certain boyhood pranks he had pulled off with the help of the very ladder that eased his way today.

It took a moment for his father's servant to answer the bell. And, when the lad did open the door, he did not greet his master's son with the usual bow and short prayer for his happiness and everlasting good health. Instead, he grabbed Danilo by the shoulder and all but hauled him into the vestibule.

"You are late. Very late. The doctor is worried. Very worried." The servant shook his head disapprovingly. This unnerved the boy so thoroughly that, when he did come face to face with his father, he was totally unprepared to deal with the opening parental scolding.

"Where have you been? Were you in the First Court to greet me? No. Were you at my door to welcome me? No. One would think that after a three-month absence..."

Now, for the first time, the doctor actually looked at his son, saw the condition he was in, uncombed and unkempt, with leaves and twigs tangled in the silk threads of his caftan.

"Your boots are filthy. What have you been up to?"

"It's my horse, Bucephalus." Danilo's rehearsed excuses forgotten, the words tumbled out of the boy's mouth in a rush. "I sent for the horse doctor, but he was too busy with the Sultan's parade horses. So I had to stay with Bucephalus myself. He is very sick, Papa. All blown up. And he moans in pain. Now he sleeps, but I think he's going to die."

Not a word of apology or regret. But the anguish on the boy's ravaged face wiped out all his transgressions. The only thing Judah could see was his son's misery.

"Sit down here beside me. Calm yourself. Let us see if there is anything we can do for the poor animal." His temper quelled, the doctor fell into the familiar role of the wise physician addressing the fearful family of a sick patient. "This Bucephalus of yours is a well-bred beast. That means he will fight for his life with all his heart. Oftentimes, that will to survive is better than any medicine. Now tell me, how was the horse when you left him?"

Somewhat comforted, the boy was able to answer coherently. "At first he bucked and kicked, and I thought he would break a leg. But I got him up and walking, and that seemed to quiet him."

Judah nodded approvingly. "If it is colic—and it sounds like colic to me—you have stumbled onto the best remedy."

"But now he lies there not moving. And his breathing is shallow. And he does not open his eyes for me."

"Is he still swelling?"

"I couldn't tell. Oh, Papa, if you could see him. I think the life is draining out of him."

"Then we must think of how we can restore him." Judah held out his arm. "Help me to the cabinet. I seem to remember a poultice. Or was it an emetic?"

Although the book cabinet stood no more than twenty steps from the bed, Judah was forced to lean heavily on his son as he shuffled across the room. Now Danilo was able to see the change in his father over the past months: the pallor, the tremor, the feebleness.

"Are you all right, Papa?"

"Just all right, my boy. Although I had to be carried across from Üsküdar in a litter." He did not add, *If you had been there to greet me, you would have known that.*

"Oh, Papa, I am so sorry. You never wrote that you were ill."

"It is only a fever. It will pass now that I am home." He did not add, *with you to take care of me*.

"What can I do for you, Papa?" Danilo asked, contrite.

This heartfelt offer was quite enough to erase the last traces of Judah's pique. "Right now, you can help me find the finest treatise in the world on the diseases of horses. It should be in a box on the third shelf in a blue linen wrapper."

After one or two false starts, Danilo located the manuscript, unwrapped it, and revealed its contents: a stack of vellum scrolls, each tied with a different-colored ribbon. And, to be sure, there it was, neatly tied with a yellow ribbon, an ancient manuscript that the doctor had carried with him halfway across the world. Like a magician, he whipped out a sheet of the vellum and waved it before his son's curious eyes.

"*Eccola!* The very thing. Hippocrates' *The Diseases of Horses*. Perhaps the father of all medicine will give us a few tips. What do you think?"

Danilo was too astonished to speak.

"Perhaps you wish to know how I came by such a valuable piece of property."

The boy nodded.

"It was a gift to me from the Marchese of Mantova, whom I served before you were born. A perfect ignoramus, that one. He had bought it before he discovered that he couldn't read it. Didn't realize until he'd paid a fortune for it that it was written in Greek. And his hired Greek proved a very unreliable translator. So he came after me to enter his service. I do believe he hired me as his body physician hoping I would explicate the fine points of veterinary medicine for him. A physician and veterinarian, two for the price of one, you see. He was as much of a bargain hunter as his wife. Well, I translated the treatise for him all right—not too challenging a job—and I did doctor him. But I ended up also doctoring his horses."

As he spoke Judah carefully piled up the vellum sheets.

"Would you believe that rascal, Francesco Gonzaga, gave me this manuscript as a gift when I finished the translation? Handed it to me like a used dishrag—said he had no more use for it now that he had a copy he could read." He shook his head in wonderment. "What ignorance." Another shake of the head and he began to page through the leaves of vellum, translating as he went. "Here we are. Colic. Called bloat when it affects ruminants. This is not a disease but a collection of symptoms: rapid standing pulse, fever, sweat, extreme pain, thrashing, kicking..."

Danilo recognized the symptoms at once.

"All that happened to Bucephalus. I was afraid it was colic."

"How did you know?" his father asked.

"I guess I must have heard about it in the stables. I'm always looking out for Bucephalus. To keep him healthy. He's highstrung. High bred. You know."

"Actually, I don't know. In fact, you probably know more about horses than I do, things you've picked up in the stables." He smiled at his son approvingly. "You've already done the diagnosis. Let us get on with the treatment." He thrust the sheaf of papers into his son's hands. "I'm finding it a bit difficult to decipher this. Why don't you take a turn."

Obediently, Danilo took the pages in hand and began to translate from the Greek.

"'Treatments for colic. There is no cure for colic. The outcome is with the gods. Therefore prayer is the best remedy. Some animals recover. Some expire. No matter the outcome, the disease runs its course within a single revolution of the sun.'" Danilo stopped to consider this. "Does that mean there's nothing we can do but pray, Papa?"

"Read on," his father replied in a firm, reassuring voice. "Perhaps we can learn from Hippocrates how to increase the odds in Bucephalus's favor."

The boy continued. "'A salt wash of the stomach can sometimes be efficacious in aiding the animal to pass gas. Also, a poultice applied to the belly. Otherwise, pray.'" At this, the boy's composure dissolved away, and try as he might, he could not stop his tears. "I don't want him to die, Papa. I love him so much."

Much as Judah wanted to gather his son up in his arms and dry his tears, the habits of a lifetime were too strong in him. Instead, he pushed on in his reassuring but distant physician's manner.

"We can still do our best to save him," the doctor said. "I will mix a poultice for you to take along and instruct you how to wash out his stomach. I have done it myself. Again, thanks to that barbarian, Francesco Gonzaga. He always called me in when one of his Arab stallions got sick. I think he felt he was doing me an honor by allowing me to treat them. Actually, I became quite fond of them. Your mother teased me about it mercilessly."

"But I thought you hated horses."

"Me? I hate no living thing. Certainly not horses. What I hate is the thought that you might break your neck on one."

"Then why are you helping me to cure Bucephalus?"

Judah stopped to consider the question. The boy waited. Then, after a few moments, Judah spoke.

"Perhaps I'd rather see you break your neck than break your heart," he said. "Now let us get on with the task."

The potion was mixed in short order, and Danilo was issued a package to take back to the stables consisting of a large bag of salt, a funnel, and careful instructions on how to wash out a horse's stomach. Eager as he was to begin treating his horse, he did stay to see his father back to bed before he left and took an extra minute to wrap him up in two blankets.

Then, resolutely dry-eyed, he leaned over, grasped his father's hand tightly, and in a voice quivering with feeling vowed: "I will never forget what you did for me this day, Papa."

"Someday you will do something for me."

"Anything, Papa."

This was Judah's chance and he took it. "Anything?" he asked, knowing where he was going and all the while thinking, *I am leading him into a trap. How can I do this?*

"Anything," the boy answered.

And Judah knew that, in his son's mouth, the offer, once

made, would never be rescinded. "Then promise me that, when you finish this term at the School for Pages, you will move out of the dormitory and stay at home with me. I am no longer required in the field. I will serve the Sultan here in Topkapi. I want my son beside me."

It was a deal made by the devil and Judah knew it. He had caught the boy at his most vulnerable moment, when the life of the creature he held most dear (yes, admit it, *most* dear) was hanging by a thread. He had exploited the boy's misery to extract a promise; at best, shoddy and dishonorable behavior. But Judah had recognized a chance to wean his son away from the seductions of the Ottoman court and could not resist using whatever means came to hand.

Danilo, of course, could see none of this. He took his leave of Judah, buoyed by the hope that his father's remedy would save Bucephalus's life, perhaps even helped him to carry his master to glory the next day in the *gerit*.

"Light the brazier and heat up a pail of water. Not too hot, not too cold, and be quick about it," he ordered Abdul back at the stable. "I am going to save Bucephalus's life and you are going to help me."

He sat down in the straw beside the animal and began to rub the distended belly in a slow circular movement as his father had told him to do. The poultice would be applied after the stomach was washed.

By the time the water was heated, Bucephalus was half awake and able to respond when Danilo stuck a hand down his throat.

"Let the horse get used to having something soft in his throat before you try the funnel," Judah had advised. "And be sure to have the stable boy hold his back legs."

Abdul was so instructed. But the precaution proved unnecessary. Danilo had placed so many tasty morsels on the animal's tongue over the years that when he thrust his bare fist into Bucephalus's mouth, the horse offered no resistance.

But the hardest part was still to come. After Danilo had

poured the bag of salt into the warm water and stirred it, he reached out to place the funnel in the horse's mouth. Gentle as a lover, he eased the neck of the funnel down the animal's throat, signaling to Abdul to tighten his hold on the animal's hind legs. This was no tasty morsel. This was a sharp, inflexible piece of metal. But again, the horse surprised them by offering no resistance.

"He trusts you, master, not to hurt him," Abdul offered.

Now for the actual procedure. Danilo filled the cup hanging from the side of the bucket and began to pour the salt water slowly into the funnel, all the while maintaining a steady flow of endearments into the velvety ear. And after an interminable time, the bucket was empty and the job done.

"Good boy, Bucephalus. Brave boy."

"What now?" Abdul inquired.

"We pray," Danilo replied. "I will ask my god to make Bucephalus strong once again so that he can carry me tomorrow in the *gerit.*"

And so they prayed, each in his own language, each to his own god, in compliance with the advice offered by Hippocrates, the pagan father of medicine.

The *muezzin's* final call to prayer came and went, and the animal remained semi-comatose, breathing shallowly. But still breathing. And before the midnight hour, the horse suddenly shuddered, shook himself, struggled to his feet, and emitted a deafening blast of gas. Then another. The odor that filled the stall drove the minders out into the night air.

"It's the gas coming out," Danilo shouted happily to Abdul, who was, by now, green with nausea. And together, holding their noses, they went back to the stall and watched while slowly, as if someone had stuck a pin in it, the horse's bloated belly began to deflate before their eyes.

17

THE EVE OF THE GERIT

I N THE CITY THE CELEBRATION OF SULEIMAN'S VICTORY
continued undiminished throughout the night. On both
the Asian and European sides of the capital, Koranic
prohibitions against alcohol were quietly ignored; women
walked freely in the streets (albeit discreetly covered); and the
young men of the School for Pages, set free from their supervised
life for a brief respite, roamed the streets at will and returned
to their dormitories at their own pleasure. It was carnival time
in Istanbul. For the next four days, the Sultan would continue
to show himself periodically outside his palace, applauding
the games at the hippodrome, tossing coins to the crowd, and
presiding over the prodigious offerings of sweets and sherbets
distributed night and day in the streets. This was a striking
contrast to the calm and quiet that prevailed behind the gates of
Topkapi Palace.

The cleanup of the palace began the very moment the
Sultan passed through the Gate of Serenity into his *selamlik*.
By the time the *muezzin* called the faithful to the final prayer
of the day, the palace grounds had been cleared of all detritus,
both material and human. In the First and Second Courts, no

evidence remained of the exploits performed there by the cavalry troops only a few hours before. Damaged patches of lawn were restored, the paved paths were swept clean, and the venerable cypress trees ruled once more. The vast crowd that assembled on the lawns to salute their Padishah were replaced by the mild-eyed gazelles that normally grazed on the lush lawns. With a thousand gardeners standing by, things happened fast.

For Princess Saida, the events of the evening began to unfold rapidly once the Lady Hürrem had recovered from her faint. This the lady did immediately after the Sultan's imposing figure disappeared into the *selamlik*. Thereupon Saida found herself being hurried down the winding stairway of the Diwan Tower, out of the building, past the guard, and into the arms of her own maid, Marisah, one of a small party of attendants who materialized at the foot of the staircase as if by magic when the ladies descended. There they stood at attention: a handful of Hürrem's personal servants—Saida's maid courteously included—plus a powerful triumvirate of black eunuchs imported to warn off any casual servants of the *selamlik* who might inadvertently glance in the direction of the harem women as they passed.

When they left the Diwan Tower, Hürrem seemed to know exactly where to go. It was she who led the way through the Gates of Felicity. And, once inside the Third Court, she demanded a bath, as·if certain that there would be a *hamam* awaiting their pleasure. Obviously Hürrem had been here before. Probably many times.

Saida, who rarely visited her father's palace, would happily have loitered in the garden-like Second Court—the tame animals especially appealed to her—but Hürrem would have none of it. And the Second *Kadin* was definitely in charge here. It was not one of the eunuchs but she who led the way through the Gate of Felicity, past the Throne Room and the Doctor's House, to a small but very pretty wooden kiosk against the back wall of the Third Court.

Once inside the little building, the Second *Kadin* immediately threw aside her headgear and cloak and advised Saida that they needed to bathe at once.

"It has been a very dirty day," she explained. "I feel the dust clogging my pores and so must you."

No mention of her imminent reunion with the Sultan. No sign of apprehension. Apparently her confiding moment had passed. But the lady could not hide little signs of nervousness like an intermittent twitch in her right eye and a slight trembling of her hands when she reached out for a water jug in the *hamam*.

Then, within minutes — or so it seemed to Saida — Hürrem had bathed and dressed and was off without even the courtesy of a "good night." It was not until the door had closed behind her that peace descended on the little kiosk. Only then did Saida realize how much tension the woman carried with her.

Could it be that, under her assured manner, the Second *Kadin* did, in truth, harbor doubts of her Sultan's faithfulness? Did she actually fear that his long absences might change his feelings for her? That another woman — a Hungarian or an Austrian prisoner, perhaps — might have taken his fancy? Was she haunted by the specter of her body ending up in a sack of stones at the bottom of the Bosphorus, as had the bodies of not a few concubines before her?

Saida suddenly recalled Hürrem's odd confidence earlier in the day. "Whereas you are a princess, I am but a poor slave. I know what it is like to be bought and sold like a piece of meat. Would you like to know?"

Without waiting for an answer the woman had continued in a harsh, bitter tone that Saida had never heard from her before, her eyes fixed on some dim, distant point in her past. "I was fifteen years old. No man had ever touched me. They stripped me and brought me to the *Kizlar Agasi*, who ordered me to open my mouth and keep it wide so he could check my teeth. He ran his finger inside my mouth and checked my gums as he would have a camel or a horse. Then he ordered another eunuch to lift my hair and tweak my nipples to make sure they held no liquid. Shall I go on?"

"Please, no."

There had been times during her presence in Hürrem's household that the girl had suffered terrible pangs of jealousy of this woman who seemed to hold such power over her father. She had envied Hürrem his letters, the poems he wrote to her, his protestations of eternal love. But now she could feel only sympathy. Hürrem had taken her in as a daughter, had brought her out into the world. Without Hürrem, she would never have been included in the royal party that would visit the hippodrome the next day.

Across the Third Court in the Sultan's *selamlik*, Hürrem was sparkling, her eyes brighter than her jewels, adoring her Sultan. Suleiman was weary. Even for a man of iron, it had been a long, trying day. But Hürrem knew how to revive him. She had brought a packet of the potions that she purchased regularly from one of the so-called bundle-women who service the harem. Applied to certain parts of a man's body in certain ways, these unguents never failed to stimulate the male member. Hürrem had been patronizing this bundle-woman ever since she first entered the harem as a young girl almost ten years ago. By the time she was called to the Sultan's bed, she had acquainted herself with the entire contents of the harridan's pharmacopeia, plus a variety of ways to administer them. As they said in the whorehouses on the waterfront, the Second *Kadin* had quite the little bag of tricks. And she meant to make full use of them tonight.

On the other side of the Gate of Felicity in the Sultan's stables, a different kind of elixir was working its wonders on Danilo del Medigo's horse. By midnight, Bucephalus was able to stand on his feet. His eyes were clear and his belly was almost down to size. Hours after midnight, the Sultan's Master of the Horse finally showed himself, just in time to witness the last of the cure. A man with a fine sense of hierarchy — and of the precariousness of his own position on the court ladder — he had made certain that every last one of the Sultan's parade horses was examined and safely ferried across the Bosphorus before he got around to answering the page's cry for help. Even so, when he finally managed to reach the stables, he had the gall to order a complete review of the problem as if he had been in charge of Bucephalus all along. He also directed that the horse be spared the stress of the *gerit* that day, a piece of advice that Danilo dismissed out of hand. He had, after all, been assured by his father—backed up by Hippocrates—that once the symptoms of colic subsided, the best medicine for the animal would be a cleansing, sweat-producing workout. What could be a better remedy than an outing in the *gerit*? Yes, Danilo del Medigo would definitely ride Bucephalus in the games, and to hell with the Master of the Horses. That decided, he left the horse in the hands of Abdul and headed for his dormitory to catch as much sleep as he could.

Actually, the boy's chances of recouping his strength were better than those of the horse. The boy was young, the horse middle-aged—truth to tell, too old for the *gerit*. But Bucephalus was now more to Danilo than just a mount, even more than a treasured thoroughbred and a gift from the Sultan. The animal's miraculous recovery had turned Bucephalus into a talisman. Danilo was now convinced that he was destined to triumph in the *gerit* on the back of this mount and no other. Why else had Fortuna kept the beast alive? Yes, Fortuna. Danilo's mind, the product of a humanist education, had no difficulty embracing both the pagan goddess and the One God of Judaism. His father, an observant Jew all his life, had for years played an active role in Lorenzo de Medici's Platonic Academy in Florence, where he had always lit a candle for Plato beside the Shabbat candles on his Friday night table and saw no incongruity in it. In emulation, Danilo slept secure in the oversight of both Fortuna and the Jewish God Yahweh—with the princess's amulet pressed close to his chest.

In the guest kiosk at the far end of the Third Court, Princess Saida was enjoying a sleep so deep that it took more than one determined poke to wake her.

"Get up, lazy girl." The Second *Kadin*, very playful this morning, reached under the silk comforter and began to tickle Saida's toes. "Wake up. Open your eyes. I have let you sleep until the last possible moment."

The girl looked up to find herself facing a glowing, wide-eyed Hürrem. What was it about this woman? She certainly was not beautiful. Her nose was too sharp. Her face was too long. And her eyes were really quite small. But her liveliness—the power of her pleasure at being alive—more than made up for her physical defects. There she stood, legs akimbo, arms stretched out like an Amazon.

This woman is as young in spirit, as hopeful as I am, thought Saida. *For her, every day is an adventure.* Then came the thought, *She must be a wonderful lover.*

"You aren't listening to me." Hürrem broke into her thoughts. "We are due to leave for the hippodrome by the end of the second prayer. The Sultan is sending sedan chairs to carry us there. Yes, sedan chairs," she repeated, relishing the words, "will carry us to the Grand Vizier's palace."

"Is it a long trip?" asked Saida, still mindful of the bouncing carriage ride of yesterday.

"Of course not. Don't you know where you are? Don't you remember coming here last night?"

Saida looked around her at the unmistakable reds and the vibrant blues of the Iznik tiles, then up at the coffers of the gilded ceiling. She had heard stories of a luxurious guest house set aside in Topkapi for concubines fortunate enough to be invited there. Had she actually spent the night in that coveted hideaway? Apparently.

Fully awake now, she studied Hürrem. Yesterday, in the incessant flow of chatter that issued from the woman's mouth, the Second *Kadin* had managed never to allude to the kiosk that was being prepared for them. Such a smooth dissembler. She may have come from some coarse Russian hovel, as they said, but she behaved as if she had been born and bred in the harem—full of secrets and mischief. Altogether the perfect odalisque. But with a difference that set her off from all the rest.

Within Hürrem burned a white-hot inner fire that no amount of training could have instilled. *If I were to get too close to this woman*, Saida thought with one long last look at her benefactor, *she could burn me to a cinder.*

18

THE HIPPODROME

THE FIRST TIME DANILO DEL MEDIGO MADE THE circuit of the hippodrome racecourse was at the age of eleven, as part of his father's efforts to entice him out of the deep sadness that no remedy in the doctor's pharmacy could alleviate. When medicines proved to be of no value he tried offerings of tasty food also, which the patient ate when he was bidden but which brought no flush of pleasure to his pale face. Nor did tasty tidbits bring a request for a second helping.

The doctor turned to nature. Long walks in the sun were equally unrewarding. But perhaps he might be able to delight the patient's eyes with wonderful sights and deluge his mind with vivid stories of long-ago events. Worth a try. But where to go? The hippodrome, of course. No question. What better place to start than that ancient racecourse whose stones still held the imprint of Greek chariot wheels? Whose walls resounded with the roar of the lions unleashed against the Roman gladiators. Whose depths echoed the cheers of a hundred thousand citizens welcoming home from one of his triumphs their emperor Justinian and his empress Theodora, former circus girl and whore.

They entered the huge space under the towering vaulted arch on the north side. It was through these majestic arches that the Greek chariots thundered into the arena from the substructures that housed the dressing rooms, stables, chariot docks, and animal cages below. For Judah, schooled in the lore of the ancients, the cobblestones still resonated with the thundering hooves.

"If these old stones could talk," he told his son as they took off down the paved central spine of the arena, "what stories they would tell."

The boy took the bait. "What kinds of stories?" It was his first question, Judah noted with pleasure.

"Stories of courage and cowardice, triumph and slaughter, great victories and great upheavals," came the reply.

And it was true. From the time of Constantine until the time of Suleiman, no important event had been celebrated anywhere else in the city but at the hippodrome. And, truth aside, no other approach could so unerringly have found its way to Danilo's heart. A didactic history of the city would have fallen on deaf ears. But tales of high heroism and great triumphs were meat and drink to a boy nurtured by his mother, Grazia the scribe — a mother now lost to him but constantly in his thoughts — on the tales of Homer.

Encouraged by a suggestion of interest in the boy's eyes, Judah beckoned him toward the eastern track, a spot said to be a thousand-year-old killing ground.

"Listen. Do you hear anything strange?"

The boy shook his head.

"There are those who swear that, when they walk over this end of the course, they hear the sound of men screaming and catch a whiff of blood." The boy's eyes widened. "It was here on the very ground where we now stand that Justinian's general, Belisarius, trapped a force of thirty thousand rebels and slaughtered them to the last man. Tradition has it that the dead were buried where they fell and that their bones still inhabit the site. Some say that when they walk here, they hear the dead calling out."

"And you, sir, have you heard them?" the boy asked.

A second question, Judah noted.

"Good God, no," he answered, "I am a scientist. But I thought you might have the gift."

The boy shook his head, no.

No matter. It was enough that he had been drawn out of himself far enough to ask not one but two questions. Sufficient unto the day, thought Judah, taking a leaf from the Christians' book.

"Let us make the complete circuit around the racecourse" — he took the boy's arm familiarly — "and head for home."

It was at the turn onto the western edge of the arena that, quite unplanned, he found himself making one final effort to unlock the boy's imagination. "This is the squarest corner of the oval and the turn where most of the chariot accidents happened. And this side of the bleachers was the most coveted place to sit. Probably because, facing east in the afternoon, you didn't have the setting sun in your eyes. See there" — he pointed to a truncated flight of narrow stone steps — "in the time of Constantine, rows of seats lined both sides of the course and reached dizzying heights. They say that, after he restored it, Justinian's hippodrome accommodated one hundred thousand people. Imagine it! One hundred thousand people yelling their lungs out as the chariots rounded this curve for the final push. If you close your eyes and listen hard, you may hear those shouts echoing down through the years."

Danilo hesitated. Then, unable to resist the lure, he closed his eyes tight shut and waited for the magic. *His hardships have taught him patience*, Judah thought. And, to be sure, after several moments, the boy began to nod slowly.

"I think I heard them, Papa," he whispered. "I couldn't make out the words. But I believe they were shouting in Greek."

After that day, the hippodrome became a place Danilo returned to again and again, sometimes with Judah on the way home from their Saturday morning prayers, often alone. In spite of hours poring over the vocabulary lists his mother had compiled for him, searching out the Greek words for "Hurrah," "Faster," and "Bravo," he never was able to identify the sounds he thought he heard in his head. But, in the course of many visits, he began to see—with his eyes shut—dim at first, then increasingly clear, the faces of the Greeks, tier upon tier of them, the cords in their necks bulging as they shouted words of encouragement to their favorite charioteers. And, after some time had passed, he began, when he closed his eyes, to see himself rounding that corner mounted on a magnificent charger, galloping full tilt across the finish line, the victor in some grueling contest.

Never in the course of those flights of fancy did Danilo come close to hoping—even thinking—that such a thing might actually happen. But when the riding master at the Harem School offered him the opportunity to join the *gerit* team, he did rush to accept. And he did practice to perfect his aim and his horsemanship with unfailing perseverance throughout his years in the Harem School and now in the Sultan's School for Pages. But this dogged pursuit of mastery, and the visions that came to him when he stood in the hippodrome with his eyes shut, ran on parallel tracks that had never met—until now, five years after he had first walked the *pista* with his father and heard a dim echo of the Greeks shouting in the stands.

And now, on this day of the *gerit* match between the Sultan's team and the Grand Vizier's team to celebrate Suleiman's great victory, the two paths converged and Danilo del Medigo's fantasy became reality.

19

THE GERIT CONTEST

I N HIS VILLA IN THE PERA SECTION OF THE CITY, THE Venetian *bailo*, Alvise Gritti, was up at dawn scratching away at the report he wrote each week for his masters in the Venetian Senate.

"The Sultan's victory celebration," he wrote, "is a spectacle halfway between our Carnival and the Roman games. Today, all attention will center on the hippodrome, where a contest is planned, named after a three-foot javelin with a steel dart at the business end called a *gerit*. It is played by two teams on horseback: one from the Sultan's School for Pages, the other from the Grand Vizier's school of his pages.

"The *gerit* is the favorite sport of the Turks, and they play it the way they fight their wars. There is no manoeuvering. Each rider simply charges boldly and directly and, up close, hurls the *gerit* at his selected opponent with enough force to knock him off his horse. All hangs on the accuracy of the throw. Success is judged by the aggregate number of hits scored by the winning team and depends not on leadership or team play, as it would with us, but solely on horsemanship and the raw guts of each player. So once the match begins, it quickly turns into a chaotic melee with riders hurling their weapons wildly in all directions and often—because they wear no armor other than a leather jerkin—results in serious injury and sometimes death. The randomness of it all defies the reason of a thinking man.

"I know of nothing in Europe to compare with this *gerit*," he continued, "which resembles a battle more than a jousting contest. That it should be the favorite sport of the Turks in both town and country, played enthusiastically by artisans and sultans alike, should tell us something about these people. By now, I have witnessed countless of these contests but have yet to fully grasp the point. To one not caught up in it early in life, the *gerit* is simply a war of each against all.

"To this mad display I will shortly repair. There is no avoiding it. I have been assigned a preferred seat in a balcony on the east side of the Grand Vizier's palace overlooking the hippodrome. At least I will not be blinded by the setting sun at the end of the day. I am further honored by an invitation to dine in the Great Hall of the Grand Vizier's palace, where those members of the winning team who have not been mutilated or killed will be rewarded by the Sultan, this to be followed by the typical Ottoman banquet of twenty courses or more. If I do not fall ill from sun poisoning or the surfeit of rich food without the digestive amelioration of even a single glass of wine, a report on the damned *gerit* will follow."

Such were the expectations of Signor Gritti, a typical Venetian—vain, dyspeptic, and convinced that there was no other civilized spot on earth except his beloved Serenissima. For most Istanbulians—the citizens who would overfill the bleachers and bellow their hearts out that afternoon as their Greek and Roman predecessors did before them—the day held the expectation of a splendid entertainment. To Princess Saida, it promised rapturous fulfillment. To the Second *Kadin*, it meant her first time ever riding in a sedan chair like the Valide Sultan she intended to become. For Danilo del Medigo, today was the day he had been preparing for all his life.

Among his teammates, Danilo was known to be mild-tempered, even phlegmatic. Not one to give way to anger, cry out from pain, sulk in defeat, or gloat in victory. But, with it all, a fierce competitor. In his years on Suleiman's *gerit* squad he had become something of a pet. "The kid with bronze balls," they called him. But no one, not even the most hardened veteran, was ever totally immune to pre-game nerves. Danilo knew this. He had seen the evidence of it in the changing room. Still, he was unprepared when he lost his nerve for the first time.

On the short walk from Topkapi to At Maydani (or Horse Square, as the hippodrome was still known to born-and-bred Istanbulians), his stomach abruptly turned into a hard knot and his breath began to come in short bursts. He barely made it through the giant arches that led to the dressing rooms underneath the course without stumbling. By then, his knees were weak and he felt a rising gorge of vomit in his throat. When the other contestants peeled off to check up on their horses, he quietly continued alone down the wide tunnel to the dressing room, hoping that his absence would not be noticed. He managed to get to the bucket just in time.

Panic was not familiar to him, but he recognized its symptoms. *This is not fear*, he told himself. *This is the fear of fear. The time to be afraid is when you are lying on the ground, too hurt to move, hearing the pounding hooves of the horses that are going to trample you to death. That is fear. What you are feeling now is a phantom. You can blow it away. Fill the belly with air, like a bladder. Suck the air in all the way down to the crotch. Hold it, hold it, hold it. Blow it out slowly. Repeat until the breath flows evenly.*

Summoning the last of his resolve, he lay down flat and began a series of deep belly breaths. A few minutes of this drill and he was breathing normally. But he was still nauseated and woozy when the team began to arrive in the dressing room.

The captain, a giant who went by the name of Oxy, saw immediately that something was wrong. Danilo felt a comforting arm around his shoulder and heard softly in his ear, "Is your gut in a twist?"

He nodded, eyes downcast, ashamed.

"Here's what I used to do. Lie on the bench. Flat. Now sit up. I'll hold your feet so you don't cheat. Up!"

Danilo groaned with the pain.

"Lower yourself slowly. I know it hurts, but do it. Again." Oxy was implacable, impervious to the grunts and groans that issued from the bench as Danilo forced his rigid muscles to flex and relax, flex and relax. He had seen other athletes suffer through this exorcism before a match. Now he understood why they did it. He was not the only one who had ever panicked.

Slowly, as he gained control over his balky muscles, the cramp lessened and the only pain he felt was the terrible weight of Oxy sitting on his feet. Best of all, the whole thing had been handled so smoothly that nobody seemed to have noticed.

"Drink some water. No wine!" And Oxy was off to attend to captain's affairs.

He sounds like my father, Danilo thought.

By now, the temporary stands along the western side of the racecourse were filled, and those who missed out on the seating had spread out into the standing room above the north and south substructures. In bygone days viewing stands were permanently maintained on all four sides of the course and could accommodate a hundred thousand spectators. But that accommodation was abruptly cut in half when, just a few years into his reign, Suleiman appropriated a wide swath of land on the eastern border of the hippodrome for the site of the palace he was building for his Grand Vizier and boon companion, Ibrahim the Greek. Now, all that remained on the east side between the track and the magnificent stone edifice that housed the Grand Vizier was a narrow strip of lawn roped off today to give space and air to the Sultan's viewing platform, thus reducing even further the seating capacity of the stadium. Still, from the vantage point of the riders emerging into the daylight from the underground vaults, it seemed as if the entire city of Istanbul was here today.

For all their numbers, it was a fairly quiet crowd that had

been gathering since early morning. But when the first rider of the Sultan's team galloped out of the cavernous depths of the substructure and stood before them framed in the center vault, the shouting began. Each player would have his moment of recognition in the stone doorway before he galloped around to take his place in the starting lineup—the Sultan's team at the southern end of the arena, the Grand Vizier's men on the north. Since there were twelve members on each team, the process was somewhat tedious, certainly a far cry from the farrago that Signor Gritti described in his report. But this was only the beginning. Like many events in Ottoman public life, the *gerit* tended to start slowly and gather momentum gradually until the moment when all hell broke loose.

Once the riders lined up at either end of the oval, the huge front doors of the Grand Vizier's palace swung open and out came the Sultan's musicians blasting appropriately raucous music (that is, Turkish rather than Persian). They were followed by a group of the Sultan's senior pages, magnificently attired in crimson caftans, carrying a rolled-up length of cloth-of-gold fabric, which they unfurled and tossed expertly over a set of poles already in place around the raised platform, thereby creating a golden canopy for the Padishah.

Next to emerge, a second platoon of pages, holding high a golden throne, which they placed front and center under the canopy.

Now came the Grand Vizier, Ibrahim Pasha, accompanied by his own attendants, even more gorgeously dressed than the pages who preceded them. Compared to his attendants he was nothing special to look at—medium build, greasy hair, and a trace of kohl around the eyes—a typical Greek. But appearances are deceiving. He made his way to the platform and stood respectfully at the right of the throne. It would be unthinkable for anyone to seat himself ahead of the Sultan.

Now, for a change of pace, a contingent of Janissaries shambled in from the south end.

"Make way, make way," bawled the heralds.

And the standing crowd, always respectful of Janissaries, parted like the Red Sea to let them through as they make their way along the *spina* and proceeded to surround the royal enclosure. The Sultan's parade band played a flourish of trumpets. The horses lined up at either end of the stadium danced in anticipation. The stage was set for the chief actor in this tableau. In any setting that the Sultan condescended to honor with his presence, he was always the star attraction. Today, even his riders took second place to him.

All eyes were turned to the bronze doors of the Grand Vizier's palace when they opened to reveal the Padishah, Father of All the Sovereigns of the World, resplendent on a milk-white steed. As always the poor beast had been stretched on a strap overnight to give it a slow, majestic gait.

Whenever the Sultan went out among his people—officially—he was always positioned above them, occasionally in a sedan chair, most often mounted on a horse. Today, when he dismounted, he stepped directly onto the raised platform so that not for a single moment was he on the same level as his people. Always raised, like a god.

Elegant, unsmiling, and ramrod straight, he bent to the waist, nodding first to the crowd at his right, then to the left. He raised his right hand.

On cue the Chief Herald stepped forward and in a stentorian tone announced, "Let the games begin!"

At a signal from their captains, the riders took off from a standing start toward the center of the field, driving their mounts furiously—but not so furiously as to overtake their captains. The etiquette of the game demanded that no player overtake his leader in this first rush, a stroke of luck for Danilo del Medigo. As he urged his horse forward, he wondered if he had done the right thing when he insisted on riding Bucephalus. He had been warned that the horse at this age was no longer a viable contestant in a speed race. And, when they took off, Bucephalus seemed sluggish. Was it the after-effects of the colic? Was the animal past his prime? Should he have requested a younger, faster, more agile mount? Then the *gerits* began to fly and there was no time for thinking.

A quick glance told Danilo which of the Grand Vizier's riders had picked him out as a target. His *gerit* clasped in his bare hand—no gloves, as leather could slip—he reined Bucephalus to the right, a standard move before the swerve to the left to deflect the opponent's thrust. He narrowed his eyes to a slit, blurring his focus, rendering the other rider faceless—a crouching form, coming straight at him. Slowly, as the space between them narrowed, the eyes of the other rider were revealed. Coal black. Merciless.

At the very last possible moment, Danilo had to lean to the left to put himself out of the way of the dart that would be coming at him, while at the same moment hurling his own pole at his opponent's chest—the best way to knock him off his mount. In these moves, timing was everything.

Danilo raised his throwing arm as he shifted his body and jerked the horse to the right. This was the moment for the thrust. But before he could hurl his weapon, he was struck with terrible force on his right chest. Weakened by the blow, his right hand loosened its grip. His weapon fell to the ground. Before he could grasp what had happened, he was flat on the turf and everything that surrounded him appeared as if through a mist. He strained every muscle in his body to lift himself up, but pain pinioned him to the ground. His body, which he had learned to trust, had betrayed him.

Sprawled on the ground, a defeated warrior, he blinked to hold back the tears. "I'm sorry," he mumbled, "so sorry..."

Then through the fog he heard a voice, a voice he knew well. He raised his eyes to heaven.

"As long as you live, I will be with you." His mother's words as she lay dying. *"If you need me, call out. I will answer from a place deep inside you."*

"Mother," he whispered softly.

As if in response, a soft white hand reached down from heaven to pull him gently to his feet. He stamped his foot to assure himself that the ground beneath him was solid. And there he stood in the middle of the hippodrome, clear-sighted once again and steady on his feet but without a mount or a weapon.

Through force of habit, he lifted two fingers to his mouth, pursed his lips, and delivered an ear-splitting whistle. And, halfway across the field, a riderless horse disengaged itself from the pack and trotted toward him. Bucephalus was coming to rescue him. This was a move he and Bucephalus had practiced a hundred times, in preparation for just such a moment.

As he hoisted himself up onto the saddle, a deluge of sound washed over him, thousands of voices cheering him on. He strained to listen, but the voices were drowned out by a second sonic torrent—the pounding roar of hooves. His *gerit* lay on the ground between him and the tangle of horsemen galloping toward him. Once he had lost his weapon the rules of *gerit* would force him to retire from the match, an ignominious defeat. There was no time to think. He turned Bucephalus away from the safe harbor of the sidelines and galloped forward to rescue his honor, veering wide from a straight-ahead course so as to cut across the opposing team at an angle.

"Go," he shouted into the horse's ear. "Go!"

As they neared the spot where his weapon lay, he slipped his left foot out of the stirrup and slid down along the horse's midsection. There was nothing now to hold him to the animal but the reins and one stirrup. At precisely the right instant he stretched his body the last perilous inches to where his weapon lay on the ground and, with only seconds to spare, picked up his *gerit*, reversed his direction, and galloped away to the sidelines, clasping the weapon to his heart.

After that, the day belonged to Danilo del Medigo. Back in the game, back to himself, he rode through the tumult and the mud, his timing perfect, his aim unerring, his mind clear. He had, as they say, hit his stride. And each time he scored, the crowd rose to its feet and cheered wildly. But nothing that followed could equal for them the thrill of the first few moments of the contest when the rider lay on the ground, perhaps unconscious, perhaps even dead, then suddenly came back to life, resurrected before their eyes.

During those tense moments, the harem ladies up on the balcony edged forward and stood pressed against the balustrade, their faces squeezed between the lattices, shouting encouragement to the downed rider—a most unusual lapse for harem ladies—shrieking bravos when he struggled to his feet and remounted his horse and—most dazzling of all—deliberately thrust himself across the path of a pack of riders to retrieve his grounded *gerit*.

"This proves what I have always said," the Second *Kadin* burbled on, as was her habit, up on the balcony. "The pages in the Palace School are superior to those in the Grand Vizier's. And that is because the Sultan himself supervises every aspect of their training."

She had failed to observe that, when the rider fell, the princess gasped and turned white and was forced to retire to a divan at the rear of the balcony. Nor had it come to her attention that since the girl had come back to her seat at the railing, she had not uttered a word.

Only after some time did Saida collect herself sufficiently to speak and then only to request that she be excused.

"I am unwell," she explained, "and must return to the harem."

In vain, Hürrem tried to bully the girl out of it. She had secured permission for them to stay on at Topkapi for another night. The Sultan had expressed a desire to see his daughter. He might invite her to dine with him this evening in the *selamlik*—an honor rarely bestowed on any woman, never yet on his daughter.

But the girl would not be swayed. She must return to the old palace. She had been absent from her grandmother for too long. The Valide liked to be read to sleep by her granddaughter.

"I never forget," Saida advised the Lady Hürrem, "that my father put the Valide in my charge. He will most certainly understand when you explain that I felt it my duty to forego the pleasures of his palace to fulfill my duty to his revered mother."

Reluctantly, Hürrem agreed to summon a cart to carry the princess back to the harem. And to that haven Saida repaired as soon as the *gerit* contest was over, leading Hürrem to conclude that if this princess was ever to occupy a position of importance in the Second *Kadin's* close circle, she had better begin to understand that opportunities to kindle a light in the Sultan's eye came far ahead of any other duty, certainly one's duty to an old woman who would be dead soon anyway.

20

REWARDS OF THE DAY

WHEN A FLOURISH OF BRASS ANNOUNCED THE END of the *gerit* match, the judges credited Danilo del Medigo with four hits, the exact number by which the Sultan's team had defeated the Grand Vizier's. At this announcement Danilo's teammates hoisted him up on their shoulders and carried him off the field in triumph. Held aloft by his mates, he soared off the field as if on a cloud, with the cheers of the crowd resounding in his head blotting out the boisterous locker room horseplay of his teammates. His delirium was not shattered until his captain, the giant Oxy, grabbed him by the hair and overturned a pail of icy water on his head.

"Time to shape up, my boy." The captain whacked his protégé on the buttocks. "The Sultan awaits."

In short order the captain had his team scrubbed clean, dressed, lined up double file and on the march into the Grand Vizier's palace.

"Remember," he warned them as they approached the huge brass doors, "keep your heads down at all times. Never look straight into the eyes of the Padishah, and never, *never* speak in his presence."

"What if he asks us a question?" asked one of the younger players.

"If that happens, a short answer is allowed. But keep it brief. And low. The Sultan dislikes loud voices. But you needn't worry. Chances are he won't talk to you. I've been received twice before — and rewarded handsomely, as you will be today — but he has never spoken directly to me," the captain said. "Are you ready? Good. Let's go. Walk slowly. Don't jostle. Don't chatter. Slow. Quiet. Dignified. Respectful to the Sultan from whom all of your blessings flow."

For Danilo, there was no need to dissemble respect. Pacing the long corridor to the Reception Salon, a truly awesome space, its vault easily reaching to three times the height of any structure in Topkapi Palace, he was astonished by the grandeur of the anterooms of the palace that the Sultan built for his boon companion, each one warmed by a glowing fireplace. This vast vaulted space, hung top to bottom with magnificent Persian rugs, brought to his mind the grand Italian palaces he had known as a child and presented a striking contrast to the small, low Ottoman kiosks that made up Topkapi Palace. It was a palace in the European tradition, the like of which he had never dreamed existed in the east.

When at last the *gerit* team reached the threshold of the Great Hall where their team's audience was to take place, he was once again overwhelmed by the grandeur of the space — a striking contrast to the Sultan's own audience chamber in the Third Court of Topkapi. That was a fine place too, but it was modest by comparison. *If I were a Sultan*, Danilo thought as he proceeded slowly along the rich red carpet to the raised dais at the far end of the room, *and one of my men showed me up so blatantly, I would not be pleased*. But there they sat, the Padishah and his Grand Vizier, each man on a golden throne, their two heads bent toward each other, the Vizier's only slightly lower than the Sultan's. So intimate that they might be brothers.

As expected, the Sultan did not engage directly with any of the athletes. He left the duty of conveying his congratulations and dispensing the gold purses to his Grand Vizier. In conformity with the Byzantine protocol of the Ottoman court, each recipient marched forward stiffly, head lowered, when his name was called. At the dais he held out his hand, head still bowed, and received a "Well done!" whereupon a jingling purse was placed by an attending page in the hands of the Padishah, then passed by the royal hand to the Grand Vizier and thence to the recipient, who stepped backward gracefully from the exalted presence. An awkward and somewhat demeaning procedure, but at least the athletes walked backward on their own steam, unlike foreign dignitaries who were routinely disarmed for a royal audience, then hauled into the Sultan's presence with their arms pinioned behind their backs and roughly dragged away after they had been welcomed not by the Sultan himself, who remained a silent, remote presence elevated above them on his throne, but by his Grand Vizier.

"Danilo del Medigo, step forward."

Prepared by the example of those who had preceded him, Danilo stepped forward, head lowered. But no purse was placed in his outstretched hand and no word of commendation was heard. Instead, an ominous silence.

Above him Danilo heard a whispered exchange between the Sultan and the Grand Vizier, too muffled for him to make out. Then came the Grand Vizier's slightly Greek-accented voice: "The Sultan has a question for this page. Step up, del Medigo."

With visions of the hangman's rope swinging before his eyes, Danilo climbed onto the platform, careful to keep his eyes at the level of the jeweled boots peeking out from under the gold hem of the Sultan's caftan.

Now, a new voice, not yet heard this day—low-pitched, steady, and precise: "You have given us great satisfaction today, young man. Your father will be proud of you."

To speak or not to speak. Oxy had imposed an Oriental command of silence in the royal presence. But Danilo del Medigo had been brought up to be a European gentleman.

"Thank you, sir," he found himself saying. Then he waited for the axe to fall.

But instead, a question. "How long is it since you first came to my court?"

"It will be six years come this *Bayram*, sir," the boy replied, brief and low.

"Which makes you . . . your age?"

"Seventeen years old, sire."

"And you began to ride here in the Princes School?"

"No, sire. My mother taught me to ride. She had access to the Gonzaga stud in Mantova."

"They used to buy horses from me when Gonzaga was alive. I don't recall his name," the Sultan remarked almost as a normal person might in an ordinary conversation.

Which emboldened Danilo to reply, "That would be Marchese Francesco. His wife was my mother's patroness."

At this point a discreet cough from the Grand Vizier stopped him. Apparently pages were not expected to jog the memories of sultans. But Danilo's rebellious streak propeled him forward in spite of the warning cough.

"Please allow me to add, sire, that from my earliest days in the Harem School I received the most excellent training at the hands of Agon Effendi. He was my mentor."

He regretted the word as it slipped out. And, sure enough, it was picked up immediately by the Grand Vizier. "You name an Albanian riding master as your mentor and not your Sultan?"

If you ever need me . . . The boy raised his head and looked straight up. *Send me the words, Mother . . .*

"Yes, sire, the riding master is my mentor. But the Sultan is my benefactor from whom all my blessings flow."

Unable to resist the temptation, he snuck a peek at the two faces above him: on the face of the Greek, a frown of irritation; on the face of the Sultan, the merest suggestion of a smile. Saved.

"You have served us well today, young man," he heard the Sultan say. "We are expecting even more of you in the days to come. Remember. I have my eye on you."

Danilo felt a tug on his shoulder. The interview was over.

"What is wrong with you, del Medigo? Did I not warn you not to talk? Did you not hear me?" Oxy boomed out as soon as they cleared the audience chamber.

Before Danilo could apologize, one of his mates rose to his defense. "But he saved himself with his wit, Oxy," his mate pointed out. Oxy was well-versed in the rules of the *gerit*, but he was not experienced in the ways of courts.

There was little urging when Danilo refused an invitation to accompany his mates across the water to Galata for a celebration. As usual, they attributed his reluctance to his youth. "A little backward when it comes to the ladies" was the verdict. Besides, he had a good excuse. His father, too ill to attend the games, was waiting for him. And indeed, once out of the Grand Vizier's palace—and glad to see the back of it—Danilo made his way quickly to the Doctor's House, stopping only briefly at his dormitory to retrieve a thin silk packet nestled in the folds of his quilt. Inside: a cinnamon stick rolled in a torn sheet of copy paper, which he glanced at and tucked into his girdle for safekeeping. In his absence, Narcissus, that most unlikely of Cupid's messengers, had paid him a visit.

He arrived at the Doctor's House to find his father enjoying a late-afternoon nap. Most unusual. The doctor must really be ill to indulge himself in a daytime respite. In emulation of the revered Jewish scholar Maimonides, Judah del Medigo lived by the dictum that the two worst temptations in life were an over-indulgence in melons and sleeping in the daytime.

Carefully, so as not to disturb his father, Danilo approached the bed and laid his hand on the invalid's brow. No fever. A good sign. But there was a grayish tinge to the doctor's flesh that the boy found alarming. A pinkish flush, he had learned, was an important indicator of good health. A yellow tinge announced liver problems. And a grayish pallor foretold... Fortunately, at that moment Judah woke up, cheerful, rested, and eager to hear the details of the afternoon's doings. An altogether far cry from the dismal prognosis his complexion seemed to indicate.

Furthermore, it was clear that, in spite of himself, the doctor was pleased with his son's report. How could a father not feel pride in a son who had distinguished himself so brilliantly in front of the whole city and the court? True, Judah would have been more pleased if his son had gained distinction in a learned *disputa* rather than on a horse. Nonetheless, he was wise enough to know that to achieve mastery—to become the best in any endeavor—required perseverance, stamina, and daring. Those pagan virtues that, as a Platonist, Judah most admired.

The boy had done him proud today. No doubt of it. Which Judah, being Judah, found difficult to express directly. Instead, he said, "Your mother would have been proud of you." For kindness, financial aid, and medical advice, the doctor could always be counted on. For praise, never.

Very briefly, Danilo considered telling his father about the soft white hand that had appeared from heaven to lift him out of the dust of the playing field. But, almost immediately, he thought better of it. Instead, he retreated to safer ground.

"It was Bucephalus who saved me from disaster." A true statement and infinitely less inflammatory than a rescue by the hand of his dead mother. "And since it was you who cured Bucephalus, I owe much of my success today to you, Papa."

"I did nothing." Having been given the credit, Judah could afford to return it. "It was your skill and your courage that won you the gold." He indicated the bulging purse that Danilo has brought to show him. "And apparently your quick thinking brought a smile to the face of our Sultan. No mean feat." He paused. "It is not often that the Grand Vizier is bested in a battle of wits."

"I just repeated what Oxy had told me," the boy reported in truth, if not quite the whole truth.

"It's exactly the kind of riposte your mother would have come up with," Judah went on. "She could be quite the courtier when she chose to. Unlike me who always thinks of the perfect retort after I'm back home in bed. But I won't pretend not to be pleased that you bested the Greek. He has given me more than one serious headache since I displaced his Greek compatriot as

Chief Body Physician. Besides, he is no friend to our people. What impression did he give you?"

Never before in the boy's recollection had his father solicited his opinion of anything or anybody. He hesitated for some moments before he decided to risk a bold reply.

"I think that this Greek is riding for a fall," he answered.

"Hmm." Judah stroked his chin thoughtfully. "You know, of course, that the Sultan befriended this Greek slave when they were boys. They have shared food, a tent, even a bed. And, to give the devil his due, Ibrahim is a superb negotiator and a pretty fair general. He is the one who subdued Egypt for us. Peacefully. What makes you think he is about to fall from favor?"

"The palace, sir."

"The Grand Vizier's palace? What about it? I've never been in the place, you know. I am no favorite of Ibrahim Pasha's."

"Nor had I seen it until today, sir."

"And now that you have?"

"For one thing, it has a fireplace in every room. Not even the Colonna's palace in Rome has a fireplace in every room."

Judah nodded. The boy had a point. "What else?"

"The size of the rooms. The grandeur. His Great Hall dwarfs the Sultan's audience room. In fact, the entire place makes Topkapi seem small and insignificant."

"So?"

Go ahead, Danilo told himself. *The worst that can happen is that he'll think you a fool.*

"If I were the Sultan," he began slowly, "and one of my men showed me up like that..." He paused, then finished in a rush, "I would have his head from his shoulders."

"Bravo!" The doctor reached up to clap his son on the back. "An excellent show of deductive logic."

This was as close as the doctor would ever come to bestowing unequivocal approval on his son, and Danilo came away from the visit feeling as good as he had ever felt after a conversation with his father. He fairly bounced out of the bedroom, having assured Judah that no, he was not planning to celebrate with his teammates in Galata but was on his way to pay an evening visit to Bucephalus, from whom he did feel, in his heart, that all his blessings flowed. (Which brought another smile to his father's face.) And by the way, he asked casually, could he stop in his father's kitchen and take away some sugar for the horse? And oh, yes, might he pick up some liniment in the doctor's apothecary? To all of which the doctor gave his ready assent.

True to his word, Danilo did pick up a cup of sugar on his way to the stables. What he had neglected to include in the details of his evening itinerary was that, while in the pharmacy, he would pour into a vial several drops of a completely harmless but powerful soporific, which the doctor guaranteed would give his patients a long night of dreamless sleep.

21

THE VALIDE'S BEDTIME

THE CART SO RELUCTANTLY SUMMONED BY HÜRREM to carry Princess Saida back to her grandmother's suite in the harem was a far cry from the luxurious chariot that had brought them to Topkapi Palace. With but a single nag to pull it, shielded from the crowd by only a thin scrim of fabric strung carelessly over what seemed to be a discarded clothesline, it was a vehicle fit for a servant, not a princess. But the cart did bounce along at a brisk pace and brought Saida to the gates of the Old Palace before the *muezzin* began his final prayer call of the day, allowing her a few moments to shed her head scarves, unlace her tight little boots, and confer briefly with Narcissus before joining her grandmother for evening prayers.

Ordinarily, this was a time of day Saida cherished. Kneeling under the watchful eye of both her earthly protector and her heavenly one, she felt at these times as if no bad thing could ever happen to her. But today everything was moving too fast. And when Narcissus answered her call, she addressed him in a curt tone quite foreign to her accustomed civility. No greeting. No smile.

"Has the message been delivered?" she demanded.

"Yes." If she chose to play the stern mistress, he would be the cowed slave.

"And the caique, is it arranged?"

"Unfortunately, Princess"—he paused just long enough to make her nervous—"it will only be available for four hours. That is not enough time to travel back and forth to Princes' Islands of course. But plenty of time"—he added what Saida suspected was a slight leer—"more than enough time for a moonlit cruise on the Bosphorus."

"Then tonight we will simply have to traipse up and down the Bosphorus," she conceded briskly. "But make certain that the compartment is completely shielded."

"The craft available is one of the Sultan's favorite caiques, lady. For informal outings." Did Narcissus wink or did she imagine it? "Only four oarsmen, but well shielded from prying eyes. As secure as the throne of the empire."

"Better be," was her curt rejoinder. "Remember, if anything goes wrong, it's your head on a pike as well as mine."

"I never forget it, lady," he replied, with no suspicion of irony.

As usual, the princess and her grandmother were served a small meal in the Valide's bedroom after evening prayers. Always a loaf of the very white and savory bread made of wheat from Bithynia but grown on the Sultan's own ground, a pilaf of Egyptian rice, a quantity of preserves, some pickled meats (*basturma* being one of the Valide's favorites), sherbets, of course, and a yogurt drink with clotted cream and melons, which the Valide could never get enough of.

After the meal came the brushing of the Valide's striking red hair. When her son, Suleiman, was born, the lady swore she would go to her grave with the same flowing red locks that had so fascinated her child's father. It was a goal she had so far managed to achieve with a special dye concocted by the Jewish bundle-woman, a formula recently improved upon by the Second *Kadin*. With this expert assistance, the Lady Hafsa managed to appear several years younger than her age. But, sadly, no amount of henna could arrest the failing of her heart.

"I am winding down like one of those windup clocks they make in Europe, ready to close my eyes before sundown," she told Saida when they had finished their meal

It was hardly an exaggeration since she had already unknowingly imbibed her first cup of doctored tea, a beverage guaranteed to put anyone who consumed it to sleep by nightfall and keep that person asleep until daybreak.

In Saida's view, the soporific was a harmless deception, designed to protect her grandmother's heart from the shock she would get were she to awaken in the night to discover that her precious grandchild was missing.

A moonlit cruise on the gentle waves of the Bosphorus occupied the same role in the Istanbul imagination that a moonlit carriage ride around the pyramids played for the denizens of Cairo, carrying with it the suggestion of stolen kisses, forbidden liaisons, intrigue, seduction, and a world well lost for love. That one short span of water was the setting of countless tales of adventure — and misadventure — told and retold during the long, languorous days in the harem. But when Saida stole a glance at the night sky through the small round window of her grandmother's bedroom, there was no moon to be seen. No stars either. No moonlit cruise tonight. She sighed. But, within moments, she was reminding herself that, although not as fabulous as moonlight, darkness was a more valuable asset to those who wished to avoid being recognized. Having thus put a happier face on it, she turned her attention to the task at hand — the evening recitation.

"What shall we read tonight?" she asked her grandmother, hoping for some familiar text that she could read, quite literally, with her eyes shut. But no.

"No reading tonight," the Valide said firmly. "Tonight you shall tell me of your outing with the Second *Kadin*. Every detail. I want to know everything." A request which implied an hour — perhaps more if the lady's lively curiosity kept her alert — of careful editing as the girl made her way through the ups and downs of the day's events.

It was not too onerous a task for someone with a good memory, and the princess was able to construct an edited narrative on the spot. But when she came to the moment when the *gerit* teams galloped to their stations on either side of the hippodrome, she suffered an acute failure of nerve. Could she trust herself to relive those agonizing moments when Danilo lay motionless on the ground while the opposing team galloped forward to trample him into the dust?

Desperate to find an alternative subject, she pounced on the Second *Kadin*. "The Lady Hürrem seemed unusually chimerical today." It was a word she had heard her grandmother use when speaking of Hürrem.

"How so?"

"Well, this morning, having dined with my father last night, she told me she was the happiest woman in the world. But this afternoon at the *gerit* she seemed very sad. She even said she wished she could return here to the harem with me. To the comfort of home, was how she put it."

"Did she say what was troubling her?" the Valide inquired with ill-disguised curiosity.

"Yes. In fact, I remember her exact words. They seemed so strange."

"Strange? In what way?"

"She said, 'I feel my shame today.'"

"What has she to be ashamed of?"

"It started when we first arrived at the Grand Vizier's palace and were sitting on the balcony. There were a lot of women, perhaps half a dozen of the harem girls that my father has married off. Seeing them all married upset Lady Hürrem in some way. But she was the one who put him up to it, wasn't she?" asked the girl.

"Yes, she told me that she loved him so much she couldn't bear to share him with anyone," the Valide replied. "I wondered at the wisdom of going so far against tradition, but it certainly took a grave responsibility off my old shoulders. Those girls were a handful, always angling to get into my son's bed and keeping the others out. Do I speak too plainly, my dear?"

"Not at all."

"But we must be generous to the Second *Kadin*." The Valide resumed her all-wise, all-kindly manner. "Life has been difficult for her, batted back and forth like a shuttlecock between those girls and Rose of Spring. That rose is not without her thorns, you know."

"But, Grandmother, my father ignores Rose of Spring completely and does everything Hürrem wishes. She was the one who wanted all the odalisques gone from the harem and who urged him to marry them off. And then she complains that the girls she got rid of are free women and she is a slave."

"She suffers," the Valide answered. "You are too young to understand suffering. And, Allah willing, you never will."

"I never hear you complaining, Grandmama. And you too were a slave as long as my blessed grandfather Selim was alive. Did you suffer from it?"

It was an impertinent question, and once she had asked it Saida lowered her head awaiting a rebuke.

But no remonstrance was forthcoming. Instead, Lady Hafsa took her time in answering, rearranging the pillows to prop up her back and stretching her long neck to its height. Then, full of dignity, she answered, "I was the mother of the first prince of the realm, with every expectation of becoming the Valide Sultan when my son became Sultan. As long as Rose's son Mustafa lives, Hürrem will only be the Second *Kadin*." The way she spoke the words made them sound like a prophecy of doom. "Now then"—she waved her hands in the direction of the teapot—"it is time for my last cup of tea. I am tired."

But Saida was unwilling to relinquish the brief span of intimacy. Such moments with her grandmother were rare. So, as she poured the tea into the chalcedony goblet, she reported, "She wants to move her household to Topkapi."

"She does?" The Valide did not appear to be even slightly concerned.

"So what is to become of us?"

"Why, nothing." She felt a reassuring touch on her arm. "We will live here in the Old Palace, in my son's harem, as we always have," her grandmother announced with all the authority of a royal edict. "Now, my tea." Then she added, "You have a special way of brewing, child. I always sleep so well when you prepare my evening cup for me."

22

INCOGNITO

I T WAS CLOSE TO A CENTURY SINCE MEHMET THE Conqueror outfitted Topkapi Palace as his residence and the center of his empire — plenty of time for generations of miscreants to devise ways of getting in and out of the palace grounds without being detected. Located at the confluence of the Bosphorus, the Sea of Marmara, and the Golden Horn, the high commanding site of Palace Point offered easy access to the three waterways by boat. Of all three, the taverns of Galata directly across the Bosphorus beckoned most enticingly to the pages of the Sultan's school, living out their monitored lives behind guarded walls, dreaming of women and wine.

As devout Muslims — either born or converted — residents of the palace were forbidden to drink alcohol. But in the long history of Islam, that prohibition had always been more honored in the breach than in the observance. To the faithful of Istanbul the temptation of alcohol was exacerbated by the presence in their midst of both Christians and Jews, neither of whom were constrained by their religion from getting drunk every day of the year if they were so inclined. Always tolerant of the aberrant customs of foreigners, the Turks nevertheless did attempt to rein in the influence of these aliens by segregating them, together with their pork and their taverns, in restricted areas, much as the Venetians were attempting to do with their Jewish ghetto. But, unfortunately for the cause of sobriety, the Byzantine Greeks who comprised the majority of Christians in Istanbul were also the most passionate and dedicated imbibers and had long since settled themselves in the district of Galata, where their tower presented a constant, visible temptation to thirsty Muslims.

Besides, there were other imperatives driving the occupants of the palace to devise surreptitious paths of escape from the Sultan's Abode of Felicity. Such as sex. Contrary to what foreigners seemed to think, the Sultan's harem more closely resembled a convent than a bordello. The de-sexing of the eunuchs, who administered the Sultan's regimen, was believed to have robbed them of their desire along with their genitals. So it had first been thought. But the genitalia, no matter how carefully cut out, had an inconvenient habit of growing back, giving the geldings good reason to haunt the fleshpots of Galata.

As for the young men in the Sultan's School for Pages, they were strictly enjoined from intercourse with either sex. The monitors who watched over them through the night kept a sharp eye out for any form of sexual indulgence.

But not even three levels of enforcement could maintain constant vigilance over the vast army of cooks and gardeners and tanners and tailors and clerks and artisans—and pages—who lived within the palace grounds, not to mention the military personnel who patroled the walls and the gates. No surprise, then, that in defiance of both religion and discipline, there were literally hundreds of residents of the Abode of Felicity who wanted or needed to go over the walls at night. A sot who needed drink, a cook who needed his wife, a pasha who needed a boy, a boy who needed a girl, even a sultan who sought anonymity—all of them crawling around shoeless in the deep night, except for the Sultan. He retained his right to wear his boots, even when he blacked his face and donned the animal skin of a *sipahi* and sallied forth anonymously with his Grand Vizier to assess the mood of his people in the taverns of Galata, as he was doing that night.

Why did the Sultan go to such lengths simply to find out what his subjects thought of him? Because, even though he was a man who had everything, there was one thing the Sultan could never be sure of getting: an honest report. His subjects had seemed well content today at the hippodrome. But one never knew what seditious thoughts lurked in the hearts of men. At this moment, Suleiman felt the need of a true measure of how his people were reacting to his second defeat at Vienna (although it had been officially disguised as a victory at Guns), for which the general population had paid dearly both in casualties and coin.

Gazing into a looking glass as he went about blacking his face, Suleiman replayed the siege at Vienna one more time. What went wrong?

Bad weather, said his generals. The same thing they said two years ago when he was forced to abandon his first siege of Vienna after two harrowing months outside the walls of the Austrian capital. This year he was held up for three months at the insignificant border town of Guns. Of course, the town was finally taken. But by then winter was threatening, and once again Vienna was a lost cause.

How much humiliation could his subjects take without recognizing defeat? How much blather of victory could they swallow before they began to choke on the diet of mendacity his men were dishing out? No one—not even his trusted Vizier, Ibrahim—could give him an answer. He was surrounded by toadies, by men who did not meet his eyes and who (by his own fiat, mind you) did not open their mouths in his presence unless invited to do so.

It was time for the Sultan to go out among his people, not heroically on a milk-white stallion but secretly disguised in a *sipahi's* skins, his towering turban replaced by a skullcap and his face black as coal.

"How do I look?" he asked his companion, garbed as a dervish.

"Like a proper *sipahi*, sire," Ibrahim replied. "You'll never be suspected unless you open your mouth."

"My mouth?"

"It's your teeth, sire. They are too white. And there are too many of them." A shrewd fellow, this Greek. "What about me? Do I pass muster?" The Grand Vizier twirled delicately before his master in imitation of the dervish he had chosen to impersonate.

"You still look like a Greek to me," Suleiman teased.

"As long as I am not mistaken for a Grand Vizier," Ibrahim rejoined as he cloaked himself in a heavy woolen shawl. He then proceeded to wrap the Sultan in a similarly voluminous garment. "Shall we?" He held out his arm.

"Lead on, my dervish friend."

Arm in arm they made their way through one of the *selamlik's* conveniently unlocked doors and onto the steep path down to the Grand Vizier's dock, swathed into invisibility in their black shawls.

If the old gods were still perched up on their pantheon, as many secretly believe, they must have been amused at what they saw when they looked down through the treetops into Topkapi's gardens. The surface of the world within the walls was unruffled by so much as a ripple, each of the three courts a true abode of serenity, not a leaf out of place. But outside the walls, the banks that sloped down to the water were alive with adventurers of one sort or another, all of them furtive, all bent on concealing their movements.

If Zeus was entertaining himself by sneaking peeks at the mortals below, he must have been mightily amused by the clumsy disguises these two had chosen. Much easier—and far more elegant—to turn oneself into a bird or a donkey. But of course this Sultan, though he may crown himself emperor, king, Padishah, was still a mere mortal, not a god, poor fellow. Although he actually seemed to be enjoying his pathetic masquerade. Mortals!

On the other side of the summit, Danilo del Medigo was also heading down to the Grand Vizier's dock. But he scurried along unhampered by either cloak or veil. He had little fear of being discovered. He had made this run successfully many times before. Oddly enough, the little wheeled kiosk that circumnavigated the grounds was not on patrol tonight. He came upon it, deserted, at the edge of the summit. Perhaps, he thought, the Sultan had given his guards the night off to enjoy the festival.

As, indeed, the Sultan had done. It would be too embarrassing for the great Padishah to be accosted by his own guards while in disguise. At Ibrahim's suggestion, the sentries had been released from duty. The chance that anyone would be loitering around the palace walls was minimal, said the Grand Vizier, with free food and entertainment on offer in the town below.

So the Sultan and his Grand Vizier made their descent down the side of Palace Point opposite from the one chosen by the page, Danilo, each perfectly confident of encountering no obstruction. But because the pitch of the slope was so steep, the terrain demanded that each path to the waterway must zigzag. And, since the hillsides were a maze of paths, there was always a chance that adventurers approaching the shore from different directions might cross on the way down, a probability that increased as the paths converged toward the shore.

From Zeus' vantage point high above it all, these three figures would have seemed to be on a collision course. Were they to collide, were the page to be identified as having witnessed Suleiman's charade, there was little doubt he would be killed on the spot. People tended to blame the gods—and the Italians—for such imbroglios. The truth was that human beings had an infinite capacity for making their own mischief. And it was left to the gods to clean up the mess.

Fortune, so said the Greeks, favors the bold, often in the guise of misfortune. As Danilo vaulted down the hillside he tripped over a patch of nettles and had to stop to pick them out of his clothes. It was a time-consuming task that left his fingers bleeding and his temper frayed. But it was also just long enough to give the Sultan and his Vizier a head start, so that by the time Danilo reached the rock ledge above the dock, the black cloaks were already emerging from the heavy underbrush below the ledge onto the shore.

Still unconscious of their presence, Danilo glanced up at the palace walls to make sure he was not being observed from above. Then he stepped to the edge of the ledge and bent his knees in preparation for the jump down to the dock. But as he was about to lift off, he heard a sound below that froze him in place: the unmistakable huffing and puffing of someone out of breath. Animals did not become winded from running down hills. There was a human being down there.

Heart pounding, the boy laid himself down flat on the rock where he would be invisible from the shore. Then, carefully lowering himself over the ledge, he looked down.

What he saw was not one figure but two, impossible to identify without the aid of moonlight. Who were these wraiths wrapped in black? What brought them to this unlikely spot? And what could he do to prevent them from seeing the caique that his princess was sending to collect him?

Cheerful, lighthearted, even amused by the absurd sight they presented but—as far as they knew—visible to no one but themselves, the two men advancing toward the pier, their billowing garments flapping around their ankles, taunted each other playfully for their clumsiness.

Just then the curved prow of a caique slipped around the bend of the cove. Danilo waited for his signal: two long flashes followed by two short. But no signal came. Had Narcissus forgotten to instruct the captain? Was the signaling lantern disabled? Nothing like this had ever happened before.

"There it is!" He heard a Greek-accented voice from below. "I instructed them to douse the lights. One cannot be too careful."

The voice resembled that of the Grand Vizier, but Danilo could not be certain. *Speak again*, he implored the voice.

Instead, what he heard was a thump accompanied by a cry of pain. Then a second voice, cursing. Then the first voice—the

Greek voice—again: "Are you all right, sire?" It was the voice of the Grand Vizier for sure.

Then came the reply. "Nothing serious. Just a scratch." This was the voice that had questioned him that very afternoon about the Gonzaga stud. Unquestionably he was hearing the voice of the Sultan himself.

Suleiman was not an especially cruel or vengeful man. It was simply in the nature of things Oriental that when a forbidden line is crossed, punishment is swift, silent, and inexorable. Had the Sultan gotten there a moment later and discovered his page on his private dock; worse, had the princess's caique given its signal and a plot to dishonor the Sultan's daughter been unearthed...Danilo could envision his own head on a pike outside the Gate of Felicity. But he could not will himself to imagine Saida's body sinking into the inky depths of the Bosphorus, weighted down by a sack of stones. And he vowed there and then that if they escaped discovery this time, this must be their last rendezvous. He made this vow in all sincerity, fully believing that the next time Narcissus brought him a summons, he would be able to resist the siren call.

But for now, there was still this night to get through. At any moment, Saida's caique would round the point and begin to signal with its lantern. And there was nothing he could do to stop it. Peering over the ledge, he could make out the two black-swathed men preparing to board their craft, each tossing his cloak onto the dock as he stepped down and disappeared behind the curtained cabin in the center of the craft. Then, smooth and silent, the caique slid away from the dock.

No voices now. No light. It was impossible, from Danilo's perch, to follow the course of the Sultan's caique. But he could hear the faint sound of droplets falling onto the surface each time the eight paddles were lifted out of the water in unison. Not until that sound faded into the darkness was he assured that with each passing minute the odds were rising in his favor. But he cautioned himself to stay still and silent until he could be absolutely certain that the Sultan's caique was well on its way across open water to wherever it was headed.

He decided to count to one hundred—slowly—before showing his head above the ledge. When he reached that number, he added another hundred just to be safe. They might have forgotten something and decided to come back for it. Or changed their minds about discarding the cloaks they had left behind on the pier. He pressed his cheek against the cold stone and waited. One hundred and eighty-six, one hundred and eight-seven...

At one hundred and ninety-two, he saw a blob of light in the distance and rose to his feet. Two long. Two short. He stretched, bowed his head, and thanked all the gods for his narrow escape. By the time Saida's caique slid up to the dock, he was there to take his accustomed seat at the stern. But instead, the captain motioned him toward the curtained compartment in the center of the craft.

As he stepped forward to pull back the drape, it began slowly to part of its own accord and a veiled head appeared. Had he been tricked? Were these the Sultan's men playing games with him? A gloved hand reached around and slowly drew up the veil, revealing a pair of rosy lips. This was no man.

Next, a slightly tilted nose. Then those eyes he knew so well, velvet brown with hazel lights that twinkled in the soft light of the lantern.

"As you see," she whispered, "I have managed to escape from my tower." She cocked her head to one side and patted the cushion beside her invitingly. "Care to join me for a midnight sail?"

But her bravado dissolved as soon as she felt his arms around her. Pulling the curtains tight around them, she buried her head in his neck and clung to him like a frightened child. What had happened to his fearless princess? Had she encountered her father on the Bosphorus? Perhaps narrowly escaped an encounter?

"I feel so wretched," she sobbed. "I am so...afraid."

His first instinct was to hug her and kiss her and jolly her out of her despair. But some inchoate impulse led him to stay quiet and let her talk.

"Tell me," he heard himself saying. "Tell me."

And, after some nose blowing and sniffing, it all came out: Hürrem's plan to move from the harem to Topkapi and her grandmother's refusal to heed the consequences. "I keep thinking that she will soon be dead and I will be alone. There will be no one to take care of me."

"What about me, Princess?" he asked lightly.

"You? How can you help me?"

"I'm strong. I do care for you. I *am* your knight."

At this, she smiled for the first time. "Of course you are. But we both know..." She looked away. "I was proud of you today at the *gerit*. You were very brave, my knight."

"You were there, at the hippodrome?"

"On the Grand Vizier's balcony. I saw everything."

"Did you see me fall?"

She nodded.

"And get up?"

She nodded again.

"Did you wonder why I was not stabbed through the heart when the *gerit* hit me?"

No, she had not wondered. "I thanked Allah."

"What if I told you that Allah had nothing to do with it."

She drew away from him. "That would be disrespectful."

"Even if I told you that it was you who saved my life?"

"Me?"

"The amulet you gave me to wear against the evil eye, I was wearing it over my breast. And the point of his *gerit* shattered the jewel to bits, instead of shattering my heart."

"A miracle," she murmured softly.

"It is more than that. Don't you see? It is a sign."

She shook her head.

"Saida..." He laid his hands lightly on her shoulders to emphasize what he was going to tell her. "When I came here tonight, I meant to end everything between us. For your sake.

Because it was too risky for you. I almost collided with the Sultan at the Grand Vizier's dock tonight; I only missed him by seconds. But I did miss him. And this afternoon, the *gerit* did miss my heart. That has to mean something."

"I don't understand any of this..."

"It means that we are meant to be together forever. In my religion we call it *besheert*, foreordained. The pagans would have said that you and I are favored by fortune."

"No." She held up her hand to stop him. "We agreed not to talk about the future."

"Well, maybe it's time we did talk about it."

"There is nothing to talk about. I cannot live on false hopes. My religion tells me to trust in Allah's will and accept what cannot be changed. Don't you see that everything between us depends on my grandmother? Narcissus is her slave. He issues my orders in her name. He is my lifeline. Once she is gone, he will be manumitted, no longer a slave. There will be no safe contact for us."

She was on the verge of tears; still, he could not let go. His religion had not taught him acceptance. And his upbringing had taught him to use his brains. There had to be a way.

"Where will the slave go?" he asked.

"He will be manumitted, free. Her death frees him."

"But if he is her slave, she can bequeath him to you, can she not?"

She looked at him uncomprehending.

"Before the Valide dies," he continued, "she can will him to you. You can ask her to do that."

"I couldn't. We never talk of such things."

"That only means that you never have, not that you cannot. She is a clear-sighted woman and she loves you very much. Now that she knows the end is near, she may even ask you if there is anything of hers you want."

"And if she does not?"

"Then you must ask her. For your own sake—for our sake. Remember this, we need Narcissus. Narcissus is the link between us." Danilo paused to let this sink in, then continued: "You can ask. Remember, *Audentes fortuna iuvat.* Fortune favors the bold. Say it. Say it with me."

"*Audentes fortuna iuvat,*" she repeated. "Fortune favors the bold. I will do it. I will ask her to will me Narcissus."

23

THE DEATH OF
THE VALIDE

T HE VALIDE SULTAN SPENT THE LAST DAYS OF HER
life at peace, drifting in and out of a painless sleep with
the two people she loved most in constant attendance.

When the doctors began to count the days, her granddaughter Princess Saida ordered a rolled-up pallet to be placed at the
foot of the Valide's bed so that, after spending the day holding
the pale hand, mopping the feverish brow, offering spoonfuls of
nourishment, and whispering words of comfort, the girl could
retire to the pallet rather than leave her grandmother's side.

In this vigil she was frequently joined by her father, the Sultan, who put aside all but te most pressing imperial business
to spend most of his time seated at the bedside between his
mother and his daughter, some of it in prayer, some of it in conversation. In a sense, this unexpected intimacy turned out to be
the most valuable gift that the Valide could have left her beloved
granddaughter. Although the Sultan had always been punctili-
ous in his harem visits, he owed attention to all of his children
living in the harem with their mothers, not to mention his concubines and, of course, his mother. So although the princess
had spent many hours in the company of her father, they were

seldom alone together and rarely had the opportunity for close conversation.

Now, in the enforced intimacy at the Valide's bedside, he began to talk to his daughter, quite formally at first, but gradually taking up a familiar tone. She asked after his health. He complained about his gout. They explored their mutual passion for high-bred horses, and most importantly they prayed together, just the two of them, five times a day.

One day, as he bent to kiss his mother's cheek, Saida said, "You will miss her." It was an intrusion into his inviolate privacy that she would never have thought to presume a week earlier.

And she was greeted with a revealing dab at his eyes and a softly murmured, "More than anything in the world."

The doctors had prepared them for what to expect in the final moments — a shortness of breath, choking, possibly a seizure. But Saida was certain, and reassured her father as they sat side by side waiting, that Allah would be kinder than that, knowing that the end was near.

Everything that could be done had been done. On the previous day the Lady Hafsa had dictated the terms of her will to a scribe. At her request Princess Saida and the Sultan were present, and as she dictated, she turned to him from time to time to ask, "Does this conform to your wishes, my lion?"

To which he invariably replied, "Perfectly, honored mother," and patted her hand to reassure her that all was well with the will.

To her much loved granddaughter, the Valide bequeathed a sum of three thousand ducats, a sizeable fortune. That noted, she turned to Saida and asked, as Danilo had foretold she might, if there was anything else the girl particularly wanted. Were it not for the conversation with Danilo, Saida would likely have lowered her eyes modestly and denied any worldly wants. But now his words came back to her and she replied that yes, there was one thing. Even so, she hesitated to make the request specific, fearing to profane the solemnity of the moment, until her father intervened by whispering in her ear, "Speed it up, daughter. Every one of these seconds is precious."

So in the end she did ask for possession of the slave Narcissus, who, she told her grandmother, "has been so faithful to you and will stand as a reminder and a comfort to me."

"Only a slave? That is all? Not my pearl necklace that you so admire or my emerald coronet?"

Saida could only shake her head in reply.

The old woman reached over with some effort to pat the girl's cheek. "I am touched by your modest request," she said in a slightly faltering voice. "But then, you have never been grasping or avaricious, my child. And for that you will be rewarded. You will have my slave and my jewels as well. All of them." At which the Sultan gasped. By custom, all the jewels he had given to his mother, as well as those bestowed upon her by his father as bridal gifts, would return to the royal treasury on her death. But he had never denied his mother anything in her lifetime and he did not intend to do so at her deathbed.

"Everything will be done as you ask, honored mother." He bent down to kiss her forehead. "Now you must rest."

"Yes, I must rest." She smiled a faint smile. "It is time." And with her mind cleared and her soul at peace, she closed her eyes, never to open them again.

Moments later, her breathing stopped without so much as a shudder. She was gone.

"Do you wish to sit with her while I get the priests?" asked the Sultan.

"Yes, please," Saida answered. Then, heedless of protocol, she threw her arms around his neck. "Oh, Father, I will miss her so."

Whereupon her father, always so meticulous in keeping his distance, leapt that chasm in an instant and embraced her as tightly as she did him. And there they stood in the awesome presence of death, their two heads touching, their tears mingling.

Hours later, after the priests had taken Hafsa's body away, the princess was still sitting in the low chair beside her bed, becalmed in a sea without winds or currents. She had spent her life of fifteen years being nurtured and nursed, and guarded and guided, by this woman who was no more. Suddenly, her lodestar was gone. For the first time in her life she could pray or not, eat or not, sleep or not as she willed. Even for a girl of considerable courage, the prospect was daunting. So she sat silent and unmoving.

Into this dead zone walked Narcissus and, without waiting for his orders, closed the shutters, lit the candles, and kindled the fire. Then he turned to her.

"I hear that you have inherited me, along with some very valuable jewels."

This jab of sarcasm was not what she had expected from the normally deferential slave. Her immediate instinct was to give him the tongue-lashing he deserved, as her grandmother certainly would have. But he had more to say.

"I am now your slave, madame." He bent himself into an exaggerated bow. "I await your orders."

"How did you know?"

"News travels faster than lightning in the harem," he answered lightly but with an edge.

"I owe you an explanation," she offered.

"Slaves are not owed explanations, Princess," he retorted, still harsh.

"You were expecting to be manumitted when she died, is that not so?"

No answer.

"So I have, however inadvertently, robbed you of your freedom today. Is that not so?" she persisted.

He remained silent.

"I want you to know that I asked for you because I need you now. But I do intend to give you your freedom in the future. And I will not forget that you stayed by me in my time of need."

"Am I to be resold when you've done with me?"

"Oh, no. I will do as my grandmother would have done. I will give you your freedom."

"By turning me out into the world when I am old, to be mocked and mistreated and underpaid?"

"It is my intention to set you up properly in your new life

when you leave my service," she answered with quiet dignity. Then, because she was not quite grown up enough to hide her disappointment, she burst out, "I thought you would be...pleased."

"By your gift of my freedom?" he asked, still unappeased.

"I spent some time recently with a slave who says she would give up all her worldly goods in exchange for her freedom," she told him.

"You are speaking of Lady Hürrem, no doubt," he replied. "Are you not?"

"Yes."

"That slave," he informed her, "is Second *Kadin* to the Sultan. I am a black man and a eunuch."

"I was trying to make amends," she sniffed. "I didn't expect to get blamed for it."

She speaks like a child, he thought. And this time when he answered the belligerence was gone.

"To be fair, I cannot blame you, Princess. If I were looking to cast blame for my fate, I would have to start with God, who made me black. Or with the traders who bought me from my parents as a boy. Or with my parents for selling me. Or with the African who cut off my manhood and buried me in the sand for three days waiting to see if I would bleed to death or survive to be sold. And sold I was to the Grand Vizier. A week after I arrived in his household they pulled my feet through wooden boards, tied them, and struck my bare soles with a cane again and again until I collapsed. For days I had to crawl to and from my bed because I could not walk. For weeks I wrapped gauze around my feet to sop up the bleeding. I tell you this because what you have done is neither cruel nor ruthless. You have offered to take responsibility for my life, a life that was shaped by others, not by you. I am not unhappy to be your slave."

She allowed herself a half smile of relief.

"But," he continued, "since you are now a rich woman, on the day when you no longer have need of me, I trust you to keep to your word and make adequate provision for me in my retirement."

Now she allowed herself a full smile. "We understand each other, do we not?"

"Yes, Princess." Narcissus, too, allowed himself a smile. "I think we do."

"Good. Then why don't you hustle off and get me some food. Some pilaf and a ripe melon." Exactly what the Valide would have ordered, he noted. "I will have need of you tonight."

"A caique with eight oarsmen?" he inquired with his old mischief.

"Sadly, no," she answered. "This is not a time for pleasure. I have a duty to my grandmother, and it is a duty that I will have to fight to perform. Since I have no sword, I must use my wits. First get me food. Then paper and my writing box."

He bowed. "Anything else?"

"Later I will want you to carry what I write to the Sultan in his *selamlik*."

He frowned, puzzled.

"I need his permission to carry out my task," she explained.

"Would I be too forward were I to ask what the task is?"

"Yes, you would," she answered primly. "Curiosity is a grievous defect in a slave." Already she was beginning to sound like her grandmother. "But I will tell you my project."

Good, he thinks. *She still needs someone to tell her secrets to.*

"I intend to write and deliver a eulogy at my grandmother's burial."

"You? A girl?"

"Who better than I? Who loved her most and knew her best?"

"But a girl...Will the *Ulema* allow it?"

"I do not plan to ask the priests. I will ask my father if I may speak for the family. I know how much he detests such tasks. And my brothers are all too lazy to do the writing. I will win the right to deliver my eulogy by default."

And, to be sure, the eulogy was written, copied, and delivered before the first prayer, along with a sweet note reminding the Sultan of certain historical precedents in the long history of eulogies. And the next day Princess Saida was carried off from the Old Palace in a litter, accompanied by her maid and her slave, Narcissus, and taken by water to the town of Bursa, where her beloved grandmother was to be honored by burial alongside the tomb of Selim the Grim, the father of her son, Suleiman the Magnificent.

24

THE BAILO REPORTS

AGAINST ALL ODDS, THE DAY FOR THE VALIDE
Sultan's funeral dawned clear and calm, most unusual
for a late autumn day and most fortunate for the
mourners making their way from the capital to the Ottoman
family tomb at Bursa.

With great reverence, Lady Hafsa's coffin was borne aloft
and carried through the streets of Istanbul, lined three deep by
ordinary citizens come to pay their respects to a woman much
admired, even loved. When the procession reached Bagce Kapi
landing, the pallbearers, chosen from among the Sultan's pages,
draped the casket with white silk and placed it on a pure white
barge to be carried over the waters to the dock at Bursa. It was
followed by a cortege that stretched out along the shores of the
Bosphorus in an endless mournful string of black caiques.

Several hundred palace courtiers formed the nucleus of the
cortege, to be joined at Bursa by hundreds more — the representatives of foreign powers, members of the *Ulema* and the
divan, the entire Janissary corps, all of the pages from both the
Sultan's and the Grand Vizier's schools, and several hundred
ordinary citizens, all somber, many genuinely sad.

The Valide had amassed considerable personal wealth in her lifetime and had donated the greater part of it to a number of *madresses,* soup kitchens, libraries, and hostels. It was a custom she continued to follow, and as a testament to her goodness she was given a final resting place beside the coffin of the Ottoman paterfamilias, a stone simply engraved *Orhan, Son of Osman, Gazi, Sultan of Gazis, Lord of the Horizons, Burgrave of the Whole World.*

Watching her from his close vantage point beside the casket, Danilo marveled at his princess's poised confidence when she took her place to deliver the eulogy. This self-possessed, dignified young woman was also, after all, the same girl who had once greeted him splayed out against her infinite pillows like a painted whore; at another time, as the wily horse trader in spiked boots; on still another occasion, as the ferocious rider who occasionally beat him in a pony race; and at yet another time as the little lost girl who clung to him like a frightened child, weeping on his shoulder at the prospect of being left alone and unprotected by the loss of the Valide. And now, standing tall before a crowd of thousands, a veritable female Demosthenes.

"But, if I may," she went on, "I should like to speak a few words on my own behalf. I am the daughter of a great man. They tell me that, in the wide world, my father is known as the Magnificent for the vastness of his power. In the eyes of his subjects, he is the father of all the poor and helpless of the world, an awesome obligation. Yet he has always found the time to be a father to me, a motherless child. When I was born, he gave me into the daily care of my beloved grandmother, the second blessing I have been granted by Allah, and of course she accepted the charge. That was her bounden duty. But in no way was it her duty to love me, to cherish me, to teach me, and to guide me. That came from the generosity of her heart. She also gave me the gift of faith. It was she who named me Saida, after the granddaughter of the Prophet. It was she who saw to it that by the time I was twelve years old, I had memorized the whole Koran. I received my first pony from my father, but she was the one who insisted that I be taught to ride it with my brothers. And she found a place for me in the Harem School and on the polo squad alongside them. 'Strength of faith, strength of mind, strength of bone,' she used to say.

"On the night my grandmother died, because of the great love I bore her, I wailed and wept so much that I almost lost my senses. Not merely because we were kin but because for all the fifteen years of my life, she guided my every move.

"In all the years, I never heard her speak bitterness or envy; only affection for me, a motherless child, and for all the unfortunates of this world. Henceforth, it behooves me to shower her with benedictions. God have mercy on her soul and God be pleased with her spirit."

The eulogy was so charmingly put that even the Venetian *bailo*, that cynical reprobate, was moved to tears. Quoting from his report to the Venetian Senate:

The sweet simplicity of this girl, her candor, her humility when she spoke of her faith, made a great impression on all assembled and added a note of humanity to an otherwise grandiloquent and formal ceremony.

Mind you, let it be said in their defense that these people prefer to do their grieving in private. I am informed that when the Sultan returned from his mother's burial, he threw his turban on the ground, ripped off all his jewels, had the decorations stripped from the walls of the palace, and turned the carpets upside down. As of that moment, the court has been sequestered for a three-month period of mourning.

Topkapi Palace is now closed to all visitors. The Imperial Gate is shrouded in white. There is no music; there are no feasts, no sporting games. No government business is conducted, no trials or petitions adjudicated, no wars fought; although I daresay taxes will continue to be collected if only to confirm that there is life beyond the grave.

In these circumstances and with your permission, I too shall sequester myself in my estates on the island of Naxos, where I will feast my ears on the music of the Venetian tongue, my eyes on the unveiled beauty of Venetian women and my stomach on the comfort of Venetian cooking. Of course, I plan to return to Istanbul in good time to welcome the Padishah when he emerges from his living interment three months from the day of his mother's death, and resume my long exile from my beloved Serenissima. With a heavy but dutiful heart.

And, to be sure, on the ninety-first day of his mourning, the Sultan did emerge from his living interment to ride his horse through the streets of the capital to the mosque, thus confirming that life had begun again. Which it did in a manner totally unanticipated by anyone, even by the Venetian *bailo* and his well-paid spies. The *bailo* wrote to his masters, the powerful Committee of Ten:

Honored Senators of the Serene Republic,

As always with these people, all deliberations are held in the utmost secrecy (which is what makes it so devilishly expensive to buy information here). Then, suddenly, a covey of heralds explodes into the streets and announces with a flourish of trumpets that a certain event has happened or will happen. This is especially notable in the case of celebrations — weddings, circumcisions, funerals, etc.

Yesterday, without any notice being given, such an occasion was announced for the day after tomorrow. Two days hence there will be a festival to celebrate the marriage (!) of the Sultan and his Russian Second *Kadin*, Lady Hürrem.

My informants in the palace swear they had no forewarning of it. But once the word was out, there

followed no shortage of explanations. Sires, you understand that, since the defeat of Sultan Bayezit by Tamerlane in 1402, when the Sultan's wife Despina was made
to serve naked at the victor's table, no Ottoman Sultan
has risked such humiliation by marrying the mother of
his children. From that time on all the *kadins* have been
chosen from among the Sultan's female slaves who
have produced male children (among whom the Sultan
then designates his heir). No primogeniture here. As I
have advised you with tedious frequency, my masters,
this sultanate is not a European kingdom in any way
we would recognize.

Yet, this week, less than a month after the final day
of mourning for the Valide Sultan, Sultan Suleiman has
taken unto himself as his empress, a Russian concubine
called Hürrem. With this move, the Russian seems to
have vaulted over the head of her rival, Rose of Spring
(where do they get these names?), mother of the Sultan's first-born son, Prince Mustafa, which makes Lady
Hürrem the First *Kadin*. This marriage will put the first
born of the Russian into direct rivalry with the crown
prince for the sultancy. It is a measure breathtaking in
its elegant simplicity.

No doubt about it, a real marriage ceremony was
performed in the palace. Immediately afterwards there
began an explosion of entertainment unmatched by any
I have witnessed in my years at this court. Bread and
olives were distributed to the poor; cheese, fruit, and
rose leaf jam to the middle classes. The main streets
were festooned with flowers and banners—the scarlet
flags of the Ottoman Empire and the green standards
of Islam.

There was a public display of wedding gifts from the
outposts of the empire: camels laden with carpets, fur-
niture, gold and silver vases, and a hundred and sixty
eunuchs to enter the service of Lady Hürrem.

In the hippodrome square, a vast balcony was screened from the crowd by silk hangings and reserved for the new empress and her ladies. From there she could watch the wrestlers, archers, jugglers, and tumblers performing day and night.

Wild animals were paraded along the At Meydani — lions, panthers, and leopards; elephants tossing balls with their long trunks; and giraffes with necks so long they seemed to touch the sky.

In one of the processions a loaf of bread the size of a room was dragged through the streets on a raft by ten oxen while the city's baker threw little hot loaves to the crowd. And people climbed trees to catch a glimpse of the Sultan or to receive gifts of money or silk or fruit that the Sultan's slaves tossed into the air.

The *bailo* concluded his report with a question:

How could such a thing come about? If you believe the gossip down at the bazaar — and I do — this Russian somehow managed to worm her way into the Sultan's mourning chamber in Topkapi Palace immediately after the Valide's funeral and has been in residence sharing his grief for the entire three months that he has been sequestered, during which, I am told, she never left his side. She cooked for him with her own hands and dried his tears with her own handkerchief. In the course of which she managed, they say, to persuade him that, with the Valide gone and the Grand Vizier often away fighting, she was the only person he could trust to do his will when he is off on campaign. In short, with this marriage she has not only eliminated her closest rival, she has also, in one and the same moment, taken on the mantle of the dead Valide Sultan, Lady Hafsa.

God must be on this woman's side. Almost as if she willed it, an uprising has broken out in Azerbaijan among the Sultan's unruly Kurdish beys, who were supposed to have been permanently cured of their Persian leanings by Selim the Grim some fifteen years ago. So the Grand Vizier, Ibrahim, has had to be dispatched to quell the rebel Kurdish warlords, and I am told that Suleiman will follow his Vizier to Mesopotamia in the late spring. This will create a void at the center of governance, which I hear tell the new Sultana has both the will and the ambition to fill. Leaving us with a de facto substitute Sultan, the newly minted Sultana. Think this: it is but a small step from Sultana to Regent. And a great distance from Istanbul to Baghdad, where the rebellion is centered. In such a case a Regent who is fifteen hundred miles away from the ruler can actually become a de facto ruler himself— or herself.

Surely it would be prudent to prepare for such an eventuality. I would advise a cornucopia of bountiful gifts to the newlyweds, especially novelty items that would have particular appeal to the distaff side. To be dispatched from Venice as soon as possible.

Your faithful servant,
Signed Alvise Gritti, Venetian Bailo at Istanbul

25

INVITATION FROM
THE SULTAN

From: Suleiman, Sultan-Caliph, Protector of Islam
To: Judah del Medigo, The Sultan's Chief Body Physician
Date: May 25, 1534

Greetings from a grateful Sultan.

Today your son, Danilo, delivered into my hands a wedding
present that I recognized at once as a manuscript of Arrian's
Life of Alexander the Great, the Greek king spoken of by us as
İskender. Although I know of Arrian's biography only by reputation, the colophon tells me that this manuscript is one of the
treasures of the Gonzaga collection transcribed by your late
wife, Grazia the Scribe, during her service to the Marchese of
Mantova.

The receiver twice values any gift that is greatly treasured by
the giver. Because it was copied in the immaculate hand of your
late wife, Grazia the Scribe, this manuscript is such a gift. Be
assured, it will occupy a place of honor in my library.

Scholars assure me that Arrian's life of İskender is the one
written closest to his own time and thus, the most accurate. But

copies of this *rara avis* are hard to come by, even for a sultan. And, diligent though I have been in pursuit of it, Arrian's *Life of Alexander* has successfully eluded me until this morning when, lo and behold, your son arrived at my *selamlik* bearing the long-sought treasure in his hands. Now, according to the arithmetic of giving, the value of your gift is doubled yet again by its particular value to me as I set out to follow in the footsteps of İskender and to wrest Baghdad from the King of Persia as İskender did—*inshallah*.

Be assured your gift could not mean more to any man on earth. I intend to keep it beneath my bed pillow, which is the very place where İskender kept his copy of Homer's *Iliad*, the story of his hero, Achilles.

And each evening on campaign, I will have read to me Arrian's account of what befell the great Greek king when he ventured east to confront the Persian might centuries ago, just as I am about to do.

Of course, in the way of treasures, this one does not yield itself readily to my eager eyes. Sadly, it is written in a language foreign to me. To bring it into the light, I am now in need of a translator who is well versed in both my own tongue and the Latin in which Arrian wrote. I am also in need of a trustworthy secretary to oversee my personal correspondence. This morning when your son, Danilo, placed the manuscript in my hands, I knew I had found my man. Having observed his development during his years in my School for Pages I have complete confidence in your son's discretion. Trained by you and his mother, he is well versed in the ancient languages. Educated at my school in the palace, he is completely fluent in our native tongue. And even the briefest conversation with him has revealed to me that his enthusiasm for İskender's remarkable exploits equals my own.

So I propose to you, my trusted physician and custodian of my well-being for so long, that your son, Danilo, take your place at my side, not as a physician, of course—that is a place no one else can ever fill—but as my personal interpreter for the duration of the Persian campaign. Note that this proposal does not contravene my previous undertaking to you that I would never recruit your son as a soldier, in spite of his prowess with the *gerit*. In deference to your wishes, I have thus far honored my pledge. And I will continue to do so. But now it seems that, thanks to your generous gift, there is a valuable service that he can perform for me beyond fighting for my cause. To repeat: this would be a temporary appointment, limited to the duration of the Asian campaign, and would engage him only in scholarly and occasional clerical tasks. And you have my personal assurance, both as a sultan and a father, that the young man will never bear arms while a member of my retinue.

It is unnecessary to point out to you that this is a once-in-a-lifetime opportunity for your son to traverse the eastern lands in the footsteps of İskender, to engage in an historic campaign, to witness *(inshallah)* the final defeat of the Persian infidels by the Ottoman Empire. It is a task I have inherited from my noble father, the revered Selim, taken from us before he was able to put finish to the Persian presence in Mesopotamia forever. And note that the young man will remain within the safe haven of the royal tent and under the personal protection of the most powerful ruler in the world.

We none of us wish to be parted from our cherished children. But I urge you to bestow your approval on my plan. Be assured, your son will be grateful for this opportunity all the rest of his life.

I await your reply.
Sealed with the Sultan's *tugra*.

FOR TWO DAYS AFTER this letter was delivered to his house, the doctor left it unanswered, buried under a pile of papers on his writing desk as if it had never arrived, as if it did not exist. But when Danilo returned from his dormitory at the end of the week to celebrate the Sabbath with his father, the actual presence of his son in the house revived Judah's latent conscience, and before they set off for evening services at the Ahrida Synagogue, he slid the letter out from under the pile of books where he had—he could hardly acknowledge to himself—hidden it. Was the paper really hot enough to burn his fingers when he slipped it into his pocket, or had he imagined it?

After prayers, father and son stopped in the courtyard of the synagogue to share the customary glass of wine with the other men of the congregation. It had not been a comfortable prayer session for Judah.

Within himself, the doctor had never found it difficult to accommodate both faith and reason without contradiction. But magic was another story. How could he, a Platonist and a rational man, have felt that a piece of paper that was not on fire was burning a hole in his pocket? And to have it happen in a house of worship on the Sabbath...

This must stop, he admonished himself. Next thing, he would be seeing jinns skulking under his bed. The moment they were alone, he would take out the Sultan's letter and show it to his son, Danilo. Once he had made the decision, he was able to give himself over to the object of the evening: to worship God and give thanks for the many blessings he had enjoyed in the past week.

Still, he did not actually reach into his pocket for the Sultan's letter until he and his son had walked some distance along the Bosphorus and were about to begin the climb to the Doctor's House in Topkapi Palace. As they trudged up the hill, he had the sense that each step was carrying his son farther away from him. Then the thought crossed his mind that the letter was, after all, not addressed to his son but to him, and that he had no obligation to consult anyone. He could, without troubling Danilo, send a polite refusal citing his ill health and his reluctance to send his only child—his only living relative in the world—into danger. He could even offer to search out a replacement interpreter. And the boy need never know of it. Sending the Arrian manuscript to the Sultan had been a serious mistake.

Next to him, Danilo strolled along oblivious to the battle that was raging within his father. So the boy was somewhat taken aback when the doctor stopped suddenly, uttered a deep groan, pulled a rolled-up piece of parchment out of his pocket, and thrust it into his hand with the hoarse instruction: "Read this."

Eyes on his son's face, Judah could see the boy's rising excitement as he read the contents of the letter.

"He is inviting me to go with him? In his own retinue?" The expression of disbelief mixed with wild joy that suffused the young face confirmed Judah's worst fears. His son was about to be taken from him.

"I cannot allow you to go." The words came out of him unbidden. "I cannot allow you to become one of the Janissaries that boast about being the Sultan's slaves. To think that a son of mine would fall into such —"

"With all respect, sir," the boy broke in, "I must remind you that I am also the son of my mother. I was suckled on Homer. I knew of Dionysus before I knew of David. I played at being Alexander the Great. My mother read to me a book of his exploits to tempt me into studying Latin. Alexander is as much a part of my heritage as Abraham, Sarah, or Jacob. And this is an opportunity to walk in his footsteps."

"Point well taken," Judah said. "I spoke hastily, but I fear for your soul embedded in the toils of this Muslim *jihad*."

Now it was the boy's turn to take a deep breath before he responded. "I admit, sir, that I find a certain affinity for the Muslim pages that I study with in the Sultan's school. I was surprised to learn how much we have in common, that we all claim our heritage from Abraham, that we all kill our animals by the same ritual, that we all refuse to eat the flesh of a pig, that all of us are circumcised."

For some reason Judah became almost apoplectic at the mention of circumcision.

"Forgive me, sir; that was only a tease," the boy said in an attempt to placate his father. "But truly the idea of taking up a new religion has never entered my mind. And in his letter the Sultan agrees that he will oversee my religious practice as if I were his own son, does he not?"

If the boy had spoken resentfully or even cursed, Judah might have summoned up the will to persist. But Judah was not only a man of science, he was also a man of feeling, and he could not summon up a defense against the combination of modesty and sweet reason with which his son made his case.

A silence followed, then finally, "If you want to accept the Sultan's offer"—each word caught in the doctor's throat as he uttered it—"I will raise no objection."

That night, Judah del Medigo dispatched his son Danilo across the courtyard to the *selamlik,* to deliver to the Sultan his blessing on the venture. And the boy, taking advantage of the opportunity to walk out freely as a messenger bearing a communiqué for the Padishah, carried along with him a communiqué of his own, addressed to Princess Saida at the Old Palace. Throughout the years of hidden communication between them, all contact had been initiated by her. It was much easier to smuggle things out of the harem than into it, especially since she had the assistance of Narcissus to act as her postman.

But this time Danilo could not wait for his princess to fix a convenient time for their next meeting. The date of the Sultan's departure for the east was set for only a few days hence. So, for the first time, Danilo was faced with a task that had flummoxed generations of illicit harem suitors before him: how to slip a message past the vigilant harem doorkeepers at the iron gates of the Old Palace, who guarded the Sultan's women like a pride of fierce lions.

While he waited for Judah to compose his missive for the Sultan, Danilo turned over in his mind the disguises, subterfuges, and spurious errands that he might concoct. There was not time enough to corrupt one of the harem eunuchs. Such arrangements took months to establish. What he needed was to get a message through this very night—a hidden message. There came to his mind a piece of advice Judah had once given him: the best way to hide a thing is to hide it in plain sight. He would hide his message in an innocent letter from an old chum in the Harem School, a letter from a lowly page to a princess, a letter of condolence on the death of her grandmother!

Mind you, it was close to four months since the Valide's death. But what if he had held off out of reluctance to intrude on her great grief? Another of Judah's worldly maxims came to mind: when inventing a lie, try to include as much truth as you can. What if he was only writing now because he was about to leave on campaign? (True.) And in the Sultan's entourage. (Also true.)

At first, the harem sentry was completely intransigent. He had his orders: letters could not be delivered into the harem. In desperation, Danilo offered to break the seal and let the guard read the letter for himself.

"Read it and you will see." He held the letter out with the same hand and the same careless ease that he offered sweet carrots to his horse. Who could turn away from such a tempting morsel? The guard read and found a nicely composed note of condolence from an old schoolmate to the princess, expressing deep sympathy and the hope that, now that her mourning period had come to an end, the princess would go on to live a life of duty and grace in emulation of her revered grandmother.

I know that you will never cease to grieve for her, the message read. *But I also know that she would have wanted you to enjoy a life full of love for all Allah's creatures as she did.* The note closed, as was proper, with a formal declaration of the page's readiness to serve the princess, should she so desire. *If there is ever any service or duty, small or large, that I can offer, you need only call upon me at my residence at the Sultan's School for Pages, from which I will shortly embark for Mesopotamia as a member of the Sultan's honor guard. To serve the Padishah in the field is an honor beyond my dreams. I can only hope that I am able to live up to the faith he has placed in me by inviting me to serve as his Assistant Foreign Language Interpreter.*

It was a message that the eunuch had no hesitation in delivering—formal, respectful, no ambiguous phrases or hidden meanings. As for subterfuge and deceit, that possibility was obviated by the information that the writer was about to set off as a member of the Padishah's elite guard to fight a *jihad* against the Shiite heresy in Persia.

26

MAGIC INK

THE NEXT MORNING CAME AND WENT WITHOUT A perfumed note or cinnamon stick on Danilo's pillow in the dormitory. As the afternoon hours passed he began to wonder if perhaps the harem sentinel had been less gullible than he appeared and had confiscated his condolences to the princess. By late afternoon he found himself on the watch for a pair of husky harem eunuchs come to take him away to the dungeons for having attempted to stain the honor of a royal princess. At the end of the school day, when an acknowledgment of his letter had still not appeared, he made his way to the *gerit* field with a heavy heart, prepared for the worst. What a relief it was to find Narcissus there waiting for him.

With no time to gather rose petals or commandeer a caique, the eunuch simply muttered a curt order: "Be in your stall with your horse after the third prayer," and melted off into the sunset. Not until Narcissus was out of sight did Danilo realize that the eunuch had not even taken the time to don his silk caftan, which he took as a sign that he too had better be prompt.

Just after the *muezzin* began his third call, Danilo excused himself from hurling drill and headed for the familiar Eunuch's

Path. There was a shorter route to the Sultan's stables through the heavily manned gate that separated the Third and Second Courts. But he chose a circuitous route that took him in and out of the palace grounds by a narrow path and that made it impossible for anyone to follow him without being seen. Still, he did not feel completely safe until he was cozily tucked up with Bucephalus in the horse's stall. Bucephalus could be depended on never to give him away. After a few moments of snuggling with the silent horse, he was joined by a cloaked figure in a very badly wound turban and sporting a bushy black mustache. What she thought she was supposed to be, Danilo could not imagine. But apparently her disguise was effective since none of the stable hands paid any heed to the strangely gotten-up visitor. Nor did they take notice when the blond page and the ill-turbaned pasha retired to the back of the horse stall and barricaded themselves behind two tall hay bales.

From the first word, she was all business. "So when do you go?" she asked as soon they were well concealed.

"I report at Üsküdar in three days," he answered, equally terse.

"That soon?" And before he had a chance to answer: "But you are already gone from me."

"Am I not here?" he asked, genuinely puzzled.

"Only in body," she replied. "Your spirit is already off to war. Do not deny it. You are filled with longing for some far-away battle."

"How do you know that?"

"There may not be much to learn in the harem," she answered, "but on the subject of men and wars, harem-bred women are very well versed. As a little girl, I already knew that although a woman can sometimes pry a man loose from another woman, all her wiles are useless against the call to arms. Men are made for war as women are made for love. Tell me the truth. Are you not happy to be going off to war and leaving me?"

"No!"

"So be it." She placed two fingers gently against his lips. "There is no time for quarrels. I was able to come today on the pretext of bidding my father farewell and wishing him great success in his Asian *jihad*. His carriage is waiting to take me back to the Old Palace as we speak. But I wanted to tell you one more time that no matter how long we are apart, you will always be the love of my life."

"You don't seem to be very sad to see me go," he observed, not without some pique.

"I am not sad. I am heartsick," she corrected him in the same pedantic way she had years before when she was his eleven-year-old tutor. "Heartsick," she repeated. "But I am consoled when I remind myself that, although there may be long stretches of time ahead with no contact between us, we've endured months apart between the *Bayrams* and have always come together afterwards. Believe me, this is not a final goodbye."

This was not the distraught maiden in tears he had expected to find. "What makes you so certain?" he asked.

"Because I tell myself that, for all the time you are gone, my father will also be gone. And for me to be married in his absence is unthinkable. Don't you see?"

He was beginning to.

"It breaks my heart that we will not see each other for a year or even more. But when you return from the Baghdad campaign we will have at least one last chance to meet unobserved during the festival for my father's victorious homecoming. After that..." She rubbed her eyes as if to banish the vision of what the future held. Then she straightened her shoulders and turned to look directly into his eyes. "But I have devised a way for us to stay close while we are far apart." Even in the semi-darkness of the stall, he could make out a trace of the old devilment in her eyes. "Through letters!"

"Letters?"

"The letters in my father's pouch. He sends and receives them every day when he is on campaign."

"But letters can fall into the wrong hands and be read by the wrong people," he reminded her.

"Not if they're written in invisible ink."

This plan was beginning to sound like something she had

picked up from *The Thousand and One Nights*.

"Written in what?"

"Written in invisible ink at the bottom of other people's letters. The harem girls use invisible ink to arrange meetings with their lovers outside the walls. Love letters are a major preoccupation with them. And I have bathed with them in the *hamam* for years." She paused. Then, with a twinkle, she added, "I even know how to make the magic ink."

It did not take magic to read the incredulity on Danilo's face.

"They make up batches of it every week," she explained.

"In the harem?"

"The girls have plenty of time and it's not difficult," she continued. "First you soak a handkerchief in a mixture of nitrate, soda, and starch. Then you dry the fabric. The chemicals come out when the cloth is placed in water, and that liquid becomes invisible ink for your quill pen."

It did seem as if she knew what she was talking about. "But how do I read these messages if they are invisible?"

"Simple. The flame from a lighted taper will reveal the invisible writing. But you must be quick. Once the ink is melted it fades quickly and is gone forever."

All very well, but for Danilo that did not solve the problem of how to get their messages, visible or invisible, into the right hands and keep them out of the wrong hands.

"I've thought about the letters," she went on, as if she had read his mind. "Hürrem always writes to my father when he is on campaign. And now that my grandmother is gone, he will write to Hürrem as he did to his mother. He has promised. And my father always does what he says he will do."

"But —"

"Listen to me," she cut him off. "You forget that Hürrem cannot read or write. I am still having difficulty teaching her after all these years. So..."

"So all her letters to him are written by you." This was not the first time he had underestimated her. It was the pouts and pranks that misled him.

"And all his letters are read to her by me," she added. "They come first into my hands. And you can quite safely write anything you want on them in invisible ink, since I am the person who first breaks the seal. And I will be able to read your messages and dispose of them by taper before she ever sees the letters. That was my first thought."

"And what was your second?" He was almost afraid to hear the answer.

"Actually, my second thought was my first thought," she answered. "It came to me when you wrote your note—a very nice note, by the way. It proves what a good tutor I have been to you. Anyway, if you are to be a personal scribe to my father, there have to be times when you can get your hands on the letters that he sends to Hürrem, so you can write notes to me at the bottom of the pages in invisible ink and I will be able to read them before I show my father's letters to her."

Danilo had heard tales of the tricks and deceptions practiced by the women of the harem, but finding himself personally implicated in one was a new and oddly daunting prospect.

As she so often did, the princess read his mind.

"This is dangerous work." She fixed him with a penetrating glance. "If we are discovered, we are as good as dead. Are you certain you want to do it?"

It was one thing to have reasonable doubts, quite another to have his courage questioned.

"Of course," he replied quickly. "I will live for your messages. It's just it may not be so easy for me to get my hands on the Sultan's private mail —"

Before he could complete the sentence, she cut in on him. "Oh, you will find a way. You have to. You are my paladin. You are my knight. You are the love of my life."

Captivated as always by her sweetness, he held out his arms to her. But she had time only for a short kiss on the cheek before she went on.

"I have ordered fourteen vials of the magic ink. Plus a packet of special quills. You must wrap each vial in a pocket handkerchief to keep them from being broken. And remember, don't pack them all in the same place. That way, if some get crushed, you will have replacements. In return, you must bring me a new supply of the doctor's sleeping powder so that I can get out to meet you when you return without alerting Hürrem. Let us each bring our packets to the Grand Vizier's dock tomorrow evening at the usual time. If anything prevents me, Narcissus will come in my stead. Just do your part and it will all work out."

"You seem so sure..."

"You forget that I have been learning how to manage these things since I was a child in the harem." She held out her arms. "It's getting late."

"Wait!" Taking her by the shoulders and looking directly into her eyes, he asked, "Have you ever tried it? The secret writing, I mean."

"Of course not." Now her impatience was palpable. "How many times must I tell you that you are my only love? I have no one else to write love letters to. Nor will I ever have. But I have seen enough in the harem to know that this ink never fails. One more safety measure—we must never use our own names or speak of our love."

Once again he felt himself falling into a swamp of confusion.

"What am I to write about?" he asked "The weather?"

As she so often did when she wanted to make sure she had his complete attention, she grasped his hands in hers.

"The words don't matter," she explained gently. "I will read the real message in the sight of your hand on the page. Think of this. You have already proved that you know how to compose coded messages."

"I have?"

She reached into her pocket and held up the note of condolence he had passed through to the guardian at the harem gate.

"This note of yours was meant to be read by the sentry as a social gesture. But it was actually meant to tell me that you wanted to see me and that you were leaving the city. The harem girls have found all kinds of ways to code their messages—a couplet from a *gazel,* an old adage, a comment that seems to follow from the real letter. I have even seen a passage from the Koran used to set a date and place for a clandestine meeting."

Now her plan was beginning to make sense to him. The messages had to be encoded in the seemingly innocent language of polite correspondence. How simple. How clever. And on that far-from-romantic note the lovers exchanged a farewell embrace.

Not for the first time, Danilo was left marveling at having discovered yet another side of his infinitely various princess. Clearly she was as capable of focusing her attention on a target as a siege engine and, if necessary, of letting fly a full armamentarium of lies, secrecy, and deception.

"But you have to understand, Bucephalus," he explained to his old confidant after the princess had quit the stable, "that as a woman, those are the only weapons she has. But if she still loves me as much as she says she does, she might have shed at least one tear..."

27

JUDAH'S FAREWELL GIFTS

J UDAH DEL MEDIGO WAS A CONSCIENTIOUS PHYSICIAN
with a strong sense of responsibility to his patients, his
masters, his family, and his god: a compassionate, modest,
and generous man. But deep in his nature lurked a fatal flaw:
a lifelong habit of refusing to recognize realities that he found
too painful to face, and behaving as if they did not exist.

Just such an event had presented itself to him early in his
marriage to Grazia dei Rossi, when he returned to Venice after
the French wars to find her pregnant with a child who could
not possibly be his. All his life, he had longed for a son. To have
a beautiful baby boy thrust into his arms seemed to him like a
gift from God. His way was to accept the boy without question
and bring him up as his own son, but never to acknowledge his
awareness of the deceit, even to his wife.

Perhaps to her discredit, Grazia tacitly played her part in
the charade. So the subject of their son's fatherhood was never
broached between them, and the boy, named Danilo after his
maternal grandfather, grew up believing that Judah was his natural father and never even heard the name of his blood father until
after his mother's death, when he read of it in her secret book.

To Judah's credit, once the truth was out, he made no effort to hide the fact that not he but a Christian knight, Lord Pirro Gonzaga of Gazuollo, was the boy's blood father. Pressed by Danilo for details on what the boy called his "other father," the doctor pronounced the knight to be an upright and decent man descended from the cadet branch of a family any boy would be proud of. Further, he agreed to write to the Gonzagas in Italy to inform them that Lord Pirro's natural son had been saved from his mother's fate at sea and was safe with the doctor in Istanbul.

But, somehow, that letter never got into the courier's pouch. Time passed and no reply was received from Lord Pirro. (How could there have been when no letter had been sent?) All of which led the boy to conclude that the distant Lord Pirro Gonzaga had chosen not to acknowledge his bastard son. And Danilo del Medigo settled down to live as the doctor's son in Topkapi Palace, and gradually the "other father" disappeared as a member of the family circle.

Being a bible scholar, Judah was fully aware of the story of Jacob and Esau. He knew that he had falsified Danilo's birthright as surely as Jacob had stolen his brother's blessing. But he loved the boy past reason. And God knows he had been a devoted father to him for seventeen years.

No surprise that Judah had considered withholding the Sultan's letter inviting Danilo on his mission to fabled Baghdad to follow in the very footsteps of Alexander. It was a dream beyond the boy's wildest imaginings. But this time, his better nature did prevail, and when he finally decided to face the reality of losing his son to the lure of glory, Judah, being the man he was, gave himself over to the task with his whole heart. He would prepare his son for the venture in every way he knew, both as a physician and as an experienced campaigner.

The doctor was never one to make protestations of love. But the succession of small packets that he painstakingly put together and packed into wooden casks — a veritable mountain of remedies against snake bites, gunshot burns, knife wounds, fever, and loose bowels, together with ribbon-bound sets of candles to light on Friday nights and socks knitted from a special water-repellent yarn for wearing when fording rivers, plus foods and spices and remedies, box after box — each offered the closest the doctor could come to a love poem.

They spent their last hours together in the gathering dark of the evening labeling and annotating the items: a salve to be used for three days only (after that it became poisonous); a vest to be worn wherever bullets were flying; alpaca socks (knitted from the hair of Mongolian goats, the very socks that protected Ghengis Khan's feet from freezing); a liquid to be sprayed on pillows and quilts to ward off mites; greenish-colored sand to keep ants out of the food, only to be spread around the edges, never to be eaten; and a manuscript of Quintus Curtius' dictionary. Plus, of course, frequently repeated warnings to be on guard against overripe melons.

They worked silently, piling box upon box to be hauled away at dawn the next morning by Danilo's newly assigned porter. And finally it was time to say goodbye. But before the twine was wound around the last carton, Judah excused himself to fetch one last offering: an unlabeled vial of deep purple liquid that he sealed with wax and placed in his son's hands.

"This is my most valuable possession, my son. It is a nostrum of my own invention. To it, I owe the success of my long tenure as the Sultan's physician." Still, he kept his hands on the vial as if he could not bear to part with it.

Finally, Danilo asked, "What is it, Papa?"

"It is the physic that I concocted to ease the Sultan's gout. Yes, gout. I see you are laughing. But, believe me, gout on campaign can be worse than a bullet wound. And the Sultan has a very bad case of it. Of all his physicians I am the only one who has ever been able to relieve it. When it hits, it strikes his extremities with crippling force. The pain is so intense that he is unable even to grasp his sword. He becomes a commander who cannot sit on a horse. This is the coin"—he held out the vial—"that can buy you the gratitude of kings. Treat it as if it were pure gold. Keep it in the money purse that hangs around your waist. Never let it out of your sight."

Coming from anyone else, Danilo would have received this oddly emotional burst of rhetoric with a measure of skepticism. But coming from Judah, the sworn enemy of grandiloquence and bombast, he took the advice at face value, reached for the purse, already heavy with gold, and found a safe niche among the coins for the peculiar treasure. And later, after Judah had retired, when the practiced Argonaut let himself out the back door and set off to zigzag down the slope to the Grand Vizier's dock, he had to admit that having the amazing tincture so close to his skin made him feel strangely invincible.

Somehow, it did not surprise him to find waiting for him on the dock not the princess but unflappable Narcissus, pacing back and forth like an anxious lover.

"I was unable to make arrangements to carry her over the water," the slave explained.

So time, which had stood still for them obediently over the years, had run out and was even now whipping the slave, who, as he spoke, held out a packet in plain paper.

"Here are the fourteen vials of magic ink," he continued. "You must wrap each in a pocket handkerchief. Don't put them all in the same place. Also, there is a packet of special quills. Before you pack them away, take a few minutes to practice writing with the ink and making it visible." Narcissus tapped his foot nervously on the wooden pier. "Where is the sleeping potion?" he asked, holding out his hand to expedite the transaction.

As Danilo handed over the flagon, he noticed that the hand receiving it trembled. The slave was frightened out of his wits.

"Was it very dangerous to come out tonight?" he asked.

"It is always dangerous, master," Narcissus replied, with ill-disguised impatience.

"Then why do you do it?"

The foot stopped tapping, and Narcissus took a precious moment to think before he answered. When he did, there was just a trace of a smile around his lips.

"That is my secret, master. And hers."

With that, he turned and sped off into the prickly under-growth.

But before the deep night swallowed him completely, the slave threw back over his shoulder one last message: "May your god watch over you and bring you safely back to us."

The thin, reedy voice echoed across the water and like a lightning flash he was gone, breaking Danilo del Medigo's last link with the life he was leaving behind. A flood of dejection washed over him. Tears threatened. But behind the tears his heart began to beat faster with the heady expectation of the great adventure that awaited him on the road to Baghdad.

THE ROAD
TO BAGHDAD

LETTERS FROM THE
COURIER'S POUCH

28

LEAVING ÜSKÜDAR

From: Alvise Gritti, the Venetian Bailo at Istanbul
To: The Illustrious Senators of the Serene Republic of Venice
Date: June 9, 1534

Most Gracious Masters:

I report with pleasure that the little jeweled timepiece you selected as a wedding present for the Sultan arrived in pristine condition and has been delivered to Topkapi. My informants at the palace tell me that Sultan Suleiman and his bride have greeted no other wedding gift from a foreign power with such delight. Even more than the valuable gems that adorn it, they dote on the little figures dressed as Swiss guards that pop out to announce the hours. I recall an equally enthusiastic response from the French king when we sent him a timepiece not unlike this one to cheer him up while he was languishing in the Italian prison. Set down here in Istanbul in the midst of these Saracens, who often seem to belong to a different race of men than ourselves, I find it somewhat reassuring that our kings and their sultans do have some commonality of interest. Clocks and kings.

Ever since I first took up the office of consul here in Istanbul, I have been kept a virtual pariah like all the other foreign representatives (except, on occasion, the French). Even my request to visit the underground cisterns has been denied, although what they have to hide down there I cannot imagine. Could it be that a little gold clock is all it takes to banish the morbid suspicion of foreigners that lurks in the Oriental mind?

Customarily the Sultan responds to gifts with a formal note of acknowledgment, nothing more. This time when I received the formal note of thanks for the wedding gift, it was accompanied by an invitation to pay a visit to Üsküdar where the Turkish army is preparing to embark on their campaign against Persia. As my account books will attest, we normally employ paid informants to find out what these people are up to. Suddenly we are invited in to look for ourselves.

Only one small detail of the wedding gift fails to please. The Sultan hates the chimes. He has requested me to recruit a mechanic who can silence them without disabling the little Swiss guards. This Sultan prizes silence.

I suggest to you, my masters, that the speedy dispatch of a clockmaker with the requisite skills to still the offending tinkles would strengthen our hand at this court immeasurably. Due to the arrival of the clock, we Venetians presently occupy a position of extraordinary favor at the Ottoman court. A window of opportunity has opened. We can use it to press for the trading concessions that we have been pursuing for some time without success.

Some weeks ago when I received an invitation to visit the staging area for Suleiman's army at Üsküdar, the timing of the departure surprised me. Mid-July was fatally late for the Ottomans to launch a campaign, I thought. And so it would have been were Suleiman attempting yet a third siege of Vienna. But he seems to have given up—at least for the present—his plans to capture the Austrian capital. Now his eyes are firmly fixed on Baghdad, and in Mesopotamia the summer heat makes it impossible to fight from June through September. On that account the

Grand Vizier, Ibrahim Pasha, was sent ahead with half the army in mid-winter to reoccupy the Persian strongholds in Kurdistan and Azerbaijan. He carries with him the huge cannons needed to lay siege to the cities along the way, making his a slow, heavy slog. But it enables the Sultan to speed off with the balance of the army to join his Vizier unburdened by the weight of the big guns, so that their combined forces can march on together in late autumn. That is the best season, they say, to cross into Mesopotamia.

Once the Sultan has conquered Baghdad (*inshallah*, as everybody here says), Suleiman can spend the winter establishing himself in Iraq as the reincarnation of the caliphs of the Arab Golden Age. Then, with Ottoman rule firmly established in Mesopotamia, there will still be time to return home before the winter of 1535.

Until now everyone—including the Sultan—believed that his father had subdued the Persians once and for all at the Battle of Chaldiran some twenty years ago. But now we have a new king in Teheran, and this Shah Tahmasp has wasted no time rekindling the old Turkish-Persian enmity. All he needed was provocation, and as if on cue, up stepped Zultikar Khan, the governor of Baghdad, to make a public declaration of his independence of Persia and his fealty to the Ottoman Sultan. No doubt the rascal had been conniving with the Ottomans behind Persia's back all the while. These people are always changing loyalties. But the Khan, who seems to have had an unfortunate flair for the dramatic, had the poor judgment to follow up his defection from the Persian Empire with packaging up the keys to Baghdad and sending them to Suleiman in a golden *casque*! Naturally, Tahmasp responded by storming Baghdad, chopping off the governor's head, and sending it on to Topkapi Palace in a velvet bag—the Saracen equivalent, it would appear, of throwing down the gauntlet. This puts Turkey once again at war with Persia.

I have now paid two visits to the staging area at Üsküdar, one a week ago and the other this very day on their eve of embarkation. Before I went, I had been told that the Ottomans lodged more grandly in the field than at home. But nothing could have prepared me for what I saw with my own eyes.

The encampment is laid out in a vast field at least five times longer than the hippodrome. On my first visit, only the Sultan's private quarters were in place and they stood — a multitude of tents of varied shapes, sizes, and colors — in the very center of the field. Here I must pause to point out that what we Europeans speak of as tents bears almost no resemblance to the structures I saw in Üsküdar. In the style of their nomadic forbearers, these Ottomans create the big, important tents out of heavy felt panels suspended by silk cords from posts as thick as a man's waist and painted top to bottom with gorgeous designs. The smaller tents that surround the Sultan's entourage are made of stiff canvas panels.

But do not think that Suleiman wallows in *lusso* in his tent while his subordinates live in squalor in theirs. As I watched, a crew of workmen was dressing the rough exteriors of the smaller tents with embroidered hangings. Even the stables on the periphery of the compound are covered by canvas!

I cannot report on the Sultan's *sanctum sanctorum* — his sleeping tent, his bathing tent, his meeting tent, his eating tent. Of these I got not so much as a glimpse. But I was shown his main reception tent, a vast rotunda fully carpeted, hung all around with colored glass lanterns and capped by a huge crescent bearing his war standard, his *tugra*. Honored sirs, I have seen many bivouacs in my long service to the Serenissima, but never could I even have imagined such grandeur in the field.

On my second visit, the camp had indeed expanded to cover the entire meadow in a grid of pathways with a place for everyone and everyone in his place, including hunting dogs and camp followers. It was Topkapi re-created in felt and canvas with a palisade of red silk to serve as its fortress walls.

Allow me to remind you, gentlemen, that this temporary city houses only half of the army that is advancing toward Baghdad; the other half, under the leadership of the Grand Vizier

Ibrahim, will winter over in Tabriz, which we hear Ibrahim has already recovered from the Persians. Note also that this caravan will be joined by local governors—the *beys*—and various Ottoman feudatories who bring with them their own mounted troops, grooms, servants, horses, mules, and baggage trains as it progresses through Anatolia and Azerbaijan.

By the time I left Üsküdar today, every tent pole was in place and every man and beast accounted for, except for one: the Sultan. At the break of dawn, he will ride out from Topkapi Palace with his honor guard of pages and his Janissaries to take up his central place in the line of march. Then, at the bong of the great bronze vessel they call the Drum of Conquest, he will head east on a journey that local engineers calculate at 1,334 miles.

By noon tomorrow, I am told, the vast field at Üsküdar will be empty. By nightfall it will be cleaned of any evidence of its recent occupiers. The city that grew up in a few weeks will have disappeared in a day without leaving a trace. And Suleiman will be on the march once again, eastward this time, across the vast Anatolian plain to Aleppo, which is still firmly under Ottoman control, and then south through the Kurdish territory that abuts the Persian Empire and seems never to be under anyone's control.

There are some points on this route of march where Suleiman will be treading in the very footsteps of Alexander the Great on his Baghdad campaign. Apparently, our Sultan was brought up on some piece of Arabic invention, very popular among the Turks, titled Ahmedi's *Book of İskender* (their name for Alexander), a kind of nursery jumble of Arrian, Ptolemy, Herodotus, and Xenophon's *Anabasis* mixed in with a good deal of Muslim mythologizing. It was in this book, read to him by his mother, I am told, that Suleiman first encountered the story of Alexander and, at that early age, adopted the Greek hero as his personal model.

Respectfully, Lords, I will take the liberty of pointing out that Alexander himself adopted Homer's Achilles as his hero at an early age, and that on his Persian campaign Alexander slept with a copy of Homer's *Iliad* under his pillow, the text of which he had read to him each night by his boon companion, Hephaestus. Indeed, it would not surprise me if Suleiman — who recently received as a gift, I hear, a Latin manuscript of Arrian's *Life of Alexander* — will give equal pride of place to that volume among his bedding.

They say that Suleiman also fancies being read to sleep in his tent. Coincidentally, he too has a boon companion, the Grand Vizier Ibrahim, who, it is said, shares his bed some nights and always reads to him. But the Grand Vizier is bivouacked many miles away in Tabriz. And I would wager that some page with a good command of Latin, and an eye on the main chance, will glide easily into a place of similar intimacy as a reader to the Sultan before this cavalcade reaches Konya.

Respectfully submitted,
Alvise Gritti

29

MALTEPE

From: Danilo del Medigo at Maltepe
To: Judah del Medigo at Topkapi Palace
Date: June 13, 1534

Oh, Papa:

Four days out of Üsküdar. Riding by day, sleeping by night, always within the confines of the Sultan's command center tucked into the middle of this vast procession of people and animals, is like living in the middle of a city so large that you cannot see the end of it in any direction. And that is what makes the smooth orderliness of our march most amazing.

Each night, as we prepare to sleep, we hear the horns summoning the engineers and laborers from their beds to wake up and ride on to the next day's stop. While we continue to sleep, they ride ahead with the camels and wagon trains. At dawn we wake up, wash, eat, and set forth leaving our tents behind and all of our garbage carefully buried. By the time we arrive at the day's stop we are greeted with a new tent city marked out by trenches, latrines, and the entire array of the Sultan's household tents (some of which are duplicates of the ones we just vacated). Meanwhile, back at the previous day's site the rear guards have disassembled that village and leap-frogged past us to our next stop with their wagons full of tents and gear.

I know that this is an old story for you, Papa, who have shared so many of the Sultan's victories, but your campaigns were waged in Bulgaria, Hungary, and Austria. You had the Danube for your highway. All we have is an old, abandoned silk road.

I don't know what exactly I expected of a military campaign, but whatever it was, it was not this—the slowness of it, the daily sameness. Pack up, mount the horse, and slowly walk to the day's destination (no faster than it takes the fully loaded camels of the baggage train). The pack animals set the pace.

What did I think it would be like? How else did I think we could transport a city of men and animals from Istanbul to Baghdad? The answer is, I didn't think. My only experience of campaigning was when I rode out with Lord Pirro Gonzaga to visit Bourbon's imperial army outside of Rome. Until we set off from Üsküdar I had seen no other army on the march than that one. I was prepared to die, but not to die of boredom.

Why didn't you tell me it would be like this? To which you have every right to respond, "Why didn't you ask?"

After almost a week I have yet to catch a glimpse of the Sultan. Nor have I been told what is expected of me, what my duties are, or indeed why I am here at all. According to the official camp roster, I am a member of the highest *oda* of the Sultan's senior pages—the ones who dress him, shave him, bathe him, feed him, and on campaign stand guard over him and fight for him. They are his guard of honor. I eat with them and sleep with them, but they have made it clear that I am not one of them. In fact, they call me the Jew Page, not with malice, more to distinguish me from them. They are all Christian-born boys, taken as the spoils of conquest, enslaved, converted to Islam, and selected to be members of the Sultan's personal and governing caste, his *cul*. That is their pedigree, and to them no one without it could ever be a true member of the Fourth *Oda* of the Sultan's pages.

They even exclude Ibrahim the Greek from their brotherhood. He may be the Grand Vizier, but they refer to him as the Greek. Although he was one of the tribute boys like them, and born a Christian like them, he, being Greek, is not their kind of Christian.

So far, what little instruction I have received has come from my official superior officer, the Sultan's Chief Foreign Language Interpreter, Ahmed Pasha. But, truth to tell, I don't think Ahmed knows what my duties are any more than I do. Or why I am designated as his assistant, since he has nothing for me to do. It was he who informed me that I am prohibited from working on Saturday since it is my Sabbath. And from eating pork on any day of the week. And forbidden to shoulder a weapon. Too bad, since my talent with the *gerit* might win me some friends among the Sultan's senior pages. But I suppose I must be grateful that, even if I do not know what I am meant to do here, at least I do know what I may not do.

Lest you think that I am unhappy on the march, I rush to assure you that I am safe and warm and well fed. I have a champion horse of my own to ride on the march, a mule to transport my books and papers, and assigned stalls in the stable to house my animals. So, you see, I am far from suffering. Nor am I, God knows, in danger. The Persian king is still a thousand miles away, and the people that wave to us as we pass through the provinces of Anatolia seem very glad to see us. Why should they not be? The Sultan has packed up his entire treasury to keep him company, so we travel with wagon-loads of gold and pay cash for everything we buy. What a difference this is from my memory of Bourbon's Imperial Army that sacked Rome, his troops forced to snatch food out of the mouths of starving people so as not to starve themselves. Since we pick up most supplies as needed, we are spared the constant search for food and forage that bedevil European armies on the march. And since we are known to buy what we need at a fair price, we are welcomed everywhere with flags and smiles.

Of course, this is only the beginning of a long march, and we are still well within the bounds of the Ottoman Empire. Once we reach the border of Mesopotamia, we will have to engage Tahmasp's army and besiege Persian cities. But at least we will arrive fresh and well fed. I know that you, Papa, have suffered untold hardship during many sieges, most recently at Vienna. And I do not minimize the possibility of hard times ahead for this campaign. But at the moment, I feel much more like a member of some vast triumphal procession than a soldier enduring the privations of war.

I do not know when this letter will reach you, Papa. It is my plan to take advantage of the couriers who ride back and forth to Istanbul on the Sultan's business. Since you stand so high in his esteem, I may work up the courage to ask his permission to send my letters to you in his pouch. That is, if I ever get to see him. I hope this finds you in good health.

D.

From: Danilo del Medigo at Maltepe
To: Judah del Medigo at Topkapi Palace
Date: June 14, 1534

Dear Papa:

Just when I had begun to believe that I was doomed to spend my campaign days studying like a schoolboy for a test that I would never be required to take, a summons arrived for me to report to the Sultan's tent after the final prayer tonight.

I will not hide from you, Papa, that I was already trembling when I began to prepare for my first reading session with the Sultan. This I did by reviewing the passages about Alexander that you sent to help me with my translating tasks. But I was so nervous that when I reached for the pages, they dropped from my hand and went flying all over the tent. Lucky for me these tents are carpeted, and no harm was done to your precious manuscript.

When I arrived at the Sultan's tent, still shaking, he was seated on a throne of cushions beside a small desk piled high with papers and did not look up. Is that how he treated you, Papa? No greeting? No smile? Was I expected to announce myself? I thought not. How does one behave in the presence of princes? How does one find one's place as a small cog in this vast wheel that is rolling over Anatolia? Oh, how I wish that I had asked you more questions when I had the chance. Because I once visited a military camp — and a European one at that — I foolishly believed that I knew all about campaigning. Now I find that I do not even know how to ask permission to use the latrine, much less whether or not to open my mouth.

So there I stood in the Sultan's presence at last, waiting for a sign. And, to be sure, after several uncomfortable minutes, the Sultan did look up. But he never greeted me. Nor did he smile. He is not a smiling kind of man. He simply put down the last of his papers, withdrew from under his pillow my mother's translation of Arrian's *Anabasis* that you gave to him, and passed it over to me. I am pleased to tell you that he keeps the manuscript in a gold-embroidered bag. And that he takes great care with it. And that, in spite of my shattered nerves, I did not drop it.

Finally came the curt order: "You may begin."

And so I began with the anecdote of Alexander's taming of the wild horse, Bucephalus. But I hardly had the first words out when the royal hand went up.

"I wish to hear the Greek's version of İskender's landing on the shores of Asia. It is a tale I heard as a child from my blessed mother, may she rest in eternal peace."

To which I added, "Amen."

To tell the truth, Papa, I was more than a little surprised at the Sultan's lack of interest in Alexander's early years. Was this Sultan never a boy himself? *Perhaps he is too occupied with the here and now as he walks in the footsteps of Alexander*, I thought. But in the course of reading to him last evening, I began to sense that he does feel a kind of kinship with Alexander (whom they call İskender), but that it is more mystical than historical. I believe he thinks himself to be the reincarnation of İskender, born to assert the power of the True Faith over the heretic Persians.

Lucky for me I was able to render into passable Turkish İskender's crossing of the Hellespont and the wonderful bit where he leaps off the royal trireme and hurls his spear into the soil of the Persian Empire to claim it as his own. I cannot be certain, but at that point, I believe I heard the Sultan mutter under his breath, "Bravo, İskender!"

This gave me the confidence to plow ahead to Alexander's capture of Troy and his homage at the tomb of Achilles. Arrian tells us that Alexander and his boon companion, Hephaestion, placed wreaths on the tombs of Achilles and Achilles' boon companion, Patroclus. As I read, my Sultan nodded approvingly, if not of me at least of Alexander. But when I came to the word "wreaths," he reared up on his cushions and his face clouded over.

"Wreaths!" He spat out the word like an oath. "What about the naked dance around Achilles' tomb? What about the perfumed oil and the choir of angels?" He aimed an accusing finger at me. "You must have skipped a page."

For a moment, I wondered if perhaps I *had* missed a page — this man speaks with such authority that he inclines you to doubt your very self. But a quick perusal of the manuscript told me that I had missed nothing. Further, I assured him that, in all my readings, I had not encountered any mention of Alexander dancing around Achilles' tomb. This only put him in a worse humor, which, luckily, he chose to take out not on me but on poor old, dead Arrian.

"Who is this Arrian anyway?" he demanded. "I was told that he was the most reliable source on the life of İskender. Now I find that I have better information from Ahmedi's *Book of İskender* that my mother read to me in the nursery."

Who indeed was Arrian? And how much did he really know about Alexander? For that matter, how much did I know? And what did I have in my pitiful arsenal of learning to put up against the bedside fables recounted by the Sultan's sainted mother?

Gathering my wits, I ransacked my memory for everything I had ever learned about Alexander's life from you and my mother, then proceeded to throw at him a mixed grill of names and dates and scribes and scholars—Arrian, Plutarch, Quintus, Diodorus, Ptolemy, I threw them all in. Each of these biographers, I explained, had his own version of İskender's story. Yet not one of their original manuscript sources survives. What we have today are retellings, each one with its own gaps and errors. Of the lot, Arrian is judged to be the most complete life of Alexander.

"But we must remember," I advised him gently, "that Arrian wrote four centuries after İskender's death, when everyone who ever knew the young king and could attest to the events of his life was long dead."

We must remember . . . Had I actually spoken to the Padishah in the imperative? Nobody tells the Sultan what he must do. Even an ignoramus like me knows that.

I sat waiting for the axe to fall. Instead, I got a quite kindly request to think back over my readings in Latin and Greek about what happened to İskender in Troy. Either the Padishah hadn't heard my lapse of protocol or else he simply couldn't believe his own ears. That gave me a moment in which to redeem myself.

Think, Danilo. Where could the Sultan's mother have gotten her story of naked dancing? Very likely from the Turkish romance of İskender, translated into Arabic from the Persian and before that from the original Greek. How easy it would have been to mistake a word or a phrase—even a whole paragraph—on such a tortuous linguistic journey.

"May I ask a question of you, sire?" I asked.

He nodded his permission.

"Do you by any chance recall the precise wording in the book that was read to you as a child?"

"I do," he answered, quite affably. "I heard many times how İskender and Hephaestion approached the tomb of Achilles on their knees; how, in a gesture of homage, they stripped themselves bare, anointed themselves with sweet holy oil to purify their bodies, and then performed a traditional dance around the sacred site. I can hear my mother's voice telling it. Every word."

His mother's voice. All in a rush, my own mother's voice came back to me relating how Alexander made for Troy to honor his hero, Achilles. How he exchanged his own armor for a shield said to have been the one that protected Achilles at Troy. And how, in a traditional act of homage, he and his boon companion, Hephaestion, stripped bare and ran a naked foot race around the tomb of Achilles.

Apparently, somewhere along the tortuous route of translation, the race had become a dance. Race, dance—not too dissimilar. And in any case, who am I to challenge the word of the Sultan's sainted mother? So, as I retold my mother's tale, I replaced her word, "race," with his mother's term, "dance," adding a silent prayer to my meticulous mother to forgive the inaccuracy.

And when that was done, I begged the Sultan's pardon for my error, blaming the translators. In Latin, I explained, the word "cursus" is usually taken to mean race, as in a running contest. Almost instantly, I saw the clouds beginning to form again above the Sultan's forehead.

"But it can also mean 'dance,'" I added hastily. And got a satisfied nod in return.

I had scraped by with my reputation intact. But what about poor Arrian? His name was mud. And on this note, we ended the long evening.

I suppose I can claim to have survived some kind of test. But one thing fills me with trepidation. Not only does this man want me to translate Arrian on the spot, he wants Arrian to have written the romance of İskender that his mother read to him as a child. And I am not certain that I can perform such a miraculous transformation.

What the Sultan requires of me is a romantic tale, and Arrian is neither tale-spinner nor romantic. With his text I see the Sultan's eyes begin to flicker, then close. Arrian is lulling him to sleep. He is a dry bone, this Greek, with no good bits to chew on. And this causes me to lose hope for my future as the Assistant Foreign Language Interpreter. And to curse the day I ever heard the name İskender.

Your respectful and loving son,
Danilo del Medigo

 ⟩

From: Sultana Hürrem at Topkapi Palace
To: The *Ghazi* Sultan Suleiman en route, received at Maltepe
Date: June 14, 1534

My Adored Sultan and Master:

Five days without you are like four months. Every day the children ask, "Why is Papa not here? When will he come back to us?" They are too young to understand that their papa is a *ghazi,* and that when the *jihad* calls he must obey its summons.

It ill behooves me to complain of my lot to you who gives his very life out of duty to his people. But since you have raised me to the exalted state of Empress and have honored me by naming me Regent in your absence, you have also, my adored husband, laid upon me a set of grave responsibilities far beyond my meager ability. Not only must I perform as a regent worthy of your confidence, but also as guardian, in your absence, of our much loved children. In these endeavors I am sorely in need of all the support I can muster. We have already learned the importance of a confidential secretary who will be completely loyal to me, and I thank Allah daily for having found such a one in the Princess Saida. She is a pillar of strength to me. But, sadly, though she faithfully makes the journey across town each afternoon from the harem to serve me here in Topkapi, I regret my inability to call on her assistance, should the occasion arise, when I need her in the morning or in the evening. But she is unwavering in her determination to live out a full year of mourning for her grandmother in the Valide's suite at the Old Palace.

Surely no man has been more faithful in observance of his mourning duties than you. Yet only three months after the Valide's untimely death, you answered the call of duty and rode off to war against the infidel Shah of Persia. I have pointed out to our mourning princess that she too has a duty, hers being the care of her younger brothers and sisters as she readies herself for marriage — far too long delayed — to a husband of your choosing, thus giving you, as a future son-in-law, a *damat* bound to us by blood and also a future vizier of proven loyalty.

It is not as if she is enjoying her mournful life. I am told that she cries herself to sleep at night, driven to tears by the loss of her grandmother, whose love she still craves but who is lost to her and cannot be restored. The only solution is for her to forego her observances and take up her womanly duties as a wife and mother and the bearer of Ottoman sons.

Preparation for such a momentous event takes time. The bride's trousseau must be ordered — think of this: every pearl in the train must be hand-sewn — a palace must be purchased, and a suitable staff assembled for the household of a princess and her husband, the Sultan's *damat*. I have begun to assemble a list of worthies for this great honor, so all that remains for you to do when you arrive home — oh, blessed day! — is pick the one you favor, as is your rightful duty, and announce the wedding date.

Please write or I will die.

Signed,
Your Sultana

At the bottom of this letter is an encrypted message. A quick pass over the page with a lighted taper reveals these words:
The princess is driven to tears by longing for the one whose love she craves, not a love forever lost but a love being kept alive by a magic taper.

30

ELMADAĞ

From: Danilo del Medigo at Elmadağ
To: Judah del Medigo at Topkapi Palace
Date: June 17, 1534

Dear Papa:

We have stopped at the base of a mountain for two days to take
advantage of the excellent hunting in the surrounding forests.
Not only birds abound here but deer, antelope, and even wild
boar. When I heard this, I barely slept for thinking of bringing down a large animal with my *gerit*. Being a member of the
Fourth *Oda*, it did not occur to me that I might not be invited to
join the Sultan's hunting party along with my fellow pages. But
as I was readying myself for my first royal hunt, my superior
officer, Ahmed Pasha, the Chief Interpreter, pulled me aside to
tell me that I must stay behind. It seems that the Sultan's undertaking to you that I would not bear arms during my service to
him precluded my participation in the hunt.

"But that was in the cause of war," I protested, to no avail.
So at dawn this morning my fellow pages rode off without me,

every hoofbeat a blow to my heavy heart. Papa, I know you do not share my enthusiasm for horses or for sport. And I understand that this prohibition against my carrying arms is meant to keep me safe. But must I look forward to a year or more of being singled out from my comrades and kept in my tent like a backward child? If so, it sets me to wondering if the conditions under which I am traveling in the Sultan's army are perhaps too stringent for me. I am resigned to my alien status as the Jew Page because of my religion, but the prospect of being despised by the comrades I eat with and sleep with and ride with every day as a weakling who cannot wield a *gerit* fills me with dread.

That is why I am begging you, Papa, to revise the conditions of my service to the Sultan. At least to allow me to take part in any *gerit* contest along the road and in any other non-military sports such as hunting. As it is, I lay on my bunk all morning feeling useless and friendless and hopeless. Which is where Ahmed found me and took pity on me. Of course, he dare not disobey his master's orders, but he did have a suggestion that cheered me up. Why, he asked, did I not use these two days to acquaint myself with the camp?

"I do have the authority to offer you two days' leave from your translation work to make a circuit of the camp," he advised me. "Nobody told me you were not allowed to ride your horse. And I would estimate two days on horseback will give you time to survey the cavalcade from the most forward units at the head to the stragglers at the rear." Then he added, with a twinkle in his eye, "It is a rare opportunity, my boy, I assure you. I myself did not get a complete view of the line of march until my third campaign. And you may never have this chance again."

It was, as an Italian would say, an offer too good to refuse. So I pulled on my boots, filled up my water bottle, saddled my horse, and set off to learn something of this expedition of which I am a part, yet not a part.

Following Ahmed's advice, I decided to begin at the rear, then visit every section of the cavalcade from back to front. As if anyone could hope to accomplish this—and see anything—within two days' ride. It took only a few hours to make me realize the folly of my plan, as you would know from your extensive experience with this army. But then, owing to your loathing of horses and mules, you may well have been happy to just stay in your tent on your days off.

If so, I will risk boring you by telling you of what I saw today. And please save this letter so that I can bring my adventure back to mind when I am old and nodding by the fire and recounting stories for my grandchildren.

For the record, our route has taken us not too far from the Granicus River, where Alexander first encountered the might of King Darius of Persia in the year 334 BC. In Alexander's time, this vast countryside of Anatolia that we are passing through so peacefully was in the hands of the Persians. I made a point of this to the Sultan while reading to him from Arrian last night. We both agreed that it would have been interesting to visit İskender's ancient battlefield at the Granicus. But sadly, said the Padishah, we must move on. Duty calls. However (I remark this for your ears only, Papa), it seems that duty does not call as loudly for a visit to an historic battleground as does the hunting horn.

Myself, I would have been happy to follow Alexander's way all along the Ionian coast to Caria province, where he stopped to consult an oracle. But it turns out that the Sultan has his own oracle to consult—a Sufi mystic called Rumi, whose grave and shrine are at Konya. Is it not interesting, Papa, that these two great leaders both chose to go out of their way to make certain that the gods were on their side before setting off to conquer Persia? But I am getting away from my purpose...

As you know, the camp is planned like a city strung out in a long line of compounds, each unit fenced in by pastures and stables for the animals and assembled into neat rows of tented streets, and each street bordered by trenches, with the Padishah tucked securely into the very center of the line protected by Janissaries at both ends.

Our next-door neighbors in the line of march, a brigade of Janissaries, had already lit their fires when I crossed into their encampment, which appeared astonishingly quiet and peaceable. Nowhere did I see garbage or filth or evidence of gaming or drunkenness. It was hard to believe that I was standing in the midst of a bivouac of battle-hardened foot soldiers, and even more amazing that such tranquility continued to prevail, even while their Janissary captains were up on the mountaintop hunting with the Sultan. In my recollection of the Imperial camp outside of Rome, neither the Duke of Bourbon nor his co-captain of the German landsknechts was able to command such a high degree of order, even while standing directly in front of their men issuing orders.

Next surprise—the liberality of the commissary. Even in this parched land, where water is often as valuable as gold, I saw full cauldrons of water standing ready for the cooks. And water for handwashing after visits to the latrine. Of course, these troops are all Muslims, and it is against their religion to use paper to wipe their asses. I remember one of my first days in the Princes School being told that it would be indecent to put paper to such a use because paper is what the name of God is written on. I also recall noticing that same day that the boys removed their turbans before pissing and then kissed them as they put them back on because the head covering is a mark of devotion to Allah. As the French say, *quel delicatesse*!

Certainly, I was not surprised when I joined the Sultan's entourage to find serenity and cleanliness and a full larder and plentiful washing-up water because he is, after all, the Sultan. But to find handwashing water provided for whole companies of soldiers in the field—that shook my mind.

Of course I did not speed by the Janissary camp as I had planned to do but dismounted and walked about through the tented streets, which led to a long string of kiosks and sheds peopled by saddlers and bow-makers, coppersmiths and tinsmiths, barbers and cobblers and slipper-makers, sword smiths and tent-pole carvers, and a great number of food sellers. A fraternity of guild members set up a bazaar at each stop as they did at Elmadağ and will continue to do at every stop.

My time in the Janissary compound was truly like a pleasant visit to a busy marketplace, and I was loath to move on. But if I were to take as much time at each encampment as I did with the Janissaries, I would never reach the end of the line, or the end of this letter.

So I quickly proceeded to the next compound—the clerks and clerics of the *divan*. I knew that the entire council and their clerks and scribes were traveling with us and would be meeting regularly as they do at Topkapi. But five minutes in their environs—street after street of colored tents and what seemed like hundreds of people trudging back and forth among them with sheaves of paper in their hands—gave me a new sense of the scope of this enterprise. And I suddenly remembered one time at dinner in our house hearing the Venetian *bailo* comment with disdain that the seat of the Ottoman Empire is wherever the Sultan chooses to pitch his tent. At the time, I took this to be no more than a sneer at the Osman family's lowly origins. But today I saw with my own eyes that the Sultan is literally the center of his empire and that wherever he moves, the government moves with him, including every last ducat of his vast treasury.

Of course, keeping an eye on the treasury could be taken as concern for the threat of the pilferage and thievery that might ensue during the Sultan's long absences from his capital. After all, the Holy Roman emperor still lies in wait for us some hundreds of miles to the west. But granting the need to secure the treasury, what possible reason can there be to drag over mountains and through deserts every single member of the *divan* together with his clerks, his secretaries, his porters, and household staff so that they can meet each week, just as they do at Topkapi, to hear petitions and draft new laws or rub out old ones? I conclude that by placing himself at the center of this movable city, the Sultan becomes the literal personification of the empire as it moves out on campaign. With all aspects of government literally under his eye, there is no empire without him. The Venetian *bailo* is thus much cleverer than he knows. The seat of Ottoman power is indeed wherever the Sultan pitches his tent.

After the *divan* compound, I moved on through the several kitchens that serve different constituencies, past the sheep-slaughtering community that also tans hides (hold your nose!), and into the domain of the treasury, which is overseen, I found, by a Grand Chancellor who travels with two hundred slaves and an even greater number of huge oak chests, each one bound by seven metal straps and secured with three locks. At the stops these chests occupy six large tents (almost as many as the Sultan has). And together, they carry the entire treasure of the empire, to be at the instant disposal of the Sultan wherever he may travel.

At the rate I was going, I would be lucky to reach the end of the line before nightfall, I thought. But when I came to the hospital tent I simply had to go in and find out what kind of medicine is practiced within its quarter-mile circumference.

The answer is, they take care of every medical problem from boils to stab wounds. This early in the campaign, the place was almost completely empty of patients, but it seems there is always suffering going on of some kind or another. And I did see two teeth being pulled, a few bones being set, and a baby delivered to a whore. Did the women deliberately join the campaign, I wondered, knowing that in this finely equipped place they would receive the kind of care rarely available to their sort? (Not until I reached the end of the line did I discover the community of wives and whores. So I now know why they are called camp-followers. They follow the camp!)

Last medical note. As I was leaving the hospital I noticed a quite small, unidentified tent in red canvas that seemed to be attached to it. Poking my head in to inquire what sort of business was done here, I was informed, in the most casual manner, that I had entered the abortionist's tent. To be sure, no possible need has been neglected.

To put your mind at ease, Papa, I did not, on this occasion, tarry in the neighborhood of the camp followers. By the time I got to them, darkness had fallen and I barely had time to ride my horse back to the Sultan's compound before the stables were locked up for the night. But I went to sleep resolved to awaken early and give myself plenty of time to visit what lay ahead of me up the line—the artillerymen, the musicians, and our neighbors, the famous Ottoman *sipahis*, the very mention of whom sets the hearts of Europeans to tremble with fear.

D.

<hr>

From: Danilo del Medigo at Elmadağ
To: Judah del Medigo at Topkapi Palace
June 18, 1534

Dear Papa:

Last night when I returned from my ride through the rear half of the camp, I begged you to keep this document as a record for my children. Until now, all I knew of the Ottoman style of campaigning was that the Padishah took my father from me for seven months every year and that he always returned home victorious, the Ottoman army having added a new territory or country to the empire.

At dawn I could hardly wait to complete my survey—the forward half of the line. So I started off early, determined to visit each unit of the encampment. So much for plans. It is now high noon and I am back at my trunk-desk, confused, saddened, and bereft of any sense of decency, much less nobility, in this enterprise.

I cantered into the encampment of the *sipahis* hoping to catch them at drill, even to pick up some tricks of horsemanship, at which, you know, they are the masters. Like all the other boys of Istanbul, I have watched them performing in victory parades. And, like the others, I am in awe of their strength, their courage, and their prodigious skill; and dazzled by the flourish of their leopard-skin cloaks as they shoot off their arrows twenty a minute while facing backward and hitting the brass target every time. I could practice for a thousand years and never achieve that mastery. It has to be in the blood.

Naively, I had hoped to strike up a conversation about horses with one of them. But nature called so I tethered my horse and made my way on foot to the latrine ditch that edges these encampments. And that is where I encountered a sight that will haunt me forever: a lone tree, shorn of branches to resemble a gibbet, and swaying from it in the breeze, a *sipahi* in full uniform, with a stump leaking blood where one of his hands used to be. All this behind the tidy tents in the bright sun while his comrades went on about their business of pissing and shitting as if nothing unusual was happening.

What heinous crime could he have committed?

As I made my way slowly back to my horse, I dimly remember asking a passerby what the man had done. But there is no dimness in my recall of the answer.

"He stole a chicken," I was advised, in an even, casual tone that made the hairs on my neck bristle.

That statement, the flatness of it, killed whatever was left of my taste for adventuring, and I walked my horse back to the Sultan's compound unable to stop my tears. This man was not some street criminal. This man was a member of the Sultan's valued cavalry. His loyalty and his bravery had passed all the tests. Is this the price we pay for peace and cleanliness? And, if so, is it worth the cost?

At home, when I come up against such puzzles, I can turn to you, Papa. Or to Bucephalus, who is very wise for a horse. But this new mount assigned to me by the Sultan is no Bucephalus, despite being younger and faster. I did try to talk to him, but conversation makes him impatient. He prefers carrots.

So I hiked back to my cot and was again found by Ahmed with my face turned to the wall. Of course, he wanted to know what I had seen that day, and in a fit of candor, I told him. Now comes the reason why I am telling you this story, Papa. He agreed that the punishment was cruel. But he said the crime was very serious.

"Stealing a chicken?"

"The fellow is lucky it's a first offense. Otherwise the penalty is both hands."

"For stealing a chicken?"

"For entering private property in the uniform of the Sultan and violating the rights of one of the Sultan's flocks."

"But the peasants here are all Greeks and Christians," I reminded him.

"All the more reason why not one of the Sultan's citizens can be treated with less justice than any other," he explained. Then with a smile, "Even Jews. Have you noticed that, wherever we go in Anatolia, we are greeted with smiles and flowers?"

I certainly had.

"That is because a hundred years ago when the *sipahis* were still march warriors, they took these lands from the Byzantines with a vow of equal justice for all people. Every member of the Sultan's flock, whatever his race, is entitled to Turkish justice. No looting or pillage is tolerated. Thus the empire has earned the loyalty of its subjects. And we can boast of bringing civil order to all the lands we conquer. Now ask yourself, is the loss of a hand or even a life not worth the price?"

That answer, Papa, told me that I must curb my habit of making judgments before I understand all the circumstances. And that some disappointments turn out for the best. Had I not been left behind from the hunt today, I would not have learned these things. But, that said, Papa, I beg you to reconsider your conditions just a fraction. I am not asking you to allow me to fight in a battle. Just to have a little fun with my horse and my *gerit*.

Your grateful and loving son,

D.

31

ESKİŞEHİR

From: Danilo del Medigo at Eskişehir
To: Judah del Medigo at Topkapi Palace
Date: June 25, 1534

Dear Papa:

Thank you from my heart for the timely arrival of your Plutarch manuscript. The moment I looked into the manuscript, I knew where my mother got her tale of Alexander's foot race around Achilles' tomb. Needless to say, the Sultan still believes that the race was a dance. And who am I to spoil his pleasure?

I began reading to the Sultan from the Troy section of Plutarch's manuscript the day it arrived, and as you so cleverly foresaw our pursuit of the adventures of İskender has taken on a new life. This Plutarch really knows how to tell a story. The Sultan is lapping him up like cream.

By the way, I haven't yet told him that some of what I am now reading to him is not by Arrian but by Plutarch. Listening to him, the Sultan no longer falls asleep on me but urges me on to just one more page. Also, my task is easier as I am much more at home in Latin than I am in Greek.

I now spend every evening at the Sultan's side, reading to him. Once begun, it took no time to establish our routine. He is very methodical. Each morning, I am handed a list of selected events described in our traveling library and I am expected to appear at his tent after sundown prepared to translate any one of them. I now have my own groom — imagine! — who, while we are on the march, follows me in a small cart which carries our book depository. I need only suggest a manuscript, and a messenger is dispatched instantly to Istanbul to fetch it. Only one proviso: the book must relate in some way to Alexander the Great, whom I am slowly learning to call İskender.

Some nights after I have finished my reading, the Sultan talks to me often about İskender, who visits him in dreams. He sees many parallels between İskender and himself, and so do I. Both became great kings at a very young age. Both set out to conquer the all-powerful Persian Empire. Both have a deep attachment to a boon companion. Plutarch says that Alexander went wild with grief when Hephaestion died. When I related this I saw tears in the Sultan's eyes. Although he has never spoken the name Ibrahim to me, I sense that he thinks often of his boyhood companion, now his Grand Vizier and boon companion. Here in the camp, the pages tease me that, as I have taken Ibrahim's place as the nightly reader, I will soon take his place in the royal bed. This is jealousy talking. How could I, a mere boy with little to recommend me other than my meager skills as a translator, even begin to replace the Sultan's closest advisor and oldest friend? The idea is laughable.

To me, the explanation of my current preferment is simple. The Sultan deeply misses his friend and confidante, likely the only being in the world besides his mother whom he can trust absolutely. Lucky for me, I come to him with the mark of trustworthiness stamped on me by you, dear Papa, who has served this Sultan so well and so discreetly.

It helps, I think, that I am a Jew. The Sultan's people worship him like a god, but they do not understand him. We Jews are not slaves as are those of his pages who are educated in the seraglio. People of our race have a long history of honorable dealings with the Ottomans—Jewish merchants as well as Jewish doctors.

Just when I thought I had failed completely, you rescued me with Plutarch. I am in your debt, but I am also pressed for time.

My gratitude and my love to you,
D.

———

From: Sultana Hürrem at Topkapi Palace
To: Suleiman the Great en route, received at Eskişehir
Date: June 23, 1534

My Beloved Sultan:

I ask you, I beg you—send news very quickly that all is well with you. Because I have received no letters from you—I swear it—since your departure more than ten days ago. Do not think that it is on my own account that I am begging for words of your progress through Anatolia. The whole world is clamoring for news.

All here are in good health, albeit worn with worry. Just a few words in your hand would ease our pain and bring joy to all.

Your son, Mehmet, your daughters, Mihrimah and Saida, and the princes, Selim and Abdullah, send you many greetings and rub their faces in the dust at your feet.

Signed in her own hand,
The Sultana Hürrem
(Unsealed and resealed for enclosure in the courier's pouch.)

At the bottom of this letter is an encrypted message. A quick pass over the page with a lighted taper reveals the words:

Longing and pain would be eased to hear that the magic messages survive the miles.

—

From: Sultan Suleiman encamped at Eskişehir
To: Sultana Hürrem at Topkapi Palace
Date: June 26, 1534

Not for all the world would I cause you to shed a single tear. Steps have been taken to hasten the courier's speed in the future.

This poem is a token of my apology to ease your heart's pain, composed in a dark night of longing:

I am the Sultan of Love.
A glass of wine will do for a crown on my head
and the brigade of my sighs might well serve
as the dragon's fire-breathing troops.

The bedroom that is best for you, my love, is a bed of roses.
For me, a bed and pillow carved out of rock will do.

The heart can no longer reach the district where you live
but it yearns for reunion with you.

Signed by Suleiman with his pen name, Muhabbi, the Sultan of Love.

At the bottom of this letter is an encrypted message. A quick pass over the page with a lighted taper reveals the words:
The taper lights the way over the miles, brightening the days of Sultan and page. Write on!

32

KÜTAHYA

From: Danilo del Medigo at Kütahya
To: Judah del Medigo at Topkapi Palace
Date: June 30, 1534

Honored Papa:

The Sultan turns out to be just as much a victim of women's whims as any other man. A tear-stained letter crying over the length of time it takes for his letters to reach his Sultana is all it took to raise his ire.

Let me tell you how this happened. After some days of riding—it is hard to keep track—a courier met us at the town of Kütahya bearing a letter in his pouch that sent the Sultan into a fit of rage. I recognized the identity of the sender, actually smelled it, before I even saw it. Sultana Hürrem doses her correspondence with a powerful tincture that perfumes the entire room when it emerges from its wrapping.

This time, whatever she had to report made him furious. Probably you can still remember that cold, piercing stare of his, the one that threatens to freeze you in your tracks. Believe me, Papa, even the fearless Janissaries were shaking in their boots when they came to get me. And all because of a delayed mail delivery. By the time I was called in, the Sultan's face had assumed its normal pallor. But the fearless Janissaries were still trembling.

In an effort to be of help, I offered my assistance in speeding up the courier service. So now I am not only the Assistant Foreign Language Interpreter, I am also Page of the Pouch, Keeper of Sultan's Correspondence, and a full member of the Fourth *Oda*.

My duties require me to operate a one-man express post to and from the closest courier stop. Normally the Sultan waits for the courier to arrive at our camp to dispatch his letters, given that our caravan proceeds at the pace of a snail. But a fast gallop from our camp to the next courier stop will give the Sultan's personal mail a good day's lead on its way to the capital over any mail that dawdled along with him personally. It also provides me with the daily gallop that I so missed when I was being carted along the route with my library like an old man. No offense, Papa.

Starting the day after my appointment, I collected a letter the Sultan had written in his own hand the morning before we left camp and carried it *veloce, veloce* to the next stop for the courier to take to the capital.

My orders were to seek out a waiting courier bearing mail from the other direction and to exchange pouches with him. I am also given keys to both pouches with instructions to open the arriving pouch and sort the mail into two piles: official and personal. The official pack I am to pass on to the Chief Clerk when I arrive back at the camp. But first I must be sure to bring the Sultan's personal mail to him the very moment he dismounts from the day's march. So far, that completes the duty roster of the Page of the Pouch. But I am happy to report that my new title has already gained me the respect of the Fourth *Oda*. They now call me Pouch instead of Jew.

And here is a list of the gifts received when I was elevated to the Fourth *Oda*.

- An embroidered caftan lined with miniver
- A silver inkstand set with jewels

- A tambourine studded with five rubies
- A sable *kalpak* hat to keep my ears warm in Kurdistan, if we ever get there.

Another happy result. Being the Page of the Pouch, I can send off my letters to you in the Sultan's bundle without asking anybody's permission. And, as a kind of bonus, my daily rides through the olive plantations and the fig orchards are leading me along the very path that Alexander took on his famous ride through Anatolia to face the Persians.

My current routine is the rough equivalent of riding a twenty-mile race every day before my evening readings. They clock me and record me daily. And when I exceed my own record, the Sultan himself congratulates me. But do not fear that my success as the Pouch Page has given me a swelled head. I am aware that neither my excellent work nor my innate virtue has won me this unheard-of advancement. I just happen to be the fastest rider in the *oda*. I know you would have preferred for me to make my mark through scholarship rather than horsemanship. But, Papa, is it not better to become a somebody — no matter the means — than be a nobody?

Lest you be concerned that I might be in danger from the bloodthirsty villains who run roughshod over the Anatolian steppes, worry not. The Sultan is a man of his word and I do not carry a weapon. But I am accompanied by an armed guard of terrifying ferocity. Remember, I am carrying the Imperial Pouch.

Also let me assure you that you will keep hearing from me regularly as I promised. Maybe not every single week, but certainly every time we stay in one place for more than one night. Our next long stopover is Konya. I am told it is the holiest place in Turkey. Not much chance of getting into trouble and plenty of time to write letters.

Until then, you are in my prayers.

Your affectionate son,
Danilo

33

AFYON

From: Sultana Hürrem at Topkapi Palace
To: Suleiman the Great en route, received at Afyon
Date: July 5, 1534

My Sultan,

When your letter via the speedy new courier was read aloud
by your esteemed daughter, the Princess Saida, it brought tears
to all.

We have, in the princess, a treasure. Ever modest, she blushes
as she writes my words. How sad that the Lady Hafsa, who
imbued her granddaughter with such an array of virtues, will
not be with us to dance at her wedding—soon to come, God
willing. Again, the princess blushes, my lovely, modest daughter.

Each week, I lay aside for her the finest silks from Bursa and
the best linens that I am able to unearth with the help of my
bundle-woman, so that when you return, all will be in readiness to announce her wedding. This wedding, soon to come,
would have been the crowning moment of the Valide's guard-
ianship of her fortune-favored granddaughter. Now the time

has almost passed for the girl to become the woman she was meant to be.

As she writes these words the reluctant virgin flushes with embarrassment. But I insist that it is not fitting for her to live alone in her grandmother's quarters with no one for company other than the women of the harem, the fat slave she inherited from her grandmother, and her horse. Her respect for her grandmother's memory is admirable, but I believe that the beloved Valide—God rest her soul—would agree with me that it is not proper for a young girl to be locked up in the Old Palace with a full suite of attendants like a married woman. And at the end of each day, when her servant arrives to take her home, I think of the gloom of her solitary life with no family to turn to for comfort or guidance, no games or amusements, only the books piled up by her bedside.

It is literally true that her closest companion is her horse, which, I am told, she visits every day to feed and talk to. Surely it is time for her to take her place with her brothers and sister, and prepare herself to marry the *damat* of her father's choice.

I worry about her. She waves away my concerns, but as I have made clear to her, I fear that she may become one of those maidens who develops an abnormal attachment to their virginity if they do not marry at an early age.

So far I have not persuaded her to abandon her grandmother's cold and lonely apartments and move in with us at Topkapi Palace, where she will find warmth, welcome, companionship, and a garden of delight.

She dutifully records my words with her pen, but I can tell that they do not reach into her heart. Not yet. But perhaps with time. Let us pray.

May God protect you, my Sultan; may you undertake many *jihads*, capture many lands, conquer the seven seas, and come home safe.

Signed and stamped with the Regent's seal by Sultana Hürrem.

At the bottom of this letter is an encrypted message. A quick pass over the page with a lighted taper reveals the words:

For some, Topkapi Palace is a garden of delights. For others, it is a golden cage in which one serves a life sentence with no prospect of escape.

34

KONYA

From: Danilo del Medigo at Konya
To: Judah del Medigo at Topkapi Palace
Date: July 20, 1534

Dear Papa:

You must come to Konya if only to see the most amazing little tower ever. I came upon it quite unexpectedly just as we rounded the bend on the road from the north. And honestly, Papa, it all but knocked me off my horse.

At first what I saw was just a splash of color in the sky. As we drew closer into the town, it took the form of a dome set on a round base and tucked into the skyline like a faceted jewel. I say jewel because the entire structure is clad from top to bottom in tiles of a single color, a light bluish-green, fresher than the waters of the Adriatic and softer than the vault of heaven. These tiles must be the finest things that Iznik has ever produced.

On the approach to Konya, this gorgeous little thing acts upon the traveler as do the minarets of Hagia Sofia in Istanbul, beckoning him ever closer into the center of the town. And when our caravan stopped at the tower to pay homage, I recognized it to be a tomb. Close up I could see that the entire structure is divided into sixteen lobes that come together at the apex like the sections of an orange. The base and the dome are divided from each other by a band of calligraphy that spells out (I have since learned), *In the name of Allah, the compassionate and the meaningful.* As I recall, this is the phrase that begins each book of the Koran. I am told that this dome rises directly over the shrine of Jalal al-din Rumi, the Sufi mystic whom the Ottomans call the Mevlana.

Konya is indeed a pious town. A man can get beaten up here for smoking in the street! I shudder to think what they do to women who displease them. The place is full of pilgrims come to pay homage to the Mevlana. In spite of your repeated counsel against making hasty judgments, I quickly leapt to the conclusion that I was in for three boring and friendless days while my fellow pages devoted themselves to their Sufi rituals.

Until this week, I had barely heard of this Rumi. Then, the night before we reached Konya, as I was taking leave of the Sultan, he inquired if I had read any of the Mevlana's poems. And when I replied no, he went rummaging into a trunk for a small volume that he pressed into my hand.

"These are a few of the many poems left to us by Rumi. He lived and preached and wrote in Konya three centuries ago and is buried here. He is what a Christian might call the patron saint of our family," he told me.

That is when I found out that the little turquoise tower I fell in love with was this Rumi's shrine.

"Please understand that this is not in any way an attempt to convert you," the Sultan continued. "I have too much respect for your father's wishes to do that. But I thought you might enjoy the poetry."

Well, Papa, you know how it is with poetry and me. When I was forced to commit the Sultan's own poems to memory in the School for Pages, it was like swallowing mouthfuls of aloes. Of course I accepted the book graciously and thanked him profusely. And I thought that would be the end for me of Rumi's poetry.

But the next day, after walking my feet off among the monuments of Konya, I found myself leafing idly through the pages of the little book the Sultan had given me. And the occasional phrase did catch my eye. Then, partly in the Sultan's honor and partly because I had had a bellyful of Arrian, I wandered over to Rumi's tomb.

You know me, Papa. The combination of mystical poetry and Koranic quotations is not exactly my idea of a good time. Needless to say, I was hardly in a worshipful state of mind as I stood at the entrance to Rumi's tomb. Of course, I was careful to stop at the fountain in the courtyard to wash my hands and feet. And I did leave my boots at the door. Wouldn't want to get stoned to death.

The first thing to strike my eye was the inscription of four lines on the wall of the antechamber:

Come, come, whoever you are,
Whether you be fire worshipers, idolaters or pagans.
Ours is not a dwelling place of despair.
All who enter will receive a welcome here.

Is that not a remarkable message to put on a grave? I was taken enough with it to make a copy for you. And that is how the Sultan found me when he arrived to pray. Copying Rumi. It is hard to tell with him, but he must have been pleased because he invited me to accompany his party that evening to the *semahane*, where the Sufis were to perform a *sema* in his honor.

Ahmed Pasha tells me that the Ottomans have embraced the Sufis since they first converted to Islam and that the hall in which the *sema* ceremony took place was built by Suleiman's grandfather, Bayezid. Also, the fountain at which I had washed my feet was a gift from the Sultan's father, Selim the Grim. I guess that if I was going to wash my feet for anyone, I picked the right saint.

Of course, I had heard stories of the whirling dervishes of

Konya who make their observances by spinning around until they collapse into a trance. So that evening I fully expected to witness some kind of wild dance in which the Sufis whirl into a frenzy, then fall about foaming at the mouth. But it is not like that at all, Papa. The ceremony takes place on a circular platform surrounded by a balustrade in the shadow of the Mevlana's tomb. The Sufis enter quietly, all cloaked in black, their heads covered in high camel-colored hats. I am told that the cloak represents a tomb and the hat a tombstone, and everything that follows is also fraught with special meanings.

After passing twice before the Sultan with solemn reverence, the Sufis slowly shed their cloaks, revealing the long white skirts meant to symbolize shrouds that whirl slowly around them as they twirl. This garment marks their escape from the tomb and from all worldly cares. While this was happening, the Sultan remained standing, as did all of his party, with their hands folded over their stomachs.

Then came the music of the ney flute, a heart-rending wail that expresses a longing for the attainment of the Ultimate. It has to be the saddest instrument in the world. The Sufis say it is the sound of the reed longing for its home in the riverbed. I noticed that some members of our party were moved to tears by its melancholy.

Then came the Music of the Spheres, which transforms the dancers into heavenly bodies. It is all very stately. Very slow at first. As they turn, they repeat a chant in a whisper while the musicians sing a hymn. Then faster and faster they twirl. But in perfect control. At the end, the head of the order joins the dancers and twirls with them. Their purpose, they say, is to affect a union with God. And I swear, Papa, despite my deep-down reservations, I thought the leader was going to rise to heaven and fly away.

Tomorrow we take off for the north, and I resume my proper duties as Page of the Pouch. I will always thank you for giving me this chance to see the great world.

D.

From: Sultana Hürrem at Topkapi Palace
To: Sultan the Great en route, received at Konya
Date: July 17, 1534

My esteemed Sultan:

When you first named me as Regent in your absence I took it to
be an honorary post — greet visitors, sign documents, and the
like. Who knew that it would fall upon me to investigate each
candidate for the hand of our daughter? Or that this would
entail the compilation of several lengthy *curricula vitae*? Or that
this would be a task requiring skill and discretion beyond the
competence of my current staff?

I believe that the best place to recruit the talents I now
require would be among your eunuchs, pages, or clerks. I am
told that your Men in Black are well trained for just such tasks.
Is it possible that a pair of them could be spared to come to my
assistance in investigating these candidates? I leave the choice to
you, honored Sultan. Then what remains is for you, my lord, to
instruct your treasury officers to set up a line in my household
budget for this new security detail.

I await word of your approval and pray every day for the
strength to carry this unexpected load of responsibility.

Signed and sealed with the Regent's *tugra*.

At the bottom of this letter is an encrypted message. A quick
pass over the page with a lighted taper reveals the words:
*Three suitors came this week to look at the bride — one judge, one
admiral, and a high priest of the Ulema. All old. All grey. All fat.
Whichever the Sultan prefers will be his daughter's choice. Does it
matter?*

From: Sultan Suleiman encamped at Konya
To: Sultana Hürrem at Topkapi Palace
Date: July 22, 1534

How could I have known when I fell into the deep pools of your eyes that I would find in you such a helpmate? As of this day, my order to add two of my Men in Black to your staff is now an official part of your household budget. Would that I could lessen your burden, but sadly there is no one else in the world in whom I can place my entire trust.

Duty calls and your poet, Muhabbi the lover, suffers. Since Rumi is a great comfort to me in these days of separation and loneliness, I hope his words will speak for me until time permits Muhabbi to make his own poems once more. Meanwhile here is a *ghazal* by Rumi translated for you by my Assistant Foreign Language Interpreter.

> *My worst habit is I get so tired of winter.*
> *I become a torture to those I'm with.*
>
> *If you are not here nothing grows.*
> *I lack clarity. My words*
> *tangle and knot up.*
>
> *How to cure bad water? Send it back to the river.*
> *How to cure bad habits? Send me back to you.*

Signed Muhabbi,
The Sultan of Love

At the bottom of this letter is an encrypted message. A quick pass over the page with a lighted taper reveals the words:
As the page's pen speaks for the poet, so the poet's pen speaks for the page.

35

EREĞLI

From: Sultana Hürrem at Topkapi Palace
To: Sultan Suleiman en route, received in Ereğli
Date: July 21, 1534

My Sultan,

You wrote me once that if I were able to read what you wrote, you would write at greater length of your longing for me. That time has at last arrived. Today, I have given our beloved Princess Saida notice that from now on I will undertake to deal with intimate or private matters in direct discourse with you, my beloved, without the intervention of a third person. Under the princess's tutoring I have learned the fine style, and due to her efforts I now feel confident to express myself to you without embarrassment. Of course, I will continue to call upon the princess in her official role as secretary to the Regent, but at least this lightens her burden. For years she has toiled to teach me, and now she will get her reward—whatever her heart desires as her gift from me on her wedding day. She need only name it and it is hers.

She blushes. But it is time she had some relief from her constant service to me and is free to step forward into her own life as a wife and mother.

It gives me great pleasure to report to you that the employment of my new security secretaries has succeeded beyond our expectations. The two Men in Black that you assigned me have come forth so speedily with such complete dossiers that I was able to cull my original list of candidates for Princess Saida's hand to one judge, one high priest of the *Ulema*, and one admiral, each with a record of long and loyal service to you. The final choice is, of course, yours, to be made public when you return (may Allah make that soon).

I take it as a sign of Allah's grace that I have discovered a second and not unimportant use for the candidate *damats'* documents. In the process of compiling their lifelong records, new details of their lives — both personal and financial — have come to light. We are now in possession of information that certain of the gifts bestowed by the Sultan, such as land, slaves, and palaces, which were earmarked to be returned to the Royal Treasury upon the death of the recipients, have mysteriously fallen into the hands of others — some of them family members — who will be under no obligation to return their gifts when the owner dies. Is there such a crime as financial treason? Yes or no, the knowledge of these concealed riches cannot but benefit your treasury. My new-found ability to wield my own pen has enabled me to convey this to you in strictest confidence.

Much credit for my new writing skill is due to our treasure, Princess Saida, who has worked tirelessly to keep me at my reading and writing lessons and has persevered when my own will to continue flagged. Poor Saida. First, she loses her mother; then she loses the grandmother who took the mother's place, a role that I have tried to play with incomplete success. Of course, she is always ready with expressions of gratitude for my efforts, but her heart remains cold. Perhaps I have leaned too heavily on her family obligations to the Ottoman dynasty. Perhaps I could have made a greater effort to emphasize the pleasures of womanhood—especially for a princess.

So I have arranged an outing—just the two princesses and myself—to visit palaces that are or might be for sale along the Bosphorus waterway. When I mentioned this to Vice Admiral Lofti—with whom I met yesterday to discuss his divorce—he came to my aid with an offer of one of his small crafts (including a crew) to ferry us along the Bosphorus in the summer breeze. When I spoke of this to little Princess Mihrimah, she flushed with excitement, even though she fully understands that none of these palaces can be hers until after her sister is married and established. But Princess Saida remained unmoved.

There is such a difference between the two princesses. Mihrimah dotes on every detail of her future life; Saida remains adrift in the past. She reads. She rides her horse. She prays. She attends to my needs faithfully by day, and at night I hear that she weeps. So different from her younger sister, who at the age of ten is already half a woman. Count on it. When the time comes for our daughter Mihrimah to marry, she will welcome it joyfully without the need of any encouragement from us. Even now she plays at selecting the names of her children and the number of her servants and slaves.

I do not expect Princess Saida to take on the details of the wedding feast such as the public ceremony, the games at the hippodrome, the bands of musicians who will play for the people dancing in the streets. Those are the proper concerns of the mother of the bride-to-be, not the bride herself. However, I admit I would like to see an occasional flash of interest, or nod of approval, or some sign of anticipation. It is quite clear to me that if we do not take charge, this lovely daughter of ours will go to her grave a spinster and never know the pleasure of marriage to a fine *damat* or the joy and pride of mothering royal children. This thought has been on my mind, but I have been unwilling to express it while dictating to the very person concerned, for fear of offending her delicate feelings.

There is something—and what that is, I have been unable

to discover—that has made this girl, by nature so accommodating, stiffen into rigid opposition on the matter of her marriage. If she were simply one of the harem girls, I would have sworn she had a secret lover. But the princess lives the life of a Christian nun. And try as I may, I seem not able to bring a smile to her face at the prospect of her happy future and the life for which she is destined.

So be prepared, my love! You may have to accompany a sad, pale wraith of a princess to her wedding ceremony. But I promise you, my adored and most revered husband, that together we will lead the sad princess to a happier state whether she is willing or not.

Signed and stamped in wax with the Regent's seal

Beneath her signature, an encrypted message:
The hot flame of true love can melt the wax that seals the message, but cannot alter what is written there.

—

From: Danilo del Medigo at Ereğli
To: Judah del Medigo at Topkapi Palace
Date: July 26, 1534

Dear Papa:

I thought Konya would be a rest stop for me. Instead, not since my days in the School for Pages have I been so occupied, morning to night. I am now a clerk—a copyist, if you like—who has spent his days in Konya hunched over his desk carefully copying the poems of Rumi, for the discerning eyes of the Sultana in Istanbul (who cannot read).

Ever since he found me copying Rumi's inscription, the Sultan assumes that I share his admiration—awe is a better word—for the Sufi mystic. So I have been chosen to make a selection of Rumi's poems, translated in perfect accuracy and penmanship, to send directly to the Lady Hürrem via the Sultan's courier. What does this portend? Think of it! Will I now spend this entire campaign as a clerk? On the other hand, I do write directly to the Lady Hürrem in Topkapi Palace. Although she herself cannot read my script, the Sultan assures me that her reader can and that the reader's standards are high. Never could I have guessed that the product of my pen would fall into reach of such exacting hands.

What makes this all such a mix-up is that, having banished me to this tedious task (for which I am so ill-suited), the Sultan feels that he has honored me with a place in the Society of Poets. Result? My horse is getting restive for the lack of exercise, and I long for the pleasures of the pouch.

D.

36

KAYSERI

From: Danilo del Medigo at Kayseri
To: Judah del Medigo at Topkapi Palace
Date: August 2, 1534

Dear Papa:

In the secret book she wrote for my benefit, Mama reminded
me that the hearts of the powerful are fickle and never to be
depended upon. And I recall many mentions of the whimsical
nature of her patroness, the Lady Isabella D'Este, flitting like a
hummingbird from one caprice to another.

But I wager, Papa, that the great Gonzaga lady has met her
capricious match in my master, the Sultan.

Since our stay in Konya, İskender the Great, the Heroic, the
Cherished, has completely lost his allure. He is, alas, forgotten.
Abandoned. These days we read only Rumi. And recite Rumi.
And discuss Rumi. And copy Rumi for the edification of the Sultana Hürrem in far-off Istanbul, who, it seems, has a longing for
his verses. Either that or she has developed an urgent need to
be inspired by having his mystic visions read to her from copies

made by . . . who else? Danilo del Medigo, formerly the Assistant Foreign Language Interpreter, now Danilo, the Clerk. Together with my little desk and my pens and my tablets and the library of manuscripts assembled to assist me in my scholarly struggles with bloody Arrian and bloody Plutarch, we have been stripped of all purpose. Alexander, no longer the Great, has been tossed onto the garbage heap like a worn-out cart horse. And the former Assistant Foreign Language Interpreter is employed as copier of texts—a clerk!

The sad joke is that after weeks of travel the Sultan's army is now following in the actual footsteps of Alexander as he made his way from the Mediterranean to the very town from which I write this letter—the town of Kayseri. After he secured the Mediterranean ports, Alexander passed this way heading north to Gordium. Now our boots are treading in his steps as we too head north. And this at the very moment the Sultan has lost all interest in him. Bad timing.

Remember the Gordian knot, Papa? I first learned of it seated in your lap. And I had been planning to lead the Sultan up to the top of the Gordian acropolis, where I hear say you can see the ancient wooden-wheeled cart in which old Gordium traveled from Macedonia to capture Anatolia. Not only the cart but also the remains of the leather knot that held the yoke to the shaft, the famous Gordian knot.

As we pass through the countryside, I have seen similar rigs on the road knotted yoke-to-shaft with a leather thong. But the Gordian knot was, they say, a knot of such extraordinary complexity that no one from earliest days to the time of Alexander had been able to untie it. Because of this, the knot carried a prophecy that whoever succeeded in finding the hidden ends and unraveling them would become ruler of all Asia.

To Alexander, that must have made the challenge irresistible. To me, it seemed like a tale made to order for the Sultan. Never one to grab onto a moment of high drama if he could avoid it, Arrian simply tells us that Alexander reached in and pulled out the pin that held the thing together. After centuries? Really? But

Curtius gave me a conclusion I recognized at once to be more to the Sultan's taste.

According to Curtius' version, Alexander began, as had hundreds of men before him, by studying the knot from every angle. Like them, he stood there for some minutes, baffled. There had to be a way. Suddenly, it came to him.

"Nobody said how it had to be untied," he was heard to mutter by those close to him. And, with that, he drew out his sword and hacked open the knot with his blade to reveal the ends of it deep inside. Voila!

So confident was I that this tale would delight the Sultan, I even undertook to make my own translation of the event from Quintus Curtius' *History of Alexander*. Sad to say, by the time my translation was done, the Sultan had no time for my scholarly efforts or for the Gordian excursion. From the moment of our arrival in Kayseri, he was deep into horse dealing with the merchants of the town, a hard-headed bunch known in these parts for sharp business practices. Kayseri has passed through many hands under various names since its early days as a Hittite capital. Romans, Persians, Byzantines, Mongols, Crusaders, and the dreaded Tamerlane have all laid their heavy hands on Kayseri, leaving it, Papa, a mess of dye works, tanneries, and slaughterhouses, and ringed by herds of sheep and water buffalo raised for the sausage and pastirma industries. The town is one long smoked-meat banquet. Also, they use the hides of these animals to make the most amazing yellow Morocco leather slippers. And I confess that I gave in to the lure of fashion and indulged myself in a purchase of the same.

No question, trade is the lifeblood of this town and stories abound. A favorite is the tale — told with relish by the locals — of the man who stole a donkey, painted it brown, and then sold it back to its owner. And Ahmed Pasha has reported to me the newest variation of this tale in which the merchant now abducts his mother, paints her up, and sells her back to his father.

You can still hear versions of this story being told over teacups in the stalls of the Kayseri bazaar, just as various tales of

İskender's miraculous splitting of the Gordian knot are spun into the smoke of bubble pipes in Gordium. What does that tell you about the people who have handed down these tales over generations? What kind of people would find getting the best in a horse trade a more compelling subject to preserve for their heirs than the conquest of Asia? And what does it tell you about those—like ourselves—who choose to make their way to Aleppo by way of Kayseri rather than Gordium? We did have a choice of route. It is not by accident that we find ourselves stuck here bargaining for horses and being treated no better than if we were cattle thieves. But I console myself with knowing that there will be wonderful sights to see in Syria, and I will have a chance to sail to Babylon on the most famous river in the world—the Euphrates. And, who knows? Perhaps İskender will rise like Lazarus from the Mesopotamian ashes once we get to Iraq. At least I am seeing the world. For which opportunity I thank you, Papa.

Your grateful son,
D.

⌒

From: Sultana Hürrem at Topkapi Palace
To: Sultan Suleiman en route, received at Kayseri
Date: July 28, 1534

My fortune-favored Sultan:

The Rumi poem that your translator sent to me fell upon me like rose petals from heaven. It was a joy multiplied by a hundred when my faithful reader, Princess Saida, sat with us to read out the words. But—and this may be a reflection on my own lack of education in poetics—I prefer your poems to his and I long for just a few lines in the hand.

My Sultan of Love, Muhabbi: I live out these long days of separation tortured by longing and racked by dreams of the perils that threaten my warrior husband; not least the knowledge, shared by all women, that the campaign trail is littered with evil women only too eager to offer their charms to lonely soldiers far from home. Women know that for men, loving memories begin to fade as with distance.

Having written that, I fear my demands for reassurance of your love have made me unworthy of the great honor you have bestowed on me by making me your Sultana. As Saida reminded me while scolding me for my tardiness at my language lessons, it is all very well for a *kadin* to weep and wail for an absent loved one, but a Sultana must bear up to her fears and loneliness as befits her elevated station.

My heart jumps in my bosom when I think of your return. Pray Allah, it be soon. If only I could fly to you across the heavens just for an hour as they do in *The Thousand and One Nights*. But I must take comfort in knowing that when the day of victory arrives, my small sacrifice will have been a part of the great effort to vanquish the Shiite heretics for the glory of the true Sunni faith.

My Sultan, your sons and daughters pray daily that Allah watches over you and protects you from all harm as you pursue your holy *jihad*.

Signed, stamped, and sealed by her Regent.

At the bottom of this letter is an encrypted message. A quick pass over the page with a lighted taper reveals the words:
Is it true of all soldiers far from home that loving memories begin to fade as the miles and months slip by?

37

SIVAS

From: Danilo del Medigo at Sivas
To: Judah del Medigo at Topkapi Palace
Date: August 9, 1534

Hi, ho, dear Papa:

We are rolling up Anatolia without a shot being fired. But the life of the *jihad* is a life of surprises, and we are not on our way to Syria as expected. Instead we are riding north to join up with the Grand Vizier's forces at Tabriz.

This decision to detour north through Azerbaijan was handed down to us without expectation two days ago by the Sultan. But who am I to complain? Even though we seem to be headed in the wrong direction to reach our eventual destination (unless that objective has also been changed while I slept), we are bound to see the two great rivers of antiquity someday soon since Baghdad lies between them.

There is a rumor circulating in our camp that the reason for this change of route is a quarrel that has broken out in Tabriz between the Grand Vizier Ibrahim and his Janissary brigade, which necessitates the intervention of the Sultan. It is whispered that the Janissaries attached to the Grand Vizier's forces are on the verge of overturning their kettles. The fact is the Grand Vizier's half of the army has not seen their Padishah for many months, and many will be refusing to march into Persia without their true *ghazi* leader. Since Ibrahim Pasha is not well liked, one must take this tale with a grain of salt.

Others have a different explanation for the change of route. They say that the season is now too advanced for river travel and that currents of the Tigris are now too treacherous for barge transport. Mind you, this new alternate route to Baghdad, via Azerbaijan and across the Zagros Mountains, is reputedly perilous in its own way. But that is the route we are about to take if we proceed by way of Tabriz.

Whatever the reason for it, I tell you that this change in our route of march is mightily vexing to the Sultan. Tonight, just as I started my reading of Rumi, a messenger arrived all red-faced and sweaty with a packet from the Grand Vizier at Tabriz. I recognized his seal. The Sultan did not appear delighted with the contents of the package. He spent some time shuffling through the papers in the packet, shaking his head and muttering. Then suddenly he hurled the entire package across the tent with a mighty thrust, and we were enveloped in a storm of paper.

Of course, a group of pages materialized instantly to clean up the mess. The boys are still picking up sheets of paper as I write. Perhaps they are accustomed to these outbursts, but I have been at this man's side day and night for two months now and have never seen him like this. When one of the pages offered him a sip of sherbet to settle him down, he bashed the cup out of the fellow's hand with such force he all but knocked him down. At that moment, Papa, I wished you had been there to administer your calming-down medicine. But all I could do was to cower in a corner in the hope of dodging flying objects. And, to be sure, as the minutes ticked by, the Sultan ceased to shake and mutter and finally began to read aloud from one of the dispatches—to me, of all people.

"The contract to deliver two thousand desert camels to the Ottoman high command at Aleppo has been voided," he read and sighed. "Attached is a new contract for two thousand mountain camels to be delivered at Tabriz." Then, without taking a breath, he waggled his finger under my nose and demanded, "Do you know how far a camel can travel in a day?"

He did not expect an answer and I did not give one.

"Twenty-five miles on average in good weather," he said. "Do you know how many miles it is across the Syrian Desert to Mesopotamia from where we now stand?"

I shook my head no.

"Four hundred miles," he answered his own question. "And how many miles do you suppose my army must march to join the Grand Vizier's forces at Tabriz in order to approach Baghdad from the east by way of Persia instead of Syria?" He paused a moment for effect. "Five hundred miles. Which amounts to an additional four days' march," he advised me. "And can you guess how much it costs to rent just one camel for a single day of march?"

"No, sir," I managed to answer.

"Of course you can't. It is not your business to know. Nor is it mine. I have advisors for that. And they advise me the extra hundred miles will cost my treasury one hundred silver rupees per load in the local currency. But that is a mere drop in the ocean of expense that this new plan will cost." A deep sigh at the prospect and a dismal shake of the turban.

For a brief moment, I thought he might weep. But he is not the Sultan for nothing. Instead, he took a deep breath, seated himself cross-legged and straight-backed on his cushions, and began what seemed like a new subject.

"These Europeans know nothing of war. Nothing." It was not an accusation, simply a statement somehow connected with the cost of camels. "They call my empire the Gunpowder Empire. Because my revered ancestor, Mehmet the Conqueror, managed to bring Constantinople to its knees with a cannonade, they take the view that all we know how to do is blow things up. The truth is, we were not the inventors of gunpowder. The Chinese were the first to use it. But it was my ancestors who divined that the mixture of sulfur, carbon, and saltpeter could be put to a more useful purpose than making fireworks for festivals. Such as blowing holes in city walls. Even so, it takes more than an explosion to win a war. And let me tell you, boy, gunpowder is a most unreliable weapon. If you allow it to get wet—even damp—it won't light. And how are you supposed to keep it dry when you're carrying it over rivers on barges? Answer me that."

I thought it best to keep my thoughts to myself.

"Besides," he went on, "even if, with luck and good weather, you manage to keep your powder dry, field guns can shoot a maximum distance of only three hundred yards, and at that distance they can barely hit a barn. Compared to an arrow, gunpowder is a crude weapon. Don't talk to me about gunpowder."

Not that I would have dared. There seem to be a hundred ways in which gunpowder has disappointed the Sultan personally.

"If gunpowder were the only weapon in our arsenal, do you think we would now be masters in Tunis? Or Egypt?" He was on his feet now, pacing. "Or Hungary? Even here in Anatolia? Gunpowder served us well at Rhodes. But compared to a piece of paper"— he reached down for one of the dispatches and held it up — "yes, believe me, compared to this piece of paper and thousands more like it, gunpowder is no more than a secondary stand of arms. Here in my hand"—he was coming close now and waving the piece of paper under my nose—"here is the great secret of Ottoman warfare that the Europeans keep sending their spies to ferret out. Paper, my son. Yet another weapon we got from the Chinese. All credit to them for that. But it was not the Chinese who taught the world how to make paper a weapon of war. No, it was my people, the first Osman tribe, the ones Europeans call 'barbarians,' who thought to use paper to keep written records of distances, troop counts, food supplies, and baggage limits. And it is paper that enables us to plan an attack long before a *jihad* begins. That and having Allah on our side"—long pause—"which the Europeans call 'Ottoman luck.'"

I found his words very persuasive and could not wait to get back to my desk to write them down before I forgot them. It isn't every day you get a private tutorial in military strategy from the conqueror of half the world. But before I could rise to my feet, he took up his peroration again.

Would I like to know, he asked, what he would choose as his second most valuable weapon after paper? This time he didn't even pretend to wait for my reply.

"Weather," he announced. "Weather, my son. If I were the god of thunder, I could devise a strategy to win any war."

The god of thunder? Had I heard right?

"Take this war we are now engaged in," he went on. "We must be careful not to arrive in Mesopotamia in the summer months because the heat limits our travel time to four hours out of every twenty-four. Beyond that limit, pack horses faint from the heat and die. So much for summer. On the other hand, the mudslides and avalanches of winter can wipe out an entire army overnight. So we must plan our arrival in Mesopotamia to avoid the Zagros Mountains in winter. Any delay is perilous. Do you begin to grasp the problem, my son?"

No mistaking it, he had called me "my son." Twice!

"Weather is always the weakest link in any strategy," he went on. "But, alas, I am not the god of thunder and weather is not under my control. So I must do my best with firepower and paper and pray to Allah to bend the weather to my purposes."

Whereupon he uttered a brief *inshallah* and I began, once again, to rise to my feet. And once again he motioned me to stay.

Lucky for me he does apparently suffer hunger and thirst like ordinary humans. So, with a snap of his fingers, sherbet was brought in solid gold canteens encrusted with emeralds and rubies, and there was no talk of war for at least ten minutes while we refreshed ourselves royally. Then he waved the beakers aside and took his place on the pillows like a professor at his lectern. And, as he began again, it occurred to me that somewhere on the road from Kayseri, I had been reassigned to a new role. No longer the Interpreter or the Page of the Pouch or Rumi's scribe, I was now the Acolyte with the Sultan for my Mentor.

"You see my son," — this was the third time he called me "my son" — "as long as we are within our own empire, we can store foodstuffs in silos along the way. But after we enter Persian territory we can no longer depend on the goodwill of the people and their willingness to sell us what we need. The Kurds shift their allegiance between the Persians and us, depending on who is the most persuasive — with gun or with gold. And should the Persians outbid us for their services, the Kurds are highly experienced at burning everything they cannot carry and fading away into the mountains with their animals. So, you see, we must take with us everything we need in order to mount an offensive against Baghdad. Not only gunpowder, weapons, and siege machines, but food for the men and silage for the animals, metal for horseshoes, leather for boots — everything right down to the little seats between the camels' bumps. Else we perish."

It was a grim picture. But the drearier the forecast became, the less melancholy the Sultan became. He even managed half a smile for the little seats between the camel bumps. Then he went rooting around among his papers with what can only be described as renewed vigor. And to be sure he found the exact dispatch he was looking for and pounced on it.

"I hold here in my hand" — with a triumphant wave of the document — "a bill for hauling only four supply categories, not including grain, from Hamedan to Baghdad by camel. Once we cross into Persian territory (*inshallah*) we will need four thousand camels to supply the arsenal. Plus five thousand for my own larder. Plus two thousand for the necessaries of the Janissaries. More than eleven thousand camels in all. And let me tell you those camels are needful creatures. Everything must be made to order for them, even the saddle blankets. It costs fourteen hundred *akces* just to equip one of the beasts. Now add the purchase or rental of the horses and donkeys and the water buffalo that carry the heavy guns, and you can see what this change of plan is going to cost. And I am supposed to sign these orders" — waving his ringed hand across the sea of paper he had drowned us in — "and find the money for all of this."

With a doleful shake of the head, he motioned me to my feet. The lesson was over. And I began to back out of the royal presence in the obligatory way.

Next thing I knew, I felt the touch of his hand on my shoulder. Now, one of the first things I learned at the School for Pages was that the Sultan touches no one and no one touches the Sultan. Yet there I was standing in the middle of his tent with someone's hand on my shoulder, and with only the two of us present, it could not have been any hand but his. While I was debating with myself whether or not to raise my eyes and discover if I was dreaming, he spoke:

"When I was your age my father read to me a quote from our ancestor the great Ghengis Khan. Do you wish me to pass it on to you?"

Of course I did. And these are the words he quoted (to the best of my memory): *"After us the descendants of our clan will wear gold-embroidered garments, eat rich and sweet food, ride fine horses, and embrace beautiful women. But they will not say that they owe it all to their Chinese forefathers and to us, their fathers. They will forget us and our great times."*

I believe, Papa, that I saw a trace of mist in his eyes before he spoke again.

"This has been a long evening for you, my son." Again! "Not what you expected when you signed on for this campaign. Without a military role to play and now deprived of your interpretive duties, you appear to have no avenue of expression for your youthful ardor. I myself have often found refuge in poetry at such times. And, observing the sympathetic way you have responded to the poems of the Mevlana, I believe that I have found an outlet for your poetic soul."

My poetic soul! Lucky for me, I hadn't raised my eyes. Otherwise, he surely would have read on my face my horror at this total misreading of my true nature.

Well, Papa, I have got my ardent wish for some role to play

beyond that of a mere clerk, and, as you so wisely foretold, it has turned around and bit me in the ass.

Good night,
D.

———

From: Sultana Hürrem at Topkapi Palace
To: Sultan Suleiman en route, received at Sivas
Date: August 3, 1534

My fortune-favored Sultan:

It is acknowledged by all that generosity of spirit is one of your great virtues, my Sultan. But sadly not all hearts are as noble as yours. For my poor sake, whose whole life is only you, and for the sake of your children, who kiss the hem of your garment, be sparing with your trust. A royal court can all too easily become a nest of envious vipers. Sadly, I must remind you that your trusted viziers in council have been the source of assassination plots in the past. We must all be vigilant on your behalf and take care to surround ourselves only with those who love us most, our dear ones.

As a loving father, you want your daughter to be happy, as do we all. But as a royal family, we must continue to add new members who add strength to our house. A royal wedding is a God-given opportunity to create a new *damat*, a son-in-law of proven loyalty to sit as a vizier on your council. I have met separately with each of the candidates on our short list of husbands for Princess Saida. And I am now able to assure you that each one—the judge, the priest, and the admiral—would be only too willing to divest himself of any current domestic encumbrances in accordance with custom, and would welcome the handsome dowry that Princess Saida will bring with her and the gift of a suitable palace yet to be selected and equipped, a task I will be pleased to accomplish.

My own favorite choice would be Admiral Lofti. He has already proven himself in the Mediterranean theater. You may prefer the judge. The choice is, of course, yours. But allow me to point out that royal weddings are not created in a day. Even now, it is almost too late to plan a wedding to take place on your return. Everywhere I turn I am unable to proceed further until I can consult with the chosen *damat*, which I cannot do until a *damat* is named by you personally. Meanwhile, the days tick by and I am at a loss to begin the impossible task of making countless arrangements with a non-existent future *damat*. On my knees I beg you, Magnificent One, to take time out of your careworn life to consider the following suggestion:

What if you were to designate Admiral Lofti informally through me and then simply make the choice official the day you arrive home safely, God willing? That would enable me to put into motion the legal and financial agreements that precede any important wedding contract. You cannot know the eagerness with which I look forward to welcoming a new son-in-law into our family circle, who may start to assume some of the onerous responsibilities that weigh so heavily on you and, in your absence, on me.

I beg you, my fortune-favored Sultan, do not withhold your favor from Admiral Lofti, for the sake of your beautiful daughter, for your own sake, and for that of the Ottoman dynasty. I beg you to bestow your informal blessing on him at once as *damat* for Princess Saida. I have spoken to him on your behalf. He is your slave. Our citizens have dug deep into their coffers to support this war and, what is more, have suffered many long months of your absence without a word of complaint. Would it not be a just reward to invite them to share in your happiness at the wedding of your beloved daughter to a man of your own choosing on the day of your return?

I long for your victorious return. I pray for your safety. May Allah watch over you. I am out of ink and out of tears.

Signed and sealed with the Regent's seal.

At the bottom of the page, visible only by the heat of a taper, is written:

Today the jewelers came to estimate the quantity of pearls needed to decorate the wedding train of a princess. How many pearls does it take to embroider a shroud?

—

From: Sultan Suleiman, encamped at Sivas
To: Sultana Hürrem at Topkapi Palace
Date: August 9, 1534

Your keen eye and motherly concern have brought to mind a recollection of Princess Saida's sweet smile, which we have hardly seen in the months since she lost her beloved grandmother. Like you I would welcome the sight of a touch of color in her pale cheeks and sparkle in her sad eyes. My daughter's happiness is close to my heart, and I will be the most joyful of men to dance at her wedding.

Your efforts to bring that happy day closer are one of the many generous gestures from your capacious heart that I treasure. Not even a Sultan can always rely on such constant devotion. Your choice is my choice. I will forward an informal letter to be shown to Admiral Lofti, this document to be shared only with the necessary few.

My daughter is blessed to have her future happiness resting in such loving and capable hands as yours.

Signed,
The Sultan

At the bottom of the page, visible only by the heat of a taper, is written:

When mortals make plans, the gods laugh. Wars alter destinies. New ties are formed on the campaign trail. New bonds are forged. Forbidden pathways open wide. What has seemed impossible becomes possible.

38

ALEPPO

From: His Special Envoy, Jean de la Foret at Aleppo
To: H.M. Francis the First, King of France at Blois
Date: September 15, 1534

Majesty:

Does your Majesty wonder at the source of this letter? No more than I do at being here in Syria and still out of reach of the Sultan. I can think of no word to describe the wild chase we are embarked on other than comedy.

As I reported from Constantinople (which the Ottomans have renamed Istanbul), we arrived there for the prearranged conference with the Sultan only to find that he had departed for Mesopotamia some weeks earlier. But we were assured that we could catch up with him at Aleppo if we took the sea route to Syria. We had no choice if we were to succeed in our mission to negotiate a trade agreement. But whatever issue we might take with their attitude, be it said for the Ottomans that they did find a berth for us on one of their ships bound for Antioch and provided us with a squad of Janissaries to protect us on the land portion to follow.

The sea voyage from Istanbul went quite without incident. These Ottomans have indeed turned the Mediterranean into a Turkish lake. They own it and they know it. When they passed us on their flotillas, they waved at us gaily like hosts at a garden party.

But that illusion was shattered abruptly when we arrived at Aleppo to find no Sultan. We are now advised that, as I write, the Sultan has shifted his route and is marching north to join the Grand Vizier in Azerbaijan. We are now informed that the Padishah will be pleased to audience us not at Aleppo but at Tabriz.

We have been offered a complicated explanation for this change of route—something to do with an unseasonable current of ferocious strength in the Tigress River that would have imperiled the animals and heavy guns. Surely the engineers must have considered conditions on the Tigress before abandoning the Syrian route. One suspects that we are not being told the whole story. One suspects it may have to do with events in Tabriz. According to my informant, who has returned to us this week from a reconnaissance mission to Azerbaijan, the Grand Vizier has had two months to establish a court and seems to have used it to position himself as a kind of surrogate king. Although the capture of Tabriz may have been brought to your ears as a great triumph, it must be admitted that the victory was considerably facilitated when the Great King of Persia took to his heels and fled eastward after he learned that the Ottoman army was approaching. So Ibrahim Pasha actually walked unimpeded into an untouched town and a fully functioning palace complete with furnishings. My informant tells me that the Persians didn't even have time to douse the cooking fires.

Mind you, no one can deny the Grand Vizier's talent for organization. Think of how he set up the Ottoman administration of Egypt in the twenties—still functioning ten years later—laws, protocols, positions, appointments all in place within three months of his defeat of the Mamluks. Ibrahim Pasha is not likable, nor trustworthy—after all, he is a Greek so is naturally two-faced by birth and ambitious by inclination—but he does know how to get things done. Now he has apparently set himself up like a king in the palace that Tahmasp abandoned, and has taken up the Persian habit of accepting the full body bow as his right. He has also begun to sign his edicts as *Saskehier*, which in the Turkish tongue means king.

What will Suleiman make of all this when he arrives in Tabriz? He was well satisfied with Ibrahim's generalship of the Egyptian conquest. But Azerbaijan is not Egypt. The Mamluk rulers of Egypt were usurpers who created and left behind them new instruments of governance. When Ibrahim Pasha conquered Egypt, he had only to change their official *tugra* to the Ottoman ensign and carry on as a foreign master. But the capital that Tahmasp left behind at Tabriz is a city with a long history of service to the Shah of Persia. And thence are we now bound. Somehow what began as a diplomatic mission has turned into a child's game of tag, in which the Ottomans chase after the Great King of Persia and we chase after the Ottomans with the local Bedouins snapping like puppies at our heels.

Be assured, Majesty, you will be advised of what lies ahead for us immediately upon our safe arrival in Azerbaijan.
May God be with us, and with you, sire.

Your servant,
Jean de la Foret

39

ERZURUM

From: Danilo del Medigo at Erzurum
To: Judah del Medigo at Topkapi Palace
Date: September 9, 1534

Dear Papa:

After a hellish two-week march across the last of the Anatolian plateau, we arrived at Erzurum with just one day to prepare for the arrival of Uzun Hazan the Tall, Bey of the Akroyun tribe of Turkomen, who have come to join us in the campaign against the Persian king. Along the way we have been collecting small parties of *subashis*, who are merely the captains of towns who come with troops when called. But this *bey* is chief of an entire tribe of Turkomen, which makes him a distant relative to the Osman tribe as both go back to their origins on the steppes of Central Asia.

Being a governor, Uzun brings with him a full complement of staff—treasurers and bookkeepers, clerks and cooks, grooms and musicians and armorers—as well as fighting men. There have to be a thousand of them at the very least, all dressed in their finest as if they had come not to a war but to a party. We, on the other hand, have had only one day to wash the Anatolian dust out of our hair, not to mention our fingernails and our ears.

Starting early this morning, the barbers' lines have stretched out past the perimeter of the camp and the washerwomen's tubs even farther. So my day was spent getting cleaned up for the Turkomen.

More to come.

Love,
D.

⸺

From: Danilo del Medigo at Erzurum
To: Judah del Medigo at Topkapi Palace
Date: September 10, 1534

Dear Papa:

What a day! All morning long the heralds raced around the camp blowing their horns and announcing a gathering at eventide to make Uzun Hassan and his tribe official members of the Sultan's expedition.

Here is the scene: A vast tent at the citadel large enough to cover a thousand people should it happen to rain, which it did not. Uzun the Tall appears, sumptuously bejeweled, his musicians trumpeting his way loudly. Next, a rousing chorus of welcome from the Sultan's marching band, more numerous than the Emir's and thus even louder. Now the entrance of the Janissaries, shambling as usual but still imposing, the enormous plumes of bird of paradise feathers that sprout out of their white caps and fall in a curve down their backs almost to their knees.

Next to enter, the members of the *divan*, every clerk, imam, lawyer, and pasha. The chamberlains stand out in scarlet, the priests in purple, and the judges in their green turbans. Finally, the Sultan presents himself in red velvet and furs, and manages to outshine the emir's copious jewels with one careless spray of diamonds pinned to his turban.

As always, the Sultan commands total silence. With a wave of his hand, he beckons the Turkomen to approach his dais, and one by one they walk slowly, eyes lowered, toward his throne where each receives a purse of coins and an embroidered caftan, then backs his way out of the Sultan's presence smoothly. (Clearly, these marauders have learned something about decorum since their early days as wild march warriors.) This is a long procedure, and by the end everyone is very hungry.

The feast begins. I cannot count the number of courses. And I cannot imagine how the cooks concocted all of them in the course of one day. Easy enough with common fare such as millet, gruel, and macaroni, but think of what it takes to conjure up a meal of horse and sheep meat boiled up in *kumis*, fermented mare's milk, with the resource of only a crude field kitchen. How did they do it? And where have they been hiding the buffoons and the dwarfs and the jugglers who popped out between the courses, whom I had never seen before on this long march? It was as if they had been kept in a box at the ready, waiting for their chance to entertain us, which they did with great energy and enthusiasm, then vanished into whatever section of the caravan in which they are sequestered.

It is hard to imagine a spectacle to rival the Rite of Welcome that the Sultan provided, but when the Turkoman chief rose to respond he came very close. After praising the Sultan's lavish hospitality and praying for the success of our mission, Hazan the Tall announced that he had brought with him a gift for the Padishah, snapped his fingers, and summoned a corps of sturdy mountain men bearing an immense rolled-up carpet so wide that it took the effort of eight strongmen to accomplish each turn as they rolled it out.

This carpet, he explained, had been woven with threads dyed by the women of the Akroyun tribe. As it revealed itself, it resembled an altarpiece with eight panels. Laid out flat, each panel celebrated a single Ottoman victory, starting with their early conquests in Anatolia. The first panel—the plainest—was a simple black rectangle bordered in gold containing only lines of text, each embroidered in glittering letters. *Orhan, son of Osman, Ghazi, Sultan of the Ghazi, Lord of the Horizons, Burgrave of the Whole World*, we all read.

The next panel celebrated the early Osman march warriors, followed by the capture of Bursa from the Byzantines. Watching, I wondered how many others in the gathering were struck by the sheer gall of these nomads who had wandered down into the pastures of Anatolia to feed their Asian goats only two hundred years before.

As it turned out, the gradual unrolling of the carpet scene by scene was a ceremony of some length, since each one had to be examined, explained, and applauded. After Bursa came the crossing over to Europe seen from the banks of the Danube (a deep blue), where Orhan's warriors demolished a force of French crusaders, pictured holding crosses dripping blood (a deep crimson). Then came the Conqueror's victory over the Serbs at Kosovo, the establishment of a European capital at Edirne, and an amazing depiction of the overthrow of the Byzantine Empire at Constantinople in 1453. I get a chill even now as I think of it.

There stands Mehmet the Conqueror, his eyes fixed mercilessly on the emperor Constantine at the moment of surrender. On the shores of the Bosphorus the headless bodies of the defeated bob up and down like squashed melons. The picture of Mehmet—his thin nose curved over his red lips, his piercing eyes staring out from under his heavy, arched eyebrows—is so lifelike that it is impossible to believe it was executed with needles and silk threads. Certainly, one would have thought it enough of a present. But no! It turned out that the carpet was only gift-wrapping for an object secreted in its folds.

Picture this: the carpet now covers the floor from the entrance to the dais with only the last section left to be unfolded. Directly above it sits the Sultan on his throne looking very pleased with this magnificent tribute to his house. At a sign from the chief porter, the carpet handlers take hold of the last folded edge and throw it back to reveal what has been hidden inside: a boy in red satin pantaloons and slippers with gold buckles, his thick black curls tied with silken ribbons and the face of a black angel. He stands up smiling and walks with the kind of dignity that only a slave can muster to the edge of the dais. There, graceful as a gazelle, he prostrates himself at the Sultan's feet.

After that, all I can report is that he was quickly whisked away to the Sultan's tent and I was excused from my reading duties that night.

D.

―

From: Sultana Hürrem at Topkapi Palace
To: Sultan Suleiman, Caliph of the World, received at Erzurum
Date: August 30, 1534

Noble Lord:

I have given some thought and study to the tradition of celebrations in your distinguished family. What say you to this: that we combine the celebrations of your victorious return from Baghdad and the royal wedding into one glorious jubilee? The world remembers that on your victorious return from Austria in 1530, your humiliation of the so-called Holy Roman emperor at Vienna was commemorated together with the circumcisions of our four sons. That joint military and domestic gala—the weeks of dancing, jousting, and feasting—is remembered with affection by your subjects and spoken of to this day.

Now, the forthcoming marriage of Princess Saida presents us with a similar opportunity. It gives you a chance to reward your people for the many sacrifices that they have made in the cause of your *jihad*, an opportunity that may never come again in your lifetime (may Allah grant you a long and happy life). We might call it the Festival of Double Happiness or some such name.

To plan out and implement what will be an event of some weeks' duration will most certainly tax my abilities, but be assured my whole heart is in this venture. If you are in accord, and now that Admiral Lofti Pasha is informally chosen to be Princess Saida's *damat*, all you need do on the day of your triumphal return is to officially place your hand on his shoulder to set off a double celebration the like of which has never been seen in the world.

In these efforts I could use the help of the princess. Unfortunately, the dear girl has given more than sufficient proof of her inability to understand that the time has come for her to emerge into the world as what she is—a beautiful, dutiful daughter who will make her *damat* a beautiful, dutiful wife and will contribute new luster to the magnificent Ottoman name. I am honored to play a part, however small, in such momentous events.

Written and sealed in wax by the hand of the Sultana Hürrem.

Beneath the signature, an encrypted message:
Choosing the groom has brought the wedding day closer.

━

From: Danilo del Medigo at Erzurum
To: Judah del Medigo at Topkapi Palace
Date: September 26, 1534

Dear Papa:

This morning, before I had a chance to put last night's letter in the Istanbul pouch, we were all summoned to the same chamber as before to be briefed on the details of our journey from here to Tabriz. As ever, the Sultan took his place high above us on the dais. But this time, he brought the little slave boy with him and sat him on his lap. And to my mind the Padishah appeared even more delighted with this second gift from the Emir than he had been with the first gift of the carpet.

I heard the Aga telling my mentor, Ahmed Pasha, that the boy had been trained to please. If so, his teachers should be well satisfied with their work. But how well, I wonder, will his African blood survive the rigors of Armenia and Azerbaijan? I suppose they can keep him swaddled in furs, like a little Russian prince. Come to think of it, I wouldn't mind a bit of swaddling myself. Just joking, Papa. You have sent me off well prepared with my store of woolen socks and my sheepskin vest, for which I have already begun to thank you as we travel into northern parts.

Gratefully,
D.

40

TABRIZ

From: Danilo del Medigo at Tabriz
To: Judah del Medigo at Topkapi Palace
Date: September 28, 1534

Dear Papa:

What a revelation is the east! We haven't even reached Persia yet, but already, here in Tabriz, our eyes and ears and nose tell us at every turn that Azerbaijan is not in Europe.

Lucky for us, the Persian king did not have time to carry off his treasure when he fled in such a hurry. Believe it or not, he left us his entire treasury. There it stands in an unlocked room, guarded for safekeeping by our Janissaries who, in a wonderful twist of fate, will shortly be paid their quarterly wages out of the very hoard they are duty bound to conserve.

It appears that when he conquered Tahmasp's capital, the Grand Vizier brought the Sultan not only a military coup but also a vast fortune. And if you add this cache to the wealth already piled up by the Ottoman conquests in Egypt and Europe —remembering also that Sultan Suleiman did not exactly begin his reign as a pauper—this acquisition must make him at the very least the second-richest man in the world. The first, I believe, remains the Persian monarch, who, to hear tell, still has vast riches hidden in the eastern reaches of his kingdom. And we of the Sultan's entourage are housed here in what was his palace.

You should see the Shah's bedroom, Papa. The floor and sofas are swathed in silk and gold Persian carpets. Not an inch of common wool. The bed, which stands not on wooden supports but on columns of fluted gold, is guarded by giant crystal lions, each with huge emeralds for eyes.

I do not command the skill to describe the overhead lantern, its hundreds of drops of silver inlaid with gold, encrusted with turquoise, and dripping with rubies and diamonds. Nor can words convey the impression of the *Divan-khane*, where the Shah granted audiences. That chamber is domed in scarlet cloth with foliage cut out of it, each leaf bordered in colored silk ribbons. The delicacy of the appliqué work is even more impressive than the richness of the fabric. Every room of this palace is exactly as Shah Tahmasp left it, down to the hand-washing basins with ewers cast in solid gold.

Standing at the entrance, I was reminded of what Alexander saw when he entered the tent that the then Persian king, Darius, had abandoned to him at Issus: the solid gold throne tossed over in the rush to escape, the carpets thrown about like so many rags, and gold everywhere—gold vessels, gold trays, gold implements.

Into this waste of extravagance walks the victor, Alexander the Great, twenty-five years old and bred in the austerity of Macedonia. There he stands gazing about him at the evidence of the everyday life of the great Persian ruler he has just driven from the field. At first, he is speechless. Finally, he speaks.

"So this is what it is like to be a great king," he says. No question, these Ottomans have lessons in majesty to learn from the Persian kings.

Of course, unlike those of us in the Sultan's retinue, the rank and file of our army cannot be accommodated in such luxury.

The troops are settled in a camp of tents that has been erected at the edge of the city. Not, you will note, outside the walls. Like Venice, the city of Tabriz has no fortifications. And, perhaps for that reason, it has never been sacked. Ask any citizen and he will tell you without shame that back in 1392, when Tamerlane came rampaging across Persia, reducing the surrounding fields to ash and the towns to ruin, the people of Tabriz immediately hoisted a white flag of surrender and sent out a party of officials to bow down to him and bury their faces in the dirt at his feet. It would appear that not much has changed in Tabriz in 150 years.

Still, although there was no armed resistance this time, I sense an air of unease in this palace. Whatever the Grand Vizier has done to subdue the populace, he has done it in such a way as to set up an undercurrent of resentment that one can detect in the narrowing of an eye or the curl of a lip. And it goes without saying that if there is insurgency brewing in Tabriz, the Sultan must deal with it before he can move on into Iraq.

Understandably, the Sultan no longer has time for leisurely nightly reading. So the Grand Vizier's equerry informs me. Perhaps there is a different reason why my evening presence is no longer requested.

On the night of our arrival in Tabriz I came to the Sultan's tent and seated myself in the anteroom of his sleeping room as I always do. It is the most quiet and serene place in the entire encampment, a place where I can preview my evening's reading without distractions. Well, tonight, as I reached over to turn up the oil lamp, my sleeve caught on the edge of the chimney, knocking it over, dousing me and my beautiful caftan, and spewing shattered glass all around; and the worst gaff of all, breaking the silence. I was so occupied with trying to sop up the oil from my caftan that I hardly noticed the figure that came out of the Sultan's chamber holding a bottle of wine and now stood before me, glowering.

"Who are you and what are you doing here?" His Greek accent was unmistakable.

Before I could gather my wits to respond, a pair of powerful hands took me by the shoulders, pulled me up to face him, and demanded, "Who let you in?"

"I am the Sultan's Assistant Foreign Language Interpreter, sir," I managed to stammer.

"Did Ahmed send you?"

"No, sir, I come by after the last prayer every evening...at the Sultan's request."

At the very mention of the word "Sultan," I felt the great hands loosen their grip on my shoulders.

"Well, the Sultan will not be needing your services tonight. So you can gather up your possessions and scat," he said with a dismissive gesture. "And be quick about it. You certainly can't appear before the Padishah in that condition. Your caftan is soaked."

How I looked was the last thing on my mind, but he was right. The Sultan is particular about the deportment of his pages, and my beautiful caftan was badly stained and drenched in oil. No argument there.

So I bundled up my papers and headed for the corridor, his voice following me as I walked. "Strong vinegar is an excellent remedy for grease stains. Pity to ruin the cloak. It is a beautiful garment. How came you by it?"

"It was a gift from the Sultan, sir," I replied.

"I see." He stroked his beard thoughtfully and then walked closer to me. "Hold your head up. Have I seen you before?" He favored me with a glance that made me feel he could see into my very soul. "Yes! It was you who performed in the hippodrome with the *gerit* team."

I nodded my assent.

"So you are what we would call a double hitter, not only a foreign language translator but a master of the *gerit* as well." Then, in an abrupt change of tone, "None of which entitles you to come skulking around the Sultan's tent, understand?"

If I did not understand his words, there was no mistaking his tone.

"Just make certain that you are never again caught prowling around the Sultan's private quarters."

Then he turned abruptly and walked back toward the Sultan's sleeping room. As he pushed the curtains aside I caught a glimpse of a low table set with two tall crystal wine glasses and a bubble pipe attached to an *argulah*. It was the first time I had seen evidence that the Padishah drank wine. Normally, he is respectful of the Muslim prohibition against alcohol.

Later, in my chamber, I heard issuing from the corridor the sound of two voices singing some tavern ditty in unison, with great gusto, at a quicker and quicker pace until the notes began to trip over each other, the voices finally dissolving into peals of laughter. It was the first time I had heard the Sultan laugh out loud.

The next morning, I was advised by Selim, a page who takes great pride in having been given the name of the Sultan's father, Selim the Grim, when he was circumcised into Islam, that the Grand Vizier had slept in the Sultan's bed until morning. Since then I am no longer invited to spend my evenings reading in the royal tent. And Selim no longer teases me about being the Sultan's Persian boy.

Of course, I am relieved to be spared the teasing. Still, the thought lurked in my mind. And I would be less than honest if I were to deny that it did not entirely discomfit me to contemplate becoming the Sultan's favorite. The privilege that comes with it! The preferment! The riches (yes, the riches)! The opportunities! The Sultan's boon companion, Ibrahim, has risen to the rank of Grand Vizier. He owns palaces. He commands armies. He does not have to beg for the chance to fight. Whereas I am neither a warrior nor a scholar — just a barnacle on the great ship of state.

But I hold onto the hope that perhaps, during the visit of the French delegation about to descend on us, I can still be of some use to my superior, the Chief Foreign Interpreter, Ahmed Pasha. The French visit is a highly secret mission that seems to be known to everyone in the world except, it is hoped, the Holy Roman emperor (who we in the Sultan's service refer to as the King of Spain). Perhaps the knowledge of French that I acquired at my mother's knee will be of use. It seems you have raised me to prefer usefulness to idleness, Papa. And I do still long for the feel of the *gerit* under my hand.

Good night,
D.

———

From: His Special Envoy, Jean de la Foret at Tabriz
To: H.M. Francis the First, King of France at Blois
Date: September 29, 1534

Majesty:

It gives me gréat pleasure to report that, after a long and taxing journey, we have caught up with the Sultan, who has established himself in Tabriz in the palace formerly occupied by the king of Persia. Sadly, the cloak of invisibility in which we have taken great pains to envelop this mission has been compromised in spite of our best efforts at discretion. And by none other than the Sultan himself.

Since the moment of our arrival, he has treated us publicly with the full honors owing to ambassadors — quite beyond the limits of a trade mission. We are housed within the royal palace rather than at one of those travelers' hostels called *caravanserai* of which this country is so proud,. Most telling, our horses are bedded alongside the Sultan's own in the royal stables. This is a gesture of supreme regard on the part of the Ottomans. Also, in our initial audience, the Sultan spoke of your Majesty as his kinsman and expressed his wish to be regarded as your brother-in-arms. This augurs well for the success of our mission. The Ottomans are by no means always so hospitable to foreign emissaries. Ask the Venetians!

By a stroke of luck, we arrived at Tabriz just in time for the quarterly distribution of the army's wages, a day of good spirits for all, especially, I would think, for the Sultan, who is able to pay out this huge sum of gold from the treasury that Tahmasp left behind. Of course, we are all aware that it is the custom in these parts for the ruler to haul his entire treasury around with him on campaign. This practice astonished the Greeks in Alexander's time, and it is still an awesome sight to see thousands of men lined up in the field to receive a purse containing their earnings for the past quarter and to see each walk away jingling a pocketful of gold coins delivered three months to the day from the last payday — no matter what part of the world in which he is serving. On campaign, these Ottoman troops also receive twelve *akce* for clothing and incidentals, plus thirty *akce* for weapons with an additional allowance for ammunition.

Did I mention that the Sultan himself lines up with his Janissary troops to receive his pay as an officer in the Janissary corps? To the European eye, such a flamboyant display of chests of coins being dispensed from the very hand of the sovereign is like a scene from *The Thousand and One Nights*. But in the east it is just one of many such public gestures that serve to entrench the Ottomans so deeply in the hearts of their troops and subjects.

Of course, it takes bottomless wealth to fund a scene such as I saw here today. And with respect, Majesty, may I tender to you my congratulations on having made alliance with such a financial prodigy as our brother, the Sultan.

Not surprisingly, the payday ritual — and the lucre that accompanies it — has swathed the camp in a blanket of good cheer that has expanded to include the Sultan's pages. At the close of the payday ceremony, the troops, in the manner of all troops, hooted off to spend as much of their money as they could on liquor and whores while the court gathered together in the shah's great reception hall, where the Sultan was tendered a royal welcome by the native Tabrizites plus assorted Kurdish chiefs.

The salutation began with the entrance of the Sunni priesthood (all of them members of the Ottoman *divan* as well as jurists, making them doubly revered personages). This governmental body has traveled all the way from Üsküdar and is expected to remain with the Sultan until we reach Baghdad, meeting regularly twice a week at the rest stops. One begins to appreciate the immense size of our cavalcade as various cadres, hitherto invisible, suddenly pop up to perform a task or simply to make an appearance.

No one I speak to seems to have a precise number for the size of our cavalcade, which has swelled considerably since we left Istanbul because various feudatories and *beys* arrive at each stop with their own complement of troops to fulfill their military obligations to the Sultan. According to my palace informant, now that the two halves of the army are joined at Tabriz, and allowing for the occasional additional dilatory Kurdish chieftain, there should be just under three hundred thousand bodies preparing to enter the Persian empire, plus an equal number of animals. The animal estimate goes far beyond military horses to include dray animals such as camels, donkeys, and water buffalo. Together the total animals probably far outnumber the troops. But as these animals are often rented for limited service on particular parts of the route, it is impossible for my informants to arrive at an accurate count of the animals that belong to the Ottoman army and those that are merely being leased.

To give you an example of the fluidity of these estimates, today a multiplicity of never-before-seen cohorts swept into the meeting place, wave after wave, each group distinguished from the others by the color of their turbans. I would guess there to be half a dozen of these military units, most of them comprising up to a thousand men and animals. All very colorful. But of the lot, the judges take the sartorial prize on account of the emerald green of their headgear. Massed together, they resemble a single huge emerald green cloud.

After all were seated, we witnessed the submission of both Gilan and Shirvan—two recently acquired provinces—whose leaders literally ate the dust at the Sultan's feet. Then came the installation of the Shirvan emir's son as the new governor of Tabriz. In the custom of the country, he brought along as a kind of gruesome trophy the severed head of the rebel governor of Bitlis, who had imprudently chosen to side with Tahmasp before the Grand Vizier's army recaptured the town. Finally, we of the French delegation were recognized.

All this marching up and down and blowing of trumpets was directed by the Grand Vizier standing in for the Sultan, who must have had his fill of severed heads by now. Since it is the custom at this court for foreign visitors to conduct their business with the Grand Vizier—and frequently not even to see the Sultan in the flesh—we were quite prepared to present our credentials to the Grand Vizier alone. But no. After the bloody head from Bitlis had been retired, Ibrahim Pasha withdrew to the side of the podium, and, accompanied by the strains of the Sultan's band, there came onto the podium a most astonishing sight: a small contingent of pages holding aloft on a palanquin a very young, very shiny, very black boy dressed in white satin. The young blackamoor was holding aloft a pillow also covered in white satin on which sat a life-size turban made not from cloth of gold but entirely of gold itself, every turn edged with a row of different-colored precious stones. One got a sense of the weight of the thing by the difficulty the boy had keeping it upright on the pillow.

I learned later in the evening from Selim, the page who seems to know everything about everyone, that this monstrous head ornament was ordered by the Grand Vizier from the legendary Venetian goldsmith Caorlini, very likely to assuage Suleiman's displeasure on learning that his European rival, Charles Five, had been crowned Holy Roman Emperor by the Medici pope. Apparently the Sultan was affronted by being denied a like honor, so the Grand Vizier had a headpiece made up for him. But since crowns are not worn in the Islamic world, the Grand Vizier had this coronet cast in the shape of a turban. No expense was spared—it is rumored to have cost 115,000 ducats. And it was publicly displayed at the Doge's palace a couple of years ago to great acclaim before being shipped off to Istanbul. What no one seemed to realize was how much a turban made of gold would weigh, especially after it had been plastered with pearls and jewels.

In a word, the prodigious crown gave the Sultan a headache. From this indisposition came the notion of announcing the Sultan's appearance on state occasions by sending out his gold turban ahead of him, *in locum tenens,* as it were.

I have taken advantage of your patience, Majesty, to regale you with these details in order to convey the peculiar nature of the people you have sent me to deal with. In this society, exquisite politesse is mixed in equal measure with rampant savagery, such as the unfortunate habit of lopping off the head of someone who has displeased you with a word or a gesture, then trucking the offending member around the countryside on a satin pillow as a trophy. At such times, all I can do is express my gratitude to God for making me a Frenchman.

Tomorrow morning we take up the practical business of reviewing the details of the treaty between the Ottoman Empire and ourselves. It should take the better part of the day but does not promise to present any difficulties, both sides having initialed the draft. Once our business is concluded, we will pack up for the journey back to Istanbul. There, after I have paid respects to the Sultana, I will entrust myself to the custody of a Venetian sea captain, the safest bet in the eastern Mediterranean — at least while the Venetians and the Turks maintain their current amity.

Your servant,
Jean de la Foret

41

COUP DE FOUDRE

From: His Special Envoy, Jean de la Foret at Tabriz
To: H.M. Francis the First, King of France at Blois
Date: September 29, 1534

Majesty:

Was it Aristotle or Sophocles who warned us that no man could count himself happy until the moment of his death? This afternoon, a completely unanticipated event occurred which appeared for a time to put our entire mission in jeopardy. It seems that no treaty is truly ratified until it is signed. Fortunately, the document was finally confirmed at the last possible moment after a thunderbolt had suddenly struck down the person on whom all depended just as he was about to record the terms of the final clause. To reassure your mind, Majesty, it was not the Sultan who suffered this *coup de foudre*, nor one of our party, thanks to God, but the Sultan's Chief Interpreter who, without warning, fell into a swoon and had to be carried from the negotiating table unconscious.

We had spent the morning haggling over details, such as

precisely how many of our nationals would be accommodated within the proposed French quarter of Istanbul. The compromise agreed upon: a number equal to the Genovese but slightly fewer than the Venetians. Within these restrictions, the French now have the right to travel by land or sea and to buy and sell throughout the Ottoman Empire on the same terms as the Turks themselves.

When we gathered after lunch—many courses, all of which tasted like pilaf—the Sultan's Chief Foreign Interpreter began to record the final terms of the treaty one by one, first in Arabic, then in French. But before he could finish, he suddenly turned pale, gasped, and collapsed at his lectern. At first we treated this *coup de foudre* as a purely personal calamity. It was only after the doctors had carried Ahmed Pasha from the room that the difficulties arising from his misfortune became apparent.

As you may recall, Majesty, we were promised at the outset that the other party would supply instant translation in both our official languages. And, indeed, the unfortunate translator turned out to be more than competent. What the Turks did not anticipate was that he might suddenly be rendered *hors de combat* by an act of God. Thus, they had not troubled themselves to provide a surrogate, nor had we. Something close to panic descended as we began to perceive our predicament.

"Never mind," said the Sultan, with all the assurance of a man unaccustomed to being disappointed. "My Grand Vizier will take on the task. He has a decent familiarity with Latin, as do you Franks, and he will complete the document in that language while translating for me. Sadly, Turkish, Arabic and Persian are my only languages."

Everyone nodded with relief, except for the Grand Vizier who turned somewhat pink and refused the assignment. His Latin was rusty and not up to the linguistic requirements of such precise interpretation, he demurred. Further, even if one of us were to do a translation of the treaty into Latin, there seems to be no one on the Ottoman side to carry it on from Latin to Arabic. Or Turkish. Or Persian. Everyone was apprehensive, no one more than the Grand Vizier, who seemed to fear the future perils inherent in a falsely translated treaty even more than the reproachful glares of his master.

And there we sat, stymied by an act of God, when, out of nowhere, a hand shot up.

"Sire?"

The Sultan motioned for the page to rise and speak.

"With respect, sire, I do have a command of Turkish, owing to my fine education in your School for Pages. And, although my French may be somewhat impaired by disuse, it is the language I learned at my mother's knee during her time of service to the Marchesana of Mantova, when she translated and read aloud a number of the so-called French *romans* that the lady doted on."

The Sultan beckoned and the page made his way to the lectern so recently vacated by the Chief Foreign Interpreter. He was a young fellow, light-skinned and agreeable to look upon with an amazing mop of golden curls; probably, I thought, one of those tribute boys taken as a tithe on captured Christian families from as far away as Russia and Poland, and circumcised as a Muslim slave to the Sultan. (I later learned that this boy is indeed circumcised but not as a Muslim. He is the son of the Sultan's Jewish doctor, of all things.)

Well, sire, the page's French was not up to our standard—he started out hesitant and never did achieve true fluency. But he did have the skill and the wit to work us through the document by the end of the day to everyone's satisfaction. Correction: not everyone. Certainly, the Sultan was well pleased with his Jewish page. As the work went on, his expression changed from frowning apprehension to half a smile. But the Grand Vizier, who had started out the day brimming with good cheer, descended from élan to red-faced spleen. This episode could not fail to have damaged the esteem in which he is held by his master, the Sultan.

As I mentioned in an earlier dispatch from Constantinople, this Grand Vizier was a slave companion to the Sultan when they were boys, and since then he has risen faster than a shooting star in the royal firmament. After leading a triumphant campaign in Egypt, this Greek was named Grand Vizier over the heads of several older and wiser viziers, which does not make him a universal favorite. But that seems to trouble him not at all.

No doubt the Grand Vizier believes himself to be shielded from his enemies by his intimacy with the Sultan. And indeed, they dine together, they hunt together, and on campaign they share a tent and even clothing. What degree of intimacy this indicates I will not presume to assess. But there has been no one better positioned to fill the void left in the Sultan's life by the death of his beloved mother and councillor than the Grand Vizier. Except, perhaps, the newly wedded Sultana, now the Regent.

Lest you begin to think me infected by the Byzantine spirit of conspiracy that pervades this place, let me assure you, sire, given the lack of any checks to the Sultan's whim from a noble class, such conjecture is far from gossip. Conspiracy is the heart and soul of Ottoman politics. And whatever the outcome of this incident, the ill wind that blew the Grand Vizier into hazardous waters proved to be a fair breeze for us. For it was the lad's intervention that saved our enterprise and enabled us to accomplish our task with dispatch.

Tomorrow, the Sultan and I will bid each other farewell and go our separate ways, him into Persia to retake Baghdad (which somehow managed to slip through his father's fingers) and our small delegation to Trabzon—shades of Jason and the Argonauts—whence we will undertake the long voyage home to France.

Your Majesty's loyal servant,
Jean de la Foret

From: Danilo del Medigo at Tabriz
To: Judah del Medigo at Topkapi Palace
Date: September 30, 1534

Dear Papa:

One final piece of news from Tabriz. We take off tomorrow at dawn for the Kurdish Mountains. Monsieur de la Foret is departed this morning. He seems to be very pleased with his treaty, as is the Sultan. That is what I would call a successful outcome for any negotiation: each comes away believing he did well. Also, I was able to play a small part in the proceedings by substituting for Ahmed Pasha, who suddenly became ill.

As with all of Mama's efforts to turn me into an educated man (and I still miss her every day, Papa), my rudimentary knowledge of French came to my aid. My debt to her is boundless—as is my debt to you.

You should have seen the farewells this morning when the Frank took his leave: the Sultan decked out in all his diamonds and his egret feathers to honor the guest, and Monsieur de la Foret, arms akimbo, clad in the gorgeous caftan that was his gift from the Sultan.

And what do you suppose the Frenchman took away with him as a gift for his master, the French king? It was the black-amoor boy, the Sultan's own gift from Uzun Hazan the Tall, that the Sultan chose to hand over to the French king. I wonder what made the Sultan send the boy away. Apparently it was the Grand Vizier's suggestion. Asked by his master what gift would best express the great value that he placed on this French alliance, the Grand Vizier, always ready with an answer, replied that the most valuable gift you can ever give is the one you hate most to part with. So the boy was sent away, wrapped up in a gold-embroidered rug like a package, and we will go on without him. Everyone is sorry for the loss. The little fellow livened up the palace with his dances and his tricks. And he made the Sultan smile.

This letter will be dispatched to you far away in the Istanbul sunshine via the Sultan's courier as we head south into Persia. Think of me plodding along the bleak and chilly roads of Azerbaijan and feeling just slightly envious of your cozy situation, but still wishing you good health in the sunshine.

D.

42

SULTANIYE

From: Danilo del Medigo at Sultaniye
To: Judah del Medigo at Topkapi Palace
Date: October 12, 1534

Dear Papa:

I cannot bring myself to relive the miserable details of what happened to me after the French ambassadors left Tabriz. Something I did or said during their audience with the Sultan had offended Grand Vizier Ibrahim deeply. Last night he came to my room to berate me for plotting against my mentor Ahmed Pasha and to warn me to keep a good distance from the Sultan, because I will be watched for any inappropriate attempts to bring myself to the Padishah's attention in my "cunning Jewish way." Apparently my offense is unmitigated gall and excessive ambition—I, your son, Danilo, who has always been reproached for my lack of ambition, am now charged with an excess of it!

So now I am traveling under two constraints. First of all, since the Sultan remains totally under the spell of the Mevlana,

the Sufi mystic, my readings from the life of Alexander no longer interest him. I ought to have been prepared for such a thing.
Mama warned me often enough to watch out for the whimsical nature of the great ones of this world. "He who walks in
the train of a prince," she used to say, "walks on shifting sand."
But I did not understand that this capricious bestowal and with-
drawal of love applies to dead as well as living favorites. Once
İskender fell from grace, I lost my place as his historian, and at
Tabriz I was dismissed by the Grand Vizier from my evening
reading duties. After that, it would take a miracle, I thought, to
give new life to the moribund remains of Alexander the Great.

During the negotiations with the French ambassador, when
I was able to render a small service to the Padishah, I believed I
might have carved out a new niche for myself. However it now
seems that whatever I do to be of help to the Sultan will be
regarded by the Grand Vizier as nothing less than presumption
and a sign of my "cunning Jewish ways." I cannot write more of
this tonight. It is too painful.

Good night, Papa.
D.

—

From: Danilo del Medigo at Sultaniye
To: Judah del Medigo at Topkapi Palace
Date: October 13, 1534

Dear Papa:

Tomorrow we travel on to Hamedan. At least, that was the
next destination the last time I heard. Having been warned to
make myself scarce around the Sultan, I am no longer party to
the conversations in his tent. So I must depend on my fellow
pages—to many of whom I am now bound by our mutual
loathing of the Grand Vizier—for word of route changes,
time tables, and the like. But even the Sultan's own pages are

kept in the dark most of the time by his natural inclination toward secrecy. Surely you must have noticed this tendency in him during the many hours you spent at his side. Or was he more forthcoming with you? I believe he does confide in the Grand Vizier. As well, he does communicate by pigeon with the advance and rear guard of our army. After all, the captains must be kept up to date on any changes to the route of march, if only so they can know which way to point their horses every morning. But to the rest of us who have no pressing need to know, nothing is told.

To a lesser leader than Sultan Suleiman, the scene of desolation that greeted us here in this no man's land between Azerbaijan and Persia might have proved daunting. But our Sultan has used it as a goad to his weary troops. His speech to them on our arrival in Persia was devoted to a single theme: If the Persians, cowardly and weak as we know them to be, have run away again, we will follow them and find them and kill them.

Of course, all assume that our final goal is to occupy Baghdad and name our Sultan as the new caliph there. But never have I heard that spoken of. So, given the level of secrecy that prevails in this camp on matters of such great portent, I suppose I should not be surprised that no mention has come to my ears of what is to become of me personally. I still have my horse, my groom, my traveling library, and my position of Assistant Foreign Language Interpreter, although I haven't had anything to interpret since my encounter with the French mission at Tabriz. But I have continued to study the ancient historians just in case I should happen to be reactivated as a source of information on warfare in central Asia as practiced by the greatest soldier the world has ever known.

Tales of the beauty of the women of Sultaniye are highly exaggerated. Unlike some women we have seen, for example, in Erzurum, where they wrap their wives and daughters up in dun-colored canvas like Egyptian mummies before they let them out of the house, Kurdish women do not cover their faces, just their hair. In other words, you can actually see them. And, from all appearances, they seem to be shy, modest, and agreeable if not exceptionally good-looking. Indeed, they look no different than most women except for the prostitutes, who are flashy, money-hungry, and loud like most prostitutes. Don't worry, Papa, I am not speaking from an intimate knowledge, but I am allowed to look and listen, am I not?

It is late and I tend to make bad jokes when it gets late. So I will bid you good night and ask you again to please keep my letters for my children in case they should ever want to know what their papa was up to on his travels through Kurdistan.

Love,
D.

—

From: Sultan Suleiman, encamped at Sultaniye
To: Sultana Hürrem at Topkapi Palace
Date: October 9, 1534

My prized and deeply honored consort:

Muhabbi, the poet, writes his love poems to your beauty. Suleiman, the king, writes this paean to praise your wisdom. Of course, we will have a double celebration—a victory and a wedding. How better to reward my flock for their sacrifices in my cause? Under your wise guidance we will give our people a festival of joy beyond their imagination. And while they are feasting and dancing, Muhabbi, the Sultan of Love, who has been silenced for so long by the demands of duty, will be heard above the tumult singing his praises and devotions to his true love, the beauteous Sultana Hürrem.

Only a king secure in the knowledge that his majesty was being well guarded from his enemies both at home and abroad could afford to risk embarking on such a fated adventure as the conquest of Baghdad. With my queen as Regent and Allah beside me at the helm of my ship of state, I am such a King.

Signed by the Sultan's seal.

Beneath the signature is the encrypted message:
When is a page equal to a king? When he is joined to his princess in the jihad of love until death.

43

HAMEDAN

From: Sultana Hürrem at Topkapi Palace
To: Sultan Suleiman en route, received at Hamedan
Date: October 8, 1534

Hail to the conquering hero!

Istanbul is filled with joy at the news of your occupation of the shah's capital. The streets ring with the cry "Tabriz is ours!" I cry tears of loneliness every night, but my heart is bursting with pride that I am Sultana to the Master of Two Continents and Three Seas.

As the miles between us increase so does the heaviness of my heart. But then I remind myself that the fearsome Zagros Mountains of Persia still lie ahead before you can claim your prize at Baghdad. In the face of such trials, who am I to complain as I sit here among my pillows, warm and safe, while you shoulder the burden of conquering the world?

Still, I do have my own small labors and disappointments, which at times threaten to overwhelm my spirit. To put it simply, my excursion along the Bosphorus with the two princesses was a failure. For reasons that will become obvious, I am using my new-found writing skills to make a private account to you of what happened. This is for your eyes only, sealed in wax with my signet by my own unsteady hand.

Early yesterday morning, our party set off from the Grand Vizier's dock in the beautiful craft lent for the occasion by Admiral Lofti. The bright sun shining high in the sky and the Bosphorus shimmering in its rays seemed to be an omen that our little mission to find a palace for Princess Saida had Allah's blessing. But as those palaces up for purchase passed before our eyes one by one, the more elegant they became, the deeper became the gloom that surrounded our sad Princess Saida.

The sortie came to its end when we disembarked on the island of Kinali to stretch our limbs and enjoy the beauties of nature untamed. As we picked our way through the brambles to the little ruined mosque hidden in the greenery, Princess Saida's spirit seemed to lift. But the moment we heard the squeak of the gate that was swinging in the breeze, a change came over her. And when a little ruined mosque was revealed to our eyes, she burst into a torrent of uncontrollable weeping. Luckily the admiral was not present to witness this display.

Clearly, my words of encouragement to our precious Saida to ease off after a year of mourning have fallen on deaf ears. If we are to get this child married we will have to do it without her help. As long as duty keeps you so far away and for so long, the responsibility to guide this girl through her losses and on to a life of happiness and fulfillment falls to me. Trust me; I will not fail in my efforts to fulfill the duties of a mother to our reluctant daughter.

Signed and sealed with the Regent's stamp by Sultana Hürrem.

—

From: Sultana Hürrem at Topkapi Palace
To: Sultan Suleiman, received at Hamedan
Date: October 16, 1534

Adored, worshiped, victorious Sultan:

Was ever a woman as fortunate as I am to play a part in celebrating the greatest victory the world has ever seen? Today there arrived from you a document that will enable me to make the expenditures needed to bring to life my dream of a double festival event in your capital that will astonish the world. Your generosity is not only abundant but is a tangible sign of your faith in me.

In fairness be it said that I could never live up to these heavy responsibilities without the help of our much loved daughter, Princess Saida, who sits beside me to record my words. I am still not prepared to relinquish her secretarial services completely. Even though she has tutored me faithfully to read my own correspondence and write my own letters, my new ability to write in my own hand lags far behind the volume of correspondence I am called upon to address. Without her I am still half speechless and half blind.

If my information is correct, by the time the courier carrying this letter in his pouch reaches you, you will be in Persia. That my far-off presence is even a small part of such a glorious achievement gives me the fortitude to carry on with my countless duties as your anointed Regent and the guardian of your children. It is my honor and my privilege.

Signed and stamped with the Regent's seal by Sultana Hürrem.

Beneath the signature is the encrypted message:
Today came the dressmaker from the bazaar to measure the bridal party and the Sultana for wedding dresses. The Sultana and the bride's maids bubbled with enthusiasm. The bride was silent.

⌒

From: Danilo del Medigo at Hamedan
To: Judah del Medigo at Topkapi Palace
Date: October 31, 1534

Dear Papa:

The fleeing king, Tahmasp, has left Hamedan without a trace. When he fled, the Persians either ate or burned or carried off every edible in the vicinity. Luckily we brought along our own supplies. But we are also burdened with tons of siege equipment that will be needed if the king of kings decides to make a stand against us at Baghdad. Officially, that fabled place has been handed over to us by its governor, but this is Kurdish territory and the Kurds are known to be undependable allies. Who knows what unpleasant surprises we will find when we cross into Iraq on the other side of the Zagros Mountains?

Meanwhile, here in Hamedan, the Grand Vizier prepares to split up our unwieldy army once again, this time for the crossing from Persia into Iraq. He will be heading the advance force to supervise transport of the heavy scaling equipment and artillery. When word comes back to us that he is safely across the Zagros Mountains and that the passes are clear of Persians, we will set off to rejoin him at the gates to Baghdad.

Tomorrow he will be gone, and those of us in the Sultan's retinue will be left to enjoy a rest stop of several days here in Hamedan, the city known to the ancients as Ecbatana and the very center of the world of Alexander the Great. If ever I am to have a second chance to review the Sultan's once-loved İskender, this is it. Hamedan is only a two-hour ride from the battlefield of Gaugamela, where Alexander fulfilled the Gordian prophecy to become lord of all Asia. Here in the surround of Ecbatana is the ground on which Alexander's Persian war was won.

Hamedan is also the burial place of Hephaestion, Alexander's boon companion, who sickened and died here on their journey home. This misfortune, the historians point out, marked the beginning of a spiral of adversity that led to the loss of Alexander's own life within a year.

The junction of these two significant moments in the hero's life — the high and the low — at one and the same place is almost enough to encourage a belief in some grand closing of a fateful circle by the gods, isn't it? Just a thought, Papa.

So here we are in Hamedan, which the local Kurds still refer to as Ecbatana, and where they also speak of İskender as if he had passed by them in the street just yesterday. Time is a poor eraser of memory in these parts. When I mentioned this to Ahmed Pasha, he said that nomadic people, such as his own and the Sultan's ancestors, tend to move forward with one eye on the past. He reminds me that nomads do not own property; hence they lack an attachment to a single homeland. And, being illiterate for the most part, they have no written record to share. All they have in common is their history passed down, mouth to ear, from one generation to the next.

"Stories of the past are their only heritage," he explained to me. "With them, ancient victories are celebrated as if they happened last week and ancient betrayals are never forgotten. Any man who hopes to conquer Iraq or Persia ignores their tribal past at his peril." More tomorrow.

Love,
D.

———

From: His proud consort, Sultana Hürrem at Topkapi Palace
To: Sultan Suleiman, Shadow of God on Earth, Emperor of the East and West, Padishah of All the Arab Lands, en route to a great victory over the heretic Tahmasp, received at Hamedan
Date: November 1, 1534

My fortune-favored Sultan:

I received a visit today from Vizier Rustem, my choice as a *damat* for our loved younger daughter, Mihrimah. He will make the perfect son-in-law—wise, settled, and bone-loyal to his Sultan. Now, we must proceed with haste to provide the same future for Saida, if for no other reason than her wedding must, of course, precede that of her younger sister.

I pause to indulge myself in a sigh of relief that the next task of staging a royal wedding will be easier when Princess Mihrimah's wedding comes along. Even now she springs to life when I speak of her future. Like all young girls, she dreams of her palace and the jewels she will wear. And I am pleased to report that our choice for her husband, the esteemed Rustem Pasha, is already in consultation with me. After a meeting with the court astrologer I have set the date for a May wedding two years hence. Even two years is not too early to make a start on planning these grand occasions.

I long for your return. I pray for your safety. May Allah watch over you.

Signed and stamped with the Regent's seal by Sultana Hürrem.

Beneath the signature, an encryption:
Not all young girls dream of palaces and jewels. A princess in a tower dreams of her rescue by a paladin on a white horse.

———

From: Danilo del Medigo at Hamedan
To: Judah del Medigo at Topkapi Palace
Date: November 2, 1534

Dear Papa:

Ibrahim Pasha finally set off this morning and with him went over half of our army and most of our guns. Already the camp has taken on a lighter air, almost as if we are on a holiday. Give the Grand Vizier his due. He is not lacking in courage or ability. I only wish he liked me a little more. But there is something about my very presence that gets his back up. At times I have the feeling that he sees me as a rival for the Sultan's favor. But that is ridiculous, isn't it? He and the Sultan are, after all, childhood friends, fellow campaigners, and, I am told, sometime bedmates. Maybe it is simply that I am a Jew and he hates all Jews.

In the hours since the Grand Vizier marched away, I have seen the Sultan wandering the compound looking as if he lost his best friend. Perhaps this is the time to reintroduce Alexander. We are only a short ride from Gaugamela. And here I sit, a ready and willing tour guide to distract the forlorn Sultan with that piece of ancient history. Time to brush up on Arrian just in case.

Love,
D.

Later:

Say what you like, Papa, miracles do happen. A few minutes ago, while I was rereading Arrian on Alexander's triumph at Gaugamela—just in case—a brief note arrived to inform me that my presence was required to prepare for tomorrow's visit to the battlefield at—yes—Gaugamela. How has this happened?

I know your opinion of what people call extra-sensory interlocution—it falls into the same pit as thaumaturgy, sorcery and alchemy. But among the many things you have taught me, Papa, is always to keep an open mind. Now I beg the same of you. Last night I had a thought that flew through the air into the mind of the Sultan. My proof? We are off to Gaugamela by dawn's light to relive Alexander's victory there.

"I will require a summary of the battle tomorrow when we reach the site," the Sultan informed me, as if our last conversation on the subject had occurred the previous day, instead of the previous month. "So you must bring along any books we have in our library on Alexander's battles. He was headed for Baghdad when Darius confronted him at Gaugamela, was he not?"

"Like ourselves, sir," I replied.

"We will be walking in his very footsteps. From Gaugamela, across the Zagros Mountains to Baghdad," —he paused— "and from there to the edge of the world," he added.

Which gave me the courage to ask the question that had been on my mind for many days: "And what of our expedition, sir? Will we continue in his footsteps beyond Baghdad?"

"After Baghdad?" You can see eagerness in a man's eyes as easily as you can see fear or love. Clearly the prospect held more than a little charm for him. He smiled a smile that I can only describe as mischievous. "After Baghdad?" he repeated. "Who can say?"

On that note the interview ended, and I repaired to my tent to spend the night with Arrian, Quintus Curtius, and good old Plutarch—in preparation for my turn as a battlefield guide.

Oh, if Mama could only see me now!

Love,
D.

44

GAUGAMELA

From: Danilo del Medigo at Gaugamela
To: Judah del Medigo at Topkapi Palace
Date: November 3, 1534

Dear Papa:

This day I accompanied the Sultan to Gaugamela to lead him through the events of the battle on the very ground on which it was fought. As always, the Sultan's baggage train went ahead to prepare a resting tent and an eating tent for him at the battle-field. But no beds. This was a day trip like a day of hunting. But here we were hunting for echoes of the distant past. How best, I wondered, to prepare the Sultan for his return to the world of Alexander? Immediately I thought of Mama's way of introducing me to history. Why not try to rekindle his interest by telling him a story? So as we rode I told him about the exchange between Alexander and his father's general, Parmenio, on the eve of the battle at Gaugamela. Old stuff to you, Papa, but it was new to the Sultan and I admit I did enjoy delivering it, making sure, as Mama had taught me, not to burden him with too many facts.

I simply explained that by the time Alexander reached Hamedan, he had overrun Darius' army at Issus and had seized the great king's mother, wives, and daughters along with thousands of prisoners. The wealth of these ancient Persians was unimaginable. Even after his army was decimated, Darius returned to the fray from his eastern empire within a few months, leading a full fighting force complete with elephants and scythed chariots.

But first, honor demanded that he rescue his women. Twice, he sent messengers to Alexander to offer money and land in exchange for them. Twice, he was refused. The third time Darius offered Alexander all his territories west of the Euphrates, plus thirty thousand talents as ransom for his women and the hand of one daughter in marriage.

A long-standing member of Alexander's close council, Parmenio observed that dragging around all the prisoners they had acquired — not to mention feeding them — was a great expense, so why not ransom the lot and have done with it?

"If I were Alexander," Parmenio concluded, "I should accept the offer from King Darius."

"So should I," answered Alexander, "if I were Parmenio. But" — he paused to make his point — "I am Alexander. I need no money from Darius. Nor do I need to receive a part of the country in place of the whole. This country and all its treasures are already mine. If I choose to marry his daughter, I will marry her if he gives her or not. But let him stand warned: Asia can no more support two monarchs than the earth can exist between two suns."

When Darius received this reply, he withdrew all proposals and began to prepare for battle.

This is the story I told the Sultan as we rode to the plain where the two kings faced each other for the last time. In less than a three-hour ride from Hamedan we were standing in Alexander's footsteps on the low ridge of hills above the village of Gaugamela. And from that vantage we replayed the battle with me echoing Arrian's description of Alexander's crucial victory. Just as the Gordian seer had predicted, Alexander was now lord of all Asia.

Up to this point in the story I had hewn faithfully to Arrian's narrative. But suddenly, I was overcome by a wish to speak in my own voice. When I first read the ancients' accounts of Gaugamela and its aftermath, it seemed quite clear to me that although Gaugamela appeared to be a great victory at the time, it turned out to contain within it the seeds of its own defeat. And I somehow found myself expressing my opinion to my master.

"With his victory in Gaugamela, İskender had accomplished his mission," I informed the Sultan (without acknowledging authorship of my observation). "After seven years away from home, three of those years in the seemingly unconquerable highlands of central Asia, the Macedonian troops felt they had won the right to pack up their share of the booty and begin to enjoy it with their families at home."

"Even the most loyal of troops reaches a limit at some point," the Sultan commented with a nod of understanding. Although he is still young in years, he has already chalked up a decade of campaigning and has gained a feeling for the state of mind of his men.

"But İskender's vision of becoming the king of all Asia overwhelmed his good sense," I made bold to opine. "It was that vision that drove him to drag his troops past the central Asian frontier from victory to disaster."

At that point I was prepared to relate the succession of victories that Alexander had enjoyed crossing Central Asia before he was turned back at the Oxus River in India. But now the Sultan's attention was fixed on my ill-advised remark that İskender's triumph at Gaugamela contained within it the seeds of his defeat. And he began to pepper me with a series of questions so pressing that, on the return ride, we had to slow down to a languid canter in order to conduct our conversation and ride at the same time. The Sultan is not a patient man. Victories had begun to bore him. He wanted to get to the end of the story, to Alexander's last days, which, as you know, Papa, became a catalogue of disasters.

"What turned İskender's last days on the return journey into defeat and disgrace?" he wanted to know. "What elements conspired to give this magnificent conqueror such a sad and dispirited ending?" When no answer was forthcoming, he simply demanded, "Tell me!"

So I was forced into reporting the disaffection of the Macedonian old guard and their belief that Alexander was betraying his Macedonian heritage, that he had "turned Persian"; that he had given all the plum assignments to local Persian dignitaries; that he had encouraged them to prostrate themselves at his feet in a subservient manner which no respectable Macedonian would abide; that he had even begun to dress himself up like the king of kings with a gilded belt that he wore in the style of a woman. I even repeated the gossip that Alexander's Macedonian generals had poisoned him, though I was careful to add that Arrian says this rumor remains entirely unproven. Even so, that scurrilous morsel proved more tempting to the Sultan than all my careful research on the battle of Gaugamela.

I remember you telling me once, Papa, that the Ottomans have an insatiable appetite for deceit, plotting, and treachery.

"They are Orientals," you reminded me. "It is a part of their view of the world."

Well, I saw good evidence of that yesterday. A flush of excitement suffused the Sultan's pale cheeks at the very mention of poison. And I must admit that, like some compliant Scheherazade, I went on to supply him with a few more bits of scandal and rumor that I had gleaned from my readings. Such as, that by the time they reached the Oxus, the Macedonians were on the verge of mutiny; that Alexander had taken to drinking himself into a stupor every night; that on one such occasion, he had so far lost control that in a drunken rage he had run through one of his veteran captains with his sword. The officer, called Black Clitus, had served under Alexander's father and had saved Alexander's own life at the battle at Granicus in the early years of the Persian campaign.

I cannot forget the Sultan's response to this piece of information. "No great leader kills in a rage, drunk or sober," he informed me. "I want to know what happened to drive this brave and noble king to such a desperate act. What had Black Clitus done to deserve such a punishment?"

He wanted me to provide Alexander with an excuse—after two thousand years. As the seconds ticked by, I could feel all the good will I had built up at the battlefield melt into impatience and disappointment. Only by luck did my horse, at that moment, toss a shoe, giving me a pretext to drop out of the rank and provide me with an evening to devise a good reason why Alexander the Great, in a drunken rage, should have killed the man who saved his life.

But first, I will sleep. Maybe the answer will come to me in a dream. If not I will at least have a night and a day to bone up on the story of Black Clitus.

Good night,
D.

＿

From: Danilo del Medigo at Gaugamela
To: Judah del Medigo at Topkapi Palace
Date: November 8, 1534

Dear Papa:

Last night I wrote that I would have a day to catch up on the story of Black Clitus. But no! My summons to read arrived with the first prayer, before breakfast—before I had time to prepare. It's almost as if I had succeeded too well in my effort to revive Alexander. Now the Sultan is so besotted with my tale that he wants his İskender in the morning. Did such a bizarre turn ever happen to Scheherazade?

Today the camp is a jumble of rolled-up tents, supply chests, horses, and camels, as preparation is made for tomorrow's departure to Baghdad. But no elephants or cannons. They have gone ahead with the Grand Vizier. Still, the camp is in disarray. Not the Sultan's compound, of course. It, like his *selamlik*, is an oasis of serenity. His slaves will not begin to pack up our tents until we ride off tomorrow morning. His second crew has already left to prepare a camp in the Zagros Mountains for his arrival there tomorrow night. And when I responded to my summons this morning, there he sat, cross-legged on his pillows, calm, unruffled, scowling, intent on pursuing Alexander through the turmoil of eastern Persia. He is completely caught up in Alexander's turn from triumph into tragedy. How did this paragon of nobility come to end his days as a drunken murderer? He chews on the question like a dog on a bone.

You will be able to gauge the intensity of the Sultan's passion when I tell you that he could not tear himself away from this feverish pursuit even to respond to the messengers that continued to arrive from all parts of the empire throughout the day. You know the protocol, Papa. These relay riders, who boast that they never fail to complete their journeys in snow, rain, blazing heat, or pitch dark, are, the Sultan once told me, the lifeblood that flows through the veins of the empire. These couriers keep him constantly in touch with goings-on from the Nile to the Indus; they are always admitted to his presence the moment they arrive, no matter how late the hour, and their reports are always read by him the moment they come to hand. Knowing this, you will be amazed, as I was, by the scene outside his tent this morning: three couriers lined up, pouches in hand, awaiting his nod, while he had eyes and ears only for my tale of the tribulations that Alexander underwent a thousand years before the birth of the prophet. If anything, he wanted the story even more eagerly this morning than he did yesterday.

"I still do not have the whole story," he complained. "Exactly what was it that possessed Alexander to kill a man who had saved his life? What could have driven him to such a dastardly act?"

As you know, Papa, no historian who has turned attention to Alexander has missed out on the story of Black Clitus. Except, perhaps, the one that the Sultan encountered in his nursery. Otherwise, of the lot—Arrian, Plutarch, the Roman called Quintus Curtius—each tells a different story of what happened on that much chronicled night in Marakanda.

Before I could wade into this morass of conflicting evidence, I felt a need to set the scene. With ill-disguised impatience, my master gave a grudging nod of permission. "But make it brief," he said. Which I did, as follows:

After a brutal year of fighting the border tribes of Bactria without a concrete victory, I explained, the Macedonians were frozen, famished, and worn out. By now, there was a split in the ranks between the old Macedonian veterans and the young Turks. The campaign was going badly. Like the Kurds, the local tribes would not stay beaten. Once pacified, they sprang back into action as soon as Alexander turned his attention elsewhere. In a word, he could not rule the empire he had conquered. And, to complete this litany of obstacles, the water was polluted, which meant that the only liquid fit to drink was the harsh, potent wine of the district.

"And what of Clitus?"

My moment was up. "Arrian does not approve of Clitus," I told him, "but he blames what happened on the drink and those types of men who, he says, can always be found at court currying the king's favor with flattery."

This observation earned an affirmative shake of the royal head. "Even otherwise gallant veterans can be looking to add a final laurel to their old exploits," he said. "I could name you one or two."

But he did not and I continued. "These flatterers went so far as to compare Alexander to the gods, even to Heracles . . . with Alexander's encouragement." I had to add that because all three historians make a point of Alexander's claims to be the child of Zeus.

"And what of Clitus?"

According to Arrian, I told him, Clitus had been aggrieved by Alexander's change-over to what he saw as the barbaric Persian style, and now under the influence of the wine the veteran warrior could not tolerate disrespect for the deeds of the heroes of old. But then ... I hesitated.

"Yes?"

Nothing for it. I had to tell it as Arrian told it. "Clitus reminded the king that he had not achieved his great deeds by himself but that they were in great part Macedonian achievements dating from the times of his father. And, heated with wine..."

"Go on." This is what he had been waiting for, I knew.

"What is more"—I might as well tell him the whole terrible story and be done with it—"Clitus held up his shield, waved it in the king's face and, in front of the whole Macedonian assemblage, began to taunt him."

A gasp from the Sultan. "Did he curse? Did he shout? What does Arrian say?"

"Arrian says that Clitus challenged the king to take note of the shield he held in his right hand. He reminded the king that it was the very shield that had protected Alexander when he was dumped bareheaded while fording the river. Then Clitus held up his sword hand and announced, 'This very hand, Alexander, that saved your life at the Granicus.'

The Sultan fell back as if wounded by the words Clitus had hurled at his king. After a moment he raised his eyes to mine, black as tar and cold as ice.

"İskender had to kill the villain, he had no choice. That speech is sedition pure and simple."

It was a judgment spoken not in the tones of Suleiman the *ghazi*, but in the tones of Suleiman the law-giver.

"Plutarch agrees with you," I told him. "He calls Clitus an evil genius. Do you wish to hear from Plutarch?"

"No," he answered. "I have heard enough. The man put a stain on the king's honor. He had to die." He lowered his head reverently, not, I think, out of respect for the death of Clitus, but in sympathy for a king who must kill to preserve his honor.

Then, as suddenly as the mood had come upon him, it was

over. I was dismissed without thanks—kings give no thanks for services rendered—but with what I took to be a king's way of gratitude.

"You have already given me much to ponder," he said. "To such a valuable member of my entourage, I cannot deny the pleasure of the chase. From now on, when we take a day to hunt, I will look forward to your company."

"And my weapon, sire? Will I be permitted to carry my *gerit*?"

His answer was a brusque question. "How can a man hunt without a weapon?"

"But my father, sire?"

Luckily, he did not take my query amiss. "Ah, yes, your father."

Perhaps he had forgotten his promise to you that I would not be permitted to carry a weapon. But I doubt it. Whatever the case, he brushed it aside as if the matter had simply slipped his mind.

"I will write to your father to clarify the difference between using a weapon to hunt animals and using it to make war. The doctor is a rational man. He will, of course, understand."

Of course I agree with him, Papa. I trust that you do, too. The prospect of a royal hunt in the Zagros Mountains is something I never dared to dream of. Certainly it is more than enough reward for the weeks I have spent questioning the point of this venture, ever since Konya. And, truthfully, Papa, I will be happy to leave Persia. Despite the richness of its past, it is now a forlorn place. Wherever you look, your eye falls on piles of trash that mark where houses and barns and chicken coops once stood. There are signs of abandonment in every street. When we arrived, laundry was still hanging on the tree branches by the river. Tahmasp's men did not even take the time to set proper fires, and many of the buildings are still standing. But with no people in them. Hamedan is like a corpse from which the soul has escaped. This is an aspect of war I was not prepared for. But the Tigris and the Euphrates still beckon.

And something happened tonight that made me hope that my bumbling translations may not have fallen on deaf ears. As

I was stepping out through the tent curtain, I was stopped by the sound of the Sultan's voice. At first I thought he was talking to me, but then I realized he was talking to himself — about Gaugamela. And you know what I heard him say, Papa? Let me tell you his exact words: "The boy had it right!" I heard him say. "After Gaugamela, İskender was king of Asia. If he had been satisfied with that and stopped at Baghdad, none of the bad things would have happened to him." His words.

Don't be surprised if this is the last letter you receive from me for some time. The trek ahead takes us over mountains where the courier service between our encampment and the capital does not operate. But there is no cause for you to worry. The Grand Vizier has prepared the way. The passes are clear of Persians. And this is the preferred season in which to cross the Zagros Mountains.

Next stop, Baghdad.

As always, your devoted son,
D.

45

HANIKIYYE

From: Danilo del Medigo at Hanikiyye
To: Judah del Medigo at Topkapi Palace
Date: November 23, 1534

Dear Papa:

By the time you read this, word of our misadventures will have reached the capital via the Sultan's courier system. But I doubt what is reported by the Grand Vizier's staff will tell the whole of our calamitous encounter in the mountain pass. Remember, he is the one responsible for the change of route that brought us to this pass—excuse the pun, Papa. So his report will have every reason to discount the effects of his decision.

First, let me assure you that I am writing to you unharmed from the town of Hanikiyye, where we are now camped on the western slopes of the fearsome Zagros. This is the spot we hit when we finally blasted out of the Manisht pass.

Breathe easy, Papa. We were not waylaid and attacked by Persian snipers. In fact, after what I have lived through in the last two days, I would most certainly rather have been menaced from the mountaintops by Persian sharpshooters than by what fell upon us with such pitiless ferocity in the Zagros pass.

Understand, there are two routes from Hamedan through the mountains that divide Persia from Mesopotamia. One is the winter route near the high desert in the east. The other is the easy summer route through the foothills. This being November, well before the onset of winter, we naturally took the easier one, and our journey along the Zagros foothills began uneventfully in mist and drizzle, normal for November in these parts.

On the third day out from Hamedan, the peaks of the Zagros loomed ahead of us like gods guarding the entrance to the pass on the eastern rim of the plain. Huge limestone, dolomite, and sandstone rocks a thousand feet straight up, they seemed closer to heaven than to us. But we were, after all, following the much traveled Silk Road to and from China that had been used for hundreds of years. And when the sun peered out from behind the peaks to welcome us to the land of the caliphs, I think I was not the only one who took it as a good omen as well as a source of warmth.

We moved quickly into the network of gullies that spreads out through the foothills. On both sides, the wind has stripped the ridges bare and blown furrows of snow into the shallow depressions left between the rocky outcroppings. Those patches might have served us as little flags signaling more snow to come, but these mountaintops are snow-capped year-round so the presence of a few loose flakes on the hillside was hardly noticed. Besides, the Grand Vizier had passed along this same route less than a week earlier and sent back a favorable report with only one warning: when we reach the tall mountains, we are to watch out for concealed Persian snipers.

It was afternoon when a breeze began to gust in from the east, but we were too busy setting up camp to pay it any heed. And by the time the tent poles were sunk, the animals safely tethered, and the food supplies distributed, everyone was much too tired to bother about the gusts of wind that, by then, had begun to seem more like blasts. It was an exhausted corps that bedded down behind our canvas walls into a deep sleep, too worn out even to think of weather.

The avalanche announced itself while we slept in a series of lightning strikes, which disrupted our slumber with a crackling that sounded like a giant with huge claws tearing up the sky. Then came a boom, as from a long way off. Then another, closer this time. Then another that sounded like a musket shot.

Now fully awake, we heard chunks of the cornice above us shearing off, breaking, tearing, cracking, the sound earsplitting, and picking up speed as they roared by us tumbling down the bank. You could tell when they were getting close because the ground under us began to shake. No one but the god of thunder himself could have created such a roar. At that moment I was certain I was going to die. Isn't it odd what comes to your mind at such times? What came into mine was the voice of the Sultan speaking as he had many weeks ago in this very tent while we were encamped at Sivas.

"If I were offered a choice whether to be the god of gunpowder or the god of weather, I would choose weather every time." That is what he said, Papa. Could he have had a premonition? Knowing your abomination of all forms of soothsaying and augury, I will not pursue this thought.

How long the avalanche lasted, I cannot tell you. I only know it seemed like hours that we lay there in the dark with only the sounds that filtered into the Sultan's tent to tell us what was happening outside. Each time a piece of the snowbank broke off, there was this aching crack, then the beginnings of a rumble as the slab began to thunder down the mountain, getting bigger and noisier as the ice cake gathered snow and got closer and closer. And there was no way to judge whether it would roar right past your tent or gather you up and bury you alive in the snowpack.

Until that night, Papa, I had never really imagined that I might die. Yet, as we lay there in the path of the monster, aware at every moment that our shelter might be the next to cave in, I was convinced that I would not live to see the sun rise. And here is a strange thing. All I could think was, *Please, God, don't let me die alone so far from home.*

By morning, the wind had subsided, but the silence was somehow even more unearthly than the screams in the night. I do believe that I am not the only member of this party who awoke believing that I had died and gone to heaven. After all, we had been told that death by freezing is painless — like a slow, deep descent into sleep. But, after a bit, we could make out the muffled little cracks that ice makes when it starts to thaw. Then, a faint twitter. *Are there birds in heaven?* I wondered. Then came a shout. Then, a curse. Definitely, this was not heaven. And when we ventured out, what we saw began more and more to resemble hell.

Overnight, great mounds of debris had created hills where none had existed the day before, some man-sized, some large enough to bury several bodies — human and animal. Men drifted through the mist, silent as ghosts. Some managed to find shovels and were clawing away at the snow trying, beyond all reason, to release a comrade, or pulling with their bare hands at the reins of horses encased in snow. Whole regiments had been buried in the snowpack, along with flocks of animals and innumerable carts and wagons full of supplies, arms, and food.

Everywhere, pieces of canvas waved in the wind like the torn banners of a defeated army. Had it not been for the Sultan — his strength, his comfort, his inspiration — most of us, facing the burial of half our army, would simply have bowed to fate, curled up, and given ourselves over to the lure of painless sleep.

What stays in my mind are the small things. I shall never forget coming out of the tent and seeing directly ahead a pure white shape, similar in form to a sarcophagus, its top surface smooth as satin and marred only by what seemed to be a twig growing out of the center. As we approached, the twig began slowly to wave back and forth, and, lo and behold, when one of the pages jumped on top of the mound to examine it, he announced it was a human finger. No one said a word. All simply scattered in every direction in search of a digging implement, and within moments there was a crew burrowing into the snow to release the owner of the finger.

The body appeared as if conjured by a magician—a hand, an arm, an ear, a lock of hair. Pouring sweat, snow flying wildly, we were finally rewarded with a grunt. Whoever it was, was alive.

We kept on digging even after the grunting ceased and we couldn't hear any breathing noises. Without being told, we somehow understood that seconds were important. I know that all of us were praying while we dug. And, as if in answer, a face came into view. It was the face of Selim, the youngest of the pages, who must have headed out into the night for the latrine, his need stronger than his fear. He was unconscious and did not appear to be breathing.

Behind me, Ahmed Pasha shouldered aside the diggers who had now stopped digging and were staring at the bluish face, transfixed. Ahmed was barely recovered from his seizure, but he managed to jump in beside Selim's lifeless body and scoop his fingers into the boy's mouth to clear it of snow. Whereupon, miraculously, with a weak cough, Selim sputtered back to life.

It must have been the cheer that echoed up and down the valley that drew the attention of the Sultan, who appeared just in time to see Selim open his eyes.

"My compliments, Chief Interpreter." The Sultan swept his caftan over the snow in a rare gesture of respect for another human being. "If this boy had been buried many minutes longer, he would surely have died." Then, turning, he bowed to us. "To all of you, my congratulations. By saving your colleague, you have bested the avalanche."

The Sultan's tone was even, his voice strong. From that moment we knew that we were destined to wrestle ourselves free from the jaws of the monster, no matter what else it had in store for us.

A troop of Janissaries was dispatched to dig a path the length of the encampment, which they accomplished with amazing speed. (Never again will I make fun of those little spades they dangle at their waists.) By noon the line of march was in touch with itself, and reports were beginning to come to the Sultan from both the head of the line and the rear. The snow had inflicted its damage in a wanton—godlike, you might say— manner, burying the food supplies but sparing the hospital tent and the pigeon coops and the treasury. (Was I the only page who thought of King Midas starving to death because everything he touched turned to gold?)

By the end of the day, the Sultan's fatwa was being passed on up and down the valley reassuring all that, although our food wagons were lost, we were not condemned to death by starvation. We were in real need of only three things, said the fatwa: food, water, and warmth. For water, Allah had provided us with an unlimited supply of snow to melt, for which we must offer a prayer of thanks. Allah had already split loads of broken trees to be gathered for firewood, the fatwa continued. And tomorrow, with Allah's help, the Sultan promised us food.

"Look up at the side of the mountain, through the break in the cornice," he ordered us.

All we could see was a forest of shattered trees. Then one of the pages spoke. "The forest is destroyed, sire."

"Correct. However, it remains the home of birds. And where there are birds there are gazelles, ibexes, and certainly wild pigs for us to eat. All we have to do is hunt them down."

"But how do we get up there, sire?" another of the pages asked.

"We climb up on the backs of the horses we have left. I will lead the way. I need not remind you that the Osman tribe has been on intimate terms with the horse and saddle for many generations. Long ago my ancestors survived the steppes of central Asia by their hunting skills. And, to this very day, the Ottomans are known to be the finest horsemen in the world."

"Hear, hear!" echoed through the valley.

"In happier times," he went on, "we hunted for sport. Now we will hunt for food, the stuff of life itself. Tomorrow at dawn, *inshallah*." He lowered his head in reverence. "I will lead you up the side of the mountain to conduct the greatest hunt in history. And I have complete confidence that we will succeed because I am accompanied by a group of hunters renowned in the world."

The shouting and stamping that followed reverberated against the walls of the pass, giving his words the air of an ancient prophecy. And for the next hour, cheering echoed through the valley each time the fatwa was read out to a section of our bedraggled force.

What the Sultan did not disclose — and what we in the Sultan's entourage learned only by whispers as the day went by — was that, at the end of the valley, the Janissaries had encountered a wall of snow as high as a small mountain that sealed us off from rescue more effectively than any Persian general could have. Furthermore, the depth and heft of the barrier were far beyond the reach of spades and shovels. Dynamite was needed. And we learned soon enough that, by a twist of fate, our supply of gunpowder had been sent ahead with the Grand Vizier to prepare for the siege of Baghdad. Was it possible that the great army of the Gunpowder Empire would perish in the Zagros passes for lack of explosives to blast its way out? That was the bitter jest that circulated among the pages as we prepared for the grand hunt the following day. Yes, Papa, the Sultan had sent a runner to remind me that, on account of my recent service to him, I was now an invited member of his personal hunting party.

Did I have my weapon with me, he wanted to know. I was able to answer, yes, I did. You know me, Papa. I had slept with my *gerit* at my side all through the campaign, even during the avalanche. And I was ready to use it. More to come.

Love,
D.

Enclosed, the letter I wrote to you while we were bottled up in the Manisht Pass.

46

THE HUNT

From: Danilo del Medigo, snowbound in the Manisht Pass
To: Judah del Medigo at Topkapi Palace
Date: November 12, 1534

Dear Papa:

Even though our regular courier service has not resumed, the Sultan's pigeon post may have already brought news to the capital of the big hunt in the Zagros Mountains. But I suspect that there is a part of the story you will never hear as long as Ibrahim the Greek is forwarding the reports. Besides, who knows? I may have forgotten how it went by the time we are freed from this frozen hellhole.

Note that I have written, "by the time we are freed," not "if we are freed." For I have no doubt we will be rescued as soon as the Grand Vizier gets news of our entrapment and sends a party of sappers to blast us out. But for now we are still imprisoned by a wall of snow, and as yet there is no sign that anyone is aware of our predicament. You see, the couriers and their horses are boxed in here with us. So our only contact with the rest of the world depends on the carrier pigeons that the Sultan always insists on bringing along just as his ancestors did. Clever Sultan. Clever ancestors. Ahmed Pasha says these birds travel eighty miles in four hours, about three times faster than our couriers. Clever pigeons.

Some of the pages—more than a few—fear that a second avalanche may engulf us, set off by the noises we make in the forest with our muskets while we hunt for food. As if a burst of gunfire could unleash a snowslide. Some people will believe anything.

What I did find slightly alarming is that this morning the Sultan issued each of us an oilskin envelope into which anyone who wished to do so could insert his last will and testament, to be strapped on his person. I need not dwell on what this gesture implies. But I assure you, Papa, I do not intend to be found frozen to death with my last will and testament stuck to my chest. Besides, I have nothing to leave behind except an eyewitness account of this accursed campaign, so why not write about it? I urge you to keep these scribblings of mine in a safe place for the children that I know I will someday produce. But if by some chance we do not get out of here safely, please make sure that my horse, Bucephalus, is treated well and not put down until his natural lifespan has been lived out. That is my testament.

You know as well as anyone how much it meant to me to be included in the Sultan's hunting party. I found myself whistling as I set about my preparations. But while I was sharpening my *gerit*, my mind was invaded by a vision, not a dream but like a dream. I was on my horse, moving through a forest knee-deep in leaves, nothing stirring. Then came a rustling in the brush and a brutish head thrust through the branches. It was a wild boar coming at me head-on, and I was paralyzed with fear because I had no idea how to kill it.

You know me, Papa. I am not a pretending sort of person. When I come face to face with new text, I know perfectly well that, given my inadequate scholarly skills and in spite of your efforts and Mama's to educate me, it will be difficult for me to decipher the meaning. On the other hand, I also know that, when I line up at the shooting range, I am the best marksman in my *oda*. But, faced with the snorting, snarling creature in my vision, I was suddenly aware that I knew nothing about hunting, and even less about hunting pigs. Cavorting in the riding ring or even in the hippodrome while the crowd cheers on is a far cry from hunting wild animals in the forest. Until now, all my training in horsemanship has been for tilting and racing against other riders in places with fences around them. And there are rules. But in the forest there are no fences. Or rules. Even if there were, I had no time to learn them and no one to teach me. I could hardly wake up Ahmed in the middle of the night and beg him to teach me how to kill a wild pig in a dense forest before morning.

For a moment, I thought of avoiding the hunt by feigning a fever. But I am such a bad liar that I was bound to be found out and disgraced. All I really needed was a quick lesson in pig-sticking. A few good tips like, what is the best moment for the thrust, what part of the body to aim at, how close you have to get—some things I know in my bones about *gerit* tilting but which may not apply to pig-sticking. Yet for the lack of them I could end up not only disgraced but dead.

Then it came to me. There in the tent in the middle of the night I heard my mother's voice reciting, in unison with me, the portion of *The Odyssey* where Odysseus comes back to Ithaca after an eleven-year absence and can't get his wife to recognize him. She asks for proof that this ragged, grizzled old man could possibly be the handsome, heroic husband she sent off to Troy a decade earlier.

Odysseus turns to his old nurse and reveals a scar on his leg from a wound he received in a boar hunt when he was a boy.

"Oh yes!" she says as she caresses the scar. *"You are Odysseus!* Ah, dear child! I could not see you until now—not till I knew my master's very body with my hands!"

She then describes the hunt in which the boy was wounded. That is the canto that Mama made me memorize and I remember it to this day.

Before them a great boar lay hid in undergrowth,
In a green thicket proof against the wind
or sun's blaze, fine soever the needling sunlight,
impervious too to any rain, so dense
that cover was heaped up with fallen leaves.
Patter of hounds' feet, men's feet, woke the boar
as they came up — and from his woody ambush
with razor back bristling and raging eyes
he trotted and stood at bay. Odysseus,
being on top of him, had the first shot,
lunging to stick him; but the boar
had already charged under the long spear.
He hooked aslant with one white tusk and ripped out
flesh above the knee, but missed the bone.
Odysseus' second thrust went home by luck,
his bright spear passing through the shoulder joint;
and the beast fell, moaning as life pulsed away.

As I repeated the words aloud to myself, I realized that I had actually picked up a few pig-sticking tips from old Homer. I had learned that boars use their tusks the way we use the *gerit*, for one massive thrust. What this said to me was, better be very careful with your aim because you may not get a second chance at this beast. Odysseus was lucky. He missed his first go at the boar and was wounded. Still, he lived to kill his prey. Then again, he had the gods on his side. I couldn't count on either luck or the gods. But I did have a strong feeling that my mother was watching over me from heaven as I made my way to join the hunting party.

It took an entire morning for us to climb up to the shelf where the forest began. Toward the last of the climb the pitch was so steep we had to dismount in order to unburden the horses. We were followed by a detachment of muleteers, each leading a string of pack animals to carry back to the camp enough wood and meat needed to roast and feed the thousands of mouths waiting below. We must have looked to them, as we headed to the peak, like the longest snake in the world, slithering up the mountain. The odd horse took a fall, but almost all got up there safely. And, of course, mules are almost as good as goats at climbing rocky cliffs.

Luckily, we managed to reach the clearing in time to gather up a quantity of firewood before dark, to be sent down the mountain so that fires could be started below. We even had the time to roast the birds that the hunters had flushed out at the edge of the treeline as soon as we arrived. Fresh melted ice, fresh-killed quail, and a bonfire of juniper branches — we already had our share of bounty and the serious business of the hunt had not yet begun. That task was, of course, the wholesale killing of large animals — some bears but mostly boars — with which the forest was reportedly teeming. Our guides also reported that these animals were stronger than oxen and ferocious in protecting their young.

We kept the fires in our makeshift camp burning all night, but even so in the morning water that had been left in cups near the fire was frozen over. Not at all balmy weather, but we hadn't climbed up there for a picnic. We were there to provide food for an army, and that business began without delay by the light of the rising sun.

As promised, the woods were literally teeming with wildlife — running, jumping, hooting, crowing, swooping. A hunter's paradise. We had been told to use arrows on the smaller game and save our *gerits* and the lances for the big animals. I myself killed four piglets that walked in front of us in a single file just as we entered the woods. We hardly had time to truss them up and call for the muleteers when along came four more. These I left to my fellow marksmen. When the first one fell, it was wounded but not dead. Then the other three gathered around it as it lay kicking and squealing on the ground and just stood there until one of the Janissaries rode over and finished them all off, *bang, bang, bang*. Unlike those of us trained for competition, the Janissaries are all skilled and enthusiastic shooters.

So it went all day, the mules hard-pressed to keep up with the kill and no resistance on the part of the animals. But on our way back to camp, when we had turned our horses loose to graze in a clearing, we spotted a sow herding a clutch of calves. This female turned out to be quite a different type of pig than the males, who had seemed more bewildered than hostile. Possibly, like me, they had never before faced off against an opponent of a different species. But I guess certain kinds of feelings are common to all living creatures. When the female caught sight of us, she quickly reversed direction and bumped her charges off to a nearby cave. One of the pages on horseback took after them to finish the job, and for a few moments nothing was heard. Then from deep in the woods came something between a shout and a scream: "It's killing me! It's killing me!"

We all jumped back on our horses and galloped to his aid, only to find the poor fellow face down on the ground with blood spurting out of his backside. And no sign of the pig. The wound told the tale of what had happened. It was a sickening mess with torn ends of muscle sticking out from his pulsing flesh.

"Lucky it was a sow that got him," my partner muttered to me as we hoisted the wounded page's prostrate body onto an improvised stretcher. "A male boar would have had better aim."

Probably so, but cold comfort to the page whose lower parts were now covered with blood.

We had been amazingly lucky earlier in the day, and now we were seeing the dark side of pig-sticking. Apparently, these big animals are often slow to react, but when they do they are deadly. Myself, I didn't take it personally. It was just the law of the jungle. Not so my fellow hunters. The moment they caught sight of their bloodied comrade, the cries went up.

"Kill the pig!"

"Get the sow!"

"Kill! Kill! Kill!"

They were after vengeance. They even prevailed on the Sultan to track down the culprit, in revenge for the wounding of their bleeding comrade. I do not believe his heart was in the venture. With piles of carcasses to be carried down the slope to his hungry troops below, a delay at this point was surely the last thing he needed. Perhaps he wanted to give the men some kind of reward for a hard day's work far beyond the call of duty. Whatever his reason, he did lead us all back into the darkening forest in search of the sow, and, amazingly, we soon found her, this time with two huge males standing guard over the lair.

Beside me, a Janissary with a musket fired and hit the larger boar. The animal spun around but did not go down. Instead he took off straight at us. I heard another shot but the beast never faltered. Then another and still he came on. You could not help but admire the courage of the animal.

Now he was very close to those of us at the front of the column. Out of some kind of instinct, I positioned my *gerit* on my hip. From the corner of my eye, I could see the second boar leap into the air to hurl himself at the Sultan. No time to measure the distance, or calculate the angle of the thrust or the timing of the throw. I let go with my *gerit*. Then everything slowed down as if the whole world was moving at half speed, and the beast literally fell from the air at the Sultan's feet. A moment earlier, I would have missed him. An inch of play in the angle, I might have killed the Sultan with my *gerit* instead of the boar.

After that I went into a swoon and fell off my horse, so they told me, for I remember nothing of it. My last memory as I lay on the ground is of the Sultan leaning over me, reaching for his jeweled dagger—was he about to kill me?—and then, as my sight faded, I felt his fingers tucking the weapon under my waistband and heard his voice say, "Keep this with you always. It will protect you from harm. And remember this: if ever you have a need for anything within my power to bestow, only ask and your wish will be granted."

I reached down and there it was—the Sultan's own dagger inset with jewels worth hundreds. I heard him say something about Allah—then blackness and silence.

When I came to, I was back at the foot of the mountain on my bedroll, covered by a downy quilt with men crowded around me. And when I greeted them, they began to applaud me like the spectators at the hippodrome. Then Ahmed told me I had saved the Sultan's life. But what I have written here is only my recollection of it.

Now you see why I wanted to tell you the story myself. Today, I saved the Sultan's life. Tonight I was fêted throughout the camp. But I know that I acted without thought, without intent, without true courage.

This venture has set me to wondering how much of our life is spent fearing and preparing for dangers that never happen. While men were quaking in fear of being bombarded from above by Persian bowmen, they were almost destroyed by an avalanche. While we were hunting for food in the age-old way, our leader was almost killed by a chance encounter with a wild animal. And I am saluted for an act beyond my control. We have much to talk about, Papa.

Last thought. The Sultan once said to me that, given the choice, he would rather be the God of Weather than the God of Gunpowder. Today, if I were offered a choice, I would choose to be the God of Timing.

I miss you, Papa.

D.

___

From: Sultan Suleiman, encamped in the Manisht Pass
To: Sultana Hürrem at Topkapi Palace
Date: November 12, 1534

Allah is kind. Allah is merciful. At the darkest hour, the troops of the holy *jihad*, snowbound in the Manisht Pass, were beset all around by wild animals. Suddenly a mad pig, poised to kill, sprang out of the underbrush to impale me. But, as the beast flew through the air, Allah guided the hand of a nearby page to bring down the crazed animal, and in a flash it lay dead on the ground, pinned to the earth by the page's *gerit*. Allah be praised. You, my beloved, are the first to know of this miracle, thanks to my pigeon post.

The Zagros Mountains have not been kind to us. The campaign has brought much glory to the empire but at great cost. Thirty-nine hundred dead and some twenty thousand horses and camels lost.

Baghdad beckons.

Signed with the Sultan's seal.

Beneath the Sultan's seal, an encrypted message:
The Sultan was saved by the strong arm of a lowly page of the Fourth Oda. He is to be granted his dearest wish. Hope lives.

47

ABI-NERIN

From: Danilo del Medigo at Abi-Nerin
To: Judah del Medigo at Topkapi Palace
Date: November 26, 1534

Well, Papa,

I have had my moment of glory. It lasted three days. As you can see by the date and place of this letter, we are well out of the Manisht Pass, but the real story of our release may not be the same as the news now winging its way to you in the capital. That report will have been authored by the Grand Vizier Ibrahim, who is by no stretch the hero of our rescue. Not even close. To be precise, while we were walking to safety through the blowout in the snow wall, he was still at Baghdad preparing his men to come to our rescue.

I believe that I left off writing to you after I killed the boar, fell off my horse, and was carried down the mountain from the hunting grounds. That evening came the great feast. There we were—those of us lucky enough to have survived the hellish crossing of the Zagros—spread out in the valley of the pass from one end to the other, warm and well-fed, unharmed by either Persian sharpshooters or wild boars, a little pleased with ourselves for having survived nature's onslaught.

It was the perfect moment for the Sultan to bring everyone down to earth with the information that we were not yet out of the woods, still imprisoned by an ice wall with no means of blasting our way out. "So eat hearty," he said, before warning us that after tonight we would be on short rations until we were rescued. Nobody even grumbled. So when a beefy fellow began to shoulder his way up to the Sultan's dais in a very bellicose way, shouting, "Make way, make way!" he was greeted on all sides with jeers and calls of "Sit down, ungrateful pig!" But something he told the Janissaries who were guarding the Sultan must have impressed them, because after feeling him up and down for weapons and relieving him of a knife, they let him through the crowd to the space in front of the Sultan's dais. And the mere sight of this ruffian in such close proximity to the royal presence brought him the attention of the entire assemblage. Lucky for him, the fellow did have the sense to keep his head lowered when he addressed the Sultan.

"My name is Orhan," he began. "In early days, my father Korkud was the Sultan's Chief Butcher and now I am the Sultan's Assistant Chief Butcher."

For this common worker even to be standing in the vicinity of the Padishah was such a total breach of custom that the crowd had no notion how to respond. So they sat silent. But the Sultan leaned forward, which the butcher took as a signal to continue.

"How does a humble butcher best serve his Sultan?" the man asked.

Again, silence greeted the question. But this time, the Sultan leaned a little farther forward.

Encouraged, the butcher answered his own question. "If called upon I would gladly have sacrificed my life for my Padishah. But I am a humble butcher. So today I butchered two hundred carcasses in honor of his great hunt in the forest. It was the best service I could render. Then tonight at the feast I was told that we were hemmed in at the end of this pass by a wall of ice with no gunpowder to blast our way out. This was the first I had heard of it. No one ever tells us anything."

He had a point. The Sultanate does not make a practice of giving out information to anyone, not even to the members of the *divan*. Was this perhaps, I wondered, a ploy to lighten the bad news of what we had still to face? Had the butcher been rehearsed to play his part? No, this Orhan did not have the wit to carry off such a jape. The way he spoke gave the impression of a man not on intimate terms with words, much less a speechmaker.

"So, when I heard of our"—long pause—"predicament, I gathered up my courage and requested an audience with the Sultan." And indeed it must have taken some courage for a butcher to approach the Sultan's Janissaries, who, everyone knows, are trained to shoot first and ask questions afterwards. Mind you, they did hold onto his knife. And the household guard may have recognized him as a lifelong member of the kitchen staff. Whatever the case, say this for the man, he did know enough to fall on his face and eat the dust at his sovereign's feet before he looked up and faced him eye to eye.

"I understand, sire," he continued, "that you have a shortage of gunpowder."

What was this? A mockery? A threat?

The Janissaries stepped forward to heave the fellow out, but the Sultan waved them away. And then, the unthinkable: the Sultan spoke directly to the butcher; almost as if to an equal.

"You heard correctly, my good man. Our entire supply of explosives has gone on ahead with the advance party."

"Well, sire, I have something here that might help you out." With that the butcher began to paw at the odds and ends of shawls and wools that he had wrapped himself in to ward off the cold.

Once again, the Janissaries moved to stop him and once again the Sultan warned them off. I wonder if someone who has spent a lifetime under the threat of assassination from the very day of his birth develops a special sense of whom he can trust. Certainly the Sultan seemed sure from the beginning that he had nothing to fear from this man. He allowed the fellow to disrobe, rag by rag, waiting patiently until, at last, the butcher reached down below his belly button and fetched up an oilskin pouch filled to overflowing with some yellowish, powdery stuff.

Of course, the Janissaries rushed in to grab it, but the Sultan again motioned them away.

"What have you brought me, Orhan?" he inquired politely.

The butcher, equally courteous, replied, "It is a gift I got from my pa, sire. When I came of age, he gave me two things: this sack and his best butcher knife. 'Strap these to your belly, my boy, and you will never be without protection in the world,' is what my pa told me." Then, with a sideways glance at the Janissaries, he added, "Your men took the knife away when they let me through."

"Don't worry, you shall have your knife back," said the Sultan. "Now, what of the sack?"

"I give it to you, sire, with my heart's wishes that it may be of some use. Not much of it, but my pa swore to me there was enough gunpowder in this sack to blast me out of any jail in the world."

Well, Papa, there was enough gunpowder in that sack to blast a giant gap in the snow wall. And the next morning we all marched out of the Manisht Pass in single file to freedom.

When the blast went off, the butcher stood in a place of honor at the right hand of the Sultan, the place normally occupied by the Grand Vizier. Only this time Ibrahim the Greek was supplanted by Orhan the butcher, hoisted on the shoulders of the Janissaries by the Sultan's order and conveyed to the end of the pass while the crowd cheered him almost as loudly as they had applauded me earlier. They had a new hero now.

On the far side of the pass, the villagers had been alerted by the explosion and were lined up on both sides of the path, their arms full of fruits and bread and pure white yogurt in gourds.

They knew we would be hungry. The army stayed two days at their invitation, bathing and eating and giving thanks, while I sat tucked up in my downy quilt being visited and cosseted by my comrades. Prince for a day.

More tomorrow,
D.

━

From: Danilo del Medigo at Abi-Nerin
To: Judah del Medigo at Topkapi Palace
Date: November 27, 1534

Dear Papa:

Here is what it is like to be a hero. The admiration and praise are sweet. But then comes the bitter aftertaste.

The Grand Vizier Ibrahim has arrived with his rescue team — a little late. Very soon after his arrival, he paid me a visit at my tent. He brought with him a purse full of coins from the Sultan, which I refused to accept. I handed it back to him and thanked him politely but explained that I had done nothing more than my duty and that every man there would have been honored to do the same service if he had been in my place. Believe me, Papa, this sentiment came straight from my heart. But it caused the Grand Vizier to grab me by the shoulders with venom shooting out from his eyes.

"Do you not know that no one refuses the Sultan's gifts?" he demanded. "The gifts that the Sultan offers for services rendered are his way of erasing any debt that he may have incurred. The Sultan can remain under obligation to no man. Are you so ill-bred that no one taught you that such a refusal is an insult?"

Without waiting for my answer he began to shake the bag in my face. "Or is this some Jewish ploy to get the Padishah to raise the sum of your reward? Is that it?"

I was too astonished to answer. But whatever he saw on my

face made him tighten his grip and lower his voice to a steely tone.

"Well, my boy, your ploy may well succeed. Perhaps I may be ordered to bring you a new purse that contains twice the amount of coins than the one you so disrespectfully returned. But do not rush to congratulate yourself on the cleverness of your scheme. You may have multiplied your takings this time, but you have much to learn, boy." He took my head in his hands and glared at me. "I thought I had made it clear to you after the episode at Tabriz that there is no room in the Padishah's suite for showy gestures on the part of underlings. Are you deaf? Are you a slow learner? Or are you just stiff-necked? That is what God called your people when they challenged him. Stiff-necked. But, be warned, this is the last time you will give offence to the Padishah and not suffer severe consequences."

With that he whirled out of the room. And now, I sit here in my tent, disgraced and cheated of the only prize I ever wanted — not gold or even thanks, just recognition that I had some small part in our victory over nature in the Manisht Pass. Instead, I have coins thrown at me as if I were a dog. And I sit here alone, humiliated, and, Papa, there are tears in my eyes.

As I write, a scene comes into my mind: a picture of Achilles alone on the beach at Troy, weeping as he watches the beautiful young virgin he earned as his prize for his victory at Lyrnessus, being led away from his lodge into the arms of King Agamemnon. With her goes the honor he earned in battle, snatched from him by an envious rival.

"*The man disgraces me,*" Achilles cries aloud in anguish. "*He should at least give me respect, but now he gives me nothing.*"

Raising his arms to the heavens, Achilles reaches up to his mother, the goddess Thetis, for solace.

At that moment I found myself raising my arms to heaven. And I swear I heard my mother whisper my name as Achilles' mother did. But, even as I implored her, I knew that, like Thetis, she was powerless to change the course of events. For, as the poet says, no one controls the honors bestowed by a king.

So here I sit sulking in my tent, reminding myself of Achilles on the beach. He was good at war. A lot better than I am. And, by some odd coincidence, he too was robbed of his prize. But there ends the likeness. For I am resolved never again to play the role of Achilles to the Grand Vizier's Agamemnon. Never!

Good night, Papa.
D.

From: Danilo del Medigo at Abi-Nerin
To: Judah del Medigo at Topkapi Palace
Date: November 29, 1534

Dear Papa:

At last the Tigris, the oldest river in the world. You cannot look at it drifting by, as I am now doing, and not get a new lease on life.

Also, I was somewhat lifted out of the miseries inflicted on me by the Grand Vizier when Ahmed Pasha took pity on me after I confided in him. His judgments are often harsh, but they are always just. He listened to my tale of woe without comment, and when I came to the end, he pulled twice on his beard and responded in a way I would have taken ill from another person, but I have come to know his stern manner cloaks a warm heart.

"My boy, there is no question that an injustice has been done you," he began. "But, believe me, worse things have happened to nicer people. Remember," he reminded me, "that you did not embark on this venture in search of glory but to add experience to your education. You wanted to visit the palaces of the caliphate and you will. You wanted to sail the waters of the oldest rivers in the world and you will." And, to be sure, today I am sitting on the banks of the Tigris with the towers of Baghdad just visible in the distance and feeling—I can't say how I feel, Papa—awed, maybe?

After we blew a hole in the ice barrier at Abi-Nerin there followed three days of slogging through the Amara marshes, a thicket of reeds six feet high in chest-deep water, a great trial for the animals but perfectly calm and safe for those of us on their backs. Then just when we were beginning to think ourselves becalmed in the reeds forever, we came upon a broad thoroughfare full of carts and wagons and people — strolling, running, walking free with huge heavy sacks on their heads — all moving along the riverside of the great Tigris, the most ancient waterway in the world, a waterway that I had never in my life even hoped to see. The river was teeming with every kind of craft from graceful gondolas to great sailing ships packed to the hilt with cargo — silks and satins and fur pelts, gold and silver, pepper and spices with names I have heard of but never tasted. I swear to you, Papa, as I watched those crates sail by, the fragrance of cinnamon and cloves and coriander wafted by my nose and I could taste on my tongue the tang of saffron.

You might point out that, from where I sat on the shore, I could not even see the cargo bales in the holds of those ships, much less smell or taste what is in them. But I did, Papa. I did. And every taste and sniff reminded me that the world is full of wonders yet to come. All I need to do is turn my head southward, and I can see ahead the towers of Baghdad.

Will we be welcomed at the gates or shot at? Our spies are not agreed. But don't worry, Papa. I still have my place in the Sultan's guard, surrounded on all sides by Janissaries, just as you were when you campaigned with him. And you know that is the safest place in the world to be.

Love,
D.

48

BAGHDAD

From: Sultan Suleiman, encamped at Baghdad
To: Sultana Hürrem at Topkapi Palace
Date: December 4, 1534

My Regent:

The long march is over. Baghdad is officially ours. Once again, a Sunni *ghazi* sits on the golden throne of Persia. The Shiite shah cowers behind the far eastern mountains of his empire. Yes, victory is ours. But sadly, the conqueror does not have his queen at his side. However, he takes comfort in knowing that this triumph resounds throughout the world to the glory of the Ottoman name, while in Istanbul there sits a Regent dedicated heart and soul to the future interests of his empire and his family.

Signed by the Sultan

Beneath, an invisible encryption:
Under Allah's watchful eye the Great Ghazi's life has been preserved

and the jihad has been saved from disaster. With renewed hope of victory for the jihad comes new hope for the page who made the thrust that saved his ghazi. Surely, this deed will raise him to the heights of his heart's desire.

—

From: Danilo del Medigo at Baghdad
To: Judah del Medigo at Topkapi Palace
Date: December 4, 1534

Dear Papa:

Finally, we are encamped in fabled Baghdad. I assume word has reached you that the city fell to us without a shot. Quite so. Tahmasp's governor, Mehmet Khan, met us at the gates accompanied by a cortège of nobles to escort our army into the city. Once again this province is back in Sunni hands and our Sultan sits officially as the Caliph of Baghdad, seated high on a solid gold throne in the caliph's carpeted throne room, wielding the caliph's scepter and wearing the caliph's crown.

In the midst of all this grandeur, there is no place for me. The Sultan is fully occupied with readying the restored province of Baghdad for its place in the Ottoman Empire. Already he has organized the government of the new province under an Albanian pasha—also named Suleiman—and has bolstered him against future Persian attacks from the east with a garrison of one thousand harquebusiers and one thousand cavalry. He is also building a citadel to repel the shah, should he return to Iraq, and has assigned a total of 32,000 troops to guard the province. All of this, says Ahmed Pasha, may well make Iraq the most expensive to maintain of all the provinces in the Ottoman Empire.

But Baghdad is still Baghdad. So each day, I mount my horse and I set out to see what is to be seen while I await a summons from the Sultan. Sadly, little of ancient Baghdad remains. Of course, the fabled city had lost much of its splendor long before we got here. Genghis Khan is said to have razed it to the ground just a few hundred years ago. And Tamerlane, they say, decimated the population a hundred years later. But great cities somehow stay alive, don't they? And, ravaged or not, this city, built on the bricks of ancient Babylon, has the air of a place held aloft by the sheer power of history. The souk is still soaked with the scent of cardamom. And the streets still hum with the accents of Arabs, Russians, Aramaeans, Turks, Jews, Christians, Nubians, Laristanis, and all the rest who keep trade flowing between east and west.

But as day follows day with no word from the royal enclosure, I cannot help but believe that I have unwittingly done something to offend the Sultan. And I wonder if, as the cynics say, no good deed goes unpunished. For in my admittedly sketchy knowledge of the history of kings, I cannot find a single instance when the act of saving a king's life (and I did save his life) is rewarded with stony silence and disfavor. I find it more and more difficult to keep myself ready for the summons that never comes.

Truthfully, Papa, I am very discouraged.

Your loving son,
D.

—

From: Danilo del Medigo at Baghdad
To: Judah del Medigo at Topkapi Palace
Date: December 13, 1534

Dear Papa:

Finally, today, for the first time since we arrived in Baghdad, I was summoned to the Sultan's apartments in the traditional residence of the great caliphs of history and legend. At Tabriz, Tahmasp fled too hurriedly to carry anything away with him. Here at Baghdad, he had time to pack up, or smash up, every portable thing in the palace. So what greeted us on arrival were bare walls and empty rooms. But not for long. Knowing the Persians, our foresighted leader anticipated finding his captured strongholds stripped bare, even burned. And so now I am beginning to comprehend what filled up the hundreds of wagons and carts that made up the bulk of the Sultan's personal caravan. Pillows! I swear to you, Papa, I have never seen so many pillows and carpets and braziers and lamps and lanterns crammed into one space, each of them so carefully packed that not a single pane of glass was shattered in transit. And enough of them to fill, beyond overflowing, the confines of the Baghdad *selamlik* where the likes of Harun al-Rashid and Saladin ate, bathed, took their leisure, and greeted their guests in the glory days of the caliphate.

I thought of you, Papa, when I took my place beneath the caliphs' ancient throne and gazed upward into the huge green cupola that shelters the ruler's throne, still awesome after centuries of neglect. Standing there, I remembered you putting me to sleep with stories of olden times when Baghdad was the most powerful city in the world, the heart of an empire that stretched from the Mediterranean to India. And Mama stuffed me with the doings of Harun al-Rashid, the caliph who rewarded poets for a good sonnet with gold pieces, Greek slave girls, and horses from his royal stables. Can you imagine the Christian emperor giving a valuable horse to a poet? As you have often told me, Papa, things do come to those who wait. But not, I have found, necessarily good things. So, yes, I was called. And treated kindly. But I was also dismissed. Not by the Padishah himself but by the Grand Vizier, who had apparently been delegated to deal with me.

During my audience, the Sultan continued to consult with his pages in another corner, leaving me to the mercies of Grand Vizier Ibrahim. Mind you, the Grand Vizier was very polite. The Padishah, in deep gratitude for my quickness and agility during the avalanche in the Zagros Mountains, he explained, was graciously granting me a fully honorable discharge from his service and a quick return to my ailing parent, plus a second purse of gold.

For a moment I stood stunned, clutching the heavy purse that the Grand Vizier had thrust into my hand. Then I found myself walking as if propelled by an unseen hand toward the Sultan at the other end of the room. As you well know, Papa, one does not approach the Padishah unless invited, yet I heard my own voice issuing from my throat as I sank to my knees and kissed the hand that had bestowed the coins and thanked him for it.

"However," I explained, looking the Sultan full in the face, "I cannot accept a reward for such a small service after the many benefactions you have bestowed upon me. What I did was nothing more than what duty demanded. But, sire, the skill I used to kill that animal, the skill for which you have so generously praised me, I learned through your good offices, in your schools, which I attended at your invitation."

I waited. When no one came forward to garrote me with a silken bowstring, I plunged on. "It is I who owe you thanks, sire — for my excellent education, my equestrian training, my language skills. Under your generous benefaction, I have enjoyed schooling that would be the envy of any boy in the world. As for these past months in your campaign retinue, I will remember them all the rest of my life with gratitude for the wisdom I have received from your own lips."

From his expression, I gathered that I had not entirely displeased the Sultan with my unauthorized utterances. But I also knew that, since this might well be my only chance to speak face to face with him, I had better get to it before I was hustled off. Thus far, the royal pages had been so taken aback by my audacity that they had made no moves. The Grand Vizier simply glowered.

"With your assent, sire," I continued, "I would, however, ask one single indulgence..." If he indicated the affirmative, I was, as we say in the stables, home and dry. If not, I was cooked. But what did I have to lose other than a packet of gold coins?

Fortuna was with me that day. The Sultan nodded graciously. He even spoke.

"Ask what you will," he said.

"All I want in the world, great Padishah," I told him, "is to remain in your service, to finish out this campaign with my comrades, and to return home victorious in your train."

As I had hoped it would, my offer so pleased the Sultan that he announced in a booming voice, "Request granted and double the purse." Whereupon he went on to acknowledge what he called my extraordinary service at the hunt right there in front of the entire court. And as I prepared to back away he added, "Such loyal service as yours calls for a reward beyond mere coins to mark the place you have earned in my heart." Then, with a nod to his Grand Vizier, "Tomorrow we will search for a place in our entourage where such skill and devotion are made full use of."

And to be sure, today I was summoned again. There was no mistaking, I was once again in the Sultan's favor. Had I any doubts, his greeting when I arrived at his audience tent the next day was, if not effusive, at least cordial. More than cordial. He actually rose from his nest of pillows to greet me. "We are having a discussion on how to deal with the Persians from now on," he advised me, as if speaking to an old friend or a trusted advisor. "And it occurred to me," he went on, oblivious of the Grand Vizier's annoyance, "that we might learn something from the eastern campaigns of İskender, who was faced with similar choices. We are, after all, walking in his footsteps. Do you by chance have a helpful passage from Arrian's *Life of İskender* firmly in your memory, my boy?"

Did I? No, I did not. Should I admit the imperfections of my scholarship or should I prepare to bluff it out in case I was called upon to recite whole passages from Arrian? Too risky, I thought. Better stick with the truth.

"My memory is imperfect, sire. But the text itself is in my cabinet only a few steps away along the corridor."

"Go get it at once," the Sultan ordered. Then, before I had

time to make it to the door, "No, stop. My business with the Grand Vizier is done for the night. Bring the Arrian manuscript to my bed within the hour. You can read me to sleep."

"But, sire," the Grand Vizier protested, "our discussion is not over. We have yet to reach a clear strategy for dealing with the Persians. And I must leave for Persia before dawn."

With hardly a pause for thought the Sultan quickly turned the Grand Vizier's point to his own advantage.

"Exactly!" He swooped down on Ibrahim Pasha like a bird of prey. "You will be much better prepared to advise me on a Persian strategy after you are on the ground in that territory and have gained close-up knowledge of Persian resources and intentions. Is that not the very reason I am sending you off on this dangerous mission at a time when I am so in need of your vast experience in settling the occupation of Baghdad?"

As always, his logic was irrefutable. He did not wait for a response but simply turned to me at the door. "Give me time to bid farewell to the Grand Vizier, my boy, then appear at my bedside with the Arrian manuscript."

As I crept out of the room I caught a glimpse of the Grand Vizier's face that seared my soul. Believe me, Papa, I have seen men in battle lusting after blood and riders, consumed by a passion to destroy an opponent with a *gerit*, but never have I seen a more palpable expression of venom on a man's face. *This man will not rest*, I thought to myself, *until he sees me dead*.

With that happy thought, I bid you good night.

D.

━

From: Sultana Hürrem at Topkapi Palace
To: Sultan Suleiman, encamped in Baghdad
Date: December 15, 1534

Glorious Sultan!

So many tasks, so many details. Duty calls to me as it does to you. Small chores in my case, the conquest of the world in yours. From time to time I think back to my early days in the harem as your Second *Kadin*, and of my delight at receiving the early poems of the Sultan of Love. Will those days ever come again? Perhaps, as I have heard the Christians say, for everything there is a season. Perhaps this is my season of service and obedience to a great *ghazi* who labors in a great cause.

One source of comfort to me is that all the omens are in place for the glorious occasion that is in prospect! When I consulted with the royal astronomer he confirmed that the very time we are planning for Princess Saida's nuptials is the most felicitous period in which a woman can marry. During any of the last ten days of January, he says, Jupiter is in good aspect to the princess's sun. So, under the benign goodwill of the gods, the princess will be married within two weeks of your victorious return. The Festival of Double Happiness will memorialize not two but three milestones: your great victory over Persia, your long-awaited homecoming, and a family wedding to warm the hearts of your people. The whole world will watch with awe and respect the total success of the Ottoman Empire.

Signed and sealed with the Regent's stamp by Sultana Hürrem.

At the bottom of this letter is an encrypted message. A quick pass over the page with a lighted taper reveals the words: *The noose is tightening.*

49

BAGHDAD REVISITED

From: Danilo del Medigo at Baghdad
To: Judah del Medigo at Topkapi Palace
Date: February 13, 1535

Dear Papa:

So, I am finally back in the Sultan's daily service, not only as a scribe but once again as the Assistant Chief Foreign Language Interpreter. And I am once again the first, rather than the last, to know the news of the day. The Grand Vizier is off to Ispahan. In today's dispatch, he informs us that city is bursting with treasure and is ripe for the taking. Ispahan, he says, will welcome us with open arms.

"That is what İskender must have been told before he went into Persia on the trail of Darius," the Sultan remarked to me. Then, pointing to the Grand Vizier's dispatch, he added, "It was just such thinking that drove İskender deeper and deeper into the heart of Asia, farther and farther from the source of his supplies, less and less able to defend himself against the brigand tribes on the Indian border. And none of this would have happened if he had been satisfied to stop at Gaugamela."

My thoughts, exactly.

"I know these people of the steppe," he went on. "They are kin to my people. Their territory is never truly conquered. Against them, no battle is ever won. Like us, they learn to ride before they are able to walk. They can approach without making a sound. They can swoop down on a marching column without warning and then vanish into the steppe like smoke. They will always live to fight another day. That is the trap."

Since I am now back on my old footing, I summoned the courage to tell the Sultan, "That is exactly what my mother taught me, sire. 'This anabasis,' she used to say, 'is a trap. It was a trap for Alexander. It was a trap for Xenophon. Always has been. Always will be.'"

"Anabasis?" I could almost see him turning the word over in his mind. "I have heard you use that word before. Can you give me a precise translation?"

"Anabasis is a Greek word, sire," I explained. "My mother translated it as a 'going down.' In ancient days, Xenophon went down into Persia. He had been hired by the shah, Cyrus the Younger, to fight his brother Artaxerxes. Xenophon calls his account of the venture an anabasis."

"And this Xenophon, did he fall into the Persian trap?"

"The Persian army was defeated. Cyrus was killed and the Greek army, the Ten Thousand, had to run for their lives."

"Did they get away?" he asked.

"Only just. Xenophon had to march his men all the way to the Black Sea to sail them home to Greece."

The Sultan took a moment to digest this information. Then he nodded and smiled one of his rare smiles. "So my incursion into the Persian Empire would be my anabasis. Is that correct?"

I thought it best to be noncommittal on the point. "If you say so, sire."

"Xenophon." Pause.

"İskender." Pause.

"Suleiman." Long pause.

"At least I am in good company." Long silence.

Finally, with a straightening of his spine, "But I need not fall into the anabasis trap." He was becoming more decisive in his speech and more upright in his bearing as he spoke. "Indeed, I need not and I will not." A definitive shake of the head. "This campaign will stop at Baghdad."

I believe I just witnessed the most powerful ruler in the world making up his mind about an exit strategy for this campaign. But I was too taken with the implications of what I had heard to think beyond my own self.

"Does that mean, sire, that we are going home?"

"Not so fast, young man." Lucky for me, he was in high good humor and did not take offense at my bold question. "I cannot and will not abandon this ancient city to the vultures. Baghdad will serve us well as an outpost of the empire from which we can keep our eye on Persian moves and Persian plans. I must still visit the tombs of Ali and Hussein. And a tax-collecting apparatus must be set up. No government can exist that is not sustained by taxes. Also, the scribes have yet to take a census or allocate the *dirlik* magistrates. So, you see, there remains much work to be done here in Baghdad—the work of peace. But no more war. This is the end of our military campaign in Mesopotamia. We have defeated Tahmasp. True, we do not have his head on a pike, but it will be many years before the Persians threaten our eastern borders again. We are once again in possession of the golden triangle—Mecca, Medina, Baghdad are ours." He allowed himself a rare smile of self-congratulation. "We will learn from İskender. We will stop at Baghdad."

Can I be forgiven for thinking that my efforts at scholarship had some small influence on this decision? Common sense tells me that a ruler as clever as Suleiman would have come to the same decision without the benefit of my help. But he did make mention of the excellent translations I had provided for him: "In spite of your youth, you have managed to provide me with wise counsel." Those are his words, not mine. "And in a time of great peril, which calls for skill, courage, and quick judgment, you rose to the occasion and rendered me the greatest service a man can render his master."

Then he drew me in close and put his hand on my shoulder. (He touched me!) I can hear his voice in my ear as I write his words: "Believe me, there will always be a place for you in my court, and if you continue to serve me there are no heights you cannot attain in the Ottoman Empire."

I am aware that such offers are purely rhetorical when made by kings. I remember Mama telling me that kings, by their very nature, have short memories. I would never know unless I put his words to the test. And this was my chance.

Carpe diem. Full of trepidation I took a deep breath and inquired in what I hoped was not too shaky a voice, "No heights, sire?"

"No heights."

"To become a vizier? Even someday a *damat*?"

"Anything is possible."

I have heard all the warnings about the fickleness of kings, but this surely is a mark of the Sultan's high regard for me, is it not, Papa?

Love,
D.

50

THE SULTANA REPORTS

From: Sultana Hürrem at Topkapi Palace
To: Sultan Suleiman, encamped at Baghdad
Date: December 18, 1534

My Sultan, Anointed Caliph of Baghdad, Lord of All Asia:

The good news of the conquest of Mesopotamia has arrived.
God knows that I have died of anguish waiting for word, and
have now been granted a new life in victory. Thousands upon
thousands of thanks to Allah! My Padishah, my Sultan, my
Caliph: may you sit in peace and comfort on your throne and
be returned soon to those who weep for you every day of your
absence.

A few details. Admiral Lofti, your informal choice as *damat*,
has already taken steps to divest himself of his present residence
and his wives. He has offered to come to my assistance by
helping to find a suitable palace in which to take up his new
life as son-in-law to a sultan. Tomorrow, we will visit two
possible choices. One in particular, fronting on the Bosphorus,
seems preferable. It will require less work to be made habitable.

Admiral Lofti has offered to initiate discussions with the owner since the price would certainly be higher were it known that the great Padishah himself was the purchaser. I have no doubt that our poor mournful girl will recover her old joyous ways when she begins her new life as a wife and, *inshallah*, a mother.

I eat the dust at your feet.

I am ever devoted, ever loyal.

Signed and stamped with the Regent's seal by Sultana Hürrem

Below the Sultana's seal, visible only by the heat of a lighted taper, is written:

The mournful girl is consoled by the prospect of one last night in paradise before the descent into a life of duty and obedience.

51

DANILO'S REWARD

From: Sultan Suleiman, encamped at Baghdad
To: Sultana Hürrem at Topkapi Palace
Date: February 16, 1535

Most trusted and devoted Queen:

My heart is touched by the affection you show for my daughter—our daughter—Princess Saida, and I am overwhelmed with gratitude for your efforts to move her out of the doldrums of the Old Palace and place her firmly on the road to happiness. Naturally, I wish her well with all my heart. But as a woman you quite naturally see her happiness in terms of love and marriage, whereas I, being a man, am guided by my duty to a greater concern—building a lasting dynasty.

Of course I would welcome as Saida's bridegroom a son-in-law of unquestioned loyalty and a strong right hand on my council. But since the day that Ibrahim Pasha was married to my sister Hatice, I have tended to think of him as filling the role of such a *damat*. God knows he has devoted himself with notable success to my interests. Certainly he did perform nobly for us in Egypt, and most importantly he gave me the greatest gift of my life—you.

Even as I write he is off on a perilous journey into the heart of Persia. And, yes, it is my duty as a father and a dynast to seek out future sons-in-law. This is a duty that I have neglected in my consuming effort to serve my *ghazi* calling of Defender of Islam. Upon reflection, I see that I have thoughtlessly allowed to fall on your delicate shoulders not only a grave responsibility as my Regent, but also the entire burden of acting as both mother and father to our children. And you, my Queen, have taken on that burden without a word of complaint. But you must not also be charged with the task of selecting my first minister, or a vizier in my cabinet, or the *damats* who will take their place as the husbands of Ottoman princesses. For me to place that onus on you has been a thoughtless act for which I beg your pardon. Forgive me, my dear one. My only defense is the age-old soldier's excuse: I was overwhelmed by the task of saving the world. And indeed, thanks to Allah, I have succeeded in preserving the Sunni purity of Islam from the Shiites' apostasy.

As I write, I sit upon the caliph's golden throne and I am daily restoring the ancient glory of the Sunni caliphate. This is not a light task, but it does leave me some time for other concerns. In a word, I am once again prepared to resume my stewardship of empire and family.

So I hereby release you from the onerous task of overseeing the marriages of our daughters, the selection of our future sons-in-law, and the planning and supervision of the wedding celebrations that accompany these happy events. On the day of my return from the field, only one event will be celebrated: the victory of the Ottoman Sultan over the Persian Shah. That ceremony, in all of its grandeur and glory, I leave in your most capable and gracious hands. In the fullness of time we two will confer together, as parents do, on the selection of a possible *damat* for each of our daughters. As tradition dictates, I will personally meet, examine, and evaluate the candidates; set the dates for the marriages; and purchase residences for Saida and

Mihrimah befitting their status as Ottoman princesses.

Certainly the admiral is a qualified candidate. Still my obligations to the Ottoman dynasty dictate that a less hurried and more thoughtful selection process be followed. While searching, I may happen upon a younger man: one equally loyal, whose courage and quickness to respond to challenges would merit consideration and whose youthful ardor might better serve the dynastic demands of the Ottoman Empire. I understand how troublesome it will be to change the plans you have made for Princess Saida's marriage to Admiral Lofti at this late date. And I certainly do not wish to offend the admiral in any way or tarnish his fine record. Perhaps a new plan can be made to seem as a postponement rather than a cancellation.

I leave that decision to you. There is no one more practiced in the art of diplomacy.

Step by step, we are moving toward a spring departure from Iraq. Already the slowest parts of our expedition—the siege equipment and the big guns—have been dispatched homeward by the southern route along the Euphrates. Meanwhile I, myself, accompanied by the Grand Vizier, will proceed to Tabriz and from there return to Istanbul via northern Anatolia.

Believe me, my love, had I a pair of wings and only my own desires to think of, I would fly home to your arms at the speed of an eagle. I am sorely tempted. But it is many months since my subjects in Mesopotamia have caught so much as a glimpse of their new emperor—the reincarnation of their hereditary caliph, once again the Defender of Mecca, Medina, and Baghdad, and, most important, the being to whom they must render fidelity and taxes. So you see why I feel it necessary to take advantage of this opportunity to make myself highly visible and not simply pass them by. But you have my pledge to be in your arms by the end of this triumphant year.

Be patient, my darling. Think not of the lonely months ahead but of the glorious future to follow.

I am, ever, your Sultan of Love.

Beneath the signature, an invisible encryption:
Aided by perseverance, fidelity, and patience, the goodwill of the gods can overcome what has been fated and transform what seemed to be the impossible into the possible.

———

From: Danilo del Medigo at Baghdad
To: Judah del Medigo at Topkapi Palace
Date: February 17, 1535

Dear Papa:

If you recall, the Sultan left me a few nights ago with the impression that he was more than pleased with my service. Then, tonight, he announced that he had a further reward for me. *What is it?* I wondered. *Another gold-embroidered caftan? A permanent appointment to the Fourth* Oda?

No, it was none of these. As a reward for my excellent service, he is sending me home by the short route across the Syrian wilderness, along with the heavy cannons and unused siege equipment. Also, he has given me an advance in rank to captain in the new Heavy Armament Brigade and a huge raise in pay. He and his Janissaries, his *divan*, and his treasure — and his Grand Vizier — will return via Tabriz and from there march home victorious across the top of Anatolia to Istanbul.

To hear the Sultan tell it, the idea of assigning me to the Heavy Armament Brigade is his own. But I hear the voice of Ibrahim Pasha in his words. And I do not doubt that it was the Grand Vizier who implanted this notion in the Padishah's mind. As the Sultan tells it, he made a solemn commitment to you, when he invited me to join him as an interpreter, that I would not be gone for more than a year. Now that year is coming to an end. He has been made aware that I am deeply homesick and worried about my ill father. (And who do you suppose has made him aware?) And he has found a way to gratify my wishes by giving me this position in the Heavy Equipment Brigade, which will bring me home sooner than if I had continued as a member of his personal retinue. It will also put a stop to the growing warmth between us.

If that was his intention, the Grand Vizier may have outsmarted himself. By now, I am as pleased to see the end of this court as Ibrahim Pasha is to see the last of me. I no longer wish to study war. I no longer find any nobility in it, if ever there was. I thought that our enemy was Tahmasp and his Persians, who have danced on ahead of us burning everything behind them. But I have learned that our true enemies have been cold and hunger and geography, and weather and deceit and history.

The great king of Persia must have read Arrian because what he is doing to us is exactly what his ancestor did to Alexander—refusing to engage. And here in Iraq we have been dutifully replaying İskender's role as the conqueror in a strange land, where we are regarded as invaders at worst and, at best, as dupes to be trapped, snared, milked, and bilked as these Persians know very well how to do.

So, Papa, I am on my way home by the short route. I cannot contain my eagerness to see you. The trek ahead will take us on the old Silk Road that follows the Euphrates River along the rim of the Syrian desert, then over the Taurus Mountains into southern Anatolia. It is slow but secure—chosen more out of concern for the valuable cannons, each of which cost the earth, than for me, I am sure. Still, you need have no fears for my safety since the entire route lies within the bounds of the Ottoman Empire—no threat from lurking Persians.

On the other hand, once this portion of the army is separated from the Sultan, it is also out of range of his courier service. But I will try to get a letter through to you when I can.

Love,
D.

P.S. I trust that the tale of your illness is an invention of Ibrahim Pasha's fertile mind. But, if you really have fallen ill,

Papa, please send a message to the Sultan and ask him to send me home. He is the only one able to pluck me up out of the Heavy Armament Brigade and speed me to your bedside. And he would do that, Papa. He never fails to repeat to me that he holds you in the highest esteem and that he owes his present good health—including the cure of his gouty toes—to your expert ministrations. And, as you know, he is a great one for repaying every act of service—both good and bad—to the full.

52

MAYADIN

From: Danilo del Medigo at Mayadin
To: Judah del Medigo at Topkapi Palace
Date: April 29, 1535

Dear Papa:

After the last letter I was able to send, everything happened so fast that I didn't have time even to search out the yellow pigskin slippers that I meant to bring home to you. And now I am halfway to Aleppo, traveling an ancient road that hugs the shore of the Euphrates and stretches over a brown sea of dust—teeming with gazelles and even wolves. Mind you, I haven't seen a wolf yet.

Oh, yes, since I am no longer in the Sultan's retinue, I no longer have the use of the Sultan's courier post. Too bad to be out of touch, but think of this, Papa: I am getting my chance to travel the length of the fabled Euphrates on my new assignment to the Heavy Armament Brigade, in which I am now a captain.

By the way, the sudden departure of this brigade from Baghdad was not because of strategy, as you might expect, but because of money (as everything seems to be in military life). It came about because of the huge financial penalty we would have to pay for hanging onto leased animals past their return delivery date. In this case, the animals are water buffaloes, ten thousand of them rented at a discount by the Grand Vizier to carry our heavy weapons, which have never been used — not once! — in the entire Baghdad campaign. Well, by some mishap, these creatures were overlooked when it came time to return them to their owners.

Don't ask me how anyone can simply forget ten thousand water buffaloes, but the Grand Vizier somehow managed it, and the fines for holding onto the animals past their breeding time mount up at the rate of a hundred gold pieces a day.

I must add that these excessive charges are not some dastardly Arab plot to bilk the Sultan, no matter what the Grand Vizier would have you believe. I am told that the buffalo merchant will actually lose many hundreds of gold pieces if he is unable to breed his herd in season, because the cows come into heat only once a year and each cow produces only one calf per breeding season. Important point: the sale of calves constitutes an even bigger profit to their owner than the leasing or slaughtering of the beasts, which makes it all the more important to have the herd back in the breeding yards on time.

Until now I hardly knew that water buffaloes existed. So far in this campaign, our pack animals have been mostly mules and camels. But I now know that it takes twenty buffaloes to transport one of the big cannons. Expensive, you say, but water buffaloes can survive on whatever grows wild in muddy terrains like riverbanks, so it costs nothing to feed them. Which is why we are transporting them via the Euphrates.

Luckily, our Sultan is a great one to create advantage out of adversity. Within a day, after the affair of the forgotten buffaloes was discovered, he had devised an ingenious plan for the quick return of this expensive herd.

Instead of remaining idle in Baghdad while the court readies itself to quit Iraq, the buffalo herd can make themselves useful by carrying the big guns back to their breeding grounds in

Aleppo. There, the Heavy Armament Brigade is authorized to purchase a herd of mules to carry us and our heavy baggage homeward over the Taurus Mountains, a chore that mules are much better at than buffaloes.

That is the important difference between camel strings and buffalo hordes. While buffaloes navigate the muddy edge of the river with ease, it is a terrain into which camels tend to sink and die. And I have learned that it is of such calculations that this war effort consists. Forget marksmanship, horsemanship, courage, and honor. Think of account books, abacuses, records, and calculations. These are the very heart and soul of war. I finally understand the lesson that the Sultan was trying to teach me when he unleashed the storm of papers over us at Sivas.

And I am daily reminded as we plod along this old river of your warning to be careful what I wish for.

I wanted to see the great rivers of antiquity. Well, I am certainly getting my chance. These beasts may be the strongest and the cheapest, but they move very slowly — very, very slowly. I mean twice as slowly as a camel and at least four times slower than any horse. (I don't know about donkeys.) As for the Euphrates, I report to you that it has the muddiest banks of any river I ever saw.

Love,
D.

———

From: Sultana Hürrem, Consort and Regent, at Topkapi Palace
To: Sultan Suleiman, whose glory resounds throughout the world, encamped at Baghdad
Date: March 25, 1535

My beloved Sultan,

I can only hope that this letter reaches Baghdad before you depart. The vast distance and the weeks that separate us make what is not easy more difficult, but these petty annoyances are melted away by the warm words of trust and concern in your recent letter postponing Princess Saida's wedding.

A postponement there will be. I have begun to advise the countless people concerned. Of course I will not cease my efforts on behalf of Princess Saida's future happiness. I will most certainly continue to cultivate a familial relationship with our chosen *damat*, the Admiral Lofti Pasha. And I will keep up the search for a suitable palace in which the couple can establish a residence and begin to raise a family. I owe it to the blessed girl not to desert her at a time when she most needs the advice of a mother.

Your magnificent leadership of the Baghdad *jihad* continues to give me the strength and fortitude to do all of this and to take on any other task or duty that you might wish to charge me with.

All hail the Conqueror of the Known World.

Signed and sealed with the Regent's stamp by Sultana Hürrem.

Beneath the signature, an encrypted message:
It is a great comfort that nothing has changed the order of events on the day the Sultan rides through the streets of his capital or the night of bliss that follows.

53

RAQQA

From: Danilo del Medigo en route to Antioch–Raqqa
To: Judah del Medigo at Topkapi Palace
Date: May 26, 1535

Dear Papa:

As we struggle along the banks of the great Euphrates, I am beginning to get a glimmering of why men study geography. We are bedded down for the night above the muddy banks of the river in a campsite that has accommodated caravans of merchants traveling between Europe and Asia for centuries, and is now all but abandoned in favor of sea routes—much faster and safer. But not for the likes of this detachment, since we are hauling heavy cargo more suited to mud than to water and thus to pack animals rather than to sail.

These huge cannons—hauled across Anatolia right up to the gates of Baghdad and never used—were much too valuable to be left behind in Mesopotamia. Powered by gunpowder, each of these monstrous *bombards* can shoot stone balls close to a mile, traveling at 284 yards per second. And even though we had no need of them to capture Baghdad, there may well be cities in future campaigns less yielding than those in Azerbaijan and Iraq, where big guns will once again win the day.

Whatever the reason, the powers that decide such matters would never think of going off to war without their big guns. Though they do not seem to have given much thought to the means of transporting these huge, heavy ordnances over vast distances, nor the effort it takes to carry the *bombards* home when the fighting is over.

I think I can truthfully say that until now, I had never given much thought to any animal other than my horse. Now suddenly these huge beasts have become the center of my existence. We of the Heavy Armament Brigade ride at the top of the riverbank along the old Silk Road from Baghdad to Aleppo, overseeing the buffaloes and their cargo from a great height and pitching our tents at night on the high ground far from the water and the bugs. But you have to watch yourself up there because the whole region bordering the Syrian Desert is beset by Bedouins who make a specialty of harassing river traffic. Mind you, Bedouins will always take you in if you are hurt or lost. However, once you get beyond the confines of their hospitality, they will turn on you and slit your throat. But don't worry, Papa. We have thousands of *sipahis* to guard us.

After my experience in their enclave at Elmadağ, I have been inclined to keep my distance from the *sipahis*, but that is impossible this time. Their brigades bracket us at both ends in the line of march. They are, we are told, positioned to keep a sharp eye on us for our own protection. One wonders if this heavy shield has not been laid on for the sake of the valuable armaments we are carrying rather than for us. Perhaps that is a cynical thought. Whatever the reason, the *sipahis* take their charge very seriously, keeping a constant watch out for stragglers and herding us along in clusters as we do the water buffaloes.

But last night, while the *sipahis* were at evening prayers, I managed to escape briefly and stroll down to where the beasts spend their off-hours in the care of their Bedouin boy handlers.

Had I the world enough and time, Papa, these boys who serve the herd of buffaloes deserve an entire report to themselves. They are all young—many, I would bet, no older than ten years—but perfectly trained and totally lacking in fear of their beastly charges, who are twice as tall as they are and fifty times as strong with huge, curled horns, the better to tear you apart.

God must have had these creatures in mind when he created the Euphrates River. It was made for them. In the evening, as soon as they are detached from their harnesses and released from their burdens, they gravitate to the river, and there they satisfy their hunger with the vegetation that grows profusely in the muddy shallows. Once sated, they set about to beautify their bodies with mud that they dig up and spread over themselves.

Then they sink into the muck until all you can see of them is the tips of their horns poking up out of the water. When they are thoroughly soaked, up they pop to enjoy the evening, looking for all the world like groups of harem beauties taking their ease around the pools of the *hamam*.

The picture so entertained me that it wasn't until I was standing directly above them at the edge of the treeline that I noticed, hidden under the ledge of the bank, a long line of much smaller buffaloes loosely tethered to a rope, as placid as a herd of cows waiting to be milked. Between them, the shepherd boys scurried back and forth carrying pails of liquid that they poured into a series of huge copper cauldrons suspended over the fires dotted along the riverbank. Of course, when I leaned over for a better look, I was able to make out that I had stumbled into exactly what it appeared to be: milking time for the females of the herd (hence their smaller stature).

By then, I had made some effort to acquaint myself with buffalo lore, easy enough to pick up from those members of our brigade who had done similar duty with these beasts in past campaigns. And I had come by a raft of anecdotes, all respectful if not downright admiring of these creatures, telling of their great strength, their tolerance for fourteen-hour marches, even their ferocity as fighters. And not a single joke at their expense. But no story I had heard suggested to me that as well as their utility as beasts of burden and suppliers of meat, they were also a source of mother's milk. However, once I understood this, I was consumed by the prospect of getting a taste of the stuff.

What harm could there be in asking? The Bedouin boys had always shown the utmost affability in our few encounters with them. So I marched myself over to the closest cauldron and gently tapped on the shoulder of the first shepherd who passed by with a full bucket to ask for a sip.

To my surprise, he refused flatly. "No, no, you cannot drink this milk, sir. This milk is not for humans, only animals." Then, as if to forestall an argument, he quickly added, "Even a small taste would make you sick. Very sick."

Which led me to the obvious question: "Then why are you collecting it?"

"For cheese, of course. Why else?"

Have you ever been patronized by a ten-year-old shepherd boy, Papa? The look I got for my question was the look I richly deserved for not using my brains. And I must admit, I blushed for shame. Perhaps that is what made him take pity on me, for he added with a friendly smile, "This cheese will roast over the coals all night, and by morning it will be fit to eat. If you wish to taste it, be here at sunrise to share in our feast."

Well, I was there, Papa. I sneaked away from our minders during their absence at morning prayers. Somewhat foolish of me, I suppose, but the taste of that cheese lingers with me as I write. Delicate. Milky. A sort of lightly salted *pannacotta*, quite unlike any flavor I can remember. Except that as I ate it, I became convinced that I had met this taste before. But where? Not in Turkey. Perhaps in Italy. Yes, then I remembered—in Rome, at Madonna Isabella's table. She had presented this same cheese as a delicacy because it had to be eaten within four hours of emerging from the boiling pot. *Buffalo mozzarella fresca!* Fresh cheese just as the Bedouin shepherds had presented it to me. But, being peasants, they keep the cheese left over from breakfast and stuff it under their saddles in packets of oilskin to stew in horse sweat, as an evening delicacy.

I don't quite know why I was so eager to tell you this tale, Papa. But I have the feeling that it says something about the world we live in, that what passes for crude shepherd's fare in one country is considered a rare delicacy at the table of a great lady in another. Let us have a conversation on this subject.

At Aleppo we say goodbye to our ever good-natured and ever accommodating buffaloes and transfer the weight of our cannons to the backs of hundreds of stubborn, bad-tempered mules. I miss the great beasts already.

Love,
D.

54

ANTIOCH

From: Danilo del Medigo at Antioch
To: Judah del Medigo at Topkapi Palace
Date: July 9, 1535

Dear Papa:

Well, here I am in the ancient city of Antioch, and there is almost nothing left to see. Back in Roman times, Antioch was the third-largest city in the western world, rivaled only by Alexandria and Rome itself. Today a single monument remains. Gazing at the great empty spaces, there came to mind the quote from Tacitus that either you or Mama taught me: *Solitudinem faciunt pacem appellant!* They have created a desert and called it peace. That is how this old city looked to me when we came upon it at the easternmost tip of the Mediterranean.

As I write, I see what the Romans—and the Christians—have done to the city of Antioch. Very likely it is the same thing that the Assyrians did to the Hittite monuments when they conquered this place. And what the Greeks did to the Assyrians in their turn. I see here the same ruination that I observed in Baghdad. And I am reminded of great Carthage burned to the ground and Alexander's magnificent library at Alexandria consumed by flames, manuscripts and all. Food for thought on the long ride home.

Once we had loaded up our food and supplies and prepared our newly acquired pack mules for the journey across the Taurus range, we were free to explore the neighborhood. For my part I chose to disappear down a hole into the bowels of the Roman Empire. The name of the place is Zeugma. It is buried under fifteen hundred years of mud and debris. This is where the rich Romans of Antioch built their summer villas. Today, all that can be seen of Zeugma above ground are a few stone tombs scattered around what might have been a necropolis, and surrounded by huge earth mounds that may conceal great treasures buried forever.

But while we were traveling here from Baghdad, we heard quite another version from a boy named Ali, one of the Marsh Arabs who have been guiding us. These guides are young like us, and the nights on the edge of the Mediterranean are not good for much more than storytelling. So this Ali fell into a conversation with one of our pages and told him a wild and improbable but, as it turns out, accurate tale of the depredations of grave robbers who, it seems, have been practicing their profession as long as the historians have. Perhaps even longer.

In a word, Ali offered to lead us to the holes dug into the mounds, some to a depth of thirty feet, that members of his tribe have been systematically "exploring" for hundreds of years. It is not easy, he explained, to take frescoes off the walls or dislodge mosaics from floors. So those things, he says, are still there to be seen by anyone with the nerve to venture into the subterranean depths. This morning we set off—just three of us pages and two of the Arab boys. I well understood that this venture was dangerous and ill advised and probably illegal—just the kind of challenge you know I can't resist.

So down we went, like Dante into the *Inferno*, only we were lowered on a rope. It was dim and airless down there, not stifling, but close. And after navigating a tunnel or two, we were in a Roman house. We knew it was a house because directly in front of us we could see through an arch a room whose walls were not lined with sarcophagi, as would be the walls of a tomb, but with painted surfaces. And the entire floor space was occupied by a single scene rendered in mosaic tiles.

Before allowing us any closer, Ali took pains to explain to us that this was only one of countless such houses—he was familiar with seventeen of them—but that we would be limited on our foray to only a single pair of rooms close to the entrance. Our time was limited, he explained, because the air was poisoned with underground gases. Very reasonable, we thought. Also, he warned us there were ninjas hidden in niches in the walls. There could be no doubt as to which of the two—the poison gases or the ninjas—he found more menacing.

Now with a grand gesture he waved us under an arch, and we found ourselves on the edge of what can best be described as a mosaic carpet, divided into two scenes. At our feet stood Dionysius (identified by his name in black Greek letters) driving a gorgeous gold chariot drawn by two prancing leopards with Niobe at his side. It was amazing seeing the scene in motion, the animals prancing, their front hooves raised as they rushed forward, and Dionysius' muscles bulging with the effort of clutching the reins. It was lifelike to the bone, yet the whole scene had been created out of little chips of stone and metal. The other half of the floor was occupied by seven figures also in motion, walking along as if out for a stroll on a Roman street.

Ali allowed us only one more room. There at our feet sat the god Poseidon, the points of his trident sharp enough to stab you and his beard tinged grey as old men's beards tend to be. The god is seated on a golden chariot, the horses again with forelegs raised, the hooves coming right out at you. He is surrounded by Oceanus and his sea creatures, floating, wriggling, swimming, as in life. You have to go there someday, Papa, and see it perfectly preserved, even to the blush on the cheeks of the maidens after a thousand and a half years.

When Ali signaled that our time was up, our disappointment must have touched his heart because instead of taking us toward the exit, he agreed to brave the wrath of the ninjas and led us forward to yet another low arch.

"This floor has been ravaged," he explained. "The figure you see has been damaged. But it is our treasure of treasures, the Gypsy Girl. She is our Venus."

As he spoke he pointed to a half-destroyed panel studded with bullet holes. (What encounter could have happened here?) Most of the girl's lower body has vanished. But her face is perfectly present. It is the eyes that haunt you. They seem to see into your very soul and bring to light all the secret thoughts that you have kept hidden away.

I know an Italian painter called Leonardo from Vinci famous for painting eyes. In fact, I once saw a crayon sketch of Madonna Isabella that he left behind at Mantova as a kind of thank-you for dinner. It was an excellent likeness. And I hear that he has since made an easel picture of a Madonna Lisa that has become famous in the world for her remarkable eyes. Maybe so. But if one day someone boasts to me that he has seen this Leonardo's Mona Lisa, I will tell him, "Good for you. But I have seen the gypsy Venus of Zeugma."

After today, we will have no regular contact with the capital. So you cannot be certain of hearing from me until this brigade arrives at Üsküdar field many weeks hence. But have no fear for my safety. Traveling through southern Anatolia I will be clasped firmly within the bonds of empire. Our only enemy will be every traveler's complaint, dysentery. And I intend to follow your dietary dictum as I have from the beginning of this long adventure: eat plenty of yogurt every day; no ripe melons, however tempting. Your wise advice has kept me healthy all this time, and I am cheered by the prospect of holding you in a tight embrace at the doorway of the Doctor's House in Topkapi Palace before the year has reached its end.

See you in Istanbul, Papa!

Your loving son,
D.

HOMECOMING

55

COMING HOME

AT NINE O'CLOCK ON THE MORNING OF JANUARY 3, 1536, the members of the Sultan's Heavy Armament Brigade were assembled in Üsküdar field and officially dismissed from duty. By nine-thirty, Danilo del Medigo, no longer on loan to the brigade but once again a member of the Fourth *Oda* of the Sultan's School for Pages, had stowed his gear, strapped his money pouch to his waist, and set out for the docks. There he spent an excessive amount of money for a private barge to ferry him across the Bosphorus to the Galata pier.

Once ashore, he headed directly to the stalls built up against the wall of the Grand Istanbul Bazaar, where Jews and Moors and Franks and black Africans and Arabs of all sects competed to provide customers with whatever their hearts desired. Anything from a balas ruby to a ripe tomato could be had for a price.

At the bazaar Danilo's wants were simple and easy to satisfy. He made his way past the valuable offerings in the domed *bedestan* to the shed behind it known to the locals as "Belgrade," because a group of Serbs had adopted it as their market. There, from three different vendors, the page purchased one cinnamon stick, one rosebud cutting, and a bunch of carrots, each neatly wrapped. These he carried across Beyazit Square to the Old Palace where the Sultan's harem was housed.

Correction: before he crossed the square, the page took the time to climb up Palace Point to a stall in the Sultan's stables at Topkapi Palace, where he offered the carrots—gratefully received—and exchanged extravagant expressions of affection with the occupant of the stall, a horse named Bucephalus.

The climb to Seraglio Point was steep, and once the page set foot in the stable, he was sorely tempted to bed down in the straw beside Bucephalus as he had done so often in the past. But he did not linger. With an affectionate pat, he bade his horse good day and sped off down the hill to the Old Palace, where he presented himself at the harem gate. There, he deposited his two remaining purchases with the guard to be delivered to Princess Saida as soon as possible.

The next stop on his itinerary was the Doctor's House back in the Fourth Court of Topkapi Palace. But on the heels of that thought came the seductive idea that if he were to turn left instead of right after entering the gate, a few steps would land him back in his old bed in the pages' dormitory where he was expected today. The cozy feather quilt beckoned. He succumbed. The moment he laid his head on the pillow, he drifted off into a deep sleep.

Danilo del Medigo was not a dreamer. The few dreams he had left his mind the moment he opened his eyes. But today's dream was unusually sticky. Even when he blinked, the round, smiling black face with its large white teeth and the gold earrings did not disappear.

"Sir! Sir!"

The page rolled over and rammed his head into the pillow. Surely the Sultan had not arrived in town so soon.

Now came a shake of the quilt, not rough but not gentle either. Slowly he turned his head and squinted at the figure looming above him.

"Narcissus!" This was no dream.

"Narcissus it is, sir, with a message for you."

The slave leaned over and held out a folded piece of copy paper, pressed the note into the sleepy page's hand, and was gone. Unfolded, the note revealed a message in red chalk: *Same time, same place*, he read. *Two long. Two short.*

The light streaming in from the skylight told him that it was still many hours until the "same time." And the fluffy quilt beckoned him to return to sleep. But, although this morning he had not put his filial duties ahead of his other concerns, Danilo del Medigo was, at heart, a dutiful son who knew how offended his father would be if he somehow got news of his son's return from a stranger. So with some reluctance he left his warm bed and set off to pay his respects to the doctor.

The doctor retired early these days. He tended to run down soon after his afternoon nap. That would give just enough time, his son calculated, for a fond embrace and a taste of supper before he clambered down the hill to the Grand Vizier's dock to await the familiar signal—two long, two short flashes of the lantern—that would announce the arrival of a sleek black caique.

His timing was perfectly calculated. He did indeed arrive at the Doctor's House in time to find a place at his father's bedside, where his face was the first thing the doctor saw when he opened his eyes. And the boy was well rewarded for the sacrifice of his own sleep by the look he saw on his father's face when he bent over to kiss the withered cheek.

After a brief meal Danilo was able to leave his father content with his promise to return two days hence to celebrate the Sabbath, if not before.

So it was with a clear conscience and an eager heart that he set off at a run to tumble down the hill behind the Fourth Court and lie flat on the rock shelf overlooking the cove with his eyes fixed on the spot where an incoming craft should first be spotted in the dark. Only when he had settled there did he give himself over to the wild anticipation that he now allowed to course through his body in expectation of what was to come.

56

IN THE HAMAM

LTHOUGH SHE HAD BEEN IN AND OUT OF THE harem's baths since childhood, Princess Saida had never completely mastered the skill of strolling around comfortably in the high pattens worn by the harem women in the *hamam*. She could execute complicated dance steps without losing her balance, but she could not overcome a tendency to stumble and fall when she was propped up on the five-inch platforms designed to preserve tender feet from the *hamam's* heated marble floors.

The treacherous pattens were not the only reason for the princess to evade her stepmother's pressing invitations to join her in one of her days of beauty at the luxurious spa that the Sultana had built for herself in her "temporary" quarters at Topkapi. But today Princess Saida had a reason to make use of the Sultana's cadre of expert practitioners in the beauty arts. And there she stood at the curtained doorway of the *hamam*, ready to endure whatever discomforts or indignities awaited her as the price of making herself beautiful for the long-awaited reunion with the love of her life.

Already her nose sniffed the air that permeated the place — a foggy mix of roses, musk, and amber. She pulled the curtain aside. The room ahead of her—the rotunda—was buzzing with the chatter of women coming and going and resting from their strenuous body treatments. There were women being dressed, women being undressed, and women being served sherbets and candied fruits from the baskets carried on the heads of the bare-breasted portresses who served the rotunda, while other attendants made their way to and from the laundry bearing piles of fluffy towels and embroidered robes.

The rotunda, a room of no great size, was capped with a perforated dome supported by a series of slim marble columns, a design similar to that of the other spas in the harem. But in the Sultana's *hamam*, the simplicity of the structure was more than offset by the grandeur of the furnishings. The couches spread about on the broad marble steps leading up to the central fountain were upholstered in satin, each one covered by a fine silk carpet and piled high with cushions of the softest Siberian down. The basins used to carry warm water from the fountain for the final foot washing were of hand-beaten copper fitted with gold handles. And the pitchers that hung from the washerwomen's belts were studded with turquoise stones and pearls. No question, the Sultana's spa had her mark on it.

The princess was quickly recognized and escorted to an empty couch where she was smoothly relieved of her clothing and wrapped in a huge fluffy towel. Then she was offered a choice of footwear—pattens with gold soles, pattens with jeweled buckles of various colours, and pattens strapped with fine leather or silk ribbons. The choice was immaterial to Saida. She would have difficulty walking in all of them. But she knew that the hated things would keep her feet high above the water that swirled around the drains of the rooms ahead, carrying off the soap scum and the depilatory creams and stray hairs that streamed down from the women's bodies as they were being rinsed off.

Still, in and of itself, the filthy mulch on the floors was not troublesome enough to cause the princess to risk offending her father's wife by refusing the Sultana's invitations. What kept her away was the enforced intimacy of the place. Ever since she moved her household from the harem in the Old Palace to Top-kapi, the Sultana had taken to using the enforced closeness of the *hamam* as a bully pulpit from which to preach to her step-daughter sermons on filial duty. Saida must, simply must, give up the quarters in the Old Palace that she inherited from her grandmother and move closer to her father, who needed her, and to her brothers and sisters, who cried for her. It was willful of the princess to bury herself in the Old Palace with a bunch of discarded concubines who spent their days sitting and wait-ing for a visit from a sultan who never came.

"Besides," the lecture went on, "you are bound to move to your own palace when you marry. Might as well start packing."

Thus far, the princess had managed to withstand the pres-sure of these cozy chats, clinging to the forlorn hope that Allah would spare her that day. But she felt her will slowly being worn down, nowhere faster than in the Sultana's *hamam*.

Apparently, someone had forewarned the masseuse of the princess's peculiar sensitivities, so today she was spared another of the *hamam*'s pitfalls, the frightening sensation of her arms being torn from their sockets and her legs from her torso. Administered for only half the time and with only half the force of a normal massage, the treatment turned out to be quite bear-able and Saida sank into a peaceful doze, only to be alerted by the sound of a familiar voice that rose above the hubbub of the room.

"Princess! Princess! Where is the princess? Is she not come?"

This outcry was followed by an inaudible reply. Then again came the familiar voice: "Bring her to me at once!"

And the princess was instantly wrapped up and delivered like a parcel to the private cubicle presided over by a *gedicli*, who was a prodigy in the perilous art of depilation. Because both custom and religion decreed that every inch of a woman's skin below the neck be entirely free of hair, and because the paste of *rusma* and lime spread over the skin to loosen the hair follicles contained enough arsenic to burn through the flesh to the bone, the elimination of stray hairs was a dangerous procedure. If the paste was left on too long, it would corrode the flesh; not long enough and there would be a scattering of errant hairs left to be extracted by plucking—most painful.

Splayed out on the table, her lower body as smooth and hairless as a plucked chicken, the Sultana somehow managed to convey with a single, broad gesture the resignation of a martyr as she murmured, "What we women sacrifice for the men we love . . ."

Just then, the ever-vigilant Amazon spied a single hair buried in the folds of Hürrem's labia, an insult to God, which she avenged with great vigor.

"Ouch!" the lady gasped. Quickly recovered, she turned to the princess with an expression that said, *You see what I mean by sacrifice?* Then she added, with a pitying glance at the un-beautified, virginal body that Saida was hiding under her towel, "It is always worth it, as you will soon discover. Come closer. Let me take a look at you."

The girl's chin was firmly cupped by a pair of strong hands. "Such white teeth! You smile so seldom that we do not often have the chance to see them. Sit here beside me, on that stool."

Saida sat obediently.

"I am so pleased to have you join me today for my day of beauty. I always invite you as a courtesy, but I never expect you to come. After all, it isn't as if you have to make yourself beautiful for a lover or a husband returning from the wars."

At the mention of the word "lover" the girl suddenly turned bright red, but she was able to cloak the alteration in her complexion by lowering her head modestly and remaining silent.

"The truth is that an unmarried girl like you has only a father to get beautiful for, and your father would find you beautiful even if you had wattles on your neck or hairs sprouting out of your chin."

This suggestion was followed by a hearty laugh. Still, the girl lifted her fingers to rub at her chin just in case there might be a kernel of truth in the jest. This lapse might have been noticed by someone less concerned with her own purposes than the Sultana. But Hürrem tended to unleash a veritable cascade of words once she got started on one of her frequent flights of oratory, and on she went, quite unmindful of the girl's discomfort.

Over the time Saida had spent in this woman's company since her grandmother's death, she had evolved a response to the seemingly benign, but somehow not quite kind, remarks that often issued from her stepmother's mouth: never a reply. Only downcast eyes, a shy smile, and silence. And with Hürrem, silence was always an option, she being a non-stop talker who simply talked right through it.

"For me the news of your father's imminent return is an answer to my prayers," the Sultana went on. "Four days, I am told. Four days and I will see my beloved and esteemed Sultan after all these months of separation. To hear his voice. To feel his touch..." Then, patting her hairless belly, "Of course I must have a full day of beauty to prepare." A brief, satisfied glance at her nether regions. Then, she reached for Saida's hand. "I understand that to you, my fortune-favored Sultan is simply a father. But to me he is the world. When you are married, you will understand."

Again, Saida smiled and said nothing. And, having made her point, the Sultana moved on to another subject.

"When I got your note this morning, I asked myself why, after so many absent days, is the princess coming to be with me on this day of beauty of all days? Could it be that she is finally getting ready to take her place in the world as a woman? Is she, at last, ready to leave her childhood behind? Could this be a first step toward womanhood? The thought makes me very happy"—a slight squeeze of the hand—"and it is sure to please your father." Then, with a signal to the Amazon to help her down from the high table, "Now let us go and be cleaned and perfumed."

Taking the girl's hand as a friend might, or a sister, she led the princess into the heart of the *hamam*, the tepidarium, where their bodies would be soaped, scraped, and sluiced with water, an especially lengthy process since the water had to be tipped from a series of sinks that lined one wall of the room and carried, basin by basin, to be poured over the prone bodies of the women on the marble couches. It certainly would not have challenged the ability of the royal plumbers to have bathtubs installed in which to perform this procedure, but everyone knew that bathtubs were where jinns and evil spirits liked to hide out. And so the two women endured the lengthy showering patiently, thus guaranteeing their safe departure from the rinsing room un-hexed and un-cursed.

Next came a gracious gift from the Sultana to her step-daughter: the offer of a rose-petal rub, fresh rose petals being the luxury of the few who could afford them. Now, rubbed to a fragrant rosy pink, the Sultana and her stepdaughter entered arm in arm into the finishing room where the hairdressers and the nail dyers worked their magic.

Here, Saida lent herself happily to the art of the hairdresser who shampooed her hair with fresh eggs, smoothed it with butter, and twisted it around rags into a mop of shining curls. Of the cosmetics, she did not avail herself. Her grandmother had strictly forbidden her to use skin-whitening paste or kohl or henna. Although the Valide herself had used henna to cover her grey hair and color her nails and routinely rimmed her eyes with black kohl, these things, she insisted, were tools for old women who wanted to look young, not for girls in the bloom of youth. And, out of respect, the princess continued to abide by her grandmother's dictum.

But the Sultana was under no such interdict—nothing but the full menu of cosmetics for her. First, her face was covered with a masque of almond and egg yolks, then bleached with a jasmine and almond paste. Then, a masque of henna for the hair and nails and a thick line in India ink to draw her eyebrows together. Last, beaten egg whites to banish the lines at the outside corners of her eyes. And this was only the basic beauty treatment. Still to come, to be applied at the last possible minute before coming face to face with the Sultan, a powder of ground-up pearls and lapis would be applied to the eyelids, a black beauty patch placed high on the cheek, and the invaluable kohl stick would turn the eyes into pools of moonlight. Hürrem's eyes were transformed into pools of moonlight just thinking of it. And, at her side, glancing into the rotunda mirror at her own shiny curls, Saida decided that, on balance and compared with other afternoons she had spent in the Sultana's *hamam*, this one had come to a good end.

It was in this spirit that she turned to Hürrem to thank her and bid her goodbye.

"You will not stay to sup with me?" The mouth took on a tight edge. "I have ordered a delicious pilaf because I know it to be your favorite dish."

Saida's apologies were profuse. "If only I could." She sighed. "But, sadly, I have ordered my house steward to have my horses at the palace gates in good time to get me home before evening prayers. He is waiting for me as we speak."

But Hürrem was not one to be thwarted by a mere steward. "Let him wait," she ordered. Then, in a more conciliatory tone: "I fear that you don't eat enough." She leaned over to pinch Saida's thigh. "Skin and bones." Then, in an intimate whisper: "Men don't like skinny women. If you were living here with us, we would put some meat on those bones."

It took only a breath to fill the silence that followed with more words. "Now about this steward who is waiting at the gate, I feel it is my duty to remind you, since your grandmother, may she rest in heaven, is no longer with us, that we are not meant to serve the convenience of slaves. It is they who serve at our pleasure."

"Just what my grandmother used to say when she felt I was being indulgent with Narcissus," Saida concurred.

"Wise woman." The Sultana nodded her approval.

"She was especially concerned that I be well trained in household management," the girl went on. "One of the maxims she handed down to me is that on any day that you entrust a slave with a sum of money to spend on your behalf, you must insist that a complete accounting be rendered before the setting of the sun. 'Delay is fatal,' she used to say. 'It is in the nature of coins to disappear in the dark.'"

This time, it was the Sultana who remained silent and the princess who filled the silence that followed.

"Earlier today," she continued, "I sent my steward to the bazaar with a good sum of money to make some purchases, while I was attending the *hamam*. At that time, remembering my grandmother's wise words, I ordered him to come and fetch me home in good time so that he could make an accounting of his expenditures and return the unspent coins before supper time."

"Of course." A veteran of the battle of wills, Hürrem easily recognized when she had irretrievably lost a point. She also knew how to turn defeat to her advantage.

"Very well, I will let you off tonight," she conceded. "But I must insist that you rejoin me tomorrow morning in my kitchens. I have a surprise for you. Here is a clue. What day is tomorrow?"

"Friday," Saida answered readily, into the game in spite of herself.

"And what happens on Fridays?"

Fridays were the days that the Sultan rode through the streets of Istanbul to say his evening prayers at the mosque in the sight of all. But tomorrow the Sultan would still be marching toward the capital. Saida racked her brain but could not think of another important Friday event.

"I will tell you." The Sultana had regained her good temper and was enjoying the game. "Friday is the day that the camels come down from Cyprus bearing the ice for the sherbet. I am going to prepare the secret syrup that I use to make sherbets for my Sultan. You know how he dotes on my sherbets."

And, indeed, the princess had heard praise for the lady's ices from her father's lips on more than one occasion.

"For the first time"—Hürrem leaned forward confidentially—

"I intend to share that secret with another woman. You!"

Herself an inveterate pursuer of secrets, the Sultana simply could not imagine anyone whose head would not be turned by being one of only two women in the world to know a secret way to bring light to a sultan's eye.

As she watched the princess's fleet, slim figure make off to find her steward, the lady could not help but congratulate herself on finally having found a tidbit to brighten the dull, listless eyes of the pale princess. And as Saida bounced along through the streets of the capital to her safe haven in the Old Palace, her eyes were indeed sparkling. And her cheeks flushed. But her head was not filled with thoughts of sherbet recipes. What she was seeing in her mind's eye was a cloaked figure jumping down from a rock ledge in response to a signal—two long, two short—from an approaching caique. Strong legs, broad shoulders, a mass of gold curls, a pair of blue eyes, and, after months of longing for it and dreaming of it, the embrace of the only man she would ever love.

57

THE TRYST

Two long. Two short.

Before the signal was completed, the shadowy figure on the rock ledge had dropped down to the dock and stood poised to board the caique that slid in, sleek as a swan, with its great gilt falcon, symbol of the House of Osman, rising upwards, wings spread as if to fly to the heavens. Without breaking the rhythm of the oarsmen, the princess's steward, Narcissus, reached out a hand to help the waiting passenger onto the narrow deck of the craft. Once aboard, the passenger disappeared so silently through the curtains of the center cabin that anyone watching could believe the whole scene to be imagined.

In the past, Danilo had negotiated this move on many such nights, occasionally boarding very small vessels, sometimes larger ones, but never one as imposing as this one. Powered by eight oarsmen, four at the fore and four astern, its curtained cabin was softly padded, its floor and walls strewn with pillows, like a floating canopied bed.

Danilo smelled Saida before he reached out to touch her cheek, her chin, her rose-scented breast, then locked his arms around her as they sank into the pillows. By unspoken agreement, they did not speak but simply clung to each other wordless, as if only the flesh was powerful enough to verify that they were together at last.

It had been over a year since they last met. They were, as always, slaves to the clock, and all too soon a shrill blast of the caique's whistle shattered their golden moment.

"Enough!" Saida held up her hand. "No more time for kisses. We have the caique for only an hour."

"Only one hour?" This was even a shorter break than usual.

"One hour is more time than I dreamed of," she responded. "I had given up all hope of ever seeing you again. But with Narcissus's help, we may have one more night before we say goodbye forever."

"Goodbye? We have hardly had a chance to say hello."

"We always knew it would have to end." She patted his cheek gently. "And now the end has come. The moment my father sets foot in his *selamlik*, he will be met by the *damat* that Hürrem has selected for me. All he need do to give my marriage his assent is touch the shoulder of the husband she has picked for me. And he will give it, be sure of that. The new Sultana has great influence on him. Give her credit. This *damat* is well chosen. He is an admiral, loyal and seasoned. At least he has his own teeth..." Her brave attempt at a joke sputtered out and she burst into tears. "I promised myself I would not cry."

"What if I told you there was hope for us?" He reached over to touch her cheek. "Would that stop your tears?"

"I would say what I always say to you: my destiny was written on the stars the day I was born. The pearls have been sewn on my wedding veil. The Sultana has found a palace for me to live in. Nothing can stop this marriage from taking place."

"What if I tell you that something has happened to stop it?"

"This is not a story in a French romance, Danilo."

"At least give me a chance to tell you my news," he pleaded. Taking her silence for assent, he reached out and cradled her in the crook of his arm. "This is a story about an avalanche in the Zagros Mountains," he began. "About being sealed into a mountainous pass. About the threat to our entire army of death by starvation. About your brave father, the Sultan. He was like a beacon—always shining. He organized what he called 'the greatest hunt in the history of the world.' With him leading the way, we killed enough wild animals to feed an army twice our size. He saved us from starvation."

Her eyes lit up. "Bravo, Papa!" she whispered.

This was all the encouragement he needed to continue. "But that is only half of the story. The struggle was over, we thought. We had even offered up prayers of thanks for our salvation. But as we began to pack up, we were attacked at the edge of the forest by a pack of wild beasts. That is when..." He paused and took a deep breath. There was no other way to say it: "I saved your father's life."

"You what?"

"I saved the Sultan's life."

She shook her head in disbelief. "Is this true?"

"Do I lie?"

She took a moment to consider, then slowly shook her head. "No, you are no fabulist. If you say you saved my father's life, I believe you. Tell me what happened."

And so he did, trying his best not to make himself out to be the hero of his story and succeeding only in further endearing him to her by his modesty. By the time he was done, the cloud of sadness had lifted from her face.

"My hero!" She held out her arms.

Now he was the one to resist. "Wait. The best is yet to come. The day I parted company with the Sultan, he gave me his undertaking to grant me anything within his power. 'If the day comes when you need anything from me,' were his exact words, 'you need only call on me, and if it is within my power your wish will be granted.' Well, the time has come. And on the day your father returns to his capital, I will seek audience and ask for your hand in marriage."

For once in her life, Princess Saida was rendered speechless.

This time she did not open her arms to him. Instead she withdrew to the far end of her seat and began to chew on her thumbnail thoughtfully.

"Time is short. You must be quick and clever." The little general had taken over. "It will not be easy for you to speak to my father alone. Once Hürrem has her hands on him she will never leave his side."

She tapped her fingers against her head as if ordering her brain to invent a strategy. And to be sure, within moments she had found one. "What if I make her a part of our plan? What if I get her to beg the audience for me?"

"How can you do that?" Danilo was genuinely bewildered.

But Saida was, as she said, "a graduate of the harem," where strategies were part of the curriculum. "What if I tell her that I agree to marry her candidate but that I want my father to hear it from me?" As the plan materialized in her brain she talked more and more quickly. "I am invited to her kitchen tomorrow for a cooking lesson. While we cook, I will tell her of my intention and ask her to arrange an audience for me, alone, with my father. She will be pleased to do it. She wants this marriage very much."

This line of thinking was so foreign to Danilo's nature, he found it hard to follow. "Why?" he asked. "Why should she care which man you marry?"

"Maybe she plans to use me and my *damat* against the Grand Vizier in the council. Who knows? What is important is that I think I can persuade her to arrange an immediate audience with my father." She clapped her hands like a child. And with a smile of ravishing delight, she leaned in toward him. "You are truly my paladin, come to save me after all. Kiss me."

As he leaned forward obediently, a newly soft voice whispered in his ear, "And tonight you will get your reward."

58

SHERBET

BECAUSE SHE HAD TO MAKE ARRANGEMENTS WITH her steward for the evening ahead, Princess Saida got a late start on the Sultana's culinary session at Topkapi. To make matters worse, her litter was brought to a standstill halfway up to Palace Point by the crowds gathered to witness the semi-annual ice delivery from Mount Olympus. For some reason, the citizens of the capital never ceased to be amazed by the icemen from the frozen north. In the temperate climate of Istanbul, they were an exotic novelty with their snowy turbans, frosty eyebrows, the blankets of furs they were wrapped in, and the dangling ice crystals that hung from their beards and earlobes like cascading diamond drops. Whenever they came to town, admiring onlookers lined the streets wondering at the frosty cavalcade of donkeys and wagons piled high with huge flannel-wrapped blocks of ice, dug out of pits many miles away, to be stored in deep caverns all over the town for the pleasure of the sherbet-loving Turks. Sherbet was, beyond doubt, the favorite sweet of the inhabitants of the city, rich and poor, in all seasons.

Like her fellow townspeople, Princess Saida relished the

cool, refreshing sweet and had to admit to herself that, foolish though she knew it was, she wouldn't mind learning Hürrem's secret of concocting a sherbet to please a king.

As she tapped her toe impatiently against the stool at her feet, she licked her lips as if to recall the taste of the delicacy, and the memory turned her mind to the woman behind the recipe she was about to learn. Living in her grandmother's suite in the harem, the princess had been on hand from the beginning to witness Hürrem's astonishing transformation from concubine to queen. Marooned in the sea of humanity that blocked the progress of her litter, Princess Saida amused herself by tracing the Sultana's ascent of the Ottoman ladder step by step.

Hürrem's first moves were unexceptional. As a neophyte concubine she simply emulated the tried-and-tested route taken by countless slave girls before her to attract the Sultan's attention. From her first day in the harem she was an eager student of the arts taught to these girls to enhance their charms. Although not endowed by nature with a talent for music and dancing, she attended those classes as conscientiously as she did the ones devoted to cosmetics, skin care, costume, and hairdressing. But the first purchase she made from the Jewish bundle-women who supplied the needs and wants of the harem girls was an expensive illustrated manuscript of instructions on the varieties of sexual positions — more than sixty — to intensify the pleasures of intercourse. And no matter what temptations there were to laze the hours away, as most of the Sultan's girls did, Hürrem could always be found at the end of the day curled up in her bedroll with her copy of *The Perfumed Garden*, a local version of the *Kama Sutra*. One evening Saida had accidentally come upon the girl, believing herself unobserved, lying flat on her back, her legs apart, her knees bent toward her chest, muttering aloud as she proceeded to enact the moves described in the manuscript:

"Her legs stretched, she lies down on her right side. He gets behind her and places one of his thighs on hers and the other one between her legs. With his saliva he lubricates his member and starts rubbing it on her vagina and anus; when he reaches a point close to ejaculation he

pushes to the nearest hole speedily. But since anal intercourse is wickedness he must save his semen for the proper destination."

Never having been exposed to anything like this before, Saida could not tear herself away as the concubine went on. *"In a stooped position she waits for her man. When he is there she starts her behind to dancing slowly, then faster..."*

Beneath her coverlet Hürrem was swaying from side to side as she read.

"She sucks him deep within her. This position is very convenient for an unexpected quick flight and can give amazing pleasure to the couple."

Judging from the increasing frequency of Hürrem's attendance at the Sultan's bed, Saida concluded as she crept away that the concubine had learned her lessons well. Earlier, the Sultana-to-be had also distinguished herself from the other girls lined up when the Padishah visited the harem, by greeting him with a smile while all the others were posing in the traditional manner like frozen Byzantine madonnas. On one occasion she even laughed out loud. And once she had found a way into his bed, she made sure to get pregnant as soon as possible and crowned her efforts by producing a boy child. This baby was followed quickly by two more sons, giving the Sultan a choice of heirs to preserve the succession, just in case the crown prince Mustafa should fall ill or fall from his horse, or otherwise disqualify himself by dying young.

And now, Saida reflected, only one barrier remained to prevent Hürrem—still only the Second *Kadin*—from reaching the height of her ambition: the living presence of the First *Kadin*, Rose of Spring, mother to the Sultan's first-born, Crown Prince Mustafa. So far Hürrem had managed to have Rose of Spring dispatched to Manisa, where Mustafa was serving a term as governor. With Rose of Spring out of the way, the Second *Kadin* had spent her effort persuading the Sultan to marry off the remaining favorites in the harem one by one, until there were fewer and fewer concubines left for the Sultan to visit. And finally, when the Sultan was languishing deep in grief over the death of his beloved mother, the Second *Kadin* disengaged herself from the harem and established a suite beside him in the *selamlik* at Topkapi. This unheard-of arrangement had led to the wedding that shocked the world.

Almost as shocking, the Sultan had proclaimed that the ceremony of marriage had transformed the former slave into a freeborn Sultana like the Ottoman princesses of old. And today, in the Sultan's long absences, Hürrem acted as her husband's regent, the second most powerful person in the empire.

Digging into her memory, Saida could see a clear picture of the wretched Second *Kadin* when she first arrived as a gift to the Sultan from his boon companion, the Grand Vizier Ibrahim. The girl had come to the Valide Sultan's suite as a suppliant, helpless as a child, throwing herself on the mercies of the Sultan's mother and pleading for her help. What had happened to turn that pathetic girl into an all-powerful empress? What had enabled her to make that unprecedented leap of status? There had to be a key, an event, as there always was in the Persian fairy tales read to the princess at bedtime by her grandmother. The dear face came to her mind. And with the vision came a sudden understanding. While the Valide Sultan lived no one could have taken her place. But once she was dead...

It was as if the Valide's death had released some caged creature hidden behind the tears and sighs of a weeping slave girl and let loose a lioness. And now, Hürrem sat as Regent with a household of over one hundred retainers, a private *hamam*, a sizeable security force, and even the personal kitchen toward which the princess was slowly making her way.

Eventually, in response to the driver's curses and threats, the human barrier did make way for Saida's carriage to pass. But by the time she arrived at Hürrem's kitchen the cooking had long since begun. And the Sultana was too busy by then to notice Saida's tardiness — or at least to be bothered by it.

Unlike the baths, the kitchen had always been a haven for Saida. So many happy hours of her childhood had been spent in her grandmother's private kitchen learning how to cook.

Perhaps because Lady Hafsa took pride in her Circassian roots, she was never one of those concubines who felt it necessary to erase her beginnings and invent a new birthright for herself when her son became Sultan and elevated her status to Valide Sultan. In Circassian life, women of every station were trained in all aspects of domesticity from cookery to finances, talents Lady Hafsa continued to display after becoming the Valide Sultan in her son Suleiman's harem.

Traditionally, the royal children of both genders were tutored in grammar and mathematics in the Harem School. Once she became the First *Kadin* with a large suite of her own and a young ward, Lady Hafsa took steps to augment what she felt to be a defect in the young girl's education and pass on to the orphan princess, Saida, the domestic skills that she herself had learned early in life. It was mainly to accomplish this that Lady Hafsa built a small private kitchen adjacent to her suite in the harem, the First *Kadin* on record to do so.

Thus did Lady Hafsa provide the current Second *Kadin* with a precedent for including a small kitchen in her new suite when Hürrem moved her household into Topkapi Palace.

Today, everything in the kitchen had been cleared to make room for two large copper cauldrons half filled with fruit, each pot sitting in a bed of coals on a tripod. Clearly relishing her role as mistress of the ceremony, the Sultana walked back and forth between these pots, stirring, sniffing, and tasting. She motioned the princess to a stool and without even so much as a greeting began the lesson.

"The sherbet you buy in the street is made from pits and peels and whatever fruits are cheapest at the marketplace," she commenced between tastes and sniffs. "My sherbet begins with a single fruit—the *rezacahi* grape—and these"—indicating the fruit piled up in the cauldrons—"these are the pick of the crop. They were harvested yesterday and delivered early this morning. They have been simmering—never boiling—since dawn, and if you come close you can catch the fragrance. Take note." She wiggled her finger at the girl. "The grapes are placed whole in the pot, never crushed, and heated slowly on a bed of coals, never a flame. That way, the fruit naturally gives up the fullness of its flavor. Patience is the secret of flavor."

She paused to let this maxim sink in, then continued. "The second secret is to use a light hand. No crushing or bruising the fruit, only a gentle stir, like this." She picked up a long-handled ladle from a rack next to the cauldron and began to stir the grapes in a slow, circular movement. "If you wish to get a feeling of peace and well-being into your sherbet, never do violence to the fruit."

To her surprise Saida found herself half believing what she knew to be nonsense. Probably because Hürrem herself clearly believed every word she spoke.

"Taste test!" Hürrem dipped her finger into the ladle and savored the liquid with evident satisfaction. "Excellent! We are ready for the first addition. You may not know it, but the street sellers will throw into their sherbet any seasoning that is cheap and plentiful—linden flowers, chamomile, cinnamon, cloves"—she wrinkled her nose disdainfully—"common stuff. What gives my sherbet refinement is that I use only fresh rose petals."

She beckoned to one of the attendants to bring her a crystal flagon and casually emptied half the contents into one of the pots and half into the other—a quantity of rose petals worth a good handful of gold pieces. As the petals slowly melted into the liquid, the rose fragrance filled the entire kitchen.

So it went—a pot of honey here, a pinch of sweetened vinegar there, until the time came for the sharing of the Sultana's most precious secret. At the snap of her fingers, two of the cooks carried a large tank filled with what appeared to be a kind of water lily. Reaching into the tank, Hürrem held up a horseshoe-shaped plant bearing huge yellow flowers with an almost putrid smell to them. Inhaling it deeply, she announced, "This is a *nullifier* plant. I have had men searching it out all week in marshes and swamps." She waved the noxious plant under Saida's nose. "This, my dear, is my secret ingredient."

She tossed a single *nullifier* plant into each pot. Then, in what for anyone else might be construed as a furtive gesture, she turned her back to the princess and reached into a sack hanging at her waist for a red satin purse filled with small gilded tablets, flinging a handful into each cauldron. This ingredient she need not name or identify. Everyone in the palace recognized the distinctive red purse as coming from a certain stall at the bazaar that specialized in importing and refining a concoction of white poppies and hashish, both of which grew abundantly in neighboring Mesopotamia. *Not quite as exotic an ingredient as a wayward yellow water lily*, thought Saida, *but much more likely to give satisfaction to the consumer.* In spite of the temptation to do so, she denied herself the amusement of inquiring of the Lady Hürrem which of the two ingredients was the true secret—the yellow lily or the white poppy. Although the Sultana laughed a lot, she had never been seen to enjoy a laugh at her own expense.

The slow stirring continued, and Saida must have inadvertently disclosed her inner restlessness to her sherbet mentor, because even that lady, unaccustomed as she was to notice the mood of anyone besides herself and her Sultan, broke off her stirring to place a friendly arm around the girl's shoulder.

"Next time, you will stir and I will sit," she announced, and then added, "and now, while the syrup cools, we can leave the magic lily bulb to steep in the fruits. That is another process that cannot be rushed. Let us enjoy a sip of something to refresh ourselves." So saying, she led the way to the newest of her innovations, her private sitting room.

The notion of using certain rooms for defined purposes was unheard of in this country. Even in the royal palace, all rooms were used for all purposes. At mealtimes, the diners ate off small trestle tables while sitting cross-legged on a pile of cushions. When the meal was over, the little tables were folded up until the next meal. At night the same space was spread about with bedrolls and blankets, which were also folded up and stored when not in use. Nomad tent habits died hard with the Ottomans.

But Lady Hürrem was no respecter of Ottoman precedents. Some said she took pleasure in deliberately flouting tradition. Most recently she had dedicated a room in her new suite
to sitting, sewing, and chatting. But not to eating or sleeping.
To make that clear, she furnished the room with large, bulky,
silk-upholstered sofas not meant to be folded up and put away.
Saida could not help but admire such a bold move. Having
been trained in the traditional strategies of the weak—secrecy,
deceit, and cunning—she knew that it took nerve and courage
for a woman to challenge openly even the most trivial of tribal
customs.

When they entered the new sitting room, Hürrem motioned
the princess to one of the silk sofas and flung herself onto another.

As she sank down into the cushions, she snapped her fingers
and spat out an order: "Eye pads, quickly, I must have eye pads.
My eyes are burning like fire."

In quick time, a slave arrived with a plate of sliced cucum-
bers that she placed over the Sultana's closed eyes.

"We wish to be alone," the lady announced.

"But, Your Highness..."

"What now?"

"A letter has come."

"Throw it on the pile with the rest of my mail," the Sultana ordered. Then, in an abrupt change of tone, she said to
Saida, "I have not forgotten, my dear daughter, what you taught
me: that as Regent, I must answer my mail on the very day it
arrives. But some days the pile is so high that I regret I ever
learned how to read. I fear I shall always need your help with
my correspondence."

The slave coughed for attention.

"Why are you still here?" Hürrem demanded.

"The letter is from the Sultan's headquarters in the field," the
slave responded.

At this the lady sat up sharply and held her hand out to
receive the rolled-up dispatch. But when she examined the seal
on the back, the expectation drained from her eyes.

"It's only from the Grand Vizier. He's always trying to get on my good side, the miserable toady. Throw it on the pile." A brief pause. "Better still, give it to the princess. She shall read it to me while I calm my eyes with cucumber juice."

She continued to talk as she snuggled down onto her pillows. "What has the despicable Greek got to say for himself? The man is insatiable in his lust for fame. The whole delay in Asia is his doing. He hopes to make his own reputation by pursuing the heretic shah into Persia. But for him, my Sultan would have returned to me as soon as he subdued Baghdad. Go ahead. Read it."

Saida read: "'Revered Sultana—'"

"A little louder, dear. You speak so softly that I can barely hear you."

Saida cleared her throat and began again in a booming tone.

Revered Sultana,

I would not for all the world disturb your tranquility with disquieting news, but for my certainty that, although we have our small differences, we are in complete agreement regarding the interests and safety of our beloved Sultan. Believe me, I would spare your feelings if I could.

"Insolent beggar," the Sultana muttered.

But it is imperative that you know the ugly story of deceit and betrayal that has unfolded in the course of the Baghdad campaign and could come to a disastrous end when our beloved Sultan reaches the capital.

At this, the Sultana frowned and leaned forward. More slowly now, Saida read:

Be warned. The Sultan's very life is at stake. A duplicitous viper has wormed his way into the royal confidence with a series of false displays of loyalty. In the latest of these schemes, this villain contrived, during my absence, to stage what seemed to be an attack by a wild boar, during which he appeared to interpose himself between the beast and the Padishah and thereby save the life of the Sultan. He has even recruited witnesses—doubtless bribed to attest to this invention.

Not only is this a fabrication, it is also a stain on the Padishah's honor. Already reports of his weakness and the villain's heroism are circulating in our camp. It is only a matter of time before they reach the ears of the merchants in the bazaars, doubtless helped along by this villain's followers. There are always ambitious men ready to form dubious alliances to advance their own interests.

The Sultana shook her head in vigorous agreement. Saida read on:

Because I feared what plans this ingrate was hatching to further threaten the Sultan's honor—perhaps even his throne (Allah alone knows what evil lurks in the hearts of such men)—I arranged to find a post for him in the Heavy Artillery Brigade, which I am advised arrived at the capital yesterday.

Saida was beginning to feel small stabs of anxiety, but she managed to press on with her reading.

So far I have been able to put this villain at a distance from the court, where he could not jeopardize our beloved master, who has remained safely guarded by me on our return march. But as I write, this miscreant is now in the city, and today, in a search of his toiletry case that I ordered, he was found to be carrying a vial of purple poison labeled REMEDY FOR THE SULTAN. There can be no doubt whom this deadly tincture is meant for.

Only two days remain before the Sultan rides triumphantly into his capital, thus there are only forty-eight hours in which to rid the empire of this despicable creature who not only threatens those of us sworn to protect our Sultan, but even the Sultan himself. And, believe me, he is clever enough to do enormous damage. Search out this villain, I urge you. The Sultan has entrusted you with the power to act on his behalf. You have the means to find the villain and destroy him. He is a piece of Jewish scum, by the name of Danilo del Medigo.

Princess Saida's writing tablet fell to the floor with a crash.

"Read on," the Sultana ordered. But the girl sat, openmouthed and rigid. "Are you ill? Speak to me!"

When the princess regained her voice, it was faint and wavering. "There has been a mistake," she whispered.

"Louder, Princess. I cannot hear you."

"I said this is a mistake. This is impossible."

"Oh, no, my dear, it is all too possible."

The girl took a deep breath to steady herself. "Danilo del Medigo would never do such a thing."

"You know this rascal?"

"He is no rascal. We were classmates. I was his tutor in the Princes School."

"The world is not a schoolroom, my child." The Sultana did not trouble to hide her disdain. "Apparently this schoolboy has grown up to be a traitor. After all, he is a Jew."

"But you have only the word of the Grand Vizier for this story, madam." The girl was struggling to maintain her composure. "And you yourself have called him a schemer and a liar."

"Liars and schemers make the best spies. They have a nose for treachery," rejoined the Sultana. "Think of this. Your father is in peril every day of his life. Why else must he have every spoonful of food tasted before he touches it? Because poisoners lurk in the kitchens. Why does he sleep with a guard at each corner of his bed? Because assassins are everywhere. By your grandmother's wish, you have been shielded from these frightening things. It is time for you to know."

From somewhere deep inside, Saida managed to control the waves of nausea that flooded over her. "What I know is that Danilo del Medigo is quite incapable of the crimes that the Grand Vizier has accused him of," she stated with all the authority she could muster.

"Based on what? A childhood recollection."

"He did save my father's life in the Zagros Mountains," she blurted out.

"How do you know that?"

Too late Saida realized that she had trapped herself. Her own body betrayed her with a deep flush. She lowered her head, tried to think. But Hürrem was a practiced hunter. Once she caught the scent, she was ruthless in pursuit.

"If you have not seen this traitor since you were children, how do you know what happened in Persia? And how could you be so sure that he has not changed in all the years?" She hesitated as a new thought crossed her mind. "Unless you have seen him since you left the Princes School. Of course. You have seen him and he has seen you. Foolish girl. Wicked girl. Where? When did this meeting happen?"

"At *Bayram*. We met a few times."

Even Hürrem was stunned by the girl's admission. That this meek little mouse had been meeting a man secretly for years was unthinkable. Where was the Valide all this time? Hürrem's mind, wide open to the most outrageous rumors of duplicity and deceit, could barely grasp the sheer audacity of what she was hearing. But with some effort she managed to make the leap and began to deal with the implications of Saida's confession.

"Has he seen you unveiled?"

The girl's silence was as good as an admission.

"He has seen you unveiled. You, the Sultan's daughter, who claim to love your father better than your own life."

"I do love him," the girl protested.

"This Jewish page has put a stain on the Sultan's honor, a stain that can be erased only by death," the Sultana pronounced.

"But what if the Grand Vizier is lying? What if this report is a ploy of Ibrahim Pasha's? What if Danilo de Medigo is innocent?"

"Then we will have eliminated one unimportant Jew," the Sultana snapped. "But if this story is true we will have saved the empire. No question, he must die! And he must die before he makes any more moves against the Sultan."

Hürrem rose to her feet and headed for the open doorway. "Fortunately, the Padishah has given me the means to accomplish my duty." She thrust the door curtain aside and shouted down the corridor, "Call for my Men in Black!" Then, turning back to the princess, "For you I have only one question, my princess. Take care how you answer it. Your very life may be in the balance here." She paused to let this sink in, then asked, "Do you still have your virginity?"

"Yes, madam." Seeing a hint of disbelief on the woman's face, Saida added, "I swear it on my grandmother's grave." There was no mistaking the sincerity of her oath.

"Then your life will be spared. But get out of my sight before I have a chance to regret my generosity."

As the shivering princess backed out of the room, she heard the echo of an angry voice shouting, "Where are those men? I need them now!"

Out of earshot, Saida called out to the steward awaiting her. "Narcissus, come quick!"

Ten minutes later she was back at the Sultana's doorway, suppliant, pleading.

But once aroused, the Sultana was not easily appeased. "What brings you back here?" she barked. "Did I not send you home? Have you now become disobedient as well as disloyal?"

"I could not leave without expressing to you my regret... my shame... my folly." The girl was literally groveling. "How could I have been so blind as not to see that this Jew was only using me to reach my father? Maybe to steal state secrets and pass them on for money to the Venetians. Or was he in league with the Persians, do you think?"

"They have spies everywhere," the Sultana informed her in a tone not quite as steely as before.

Encouraged, the princess raised her head to reveal the ravages of her tear-stained face. "I am so ashamed. Please don't tell my father. Please, I beg you."

After a long moment of deliberation, the Sultana replied, "I will keep this from him, not for your sake but for his. If he were to learn of this betrayal, it would break his heart. He will never know of this shame. No one will. Dead bodies wash up on the shores of the Bosphorus every night. What is one more or less? Now it is time for you to go."

"Not yet. Please." The princess reached up to grasp the woman's clenched fist. "I know I have no right to ask. You have already saved me from making a grave error. But I need your comfort. Without my grandmother to watch over me, I am so confused."

As the girl raised her hand to wipe a tear from her cheek, she caught a glimpse of softening around the Sultana's hard-set lips.

"My grandmother always told me that if I was in trouble you would come to my aid," she went on. "What can I do to make amends?" Now she was on her knees, the perfect penitent. "I would gladly marry the admiral tomorrow."

"Too late. What is done is done and cannot be undone. Your father has already canceled the wedding plans. He would not be pleased with further alterations." Once again the woman's lips were set in a thin hard line.

"Perhaps the two of us could audience him together on the day of his arrival." The girl spoke softly, timidly. Raising her head, she caught a glimmer of interest in the beady black eyes. "You are the one he trusts. He places all his faith in your wisdom. If you spoke on my behalf he would not be angry." She lowered her head and added in an almost inaudible tone, "I fear my father's wrath."

This time her tears and pleas appeared to have reached the

Sultana's heart. In a regal gesture she placed her hand on the girl's forehead like a benediction.

"Your humbleness and modesty have touched me. I will help you. We two will visit the Sultan together. Do not worry, my child, your father will not be angry and the blackguard Jew will never bother you again. My men will see to that. They never fail."

As she reached out to embrace the object of her beneficence, she failed to notice that the girl had turned ashen and was trembling.

"Now run along and dream sweet dreams of a beautiful life to come."

But the girl did not move. Graciously the older woman reached out to help her to her feet and, with the slightest of pressure, turned the girl toward the door. "Be off with you now."

Almost like a sleepwalker, the princess headed for the doorway, turned back suddenly, and once more fell to her knees. "I beg of you, madam, do not send me away. At least allow me to drink a cup of tea with you before I go. Just a sip as I used to do with my grandmother. She always said I brewed the best tea in the world. I miss her so much."

Seconds went by in silence. Then the girl felt the pat of a hand on her cheek. "You poor child. Of course I will take tea with you."

"Am I forgiven, then?" Saida's eyes were wide with genuine surprise.

"Forgiven."

"And may I spend the night close to you? I so need a mother now."

"Very well." The Sultana gave her assent with a nod.

"You are the soul of generosity, madam. I will send my slave at once to inform my household that I will not be returning this evening, and then with your permission I will prepare our tea."

"Permission granted. Before we sleep we will drink a cup together in love and forgiveness."

Saida threw herself into the Sultana's open arms for a final embrace, then hurried off to give Narcissus his orders for the night and to prepare a pot of her grandmother's favorite tea — double strength.

59

RENDEZVOUS

WALKING OFF THE PRACTICE FIELD FOR HIS WATER break, Danilo allowed himself a rare moment of self-congratulation. Four perfect thrusts out of five. It was good to know that he hadn't lost his skill with the *gerit*, and good to be back in the routine of the practice field. He was thinking that after the final thrusting drill, when the other pages had dispersed among the stews of the Galata docks, he would return to his cubicle in the School for Pages and plan how to approach his upcoming audience with the Padishah.

Tonight when he met with his princess he would have a chance to try out his words on her. Who better to consult on the correct phrases in which to address a sultan? She was, after all, his language tutor once.

His thoughts were interrupted by the sight of the round face of the princess's slave, Narcissus, bobbing up and down behind the giant water cask at the side of the field. With a barely discernible nod, the eunuch motioned him toward the shady grove behind him, where he would be waiting as always to transmit the details of the time and place for that night's rendezvous. Would they be treated again to a ride in the royal caique with its brilliant white hull and gilded mountings? Not for the first time Danilo wondered how Narcissus managed to produce these elegant surprises.

In all their years of furtive meetings, the eunuch had always kept his distance. But today he grasped the page's arm from behind and steered him with crude force toward the gates that separated the playing field from the Eunuch's Path. Danilo could feel the strength of the slave's massive body as it propeled him to the end of the field and out the gates.

"Why are you pushing me? Where are we going?" he inquired with some asperity.

No answer. Instead he was dragged along the Eunuch's Path through a small opening in a thick hedge leading to a garden in the Second Court, where he was given the terse instruction, "Keep your head down. We must not be seen."

"Why not?" Again, no response. "Where are you taking me?"

This time, he got a short answer. "To a place where you will be safe." The slave took a moment to look from side to side, and then nodded with satisfaction. "So far we have not been followed."

The garden they came into was so serene, the birdsong so sweet, and the scent of the oleander bushes so calming—so out of keeping with the frantic manner of his guide—that Danilo concluded this must be another one of Princess Saida's pranks. Why not play the game, he asked himself, at least until he got to where he was being led, which seemed to be in the direction of the stables. So he hustled along silently behind his guide through the huge, carved wooden doors of the stable and obeyed a whispered instruction to get down on his knees and crawl past the quarters of the Master of the Horse toward a long row of stalls, most of them empty, awaiting the imminent return of the Sultan's household steeds from Baghdad. Then, halfway down the aisle, the eunuch turned and grabbed him by the shoulders so abruptly that he stumbled and fell flat on his back on the straw-covered floor of a stall, where he found himself staring up at the fine, familiar cock and balls of his horse, Bucephalus.

Now the eunuch spoke, quickly and breathlessly. "Your life is in peril. Men are out searching for you all over the city with orders to kill you."

"Is this some kind of a joke?"

The slave cut him off. "Be quiet. There is very little time. I must go and make the payment for your passage to safety. But my orders are not to leave you alone until you give your word— on your father's life—that you will not leave this place until either I or the princess comes for you."

In genuine bewilderment, Danilo asked, "Where would I go?"

To Narcissus, the question was beneath notice. "There may already be men stationed at your dormitory and patroling the Doctor's House. But here, you are safe. The Sultana's guards are dolts. They cannot imagine that you might be hiding in the stable, right under their noses. And if by chance anyone does come looking for you, you can bury yourself in the straw. I must go. Do you swear?"

What did he have to lose? "I swear," Danilo replied.

"On your father's life?"

"On my father's life. But I have a question. Where is the princess?"

"She is drinking tea with the Sultana," the slave answered, po-faced, and then added, with the merest suggestion of a smile, "The Sultana has become very fond of the special tea the princess brews, and the princess always keeps a stock of the doctor's calming tea on hand should the need arise."

For the first time in the encounter, Danilo wondered if the slave's bizarre behavior was indeed more than a prank.

"What do you think, Bucephalus?" he inquired of his horse after Narcissus had left. "Is this one of Saida's tricks or are there really men coming to kill me?"

The horse's answering neigh gave Danilo the comfort he was seeking, and he settled down in the straw beside his faithful steed to await the arrival of his princess.

Before long she dashed into the stall breathless and disheveled.

"Thank God you are here." She reached out to touch him as if to reassure herself. "I was afraid you might have been carried off somewhere and I would never see you again."

"Are you telling me that Narcissus's story of men out to kill me is true?"

"Of course it is. Why would he lie?"

"I thought it was one of your pranks."

"Were it so. Hürrem's Men in Black are already out there looking for you. I saw them patroling your father's house."

"But why? Tell me."

"A letter arrived from the Grand Vizier denouncing you as a traitor. The Sultana has given her men orders to kill you."

"That can't be. The Sultan will never allow it. I am high in his favor."

"Too late. These men will find you and kill you and bury you before the Sultan arrives. By this time tomorrow you will be dead."

"Are you telling me that she has the power to do that?"

"She is the Regent. She rules in his absence. She believes you to be a threat to my father and she has sentenced you to die," the princess explained.

"But she doesn't trust the Grand Vizier. She knows him to be a liar. How can she put any faith in what he says?"

"She told me that when it comes to treason, you have to take your information where you find it."

"I can't believe this."

"You had better believe it. By the time the Sultan grants you an audience you will have disappeared, and the rumor will be spread that you went down to the Galata stews to get in trouble and found it."

"Are you certain of this?"

"What will it take to convince you?" She dug into her pocket, pulled out a satin bag, bunched up her skirt, and dumped the contents of the bag into her lap. "These are my grandmother's famous pearls. They are matched perfectly so they will fetch more if you sell them as a set. But if you need to, you can sell them individually."

"I can't take your grandmother's pearls."

"You must." Her tone was urgent. "A wanted man needs money to escape, money for food, money for bribes, money to settle somewhere. You are the love of my life. These pearls will save you. Besides" — she paused, bit her lip, and averted her eyes — "there is something I want from you in return."

"Anything."

"Listen carefully." She leaned forward and fixed him with the full power of her gaze. "I want you to make love to me tonight. I want you to take my virginity." Then she added almost in a whisper, "I cannot bear to have a stranger make me bleed."

Every muscle, every bone, every sinew in his body was pressing him to take her in his arms. But he turned aside.

"Unless I do not please you." She drew her cloak close around her body modestly. "Perhaps my body is not soft enough."

To this he had no trouble making an immediate response. "Your body is perfection."

"Then why waste time talking?"

"I am thinking of your honor," he explained.

"My honor?" She took a deep breath and straightened her back proudly. "To bestow my hymen on the love of my life is honor enough for me."

This was an aspect of her honor he had never thought of.

"But I cannot bear for you to be drowned in a sack to pay for a sin that I committed." Even the thought made him shudder.

"I see. You are afraid that if you take my virginity my father will be obliged to kill me to wipe out the stain on my honor. Is that it?"

"I will not allow you to be killed — or even punished — on my account," he replied.

"You are truly my knight," she cooed as she reached over to run her fingers softly down his cheek. "But you keep forgetting, my paladin, that I am a harem girl. Remember, I spent my childhood in my grandmother's *hamam*, listening to the concubines chatter. I know all the harem tricks."

"Such as?"

"Such as how to restore a perforated hymen at every rising of the new moon if need be."

"You learned that in the harem?"

"All it takes is an amalgam of crushed *rezacahi* grapes and ground musk root," she reported as casually as if she were passing on a recipe for pilaf. "A few dabs are enough to close off the passage, and the paste takes only takes ten minutes to harden into a perfect replica of the original membrane. Then—abracadabra! A newly minted virgin."

"And what about the bloodied sheet?"

"Ah, yes, the bloody sheet."

Now he could see lurking around the edges of her kohl-lined eyes traces of his mischievous playmate of old.

"For that I will need a small bladder of pig's blood to hide under the pillow on the wedding night, and a pin to prick it at the certain moment. The next morning a bloodied sheet will be held up by the bridegroom to show his prowess and prove my virginity." She paused thoughtfully. "Men want virgins. Women learn how to supply what men want." She held out her arms, careless of the cloak sliding down her body. "So let us strike a bargain, my knight. I will restore the lost virginity and you will take care of the lovemaking. Agreed?"

Taking her face in his hands as she had done so often with him, he answered, "When love commands, the lover has no choice but to obey."

Whereupon he set about dedicating his full attention to the task his old tutor had assigned him.

Given the relentless single-mindedness with which his fellow pages pursued their pleasure on their all-too-rare visits to the stews of the Galata docks, Danilo could hardly be counted their equal in lovemaking experience. His total sexual encounters to date were few in number. And even those had been undertaken more to prove his manhood to his comrades in the School for Pages than to satisfy his own desires.

As for his partner in the enterprise, in spite of whatever worldly information she had picked up in the fleshpots of the harem, Princess Saida herself was a virgin who lacked any practical experience. It could be said that the lovers entered into their adventure as a pair of innocents, having to find their path together in a strange and unfamiliar country. But mutual passion, longstanding trust, and above all a deep and abiding affection led the way.

Luckily, the Danilo who had proved himself a quick student of foreign languages proved an equally fast learner in the art of love. Each time he found himself making a move or uttering a word or touching a place that seemed to please his partner, he continued. If he sensed the slightest sign of discomfort or unease, he immediately left off. In short, as he gathered her in his arms and set about to make love to her, his agenda was based not on his own pleasure but on hers.

It was in that spirit that he began to explore every dimple, every curve, every bone in her perfect body. And he was rewarded by a rush of passionate kisses. But, held back by his fear of hurting or harming her, he found himself unable to summon up the power to break through the membrane that protected her virginity. Then suddenly he was aware of the feel of her hands on his body taking hold of his rigid member and guiding it slowly and carefully through the shoals and shallows of her virgin canal.

One sudden thrust was all it took to shatter the barrier. Then came her sharp cry. Was it pain or pleasure? Or a mixture of both?

Of course, there was blood. Fortunately their prior conversation had prepared Danilo for the sight of it, if not the warm ooze that seemed to suffuse his body.

And wound tightly around each other they now drifted into that warm sea of sensation where two pulsing hearts beat as one.

When at last they lay back exhausted in each other's arms, no words passed between them. There was no need. Their bodies spoke for them. Every touch, every sigh, every soft caress spoke a language more intimate than words.

Then Saida broke the silence. "Before I go —"

"Not yet," he begged.

"Yes, I must. It is time. But allow me one more moment."

"It is yours."

"I have dreamed of our last night together for a long time," she began in a quiet voice. "Tonight as I was walking in the dark to meet you I prayed to Allah to make my dream come true. I vowed that if I was granted a single wish, I would live out the rest of my days as an obedient Muslim daughter and wife. All I asked in return was one night of perfect love. Tonight, with Allah's blessing, you have made my dream come true and given me a gift that only the gods can bestow."

"I have done nothing."

She interrupted him gently. "Oh, but you have. Did you know that in ancient days the tribes kept a team of experts trained to deflower their virgins? And the deflowerers were well rewarded for their skill."

"You're teasing me again."

"No, it's true. My old *lala* told me." But as she told her tale, he could see the glint of mischief in her eyes. What spirit! Her gallantry deserved something more than empty reassurances.

"I am not a man of words. But I do have a confession," he offered. "I want to tell you something that I have never told anybody, not even my father."

"Go on."

"At my bar mitzvah the rabbis told me that coming of age was an initiation ritual, and that I was being inducted into the company of men. I was thirteen years old. I didn't understand. My true initiation was tonight when I felt your warm blood on my skin, And now I can say to you what you have said to me so many times. You are the love of my life. No matter how many years we spend apart, even if we never see each other again, I am yours forever and you are mine."

It was the longest speech he had ever made in his life, and for once it rendered the princess speechless. But all too soon the ever faithful, ever vigilant Narcissus broke into their embrace.

"You must let me go," she whispered as she carefully disengaged herself from his arms. "If Hürrem wakes up early from her sleep and finds me gone, we are undone."

Left to his own devices, Danilo would have waved off the slave and taken the consequences. But he was no match for the cool head behind the sorrowful eyes.

"Have you got his papers?" Saida inquired of the eunuch.

"Everything is in order, Princess. The *San Domenico* sails after the first prayer, and Captain Loredano is expecting us within the hour," he replied.

"Sailing to where?" Danilo asked.

"To Italy, of course," answered the princess. "To fulfill your destiny."

Try as he might, Danilo could not hide his misery at the prospect of such a fate.

"You must take comfort knowing that you have given me my heart's desire," she counseled. "But remember" — she fixed him with a piercing stare — "I am the one condemned to a loveless life ever after. For you it is not the same. You will have other loves."

When he opened his mouth to deny it, she placed her fingers tenderly over his lips. "I know you. You love glory. You love your horse." She reached up through the straw to pat the horse's flank. "It is a good question which of us you most regret leaving, me or Bucephalus." Then she added, "So I have found a way to take care of Bucephalus for you after you have disappeared." She smiled sweetly. "When you are gone, I will get my father to give the horse to me." She paused for maximum effect. "As a wedding present." She giggled like a naughty child. "That way Bucephalus and I can cry over you together. I will bring him carrots every day in my husband's stable and we will talk about how much we miss you. I know he will be a great comfort to me."

And then, with a fleeting smile, she twisted away and was gone. But before he had a chance to miss her, she was back with a final warning: "Under no circumstances can you leave the stables—or even think of returning to your father's house—until Narcissus returns to spirit you away to the Galata dock. That is where the Italian galleon awaits you."

"But I cannot leave without saying goodbye to my father." On that, he was determined to stay firm.

"Have you not heard a word I've said? The Doctor's House is surrounded by men with orders to shoot you on sight."

"I can't run away like a thief in the night."

"If you will not do this for yourself, do it for your father. He cannot be thought of as having anything to do with your escape. I know the doctor. He is an honest man and a bad liar. What he knows, he cannot hide. If you told him where you were going, he would give us away while he was trying to protect you. His safety depends on his not knowing anything of our plan. He will be heartbroken. He may even go to my father for help in finding you. If he does, that will help to convince the Sultana and the Grand Vizier that he had no part in your escape, and he will be safe from them. For his sake make no effort to return to his house to say goodbye."

"But —"

She cut him off firmly. "Maybe someday in the future the Grand Vizier will die—he certainly has it coming. But for now you need to keep yourself out of his reach. In Italy, you will be safe from him and all of us in this Byzantine court."

"Even you?"

"Even me. Remember, my love, I am the daughter of a king. I was named for the prophet's granddaughter. I have loyalties beyond my own desires."

"But you have put yourself in mortal danger on my account."

She gazed at him fondly. "I have done nothing to betray my father. My conscience is clear. And I have realized my heart's desire. Now promise me you will not risk a trip to the Doctor's House. It is bad enough for me to have to live the rest of my life with an absent lover. I don't think I could manage it with a dead one."

He promised. And she was gone.

60

MEMORIES

DANILO HAD GIVEN HIS WORD TO PRINCESS SAIDA not to leave the safety of the stable. But there were things in his father's house that he would not—could not—leave behind. So as soon as he was certain the princess was out of sight, he crept cautiously out of the stable into the black night. Saida might be a girl brought up to know the ways of the harem, but he was a boy brought up to know the secret places of Topkapi Palace—places like the grape arbor in the garden of the Doctor's House that would shield an interloper from detection as he crawled through a certain cellar window that was never locked.

This was the knowledge that came to play as he moved silently along the familiar path to his father's house, inched through the window, crept up the cellar stairs past the doctor's curtained door, and sneaked into the doctor's study.

There he mounted the set of library steps beside the bookcase and, agile as a monkey, reached up to the very top shelf for a rolled-up painted canvas tucked behind a bound set of *The Letters of Marcus Aurelius*. It was his mother's portrait rendered by Andrea Mantegna. Beside it sat the familiar cloth-of-gold book bag in which his mother's secret book was kept, tied with a velvet ribbon.

His next stop was the blanket chest in his bedroom, where he retrieved the jeweled dagger he had received with the Sultan's blessing on the day of the boar hunt. Then he stooped to loosen his girdle and to carefully wrap a canvas around his body. And after securing the book in its gold bag around his neck, he made for the cellar stairs.

As he approached the door of the doctor's room he was hit by an urge to take a chance and embrace the father he might never see again. But if Saida was right, as she so often was, that might be putting his father in danger.

With a sigh and a shake of the head, he resisted the impulse and threaded his way, without mishap, out of sight of the foot patrols that surrounded the house. He didn't look back until he was cuddled up in the straw of Bucephalus's stall, ready to be found when Narcissus came to fetch him just before dawn.

"Psst! Wake up! And take off your pants."

"But —"

"No time for buts." The slave held out a hand to help the sleepy page to his feet. "Your ship sails at sun-up and Italian captains are never tardy."

"But I don't need —"

"Oh, yes, you do." The eunuch reached into the carpet bag hanging on his arm and held out a pair of sky-blue pants. "Put these on."

"They're blue," Danilo protested.

"What did you expect? Violet? That's for Armenians. Sky blue is the Jew color. And remember this: aboard the *San Domenico* you are the Jewish son of a Jewish merchant traveling home to Italy from Persia."

Once again the slave rummaged around in his satchel and this time brought forth a pair of sky-blue slippers. "The princess went to a great deal of trouble to get these dyed for you."

Reluctantly, Danilo took off his precious yellow slippers.

"Can I wear my caftan at least? The Sultan gave it to me when I rode for him in the hippodrome."

The eunuch stood back to consider this. "What kind of a merchant wears a brocade caftan with a miniver lining?"

Years of living under constant surveillance had sharpened the page's ability to invent quick responses. "A rich Jewish merchant," he answered without a pause. "He would be bringing the caftan home to show off in the marketplace." Then he added, "Rich merchants get themselves dressed up in Italy," trying to sound as if he actually knew from personal experience how rich merchants comported themselves in Italy. Then, seeing no improvement in the eunuch's doubtful countenance, he added, "The Mediterranean is a very cold sea. I don't think your mistress would like me to catch a fever and die out there without a cloak."

"Very well. Wear the caftan. This is for your head," he said, holding out a square black headpiece with silk fringes hanging from the corners.

Danilo understood the rules of games: you win some, you lose some. He held out his hand gamely, but as he placed the hat on his head he made a counter demand: "You understand I must carry my *gerit* with me."

"You must not," the slave replied with equal conviction. "Jew merchants do not travel with lances." Clearly, the point was not negotiable. But then, because even a stone would be moved by the picture of dejection on the proud young face, the slave added, "You can buy a new weapon in Italy. You will be well able to afford it. Now put on the hat."

"Can't I even wear my turban?"

"This hat is a Jew hat. Wear it. And keep your blond Frankish hair hidden. The princess wanted me to give you a henna rinse, but there isn't time. So keep the Jew hat on at all times. Which reminds me..." Once again the eunuch dove into his capacious bag. "You don't want to get this stuff in your eyes. It stings."

He uncapped a small jar, and Danilo began to feel the fat fingers dabbing away at his face with a greasy concoction that he could see through his half-closed eyes was the color of mud.

Finally, with his wardrobe complete, his fair hair tucked into his fringed hat, and his light skin browned to a deep tan, Davide dei Rossi, the dark-complexioned son of a merchant from Mantova, followed his minder out into the night and down the steep path to the shore of the Bosphorus.

There a dilapidated barge awaited, a craft too decrepit to attract attention even at this ungodly hour. The bargeman had received his orders not to cross the Bosphorus directly but to deposit his passengers well below the Galata docks. Taking the roundabout way, the barge dipped south of the Sultan's marble quay into the quiet waters of the Golden Horn, where it was tied up at the royal shipworks, a yard certain to be deserted until after the first morning prayer.

Once on shore, the bulky eunuch and the swarthy Jew page turned into the warren of back alleys, where the only sound to be heard in the silent night was the raucous cry of the night watchman and the tip-tap of his staff on the cobbles as he made his way past the massive warehouses that lined these lanes. As the furtive pair crept along they began to hear the first sounds of the day: the spitting of camels, the meowing of cats, and the occasional plop of a wet fish being landed. Danilo felt something soft against his ankle—a cat, one of the hundreds that scavenged the docks. He was tempted to kick it aside, but on second thought if he did it would probably squeal and give them away.

At the turn into the quay stood a Greek charcoal burner with a face as black as hell—and a heart, they say, to match. And straight ahead, Danilo found himself facing a galleon clearly identified by the legend on the side of the prow: *San Domenico*.

Beside him in the shadows, Narcissus pointed at the gangway. Stationed there, ramrod straight and fully armed, stood one of the Sultana's Men in Black, his head encased in a dark woolen face-mask, his musket cocked.

Was this a single sentry, one of many scattered around the city to search out a treasonous page? Was he stationed by the ship because the eunuch's plan had been discovered? Believing the worst, Narcissus gave Danilo the sign of defeat—palms to the sky, head bowed. But Danilo del Medigo was, as his Albanian riding master once observed, of the breed that never gave up. Motioning the slave back into the shadows, the page leaned down and took a kick at the cat, which squealed.

"Are you mad?" Narcissus barked. "The masked man will come to get us."

"Exactly." For the first time in a long evening of submissions, Danilo took command. "Do as I say. When he comes over to investigate, poke your head out and back—just enough to decoy him."

"He will kill us both." The slave was shaking with fear.

"I can take him," Danilo insisted.

"Are you blind?" Narcissus pointed to the musket. "He's armed."

"So am I." Danilo reached into the folds of his girdle for the jeweled dagger hidden in a scabbard at his waist. "The Sultan promised me that if I kept this weapon with me it would always protect me. All you have to do is give that guard a quick sight of you to get him over here. I will do the rest."

With that, he gave the cat another kick. The cat squealed.

This time the guard took the bait. Weapon aimed, he marched across the quay to where Danilo and Narcissus were hidden in the shadows of the warehouse.

"Step out, whoever you are! Step out or I will shoot!"

Danilo took a swing at Narcissus's backside, forcing him to straighten up and show a flash of white turban. The sentry stepped into the darkness, his weapon pointed at the slave's white turban. As he lunged for the headpiece, a lithe figure sprang out with a dagger held high to stab the masked man full force in the chest. Once, twice . . . On the third thrust the guard collapsed into a shapeless puddle of blackness.

Moving slowly and with great care, Narcissus knelt beside the body, placed his ear against the sentry's open mouth, gave a nod, yanked the dagger out of the dead man's wound, wiped the blood off on his pant leg, and held it out to Danilo.

"You may be needing this on your journey," he muttered. "Now help me." He grabbed the inert body by the feet and started to drag it into the closest doorway. "This body will stay out of sight here until after the first prayer. By the time these places open you will be far away sailing over the Sea of Marmora."

Little glints of sun were beginning to shine through the early morning clouds, but not brightly enough to light up the two shadowy figures creeping across the wide swath of boardwalk and slithering up the gangway onto the anchored *San Domenico*.

The slave led the way along the lower deck to the stern of the ship and the ship's castle, a small, stout three-storied turret. On the top tier of the little tower sat the wheel the helmsman used to guide the vessel. The level below housed the crew's eating table surrounded by sheepskins that served as seats by day and mattresses by night. A few steps below deck there was a small round cabin with no portholes called the *pizola*, a room normally reserved for the use by the ship's owners. It was small and airless, to be sure, but the most private and comfortable space on the vessel, and, as Narcissus was at pains to explain to Danilo, it had been made available for his comfort at some cost.

"Captain Loredano has been well paid to carry you safely ashore at Venice," he pointed out.

"Venice?" Until this moment Danilo had given no thought to his destination. "I was thinking the port of Rome."

"Rome is where the pope lives. You will be much safer in Venice. Think yourself lucky. If *San Domenico* were bound for Genova you would be spending at least two extra weeks at sea."

Suddenly the voyage ahead took on a new reality. "How many weeks will it take to get to Venice?" Danilo asked, almost afraid to hear the answer.

"Only six or eight. A couple of months if the winds go against you." The slave was in charge once again as he inspected the cabin, shaking out the coverlet in search of insects and vermin. "Think of what's in store for you," he went on, oblivious to Danilo's distress. "Cruising the Mediterranean in the owner's cabin on a grand sailing ship."

Danilo shuddered at the thought. His mind leapt back to the voyage across the stormy Mediterranean a decade ago, when he and his mother took to the sea in flight from the sack of Rome. He shivered.

Narcissus reached over to cover him with a shawl thrown over the bunk and continued. "You should be counting your blessings, with everything planned for your comfort and safety." He reached into his carpet bag and held up a leather purse on a metal chain. "Spending money," he explained as he wound the chain around Danilo's neck. "The princess thinks of everything."

"God bless her," muttered Danilo, half lost in memories of the savage Mediterranean storm.

"You must never remove this wallet from your person." Danilo heard a click at the back of his neck as the chain of the purse was fastened.

"Not even when I sleep?"

"Especially then. That is when the thieves come out. Many of the oarsmen on this vessel are slaves impressed into the Venetian naval service. They will not hesitate to rob you blind. Try to remember that you are no longer a penniless page. The purse is full of gold."

Now the slave held out the carpet bag itself. "Inside you will find a set of identity papers should you need them. You are described as Davide dei Rossi, a member of the dei Rossi family in the service of the Gonzaga dukes of Mantova. These papers should see you past the Venetian customs officers who will meet the ship at the *dogana* before it docks at San Marco. Speak Italian to them. And once you are in the city, my mistress says that you will easily find fellow Jews to help you settle."

He was interrupted by a loud clang of the ship's bells.

"That," he informed Danilo, "is the warning bell. At the next bell this ship departs, and I do not intend to be on it. So listen carefully," he said, wiggling his forefinger for emphasis. "Do not leave this cabin until you are out in open water. Rest, sleep, anything, but do not be seen. And when the captain addresses you as Signor dei Rossi do not look surprised. The princess picked that name to put on your forged documents because it is the name of your mother's family. Remember you are no longer a page in the Sultan's *cul'*. If anyone asks for your name...?"

"I say I am Davide dei Rossi." Danilo repeated the name like a catechism. "My father is a merchant in Mantova."

The slave nodded approvingly and, without another word, waddled over to the ladder leading up to the deck. Then, teetering at the top of the stairs, he turned. "Think of it this way. You are a rich tourist cruising the Mediterranean in first-class style."

But, try as he did to feel rich and touristy, what dominated Danilo's thoughts was his voyage long ago en route from Rome to Istanbul through these very same waterways. As he peered out through the porthole he could feel in his bones the icy waters of the Mediterranean sloshing over the deck and sliding in under their cabin door. He could almost hear his mother's voice beseeching God not to let them drown and could feel the choke of terror at the thought of pirates in the nearby coves lying in wait for their ship.

61

THE JOURNEY BEGINS

F ROM THE MOMENT HE HAD PLACED HIMSELF IN
Narcissus's hands for the flight from the Sultan's stables
to the safety of the *San Domenico*, the sheer necessity to
remain alive had left Danilo no time to think.

Not until he was safely tucked into his bunk in the *pizola* did
his heart stop pounding. Only then did his fevered mind begin
to steady itself. Only then did his thoughts turn to the princess
whose efforts had saved him from the Sultana's men, who even
now were combing the streets of Istanbul in search of him.

He reached for the documents in the pocket of the carpet
bag and began to examine the *laissez passer* identifying him as
Davide dei Rossi. Such forgeries did not come cheap, especially
when they were needed within a few hours. And the documents,
plus the bribes that most certainly had been paid, were only a
part of the large sum it must have taken to transform him overnight from Danilo del Medigo, a fugitive on the run from the
Sultana's Men in Black, into Davide dei Rossi, son of a Mantova
merchant returning from his first business trip to the east.

Where had the princess come by such a sum so quickly?
But then she had never failed to rise to an occasion when the

occasion demanded it. What a girl! The only girl in the world for him. Now he would never see her again. Long ago his mother had offered her life for his. And when this ship set sail he would be leaving behind two people who loved him in the same selfless way: the father who had nurtured him and the princess who had risked her life for him. He turned his head to the wall to ward off the thought.

From the wheelhouse above him in the ship's castle, the captain's voice could be heard bellowing orders. All around, bells rang and winches squealed as the heavy anchor chain bounced against the side of the ship on its way to the surface — all of this unremarked by the occupant of the *pizola*, too deeply buried in the past to take notice.

It took a sudden, violent lurch of the ship as it reversed direction to jolt him out of his bunk and dump him onto the floor of the cabin into the present. Was there still time to go back?

As if they had a will of their own, his feet found their footing and carried him through the door of the *pizola*, up the ladder, and onto the poop deck. There he faced a long aisle with rows of oarsmen on either side, three to a bench. He stood there mesmerized by the rhythm of the oars as they plunged deep into the water and rose high in the air in perfect unison. The ship was underway. No chance now to leave the vessel.

Unwilling to face the prospect of crawling back into the tight, cramped confines of the *pizola*, he began to move slowly and carefully past the oarsmen toward the prow of the ship. The six cannons arranged around the mast were a sharp reminder that, although the *San Domenico* was a merchant ship, any vessel sailing the eastern Mediterranean must be prepared for marauders — Turkish corsairs, if not Corsican pirates.

But at this moment the perils lurking in the depths of the Mediterranean were in no way apparent. The *San Domenico* was cruising peacefully along the Bosphorus — a turbulent waterway but not a perilous one — and the passenger from the *pizola* managed to catch one last sight of the minarets of Istanbul as they faded from view. The sun was rising now, bathing the fabled domes of the capital in a pale pink light. Turning backward to face the city, he was able to pick out the familiar cupola of the Hagia Sophia in a corona of sunlight, its minarets waving like golden stalks in the breeze.

He blinked and clenched his eyes shut in an effort to imprint the scene on his memory. But as distance blurred the details, he was left facing only emptiness.

Now the Princes' Islands loomed up ahead. The sight of the silvery shore brought with it a fresh flood of memories and with them came a surge of loneliness. As he sailed slowly past the familiar shore, images from the past begin to riffle through his mind. He saw his princess lying on her bed of leaves in the ruined mosque on Kinali Island—her laugh, her mischief, her long strong legs wound around him. He groaned. Not so long ago he had even imagined her as his wife. But as she knew from the beginning, it was never meant to be. With that certainty came a jarring sense of loss, as if a huge piece of his self had been washed away by the sea, leaving an empty place in his heart that would never be filled.

﹏

From: Venetian Bailo at Istanbul
To: The August Senators of Venice
Date: February 7, 1536

Most Honored Masters:

When I last reported on the sudden and unexpected marriage of the Ottoman Sultan to his Russian concubine, I never imagined I would be repeating a request for your action on yet another sudden regal wedding. Today heralds emerged into the streets to announce that the Sultan's victorious return from Mesopotamia would be followed within ten days by the marriage of his much loved daughter, the Princess Saida, to a certain admiral. And this afternoon I received an official invitation to the event.

So once again a gift must be carefully chosen and dispatched with utmost haste. Allow me to bring it to your attention that this time the bride is not a jaded concubine who would be titillated by a novelty such as a jeweled clock. This bride is a young, innocent virgin — she had better be or heads will roll — raised by a strict grandmother and much loved by her father, the Sultan. That is to say, she is worthy of the finest of gifts, and delivered as close to the wedding date as possible.

It is only one day since the nuptials have been announced, and already gifts have begun to pile up in Topkapi Palace. You can believe me that to miss this opportunity to show our love for the Sultan would undermine the new ties of amnesty and friendship that we now enjoy, largely due to the amazing jeweled cuckoo clock.

Perhaps because of time constraints your eminences would prefer that I purchase the gift here in Istanbul. A set of signed tapestry bed curtains could be had. Or a blanket of sable fur with matching pillow covers. Or both.

Take note: this celebration is not an engagement to be solemnized in the future. It is a formal wedding announcement that calls for speedy delivery of an appropriate wedding gift. I need not assure you that, being fully aware of the value that the Ottomans place on protocol, nothing short of death itself will prevent my being present at the celebration of these nuptials.

I await your instructions.

Your servant,
Alvise Gritti

62

FORTES FORTUNA JUVAT

AY THREE ABOARD THE *San Domenico*. THE
Venetian galleon cleared the shores of the last of the
Princes' Islands — the little island of Kinali, so redolent
with memories. Soon the sailors would yield to oarsmen the
delicate task of navigating the narrows leading from the Sea of
Marmara to the eastern tip of the Mediterranean.

The passenger in the *pizola* had at last been given official
permission to walk the decks, but only after the ship entered
the Mediterranean. He had already been warned twice against
attempting to go ashore at any of the ship's Mediterranean
ports of call.

"The eastern Mediterranean is an Ottoman lake," the captain
informed his charge. "Every port from Istanbul to the Venetian *dogana* falls under the sovereignty of the Ottoman Empire.
And you cannot afford the risk of being recognized by the port
police. Too dangerous."

The sails were unfurled at sun-up the next day. Ahead lay
Homer's wine-dark sea. As he looked down from his perch at
the prow, the passenger once known as Danilo del Medigo was
reminded of an earlier Mediterranean voyage. He could almost

see himself as a boy arriving at the Galata docks after a perilous crossing, walking down the gangway of the pirate ship with his mother's book under his arm and her portrait by Andrea Mantegna plastered to his body like a shield. His only treasures then, his only treasures now. Except for a necklace of matched pearls, a purse full of gold, and a jeweled dagger. Not much to show for ten years of life in Istanbul.

And now, having survived his escape, he faced the prospect of weeks alone cooped up in the close quarters of the *pizola* with no relief except for his sanctioned daily walks around the deck. What he did have to look forward to: more of the hostile stares of the oarsmen, the crude jests of the crew, and the occasional bark from the captain to get back to his quarters and stay out of sight.

In search of solace, he looked to the heavens. But no helping hand reached down to lift him up and no sweet voice whispered courage into his ear. Even his mother had deserted him.

As if to mirror his thoughts, the bright sky had turned into a heavy, grey miasma. He was sailing alone into an unchartered sea. He might never see his father again and his princess was lost to him forever. Then, like an explosion, a shower of sunbeams shattered the fog. And as the mist lifted, he began to feel himself slipping free of the yoke of the past.

Now a voice spoke to him. Not the voice of his mother but his own voice muttering words his mother had taught him: Pliny the Elder's credo, *fortes fortuna juvat*—fortune favors the bold.

Like a cue, the sound of the phrase in his own tongue unleashed a fresh rush of thoughts. What if the princess was right? What if our whole life was written somewhere in a book? Or in the stars? What if fate and not chance had put him on board the *San Domenico* bound for the city of his birth? No matter that his fraudulent papers called him Davide dei Rossi, he was still Danilo del Medigo, the first child to be born in the Venetian ghetto. Could the hand of Fortuna be guiding him back to his homeland? To Italia? Was he, as his princess would have said, living out his destiny?

Perhaps it was the comfortable rocking motion of the waves that washed up against the deck of the galley as it sailed past the Peloponnese toward the port of Venice. Perhaps it was simply the passage of the day. But, in the weeks that followed, Danilo found the strength to climb out of the swamp of disappointment and hopelessness that had threatened to overcome him as his ship threaded its way through the narrows. By the time the *San Domenico* veered north to enter the clear waters of the Adriatic, his vision was no longer menaced by the dark swirling depths of the Mediterranean. Bending over the rail to look down, what greeted his eyes was a vision of the sun's rays dancing on the azure wavelets of the Adriatic heralding the dawn of a new day.

CODA

CODA

T HE PASSENGER IN THE *pizola* WAS NOT PERMITTED TO go ashore at Ragusa.

"Being a sailor myself, I know what it is to be young and looking for a spot of shore leave after a long stretch at sea," Captain Loredano explained when he stepped forward to block Danilo's descent down the gangway onto the Ragusa pier. "But you must understand that Ragusa is a nest of Ottoman spies, and your fine gold-threaded caftan would immediately single you out from the crowd as an object of curiosity and put you in danger. I cannot allow that to happen. I have given my word to deposit you safely at the San Marco dock. And I am a man of my word."

This was not the first time since the ship set sail from Istanbul that Captain Loredano had made reference to the debt of honor he had incurred when he took on the young passenger whose papers identified him as Davide dei Rossi, son of the merchant Isaac dei Rossi of Mantova. Nor was it the first time the passenger in question was moved to estimate the size of the bribe that had protected him from any Ottoman attempt to gain access to his cabin since the ship set sail and, if the captain was to be believed, would continue to shield him from any Ottoman agents that the ship might encounter at the many ports of call between the Galata docks at Istanbul and the *dogana* at Venice.

His escape must have cost the princess hundreds of ducats. No doubt she had put herself in serious danger to buy his safety. Not since his mother had risked her life for him had anyone loved him that much. And very likely no one ever would again. It was a sad thought.

But after several days of being tossed about on the wine-dark Mediterranean and now finding himself skimming along over the crystal wavelets of the Adriatic, the newly christened Davide dei Rossi began to feel the occasional surge of life. Not quite a stirring of hope but at least a flickering of curiosity about what lay in store for him.

When the ship put in at the port of Ancona, the captain relented so far as to set up his passenger in the helmsman's chair at the top of the ship's castle, from where he was able to enjoy seeing ordinary people going about their everyday business on the pier below. The sight of their genial faces was a welcome change from the sullen, angry glares of the oarsmen of the *San Domenico*, not one of whom had so much as met his glance when he passed by them on his daily exercise—a run from the stern of the ship to the prow, weather permitting. Even on board the vessel, as Captain Loredano made clear, the less visible this passenger was, the better for both of them.

"Since I have neglected to include you on the passenger manifest, it would be awkward to explain your presence on my ship should anyone see you come ashore," the captain explained.

Nor did the captain's efforts to conceal his charge diminish when they finally entered the Venetian lagoon. Quite the opposite. As soon as the ship's sails gave way to oars, Danilo found himself bundled up in blankets and stuffed into the back of a closet in the *pizola* on the off chance that the customs officers at the Venetian *dogana* might take it into their heads to make a search of the ship's castle before clearing the cargo to be unloaded at San Marco.

As it happened, the custodians of Venetian security who met the ship at the *dogana* showed no interest whatsoever in the private cabin in the ship's castle. Nevertheless, the passenger was not released from his hiding place until the ship had crossed the Grand Canal and dropped anchor under the watchful eyes concealed high in the Serenissima's fabled clock tower. Only after the *San Domenico* was securely moored did the captain appear at the *pizola* to accompany its occupant ashore. But not before that man of honor had imparted one final, stern admonishment to his charge.

"Remember to keep your papers close to your person at all times." He wagged his fat finger under his passenger's nose. "And for God's sake try not to be noticed. If you take my advice, the first thing for you to do is to get rid of that outfit you are wearing and get yourself some new clothes. Those balloon pants and that gold-threaded jacket spell out the word 'Ottoman' to Venetians in capital letters. Remember, in Venice all Ottomans are spies. So, for your own sake, do not take it into your head to take a stroll into the Piazza San Marco dressed as you are. Your life may depend on it."

It was a stern warning but not an unkind one, and the passenger took it in that spirit.

"Thank you, Captain," Danilo said. "I am grateful for your advice and I mean to follow it."

"Good." The captain patted him on the shoulder. "By the way, try not to be caught with that weapon you have so poorly concealed in your waistband. This is Venice, boy, a city of suspicion, skullduggery, and deception. There is a metal box on a pole in every *campo* inviting citizens to drop in reports of strangers who look to be carrying weapons, with substantial rewards offered. And, believe me, you do not want to find out what will happen if you are taken over the bridge to the Doge's dungeon. Not for nothing do they call it the Bridge of Sighs."

Then, fearing that he had not made his point well enough, he took his charge by the shoulders and shook him, not roughly but firmly. "Understand, Signor dei Rossi, once you step off this vessel you no longer have me to watch over you; once I have fulfilled my commitment I have no stake in what happens to you. But you have behaved well on this journey and I wish you Godspeed."

All very well. But not having set foot on Venetian ground since his parents carried him away to Rome as an infant, Danilo had no familiarity with the city. Where better could he conceivably melt into the crowd than in the town's main piazza?

"If I may not walk into the Piazza San Marco, where shall I go?" he asked.

The captain had a ready answer. "When you leave the ship, I suggest you walk along the Grand Canal with your head down until you come to the gondola jetty. That way —" with a vague gesture to his right. "There you can ask to be taken to the Rialto. That is where you will find the stalls for *strazzaria*. You will also find your countrymen. The Jews have a monopoly on the sale of second-hand goods in Venice, and they will sell you an outfit that a well-to-do Italian merchant's son would be wearing. You can tell the Jewish stalls by the striped pole at their doors. They may even give you a good price for your fancy jacket. I hear you Jews stick together. Come to think of it, you may want to go through the Cannaregio district from the Rialto to the old foundry. That is where the Jews live now. They still call it the *ghetto vecchio*."

"I know it," Danilo told him.

"You've been there?"

"I was born there."

"You were born in the *ghetto*? Well, then, this is something of a homecoming for you, is it not?"

"I left there at a very early age," Danilo replied.

"Even so, you are returning to your birthplace. You are coming home."

And, seeming very pleased to have found such a happy ending to their long journey together, Captain Loredano made for his ship, only to turn back halfway there and add, "For God's sake, boy, do not go into the *piazza* dressed in those Ottoman clothes. Any man of sense knows that if a spy were sent by the Sultan to steal Venetian naval plans, he would hardly be wearing a pair of Turkish pants. But the spy catchers of Venice are hardly men of good sense, and any one of them might easily see his advantage in arresting such a person in hopes of collecting a reward. By the way, don't even think of walking to the Rialto. Hire a gondola to take you there. And don't try to economize by engaging an open craft, even though they come cheaper. Get yourself one with heavy *felse* at the sides. That way, if you sit back in the seat, the canopy and the curtains will hide you from curious eyes."

And, finally the captain whirled away into the bowels of his ship with a quick *bona fortuna,* leaving his young passenger to find his own way to the Rialto.

Ahead of Danilo lay the Piazza San Marco, forbidden territory. Behind him flowed the broad expanse of the Grand Canal. That left him only two choices, right or left. He was about to flip a coin when he recalled the captain's gesture. Left it would be. Within a few moments he came upon a clutch of gondolas bobbing up and down beside a short pier. The price for the journey was, as Captain Loredano had warned him, steep. But the captain's warnings had made their impact on his passenger. He did not hesitate to open his purse to pay the gondolier fifteen gold ducats for a ride to the Rialto under cover of the heavy curtains, which did indeed shield him from curious eyes as long as he sat far back in the canopied chair in the center of the craft.

But the canopy also prevented him from seeing the line of Venetian landmarks that bordered the fabled Grand Canal as they were extolled in a sing-song by the gondolier.

"*Ca Foscari, Palazzo dell'Ambasciatore, Ca Vendramin-Calergi, Palazzo Giustiniani. . .*" The boatman called the names as if singing a lyric, names that conjured up visions of elegance and romance so intriguing that his passenger could not keep himself from sticking his head out between the *felse* to catch a glimpse of the renowned palaces of the Canal Grande. For this bold move he was rewarded with the sight of a shoreline faced with a line of structures so elegant, so imposing that they left him convinced that the sight of them had been worth the risk.

It wasn't as if he had been catapulted into this great city after a lifetime in the provinces. He had, after all, in his early years lived with his mother among the great Roman palaces. But at that young age styles in architecture held a low place among the objects of his interest—far below armor and weapons and horses and playing fields and arenas.

Later, in Istanbul, his eyes had become accustomed to the Ottoman residences built along the Bosphorus after the Turks made the venerable city of Constantinople their capital. Even to the untrained eye, the wooden villas that the Ottomans had built on the shores of the Bosphorus, three stories high at most and cozily aproned by capacious wooden balconies jutting out over the water, could not match the stately palaces that the Venetian plutocrats had planted in the murky depths of the lagoon—each one simply called, with suitably arrogant modesty, a *casa* or *ca* in the local dialect.

So, yes, these Venetian "houses" were new to Danilo's eyes. Most of them were built entirely with gleaming Istrian marble, each one floating like a stone pontoon on its deeply sunk wooden foundations. There they stood, not a single one of them undistinguished, rendered majestic by their courses of vaulted marble columns and tall gothic windows separated by carved-out niches inhabited by sculptured figures. They were not alike in detail, yet all similar enough to create a perfectly harmonious shoreline, each *casa* featuring a decorated portal and each canal water gate displaying a sufficient number of striped poles at the portal to moor a fleet of gondolas if need be. And these portals were only the back doors. An infinitely more impressive entry could be found on the land-side of the *casa*, fronted by a garden.

Gazing at this stunning array of elegance and harmony, Danilo could almost hear the sounds of dance music issuing from the tall windows and see the whirling skirts of beautiful women behind the stained-glass windows.

He was interrupted in these fancies by the repetition of the cry, "Rialto!" The gondola had brought him to his destination. The Rialto, it seemed, was both a piazza and a bridge. Colorful, crowded, noisy, and variously peopled as if begging to be painted by some Venetian street painter. (A task he later discovered had in fact been done by Vittorio Carpaccio.)

After a few minutes of being jostled and stepped on in the bustling crowd, there came to Danilo's mind his mother's observation that you can always find the Jews in any town by following your nose. Just pick up the scent of fish, she said, and it will lead to the Jewish merchants' establishments because nobody else is willing to set up shop amid the stench of fish. Thus the Jews can move in unopposed. And, to be sure, his nose soon picked up the unmistakable stink of fish-mongering, which led him to a row of stalls marked by the red, green, and black striped poles that he had been told identified the *strazzaria* kiosks.

On a whim, he chose the middle one and found himself the only customer in a small kiosk festooned with articles of clothing—women's, men's, children's, all colors of the rainbow with an added mixture of black.

Where to start? With the cut? With the color? With the fabric? At that moment, the young man who had faced a thundering herd of *gerit* warriors unflinchingly in the Istanbul hippodrome felt himself completely overwhelmed by the cascading racks of hose, shirts, doublets, and jerkins raining down on him wherever he looked, and he was about to make his escape when he felt a tug on the sleeve of his caftan.

"Wherever did you come by such a gorgeous jacket?" The questioner was a dark-skinned Spanish-looking fellow, beardless like himself, and seeming to be about his age.

"Please don't be offended." The stranger spoke Italian with a pronounced accent, but Danilo was hard-pressed to distinguish what country's accent he was hearing.

"I have never seen a more elegant brocade," the stranger went on, fingering the fabric. "Bursa?"

His manner was so straightforward and his smile so infectious that Danilo could not resist the urge to confide. "It was a gift to me from the Ottoman Sultan, for winning a *gerit* contest in the hippodrome." Then, suddenly remembering the captain's warning about Venetian spy catchers, he added, "I am not an Ottoman spy." Whereupon, appalled by his own folly, he stood silent, waiting to be arrested and conducted to the Bridge of Sighs, never to be seen again.

Instead, the spy catcher continued the conversation in a casual tone without laying a finger on him.

"I never thought you were a spy. But I did think you might have come here to the *strazzaria* stalls to sell your caftan. If so, I will gladly pay twice what they offer you."

"Sell my caftan?"

Mistaking Danilo's hesitation for a bargaining ploy, the Spaniard leaned forward to make his bid.

"I want it for my mother — my aunt actually, but she is like a mother to me. She is a beautiful widow, a veritable fountain of generosity, very clever, and she loves exotic costumes. She was a daughter of the del Luna family, but you may have heard of her as Grazia Nasi."

Even buried far away in Topkapi Palace, Danilo had heard tell of the legendary Portuguese widow, Beatrice del Luna.

"I have heard of her," he replied, not at all certain of the reason for the celebrity of the name. Then it came to him. "She is a *Marano*," he blurted out, for which he was rewarded with a deep scowl.

"Do you know the meaning of the Portuguese word *Marano*?"

When Danilo shook his head no, his companion continued in a newly stern tone.

"I will tell you. *Marano* is Portuguese for pig. So, yes, we are *Maranos*, but we prefer the term New Christians." And then, with a friendly smile to show he bore no ill will for Danilo's semantic insult, he held out his hand. "Allow me to introduce myself. I am Samuel Mendes, nephew to Grazia Nasi and son of the body physician to the king of Portugal before the expulsion of the Jews from that benighted land."

"You are from Portugal, then?"

"Yes, I am. But I now work in my family's bank in Antwerp."

His family's bank. Danilo made the connection instantly. The Mendes family was known throughout the Jewish world as the most prominent of the Levantine bankers who somehow managed to survive and prosper in the poisonous atmosphere of Mediterranean financial practices.

Danilo held out his hand. "I am Davide dei Rossi, the son of a Jewish merchant of Mantova," he lied. Then, almost instantly he added, "That is not true. I am traveling under false papers. My real name is Danilo del Medigo. My mother was Grazia dei Rossi, the scribe, and my father is Judah del Medigo, body physician to the Ottoman Sultan."

"So you, too, are the son of a physician. Amazing! Do you believe in chance?"

"It is not exactly a belief," Danilo answered. "But in a tight corner I have found myself praying to the goddess Fortuna."

"Which makes us a pair of pagans." The Spaniard grinned with delight. "How old are you?"

"Twenty."

"Me too. It must be part of a plan that we should meet here. Same age, each of us a doctor's son..."

"Except" — Danilo felt compelled to set the record straight — "Judah del Medigo is only my legal father. My blood father is a Christian."

"But your mother is Jewish?"

"My mother is dead."

"Like mine. One more thing we have in common. But your mother was Jewish?"

"Oh, yes, born to a family of Jewish *banchieri* from Ferrara."

"According to the rabbis that makes you a Jew. At the very least, half a Jew. Like me. I am a Christian by day and a Jew by night. Maybe if we put our two halves together" — he grinned his infectious grin — "we could amount to one whole Jew. So now that we are brothers, how much do you want for the caftan?"

"Nothing. I couldn't take money from my brother," Danilo replied without thinking.

"And I couldn't possibly accept such a valuable gift from my brother," countered Mendes. "We have a predicament here. Think, Samuel, think." He drew back and tapped at his forehead with his forefinger. Silence. And finally, "You look like you could use a new set of clothes."

How could the stranger have known this?

"Actually," Danilo reported, "that is what brought me to this *strazzaria*. The captain of the ship that carried me to Venice warned me that my harem pants and caftan would attract notice and could easily result in a trip across the Bridge of Sighs to a place where no man in his right mind wants to be."

A nod of agreement. And finally, "Good advice." Another silence. "Here is my proposal: I will save your life by buying you a complete new set of clothes, and you will make my aunt the happiest woman in the world by giving her your caftan."

The ease of the transaction made it appear to be fated. Either that or cursed.

"You want this caftan for your aunt, Grazia Nasi, who is like a mother to you," Danilo repeated, playing for time.

"She is the widow of my uncle Francesco Mendes, and I am proud to be in her service," came the answer.

"In the Mendes bank?"

"Officially, yes. Also, from time to time I serve in her less Christian ventures. But, believe me, my friend, your caftan will find a good home in both worlds. So let us get you dressed. Is there anything here that has taken your fancy? A jerkin? A cloak? A hat? What about this?"

He reached up and with a flourish unfurled a short coat of red velvet lined at the neck with a blood-red binding. "Neat but not gaudy." Whereupon, assuming the stance of a bullfighter, he snapped out the garment and then leaned back to assess the effect.

"No, won't do. Too German. We are going to be more Spanish this year. Less color, lots of black." He reached behind him and grabbed a second flared coat, this one in padded black satin, faced at the sleeves with frilly black lace. "Try this on. I'll hold the caftan."

Still, something kept Danilo from giving up his precious cloak. However, young Mendes was not one to be put off easily.

"I do know what is being worn these days by fashionable young men in the highest circles. It is part of my business as a banker to know such things. I promise to select only the finest and latest styles for you," he coaxed.

When Danilo continued to hesitate, Mendes added, "If your modesty is bothering you, you can step behind that screen and I will hand your new outfit over to you piece by piece."

His hands still clasped around the caftan, Danilo moved toward the screen.

"You had better take your carpet bag with you. I can smell the presence of a dagger in there."

Slowly, Danilo felt his fingers gradually loosening their grasp on the gold clasp of his caftan as he picked up his bag and stepped behind the screen.

"Might as well hand over your pants and *camicia* too."

Now all he has to do is walk out of here with my caftan, leaving me half dressed, not even able to chase him. And who would believe my story, me, a stranger in balloon pants? While his mind played out its litany of suspicion, Danilo found his arms reaching up to toss the caftan over the rod. *Why not?* At least he still had his purse full of coins and his dagger.

"While you are at it, give me those slippers. Nobody is wearing colored shoes these days. Believe me, it's all the Spanish style, black, black, black."

This time Danilo did not hesitate to grasp the slippers that had cost his princess a fortune to have dyed for him and tossed them over.

"And hand me the pants. Your captain was on target there. Anyone wearing those pants on the Rialto might as well be wearing a sign that says, I AM AN OTTOMAN SPY."

Over the top of the screen went the pants. Next, a long pair of stockings came flying in from another direction, accompanied by a fashion footnote.

"Trunk hose come in all lengths, you know. They make them in only two lengths: one over the feet and up to the knee, another knee to waist. I am giving you a pair of each. Take your pick. I would recommend the one-piece. Once it is on, you don't need garters. Let me know if you have trouble getting the hose on. I'll come around and help. By the way, the panel in the front is called a codpiece. If it is a little loose you can always stuff it with a wad of silk."

So it went—a leather jerkin, a peaked cap, a shirt of fine linen, scores of doublets—one of them a single doublet that was a perfect fit, flared out at the waist and trimmed at the neck with a ruff of miniver. Finally, an invitation to step out and be seen.

"Excellent! Now it is time to show you off to the Venetians," was the verdict. "I know you must feel a little naked without your balloon pants, but you will get used to the trunk hose. Actually, you have the legs for them. Not every *bravo* does." Danilo could not suppress the flush that came to his cheeks. "Don't be embarrassed. Good looks never did a *bravo* any harm. By the way, how are you fixed for funds?"

Danilo was pleased to be able to reply without hesitation that, for the next few years at least, he was well fixed.

"And now that you are fit to face the world, what are your plans?" That was a more difficult question to answer.

"My father had planned for me to attend the University at Padua. But I am not a born scholar," Danilo admitted. "So my plan is to wait and see what comes along."

"A man after my own heart!" This cheer of approval was accompanied by a congratulatory clap on the back. "But actually, I wasn't inquiring after your plans for the rest of your life. More like the next hour or so. You see, I have a free hour right now and I wondered which way you were headed."

Since he had no plans and no idea of how to make any, Danilo fell back on the truth. "To be honest, I hadn't made any plans beyond the Rialto. But the captain of my ship advised me to look in at the ghetto."

"It's a good place to start." Mendes nodded his approval. "Also, you have arrived at a perfect time. Tomorrow is Passover, and it is written in the Haggadah that your fellow Jews have to offer you a place at the Seder table on the eve of Passover if they want to or not."

After so many months at sea when the days simply melted into weeks and then months, Danilo had lost track of calendar time. Not until this moment did he realize that he had arrived in Italy on the eve of the Feast of Deliverance, which made it seem to him what the soothsayers call a fortunate day. To complete the circle, Mendes added that he happened to be going in the direction of the ghetto himself.

"So let us take a stroll together through the parish of San Girolamo," he offered.

And out they stepped onto the streets of Cannaregio, two fashionably dressed young blades passing the time, seeing the sights and telling each other the stories of their lives as friends tend to do at the beginning of a friendship.

"So tell me, what was it like to fight in the best army in the world?" Mendes inquired.

"Not much to tell. I was wild to go. My blood father was a fighter—a true knight."

"I don't understand. I thought your father was a doctor like mine."

"Judah del Medigo was my mother's husband. He raised me as his son. But I take after my blood father—or so I thought before the Baghdad campaign changed my mind."

"How odd." Mendes shook his head in puzzlement. "I have known men to become disenchanted with war after a defeat, but if Venetian accounts are to be trusted, the Iraq war was a great military victory for the Ottomans. Our reports led us to believe that the Sultan won back all the lands his father had lost to the Persian king, including Baghdad. Is that not so?"

"We conquered Tahmasp without a single shot being fired,

if you call that a great military victory," Danilo replied. "The worst danger we encountered was from an avalanche, and my most heroic act was to save the Sultan not from a dagger or a lance but from a crazed pig. And for that brave deed my reward was to be sent home by a jealous vizier like a wayward child. Don't talk to me about the nobility of war."

Not until the words were out of his mouth did he realize how harsh his tone had become, and in an effort to make amends he offered a further explanation.

"I used to dream of being a knight, *sans peur et sans reproche*, like my blood father. When the chance came, I begged to go on the Baghdad campaign with the Sultan. I had always thought of war as a noble calling, a contest of courage, valor, and skill like the *gerit* contest, but I was wrong. What Mesopotamia taught me is that war is all about strategy, deceit, and weather. But mostly it is about keeping records. My Sultan is the greatest fighter in the world, but what occupied most of his attention on campaign was keeping track of his thousands of men and weapons and animals. What I did not understand until I saw the war unfold before my eyes was the constant threat, not from enemy sharpshooters but from starvation. The pack animals, the riding animals, even the herd animals brought along to be slaughtered must eat, along with the men. So a general is constantly on the lookout for pasturage to keep his army moving. In a word, fodder is a more important part of the arsenal than gunpowder, and most of the time a great general is acting as a combination of Chief Shepherd and Chief Clerk. That is what I learned about war from the Baghdad campaign."

Mendes rubbed his fist against his cheek thoughtfully. "I see..."

"No, you don't," Danilo shot back. "Believe what you like. I was in the middle of it for over a year, living in the tent of the greatest general in the world. I have seen the face of war. Have you?"

"Actually," his companion answered, taking no offence, "I am in a war right now as we speak. It is a secret war, rife with deception and lies, but it is war in a righteous cause."

"Against whom?"

"Against the pope in Rome and his Inquisition that is pledged to kill or baptize all the Jews in the world."

"And you think you can stop him?"

"We have a secret weapon."

Coming from another source, Danilo might have taken the phrase as a bit of bravado. But his bones told him that his new friend was no braggart.

"May I ask what it is?" he asked.

"Money," the Spaniard shot back, as quick as a bullet. "Money has an eloquence of its own. That is an aspect of war that you seem not to have noticed."

"If not, I do so now," Danilo responded cheerfully to the rebuke. "But I still do not understand. How can you be at war with the pope and be a professing Christian at the same time?"

"Because only Christians are permitted to practice banking in the Holy Roman Empire. And our control of the Mendes bank is what enables us to finance our war to rescue Jews. Saving lives is not a rhetorical exercise, my friend. It costs money. The escape hatch from a dungeon is greased with gold. Safe houses have to be bought. Spaces have to be booked and paid for in the holds of ships where refugees can be stowed and transported in place of cargo. It takes bribes—large sums—to persuade sea captains to make unscheduled stops at ports that offer refuge. Then we come to the matter of settling these poor, hounded, homeless Jews in places where they can bring up their children in the faith of their fathers."

This time, it was Danilo's turn to rub his chin thoughtfully and reflect.

"What about the Jewish God, the one whose first commandment was that we must have no other gods before Him?" he asked.

To his surprise, his question was answered with a sweet smile. "If you're concerned for my immortal soul, have no fears. Let me remind you that, with us Jews, survival trumps apostasy every time. Anything is forgiven in the struggle to survive."

This was not a precept of Judaism with which Danilo was familiar. "Anything?" he asked. "Even breaking the first commandment?"

"We have a biblical record of what the Lord is willing to put up with when the survival of the race is at stake," was the answer. "Take a look at Genesis 19:33, where Lot's daughters gets him drunk and seduces him — apparently with God's approval. They are hiding out with their father in a remote cave after the destruction of Sodom and one of the girls tells her sister, 'Our father is old and there is not a man on the earth to come unto us. Let us lie with him so we may preserve the seed of our fathers.'"

"I never heard this story from the rabbis," Danilo admitted.

Mendes smiled. "It is not thought to be suitable for children. But you can look it up. Sadly, I dare not carry around a copy of the Pentateuch in my carpet bag, but you'll surely find one in the ghetto."

Now thoroughly ashamed of both his doubts and his ignorance, Danilo held out his hand.

"I'm sorry," was all he could think to say.

"No need to apologize. You've been away in the east for a long time." A strong arm reached out to guide Danilo gently but firmly to a nearby bench. "Let us sit for a few moments." Not until they were comfortably settled did he speak again.

"From the beginning of the forced baptisms in Portugal," he began, "and the removal of Jews from high places, the Mendes family, being New Christians, have been able to continue as bankers to all manner of Christians, including kings. Kings are always hungry for gold, and they still needed to borrow money from us at interest after the Expulsion. But four years ago, without notice, my uncle Diego was dragged from his house in Lisbon, arrested on trumped-up charges of *lese-majeste* against God and the Emperor, and imprisoned in a Portuguese dungeon. It seemed as if our efforts to convince the Church of our Catholic piety had failed. But as soon as the lending stream began to dry up, all the Christian nations — Spain, Genoa, France, even Portugal—came together to issue a joint warning of the chaos that would overwhelm the Christian world if the Mendes bank went down. Even King Henry of England joined in. And after two months in prison, my uncle Diego was released under a caution payment of five thousand ducats." He paused and sighed. "Sadly, most Jews do not have King Henry to speak for them or enough ducats to ransom themselves. That is our task."

"I didn't know . . ." Danilo stammered.

"Of course you didn't. It is in the interest of the Holy Roman church to keep these dealings quiet. When I first heard of the plan for our family to be baptized, I asked the same questions of my rabbi as you did of me. How can we profess a belief in the divinity of Christ when it goes against the first commandment? My family consulted two rabbis before we agreed to be baptized, and both have given us absolution from the sin of apostasy. Believe me, I am not pleased with myself when I mumble the prayers at mass and bite into the biscuit. But, as you say, war is a dirty business. So let us walk on and speak no more of it."

And on they walked in companionable silence until they turned a corner and came upon an ancient figure carved into a niche, a battered stone relief featuring a camel and a heavily burdened porter with a broken nose, topped with a much less weathered turban that must have been added at a later time.

"This frieze marks the address of the Moselli family," Mendes explained. "The figure of their porter is very popular in Venice. They call him Sior Antonio Rioba, and they come here to rub his broken nose for luck." Whereupon Mendes stepped forward, spat on his fingers, and rubbed them over the rough stone. He then stepped back and motioned for Danilo to follow as he turned into the street.

"See the little bridge down the block? That is the bridge leading to the portal of the ghetto. And that is where we part company."

"You are not coming in with me?" There was no mistaking the forlorn look that accompanied Danilo's question.

"Can't risk it." Samuel shrugged. "Not that I wouldn't prefer to. My family is far from Orthodox, but there are things about Jewish observances that I miss—especially the food. However, as a New Christian I must be seen to be celebrating Easter time with my fellow Christians. To be observed and reported anywhere near a Hebrew Seder would be taken as proof of backsliding, what they call Judaizing. And what they consider to be heresy, which could very well lead to a very hot seat in a very hot fire."

"But surely you run no risk of being reported by people in the *ghetto*. They are fellow Jews."

"A poor Jew can get more money for slipping a note in the *Bocca di Leone* and exposing a Judaizer than he can earn in a year of hard work."

More striking to Danilo than the statement was that it was spoken without rancor.

"Not all Jews are heroes, and the rewards are very tempting," Mendes added sadly.

"Yet you have given me information that I could use against you in just that way. Why?"

"Simple. I knew I could trust you. You forget that I am a banker and it is a part of my job to know men. That is a skill a banker must learn just as he must master the abacus. Besides, you told me I could trust you."

"I did?"

"When I asked about your caftan I learned from you that the garment had been a gift from the Sultan for winning a *gerit* match in the hippodrome. The *gerit* is a very special weapon. Success with it marks a man as a member of the confraternity of *bravi*, of which I, too, am a member. I used to joust with the Habsburg prince in Antwerp. He is good. But not as good as me. And if you jousted with a *gerit* in the Istanbul hippodrome, I would wager that you could score points off both of us." Danilo blushed and shrugged. "But, while we're on the subject of horsemanship, a question."

"Ask away!"

"Is it true that the Sultan's horsemen are trained to fire twenty arrows backward from the saddle at the rate of three a second?"

Danilo was too proud of that hard-won accomplishment not to claim it.

"We were," he answered with some pride.

"Then someday soon, when time permits, may I ask you to teach me the trick of it?"

Delighted at the prospect, Danilo replied, "Anytime you say. But meanwhile here's a tip. Strong thighs. That's what keeps your body attached to the horse when he is galloping one way and your head is facing the other. But be warned, it takes practice."

"Strong thighs. Practice. Sounds like a way to use my spare time until we meet again. But for now, we must part."

It was a moment too painful to prolong. By unspoken agreement the young *bravi* embraced, turned their backs on each other, and sped off, Samuel to his pressing New Christian duties, Danilo to pursue whatever awaited him behind the walls of the ghetto. But suddenly, as if in response to some inaudible order from above, the fading click of their two pairs of heels paused, then resumed, and once again they found themselves face to face at the crest of the bridge.

Mendes was the first to speak. "Let me leave you with this offer. If you decide not to settle with our people in the ghetto — and they are your people since being the son of a Jewish mother makes you Jewish whether you like it or not — there will always be a place for you by my side. You might have a bright future with the Mendes family."

"As a banker?"

"Hardly. Our family provides all of those we need, but we can always use a young *bravo* with a good heart and a talent for the *gerit*."

"I am flattered by the offer," Danilo replied, "even tempted. But, believe me, I've had as much as I can take of noble causes. I thought I had explained that."

"And so you did. But I wonder if you are not too close to the Baghdad campaign to see it clearly. Why not take a rest in Italy to think about my offer? You have a lively mind. Perhaps time will show you a solution you haven't considered."

"Such as?"

"You seem to believe that you must choose between two paths — the path of your blood father, the man of war, or the path of your stepfather, the man of peace. It is possible that there may be a place between them where you can claim your full birthright from both your fathers."

Danilo found himself beginning to lose patience. "But I have already told you —"

Mendes grasped his arm with some urgency. "Don't say no! Give yourself a chance to consider. I can be reached at any Mendes bank or through our partners, the Fuggers."

It was a name Danilo recognized at once. "But they are a Christian bank."

"The biggest in Europe."

"Bigger than the Medici? Bigger than the Genovese?"

"The biggest."

"But they are Christians."

"They are also German bankers, and we are Christian bankers, so we know where we stand with them," came the reply. "What bankers care about is money. That is our bond. As long as the partnership remains profitable we can trust each other. It is a very different kind of trust than the trust between *bravi*, but bankers do trust each other with their money. Whereas friends trust each other with their wives. And we *bravi* trust each other with our lives. So remember that if you need me or if you change your mind..."

This time his footsteps did not hesitate but thudded along against the descending wooden planks of the bridge until they were all but drowned out by the sound of the water below, lapping at the shores of the canal. Then, just before the click of the heel taps disappeared completely, a distant voice cut through the fog, echoing in the void like the voice of the oracle calling out a prophesy from her cave at Delphi: "Consider this, my friend. Perhaps you went to the wrong war."

On his side of the bridge, Danilo listened with his eyes closed, willing the voice to speak again, trying to fix the image of his new friend in his mind. But the voice was not heard again, and with the passing of minutes the image of Samuel Mendes became less and less defined and the whole encounter more and more remote.

Had their meeting really happened? Was it all a dream? The trunk-hose that hugged his calves and thighs were real enough, as was the miniver ruffle that caressed his chin; both as real as the sternly printed sign hanging from the arch above the portal: JEWISH GHETTO ADMITTANCE FROM SUNDOWN TO SUN-UP FORBIDDEN ON PAIN OF DEATH.

Shivering with cold and apprehension, Danilo stood on his toes to reach up for the bell pull, then stopped, his hand in mid-air. One tug and there would be no turning back.

In his mind's ear he heard the Venetian rasp of Captain Loredano's voice: "The ghetto will be a closing of the circle for you. A homecoming."

Using the full force of his strong thighs, he launched himself into the air, grasped the bronze ball that tolled the bell, and tugged it hard twice.

On the other side of the door an unseen hand released a bolt to reveal a narrow, metal-edged slit in the door.

"Who goes there?" came the challenge.

"A Jewish merchant stranded far from home on Passover Eve seeking a place at the Seder table," Danilo replied.

"*Shalom, haver.*" The accent was strange, but hearing the word "friend" spoken in Hebrew was heartening.

As the heavy door swung open, the weary traveler hoisted his carpet bag over his shoulder and crossed the threshold into the next chapter of his life.

Read on for a preview of the final novel in
the Grazia dei Rossi Trilogy,
Son of Two Fathers.

I

CHAOS

A LONE FIGURE STANDS AT THE FOOT OF THE PONTE di Ghetto Vecchio gazing up at the portal over the entrance to the Venetian Ghetto. Tall, muscular, and fair haired, the stranger could be taken for a Frank, but his papers identify him as Davide dei Rossi, son of a Jewish merchant from Mantova, returned this day to his Italian homeland.

The stranger hesitates, trapped in a state of mind between apprehension and anticipation. Today, April 4, is the eve of Passover. Jewish law decrees that any Jew travelling far from home on Passover must be offered a place at a Seder table. All this stranger need do to gain entrance to the ghetto is announce his presence. But he cannot bring himself to sound the bell hanging from the portal.

Was it foreordained, he wonders, that he should find himself at *this* doorway on *this* day after his long Mediterranean journey?

What lies ahead for him behind these doors? A new life? Is it a life that he wants to live? And does he have the right to claim Passover hospitality?

Deceit does not come naturally to him. He is uncomfortably aware that although he *is* a traveler far from home, he is only half a Jew; that his blood father is a Christian knight; and that his papers are fraudulent. Still, as the son of a Jewish mother, by Jewish law he is a member of the Jewish race — which makes him a *Jewish traveler* far from home. Reassured by this reminder he reaches up, grasps the bell-pull hanging from the portal, tugs at it hard, and prepares to claim his birthright.

Meanwhile, across town, high above the majestic reaches of the Palazzo Ducale and shielded from the eyes of the vulgar masses below, a furious battle continues to rage between two opposing factions on the floor of the Venetian Senate. The celebration of Christ's rising is only two days away. By long-standing tradition the senate disperses for its annual Easter recess on Holy Thursday. But this year Holy Thursday has come and gone, and the august body that rules the Serene Republic of Venice cannot adjourn until they resolve the issue on the floor.

Venetians do not readily violate a long-established tradition. What can have caused this transgression of the customary Lenten recess? Is menace looming from the ever-threatening Ottoman fleet? Has the volcano on Cofru erupted? Is a flash flood rising from the lagoon to submerge the entire city of Venice? Not if the reports from our spies are to be trusted. The latest word is that the Ottoman fleet is tucked into the Golden Horn far across the Mediterranean — too far to present an immediate threat. Corfu remains untroubled. No trace of flood waters is lapping at the edges of the Piazza San Marco. But there *is* an outstanding issue sufficiently provocative to have set off today's crisis in the Senate chamber — the reoccurrence of the age-old Venetian problem: *what to do about the Jews?*

Jews have been trading actively in the ports of the eastern Mediterranean for centuries. When the tide of anti-Semitism spread into northern Europe following the Black Death, the

German Jews began to trickle down over the Alps into Venice. There they set themselves up as loanbankers — *banchiere* — purveyors of easy credit. They quickly became an integral part of the economic fabric of the city. Unfortunately, they also became so numerous, so successful, and so visible that an edict was soon passed forbidding them to live in Venice — with certain exceptions, such as Jewish doctors. The ruling went so far as to resettle the Jewish *banchiere* at a safe distance in the nearby port of Mestre, thought to be far enough from the capital to save its pious residents from being contaminated by the heretic Jews.

All this at a time when Venice was poised to become a world financial power but was being held back by the Catholic Church's condemnation of moneylending as the sin of usury. And this de facto ban had begun to stifle the ability of Christian bankers and traders to lend or borrow money at interest, which in turn was placing Venice at a disadvantage in its contest with other major commercial centers such as Antwerp and London — cities less bound by the dictates of the Catholic Church.

The Jewish *banchiere* had brought untold benefits to all sectors of Venetian society, from the merchants and traders up to the doge himself. To expel them seemed a foolhardy move, but it did satisfy the demands of piety. In the streets and squares of the city, itinerant Franciscan friars roamed and roared, preaching support for the expulsion edict. Led on by these Franciscan churchmen, pious Venetians were coming to believe that God was punishing them for the sin of nurturing heretics in their midst.

"Nothing but the total eradication of the Jewish population from the city of Venice will appease God's anger," ranted Friar Giovanni de l'Anzolina.

From his pulpit in the *Frari a Basilica*, Friar Giovanni Maria di Arezzo sermonized against Jewish doctors, singling out a certain Master Lazaro.

"This villainous Jew has frequented Christian women," he raged, "and made them dissolute. All afflictions of the state arise from their presence in this city."

"They are a perfidious people!" Alvice Grimani thundered in the Senate. "They are spies of the Turks! They are the scum of the earth!"

In the mid-fifteenth century a dissident faction of the Franciscan Brotherhood took to the streets again, not in support of the expulsion of the Jews this time, but to support their continuing presence in the city. Do not forget, they cautioned, heretic Jews had been permitted to settle in Venice in the first place, so that they could be allured to convert to Christianity. Now it was the Christian duty of Venetians to keep the Jews in residence in order to bring them to Jesus. And think of the hardship that would devastate the poor if they were unable to pawn their meagre possessions to the Jewish brokers in times of need.

The Senate voted to reinstate the *banchiere*. Not surprisingly this change of heart was not destined to remain permanent. Within two years the reinstatement was annulled.

With only the occasional eruption, the debate continued to disrupt Venetian governance for over a hundred years. But when the Venetians suffered a humiliating military defeat at Agnadella in 1509 by what Senator Antonio Coldumer reminded his colleagues was "an alliance of God-fearing nations," the Jews once again became the scapegoat. Adding fuel to Coldumer's argument, Zaccaria Dolfin brought it to the attention of the Senate that both Spain and Portugal had expelled their Jews and had been blessed by heaven for it. On his knees, he warned the nobles to fear the wrath of God if they failed to expel the Jews once and for all.

But God-fearing as they might be, the Venetian nobility were all too aware that the foundation of their prosperity lay not on a bedrock of faith but on trade, and that their trade supremacy floated on a sea of credit. This presented Venice with a seemingly irreconcilable conflict between piety and profit. The Venetians could neither live with the Jews nor without them.

GLOSSARY

AJEMI-OGHLANLAR	An apprentice page
AKCE	A silver coin — currency used in the Ottoman Empire
ARGULAH	Waterpipe (hookah)
BAILO	Venetian diplomat overseeing affairs with the Ottoman Empire
BAISEMAIN	Hand-kissing — a gesture of respect and a common way to greet elders or dignitaries
BANCHIERI	Banker
BASTINADO	A form of corporal punishment in which a person's bare feet are whipped
BEDESTAN	A covered market
BESHEERT	Foreordained
BEY	Title for a tribal leader
BRAVI	Plural of "bravo"
BRAVO	A soldier
CAFTAN	A type of coat of ancient Mesopotamian origin
CALCIO	Soccer
CAMICIA	A shirt

CAMPO	A field
CARAVANSERAI	A hostel for travellers
CUL	Ottoman slave class
DAMAT	Bridegroom — the title used for men who entered the House of Osman through marriage
DEVSHIRME	Ottoman practice of collecting (enslaving) young boys for service
DIRLIK	Estates
DISPUTA	Dispute
DIVAN	Governing council
DOGANA	Customs
ECCOLA	"Here it is"
FELSE	A cabin on a gondola with doors and windows
FERACE	A style of outdoor women's clothing
FIRMAN	Decree
GEDICLI	A prodigy in the craft of body hair depilation
GERIT	A Turkish lance
GHAZI	A title given to Muslim warriors
GHETTO VECCHIO	A ghetto in Venice
HAMAM	A Turkish bath
ICH-OGHLANLAR	A student page
IKINDI	Afternoon
IN LOCUM TENENS	Placeholder
INSHALLAH	God willing
KADIN	Mother of princes
KALPAK	A high-crowned hat
KUMIS	Fermented milk
LALA	Statesmen assigned as tutors to princes
LANDSKNECHTS	German mercenary soldiers
LUSSO	Luxury
MADRESSES	Islamic educational institutions
ODA	Chamber

PISTA	A track
PIZOLA	A small cabin
RAHAT LOKUM	Turkish delight — a sweet confection
RARA AVIS	"Rare bird" — as in a rare person or thing
REZACAHI	A type of grape
ROMAN	Novel (French)
RUSMA	A fluid used for hair removal
SANCTUM SANCTORUM	"Holy of Holies"
SARAY	Palace
SASKEHIER	King
SELAMLIK	Portion of an Ottoman palace reserved for men
SEMA	A Sufi ceremony
SEMAHANE	A room where a sema is performed
SHALVAR	A pair of light, loose trousers
SIPAHI	Ottoman cavalry troops
SPINA	Spine
STRAZZARIA	The sale of used goods
STUDIOLO	Studio
SUBASHI	An Ottoman title often used for commanders of towns
TAKKE	A prayer hat
TUGRA	A seal or signature of an Ottoman sultan
VELOCE	Fast
YASHMAK	A veil used by women to cover their faces in public

AUTHOR'S NOTE

This book, volume two of the Grazia trilogy, is dedicated to Heather Reisman, who adopted Grazia long before anyone else and has never wavered in her support.

The book would never have been completed if not for the help of several assistants and friends who stuck with me through many long years. I owe a special thanks to Dr. Alan Berger of St. Mike's Hospital, whose ongoing concern and great skill have preserved my eyesight.

All the members of the Osman family are genuine historical figures except for Saida, whose character is based on an anonymous "princess" born to one of Suleiman's concubines who died in childbirth.

JACQUELINE PARK is the founding chairman of the Dramatic Writing Program and professor emerita at New York University's Tisch School of the Arts. She lives in Toronto.